Fall From Heaven

Love and Loyalties in Ruined Realms

E.L. Dawn

cc

Where The Impossible
Becomes The Every Day

Cover Illustration by Elsie Noelle (*NightfuryNova*)
Editing by K.F. Starfell

ISBN 979-8-9930958-0-6 (*hardcover*)
ISBN 979-8-9930958-1-3 (*paperback*)
ISBN 979-8-9930958-2-0 (*ebook*)

2 3 4 5 6 7 8 9 10

To my husband who made my dream reality.

Content

Fall From Heaven

1
Fated Encounter

THE MORNING LIGHT CAST THE church's exterior in a warm orange with rich, golden shadows. The stained glass windows glittered like gems. Once she had landed on the streets of England, Estelle took a moment to gaze at the building in awe, filing away every detail in hopes of one day helping to rebuild. It was truly magnificent, even with the top of the steeple broken off amidst the chaos. She was sure, if it had still been there, it could have pierced straight through Heaven.

The sound of an explosion from the east broke her out of her reverie. As much as Estelle would have liked to admire the building's architecture, she had a job to do, one that she had sworn to carry out. She hastily moved toward the church and folded her wings against her back.

Estelle brushed her fingers along the engravings of the church's vast, arched doorway, watching the glow of her halo cast a shadow. She couldn't help but feel a sense of loss. In all likelihood, that was the first and last time she would get to see it. Like all the other beautiful things on Earth, the church would be engulfed in flames soon enough. Estelle put her hand on the door and took one last breath before entering the building.

Inside the church, dozens of believers immediately popped up from their pews and turned their heads to the newcomer, eyes blown wide at the sight. It was a normal reaction as most humans tended to pray where they sat and tried to hide from the war raging outside. After the initial shock, many of them bowed their heads in silent reverence. Though most still seemed tense, like they weren't quite sure what the appropriate protocol was when in the presence of an Angel. Which was a little odd. Usually, everyone would show a different emotion, whether crying from relief or a simple nod. Nonetheless, she needed to quell their fears.

Estelle offered a reassuring smile. "Do not be afraid." She stepped forward down the aisle, arms off to the side with palms facing forward. "I am Vegariel, a servant of God," she said, proclaiming her Holy name almost like a song.

They seemed to relax some, but not as much as usual. Estelle turned toward them all once she reached the front of the church.

"I am here to escort you all to the Kingdom of—"

"*Vegariel?*" a rough voice interjected, earning a couple of gasps from the others as they looked somewhere behind the Angel.

Estelle tensed.

"What kind of name is that? Sounds like one of those drugs you would give to human kids to force them to sit still and pay attention."

Estelle quickly turned around and paled at what she found. Behind her, sitting splay-legged on the altar with one muddy combat boot propped up on the edge, a mere twenty feet away, was a Demon—a freaking Demon with ash blonde hair, angular features, and deep, red eyes that appeared luminescent, even in the morning light. He wasn't entirely shifted. Sharp, black horns peeked through his hair, and a thin, pointed tail whipped around behind him.

The Demon looked back at her and grinned, putting dangerous, white canines on display. "You seem like you could use something like that."

She stared at him, searching for a way out. This was not supposed to happen; if it was, no one told her about it. What was she supposed to do? She couldn't fight him; she wasn't certified to do that yet, and even if she was, what good would it do? The Demon was clearly above her level. It wouldn't take a genius to figure that out. There was nothing to indicate his approach, as he seemed to come from the shadows themselves. Estelle needed to get out, but... *The humans.*

The Angel blinked and spread her wings, shielding the humans from the terrifying enemy. *Remember the humans,* she thought as she steeled her expression and faced the creature head-on.

"What business do you have here, Demon?" she asked, voice steady yet cautious.

"I don't have to answer that," he scoffed, rolling his eyes slightly. "And don't call me Demon, *Hell-bell*, it's Zylis. Stop acting like I'm anything less than you."

"You do have to answer that. You're trespassing on God's property," Estelle shot back. Why would a Demon try to reason that anything other than what they were?

"*Trespassing?* What are you, a cop?" he said, glaring. Then the expression dropped, and he looked up in thought. "Actually, yeah, I guess you are."

How did he even get in without me knowing? Estelle thought, taking a deep breath to calm her nerves. *He couldn't have gotten in after me; I would have noticed him sooner. Was he here before me?* The realization shook her to the core. If he were in there before her, that would explain why everyone seemed more worried than average.

"What did you do to these people?" she demanded.

"Do to them? I didn't do void." The Demon hopped off the altar, and Estelle instinctively put her barrier up. "It's your fault they're scared. You're the ones who fed them all that fearmongering about us." He descended the steps and strolled toward the Angel.

"Just tell me why you're here!"

The Demon, Zylis, rolled his eyes. "Same reason you're here, Star."

"It's Vegariel," Estelle sternly replied, hoping it masked her fear. "And I highly doubt that."

"Holy devil, you guys never change," he muttered right before he reached her. He stood five feet away, which was far too close for comfort. His red eyes bore into her soul, almost as if he could see everything through her golden irises. "Look, if you don't believe me, then just use your little magic trick and see for yourself, huh? You can do that, right?"

Estelle stared back for a moment, confused at his motives.

Like all Angels, she had the power to protect herself from the Demon's corruptive touch by creating a protective layer of her soul around her being. She could also look into someone's eyes and detect lies using the Truth Seer. Normally, she would use it on humans to detect if they were true believers, not necessarily as an interrogation method.

"Here, I'll repeat myself," Zylis continued, after a slight pause, stepping forward. Estelle activated her power at that moment, never leaving his eyes. "I'm here for the same reason you are, Star: Evacuation."

He was telling the truth.

She couldn't believe it, even with the 'magic trick,' as he put it. She must have screwed things up. She was a rookie, after all. She had never attempted to use the power on a Demon before. Did it even effectively work on them?

"You still don't believe me, do you?" Zylis asked, monotone. He sighed. "You get your power from God, right?" He took another half a step closer, making them only about three feet apart, forcing her to tilt her head to keep eye contact with him. "You really have so little faith in Him?"

"Absolutely not," Estelle said quickly, putting all of her strength into not stepping away from him, not to give him the pleasure of her backing down.

"Then what? You thought your powers were malfunctioning?" He snorted. "Wanna try turning it off and on again?" His voice was condescending, and the mocking smirk on his face was actively egging her on.

The Angel stared back for a moment. She loathed to admit it, but he was right. For whatever reason, Zylis was telling the truth, as far as she could tell. Estelle wasn't foolish enough to believe his intentions were benevolent, of course, but so long as he didn't interfere with her duties, she figured it would be best not to press him further.

She sighed and looked away from the Demon.

"I have a job to do," she said, stepping back. "I'll deal with you later."

5

"Sure." Zylis raised his eyebrows mockingly and snorted. "We'll see how that goes."

Estelle narrowed her eyes at him before turning back to the humans, giving them another reassuring smile as she told them, "You have nothing to worry about. As long as I am here, you're safe." The humans seemed to relax visibly, even though their eyes followed the creature, who walked off to the side. "Now then," she began again, "as I said before, I'm here to escort you all to the Kingdom of God. In return, I only need one thing from you." She paced down the aisle, looking directly at a woman with dark brown hair, huddling two small children under her arms. "When I reach you, I ask that you look me in the eyes and repeat the phrase I tell you, and when I offer my hand to you, you take it. Understand?"

Everyone nodded.

Vegariel knelt before them, directing her attention to a little girl no more than six years old, and offered a warm smile.

"Look into my eyes and repeat after me," she told the girl. "I am a child of God."

She looked up at her with bright blue eyes, and Estelle activated Truth Seer. "I am a child of God," she said.

And she was. So, the Angel extended her hand, waited for her to take it, and then wrapped her fingers around her tiny hand with a firm but gentle grip. Within seconds, all that remained of her on Earth was a pile of clothes on the floor.

She proceeded with the others in the same manner and remained quite baffled that the Demon had been silent throughout the process, leaning against one of the pews off to the side. Estelle didn't dare question it, lest she jinx the whole thing, but she kept a close eye on

6

him through the entire ritual in case he dared to try something. It wasn't until the very end that the Demon finally decided to break his silence. By then, only one person remained: A kind-faced man in his late forties.

Vegariel smiled at him. "Repeat after me. I am a man of God."

"I am a man of God," he said. And he was.

She held her hand toward him, only to falter when the creature's voice cut through the peaceful atmosphere.

"Him? Really?" he asked incredulously, strolling over with one hand shoved in his pocket. He clicked his tongue. "Yeah, I'd rethink that one if I were you."

"What on Earth are you talking about?" she asked, turning slightly to face him.

"He's not a good person," Zylis stated plainly as if it were the most obvious thing in the world.

Estelle gaped at him, but after a moment, she felt a sense of anger steadily beginning to form in the pit of her stomach. She turned to face him, ultimately, slightly shielding the man with her wings.

"And just what do you suppose makes you an authority on that?" she asked, genuinely curious to hear what excuse or crude joke he had to justify accusing the man.

Zylis quirked an eyebrow. "Wow, they don't teach you anything, do they." It was not a question.

"About what?"

"Uh, basic Demonic abilities?" he sneered. "Does the term 'Vice Detection' ring any bells? Or what I like to call the shame detector."

"This man isn't lying."

"I never said he was."

7

"Then I fail to see the issue here," Estelle said, narrowing her eyes. "He is a man of God. That's all there is to it."

"Seriously?" He stepped closer, waving his hand toward the man behind the Angel. "Is that all you emus care about? Obedience?" he scoffed. "So, what? Do you think believing in God and being a piece of trash are mutually exclusive properties?"

Estelle opened her mouth to retort, but no words came out. Her wings folded back down, exposing the man to the Demon.

Zylis smirked and took that as a cue to continue, beginning a casual stroll and slowly circling them. "Again, feel free to use your little magic trick if you don't believe me, but I'm not kidding. This guy is horrible."

The man behind the Angel took hold of her white dress.

"You're gonna have to be more specific," Estelle spat.

"He beats his wife and kids," Zylis announced.

The Angel couldn't help but glance at the man, eyes wide and brows turned in a question. Afterward, she looked back at the Demon and activated her power.

Zylis looked directly into her eyes. "Used to, anyway. Probably would still be doing it if not for the, well..." He gestured toward a window, where towers of smoke could be seen billowing on the horizon.

Estelle stared at him for what felt like hours, frozen in shock, unsure how to proceed. The Demon was telling the truth. But he must be lying, right? He just watched an entire church of people go to Heaven. He must want someone to take to Hell. But wouldn't he have tried to take more than just one man if that were true?

She turned her attention back toward the man again, "Sir, I'm going to need you to repeat after me again," she said, trying to ignore the

Demon nearby. There was a flash of fear in the man's eyes. "Say, 'I am a man of God.'"

"I *am* a man of God!" he said emphatically, gazing into Vegariel's eyes imploringly.

"You're an abusive scumbag, actually," Zylis interjected, and for a moment, Estelle saw a spark of something true in the man's eyes just before he turned toward Zylis.

"No, I am a man of God! I am a man of faith!"

"And you're also an abusive scumbag, and not just to your family," the Demon snarled, a dangerous glint in his eyes as he stepped closer, towering over the man.

His pointed tail whipped behind him, cat-like pupils contracting to mere slits, exuding a dangerous aura as he stared down at the man with a look Estelle could only describe as complete and utter revulsion.

"You think you deserve to be with them now? That *they* deserve to be with you?" he sneered, borderline hissed, showing off the sharp canines. "Why? One lifetime wasn't enough?"

The man abruptly turned back to the Angel. "Please, he's lying!" he cried, face pale and panic-stricken. "I went to church every Sunday!"

That was true.

"I'm a man of God!"

That was true.

"I've lived a proper life!"

Estelle tensed.

"I've been good to others—I'm a good person!"

That... that was a lie.

She stared back at the man in silence and deactivated Truth Seer. She didn't need to hear any more from him. She breathed deeply and

9

exhaled slowly, trying to clear her head enough to consider her options. She almost wanted to laugh at the dry, cynical feeling rising inside her because, of course—of course, her first time handling duties on her own in the Rapture Zone, she would be forced to decide that— because of a Demon, no less! The bitter irony of the situation was not lost on her, hitting her like a downpour of rain soaking through her white dress.

She was careful and kept her expression neutral. As far as she knew, there weren't any explicit rules about refusing passage to a true believer, but the consequences for any failure to adhere to the guidelines, if discovered, would be severe. But when she thought about the wife and children, about the pain she would be exposing them to if she were to let the man through.

She couldn't do it. Maybe something was wrong with her powers, and he wasn't a man of God at all. It certainly seemed more likely than what the Demon was suggesting. But in either case, she still couldn't do it.

As the last of the air left her lungs, Estelle looked around the chapel, checking to make sure it was only the three of them: the man, an Angel, and a Demon. There was no one else.

No one would have to know.

Steeling herself, she turned toward Zylis again. "What will you do with him if I leave him here?" she asked carefully.

Both man and Demon were shocked. The man instantly dropped to his knees, grasping Vegariel's clothes and pleading for mercy. The Angel ignored it through clenched teeth and stared into the vast, glowing, red eyes, awaiting his response.

"Well?" she prompted after a couple of seconds of hesitation.

Zylis cleared his throat. "I mean, I'd just take him with me. It's not my area, really, but I can transport a few people on my own."

Estelle nodded, side-eyeing the man. He was tugging on her dress like it would save him from his fate, spewing empty words and promises he should have never had to make. She couldn't bear to look at him any longer.

"Alright," she said, meeting Zylis' eyes. "I'll leave that to you, then. Heaven has no place for those who seek to make it unsafe for others." The tugging on her dress stopped.

"You're something else, aren't you, Star?"

"Not really. Given the situation, I would think anyone else would do the same."

"That's cute," Zylis shot back, sticking both hands in his pockets as they walked around each other. He lightly kicked the man in his side. "Get up, douchebag, you're coming with me."

The man didn't attempt to move and bowed his head, staring directly at the tiled floor. After a moment, the Demon clicked his tongue, grabbed the back of the man's shirt collar, yanked him to his feet, and swore profusely.

"No, please..." the man said, broken and quiet.

"Shut up, you heard the princess."

Princess? Estelle blinked several times in confusion but opted not to comment on it as Zylis began to drag the man toward the door. The sound of the door falling shut echoed within the church, and then he was gone, leaving the Angel alone in the empty chapel.

2

Opportunity

AFTER A COUPLE OF RELATIVELY uneventful rescue missions to the surface, Estelle was glad she didn't run into the Demon again, or any other. It had been eight days since she had run into him at the church.

She hadn't told anyone about the encounter. Though it was relatively rare to see a Demon stray from the battlefield, it wasn't unheard of. Estelle was stationed in the Rapture Zone, only a few short miles away from the actual fight, which made the likelihood of running into the enemy higher. Even though it was her first mission alone, and encountering a Demon was not supposed to happen, it was to be expected with the war.

Estelle had gotten into a routine of sorts. She would wake up before dawn on the days she was assigned to work, get dressed, and go outside. She would walk from the dormitories to the golden gates, where an Angel would provide her with a map marked with all the churches she was tasked with evacuating that day. Estelle would then fly down to the other realm and get to work, and if she acted efficiently, she'd finish by six o'clock in the evening, at which point, she would return the same way she had come and promptly pass out on her bed in exhaustion.

Estelle enjoyed what she did—she was helping people. And with the war raging worldwide, she wanted to do everything she could to keep them safe. For humans, it was World War III, but for otherworldly beings, it was one war that had been going on for an eternity. It only really started affecting humans around two years ago, turning Earth into a complete battlefield for the Angels and Demons.

Through the working days, Estelle couldn't help but think of the Demon whenever a human was a little too reluctant to look her in the eyes, that sense of something there, a dark secret hidden behind the well-kept exterior, lingering long after she sent them to Heaven and their clothes hit the floor. She wanted to ask what they had done, but didn't know what to ask.

It was a fascinating ability, Vice Detection. To see into the souls of humans and instantly know every shameful thing they had ever done. It made sense that Demons would have that ability, but Estelle had to wonder why that wasn't among the things Angels could do. It would have certainly made her job more manageable.

Estelle's mind was polluted by endless questions one Friday evening as she wandered from place to place in a daze, exhaustion gradually getting the better of her. She wasn't sure why they had assigned her so many locations that day. It was unreasonable, and she would have been angry if the work had not been so important. Maybe it was because they acknowledged her work ethic and elected to give her extra work. Or it could be because things on Earth had gotten worse. Either way, it was an unfortunate situation.

By the time Estelle had finished clearing out the last church in London, it was long into the night. The stars burned bright, lighting up the sky, but the structures of buildings around her cut deep, jagged shadows into the cityscape.

She was ready to go home and sleep through the weekend. Yawning, Estelle started flapping her wings, preparing to take off, only to be harshly pulled back into full alertness at a sudden flash of red light in her peripheral vision. She tucked in her wings and sharply turned in the direction, searching for the source, but found nothing. Her halo cast a subtle light above, illuminating the Angel, though it did nothing to help her see through the dark. Keeping her eyes on the shadows, she stepped backward, only for her wings to collide with something solid.

"Such a hard worker," a familiar voice said, deep and husky, behind her.

Estelle nearly choked, viscerally aware yet frozen in place.

That same voice chuckled. "What are the chances of running into you again?" He leaned in closer. "I hardly see the same Angel twice."

Heart pounding within her chest, Estelle spun around on her heel, expecting to see the Demon right behind her. But he wasn't. He was several paces behind her, nowhere near as close as she had initially thought. Zylis' eyes glowed red in the dark, and she could faintly see a smirk on his face. However, the rest of him seemed to blend into the shadow, as if he were made from it.

"How did you find me?" Estelle asked, squinting into the darkness.

"What makes you think that I found *you*?"

Estelle blinked, and he was gone. "I would never go looking for a Demon," she said, looking at every shape in the shadows.

Zylis chuckled, the sound bouncing off the walls before solidifying behind her. "We'll see about that," he rasped, leaning in further than before. "Let me know if you ever feel like taking a dive." His breath was hot against the side of her face, sending shivers down her spine as he whispered, "*Star.*"

Estelle whirled around, but by the time she'd made the turn, he was gone.

"It sounds like he's trying to tempt you," Antares said, effortless and calm. It was Saturday, the morning after the incident. They sat beside each other on a bench, overlooking the platforms in the outermost circle.

The blood drained from Estelle's face as her eyes widened, staring into her mentor's blue eyes. She opened her mouth to speak, but before she could get a word out, Antares continued.

"No, no!" he hastily exclaimed, waving his hands around for emphasis. "It's not a bad thing—well, unless it worked, but—"

Estelle's throat made a noise, strangled and involuntary.

"That's not the point I'm trying to make!" he went on, trying to quell her fears. "You have nothing to be concerned about, Miss Amadea. In fact, this could be a great opportunity."

"A *great opportunity*?" she repeated, bewildered. "Yeah, to get cast out because I'm not supposed to fraternize with Demons!"

"That hasn't happened since the Originals."

"Then what do you mean?"

"Well..." Antares made a vague, meaningless gesture with his hand. "You're in a very unique situation. Not many second-tier Angels come in contact with Demons, let alone the same one multiple times," he explained. "If you show yourself capable of resisting temptation, that will make you stand out when the Apostles review you for ascension."

The young Angel stared at her mentor, mulling over the information, before she spoke, narrowing her eyes, "You really think so?"

"I *know* so." He held eye contact with her for a while before looking away.

"Isn't it sort of dangerous?" Estelle frowned. "What if he attacks me? I can't fight him off."

He hummed, brows pinched together for a moment. "I can understand your concern," he said, sighing and leaning back on the bench. "It's a shame they don't allow us to give combat training to Angels below the third tier."

"It's not just that..." she said, looking down at her feet, idly fidgeting with the zipper of her coat. She bit her lip, debating whether she should voice her concerns, then sighed, a big puff of mist forming from the pushed air. "There's just so much I don't know about Demons," Estelle finally said, then released an awkward laugh. "Even *he* seemed surprised."

Antares hummed again. "The curriculum, as far as that is concerned, does leave much to be desired."

Estelle was a level two Angel. She could go on missions on her own, even near or in the Rapture Zone, where the battle raged nearby. Before, she was in a group with two upper-ranked Angels, levels eight and nine, watching over her and three others. Levels three to five underwent combat training and were sent to the front lines. Six through eight had clearance to learn advanced magic and defenses, and tier nine could learn all the secrets of Heaven and Hell.

"Why won't they teach us this stuff?" Estelle pressed. "It just feels unnecessarily risky... I don't know." She ran her hands through her raven black hair, collecting it and pulling it over her shoulder, then started combing it with her fingers. "I'm sure there are good reasons for it; of course, I just don't understand *why*."

"It's... complicated," her mentor replied. "The official reason is that they don't want sensitive information falling into the wrong hands. But honestly, from someone who has worked closely with the higher-ups, some of the restrictions still seem arbitrary," he said, then shrugged. "I'll be the first to admit that it can be frustrating, but that's society."

Estelle nodded and stayed quiet as two women walked by, chatting animatedly, and waited for their voices to recede in the distance before speaking. "Do you know about Vice Detection?"

For several seconds, Antares didn't respond. Estelle was sure that if she looked at him, she would find him staring at her with his mouth agape. She chose to keep her gaze trained on the ground beneath her feet.

"I do," he eventually answered, leaning down to speak quietly to her. "It's an innate Demonic ability."

Estelle nodded. "Can it be used on Angels?"

"No." The answer was quick.

She looked at him at that moment. "What if—"

"Estelle Amadea," he interjected. Staring intently at her, Antares raised his hand and slowly pointed at his eyes, then ears, before finally tapping his wrist twice. Estelle could count the number of times she'd seen the gesture on one hand, but she knew what it meant.

Others are watching. Others are listening. Now is not the time.

The young Angel snapped her mouth shut, drew her wings in closer to her person, and turned away again, staring at her shoes in silence. She shouldn't be questioning the Apostles' motives and God's will. Luckily, Antares was understanding and wouldn't get her in trouble for speaking her mind aloud. What was dangerous was saying it aloud in public.

Eventually, Antares cleared his throat. "Listen, there's not a lot I can tell you, but I can say: I don't think you need to worry too much about him attacking you without warning."

Estelle looked up and met Antares' blue eyes. A million questions raced through her head, but she didn't dare voice them; instead, she let the quizzical look on her face speak for itself.

"But—and I'm telling you this as your instructor, for your safety, because the Demon has clearly taken an interest in you, which makes the probability of you seeing him again significantly high," he prefaced. Something told Estelle the disclaimer wasn't meant for her. "If he ever shifts—shifts fully," he continued. "By which I mean, if you see wings, you need to run as fast as you can."

Estelle stared at him momentarily, turning the words over in her head before offering a soft smile. "Thanks, Antares, I'll be sure to remember that." Estelle laughed, trying to defuse the situation. "But who knows, maybe he'll get bored, and I'll never see him again."

Her mentor smiled but didn't say anything.

3
Fairy Tales

AT THE SHRILL CRY OF a whistle, Estelle shot through the air with arms firmly at her side. She kept her gaze locked on the center of the first hoop, ensuring a clean goal as she cleared it. All of it was a matter of muscle memory at that point. Her body knew exactly what to do, and subtle shifts in her center of gravity made it all second nature.

The wind whipped through Estelle's black hair as she picked up speed, her body twisting and turning as she zigzagged through each ring. The last ones were always the trickiest, as far as accuracy was concerned. With ten rings stacked vertically, forcing her to go into a nosedive for the final stretch of the course, it was only made more intimidating due to the rings' decreasing diameter, which forced the Angel to pull her wings inward.

As Estelle torpedoed through the final rings, she silently cursed herself as the tips of her wings grazed the last few hoops. Nevertheless, she managed to make the final, crucial landing, extending her white feathers as soon as she cleared the last obstacle and twisted her body upright just before her feet touched the ground.

"Thirty-five point eight seconds!" Mebsuta, the instructor, announced. "Forty-seven out of fifty rings. Up next, Giovanna Rūnnel!"

Estelle quickly stumbled off the landing platform, panting as she moved to watch her friend from the sidelines.

Heaven had a "schooling" system to make better Angel soldiers for humans. Their curriculum consisted of administering blessings, learning how to behave in difficult situations with mortals, learning the rules and regulations of Heaven, the history of the Three Realms, and flight training.

Estelle was one of the top students among the other second-tier Angels. Always on top of the assignments despite her duties in the mortal realm, she studied hard to stay near the top and had just beaten her record by a single second. The week before, she had gotten forty-eight rings. Something was missing about her technique, but she couldn't pinpoint exactly what it was.

On the other hand, Giovanna was always slacking off but still managed to be in the top twenty percent. Most of the time, she didn't even show up to class unless it was about different techniques in flight agility and maneuvering at high speeds. Estelle was sure the only books she read were ones about flying, but her friend seemed to have figured out the secret.

"Thirty-one seconds, even!" Mebsuta yelled. "Forty-nine out of fifty rings!"

Panting slightly, Giovanna made her way to Estelle. "The last hoop," she muttered. "It's always the last hoop." She flexed her wings out in frustration before they folded back into a natural position.

"You should show up to class," Estelle teased. "Maybe then you'll be good at it."

Giovanna barked out a laugh and stepped closer to the tower above, making Estelle tilt her head back. "Says the girl who looks more Demon than Angel. I have the top score in the class."

Giovanna was right about how Estelle looked. When humans are chosen to become Angels, rumor has it that they are purified of all impurities and their hair turns lighter, typically in a pastel color palette, to symbolize the cleanliness of their souls. Giovanna had cloud blue, and Issac, another friend, had lilac. Uncharacteristically, Estelle had black. It was extremely rare to have black hair, even more so than pure white.

She chose to negate the rumor. She was selected to become an Angel, and that's all that should matter.

Estelle raised an eyebrow. "Other than Lilith, you mean."

"Oh, for the love—" Giovanna scoffed. "Lil—I mean, Audelaire isn't in this class anymore."

"That's why she was the first to ascend," the raven-haired Angel said quickly.

The taller Angel playfully smacked her on the arm. "Come on, we're all passing with flying colors—"

"Up next, Issac Sterling!" the flight instructor shouted.

"Ah, I might've spoken too soon."

"Giovanna, don't say that!" Estelle chided, flicking the tall Angel's forehead. She wasn't wrong, though, as made evident by how Issac clumsily landed almost a full minute later.

"Fifty-seven point nine. Twenty-seven out of fifty rings!"

Their classmate made his way over to them with a nonchalant look on his face.

Giovanna began to chastise him on his score, being honest in the most brutal way possible. Estelle just looked at him with a sad smile.

Issac was adamant about doing just enough to get by for as long as she could remember. But the talent he had shown through conjoined missions, back when they were all level one, was more than enough to tell Estelle he was holding back during classes.

Issac averted his eyes from Estelle's.

It was early evening when classes ended, and Estelle resisted the urge to yawn as she stared into space, waiting for their teacher to hand out their reports. They received weekly feedback, highlighting their strengths and areas for improvement, along with suggestions for the upcoming days. Estelle had noticed a pattern with hers in the last couple of months. Usually, they told her she needed to work on defensive flying, weight training, and blessed healing. And, lo and behold, when Antares handed her the paper, it said precisely that.

"Ah!" the teacher exclaimed suddenly, reaching into his pocket and pulling out a scrap of paper. "Sorry to trouble you, Miss Amadea, but would you mind dropping by the library? There's a book I need for tomorrow. I'd go myself, but the administration has called for a meeting this evening."

"Of course, it's not a problem." Estelle smiled, standing up and accepting the piece of paper as she glanced at the hastily scribbled directions. "What access level is it?"

"Six," Antares replied with an air of apology. "You shouldn't have a problem carrying it, though."

"I'll go right away." Estelle gave a short nod, smiling brighter to show she didn't mind doing the errand.

"I might as well go with you," Issac said, walking up to them. "I need to get some books about flight control."

"Sounds good." The girl beamed before turning her attention back to the upper-rank Angel. "I'll bring it to class tomorrow." And with that, she grabbed her bag, and the two students left, going out into the cold December air.

The four concentric walls of Heaven kept different classes of Angels divided. The library was one of the few communal spaces, unless one counted the outer ring, wherein all were welcomed into their eternal home, and where Angels went to and from Earth. The trek to the library wasn't a long one, but the bite of the gentle breeze made it feel like an eternity.

Estelle shivered as they walked down the pathway, wrapping her arms around herself as she tried to use her wings as a buffer against the cold.

"You didn't bring a coat, did you?" Issac asked, looking at her from under the fur lining of his coat's hood.

Estelle laughed. "I didn't. I expected to return to the dorms after class, not the library." She could see her breath as she talked.

"Then why did you say you would do it?"

"Why are *you* coming to the library with me?" she countered, turning slightly to face him. After a moment of silence, she pleaded, "You would be at the top of the class if you would just show them."

"You and Mebsuta," he chuckled. "He chewed me out before we went back inside. That's why I'm getting books, an extra assignment for not doing better."

"Why haven't you done better?"

"It's not that I don't want to. I just haven't found a reason why I should."

Estelle let the conversation end there. She had tried convincing him to do more with his abilities before and given ample reasons why he should want to ascend.

If they ascend, they could read the higher-level books and learn more about the three realms: Heaven, Hell, and Earth. Learn how to command their Angelic powers, along with fighting tactics. Go to the front lines and fight against the Demons. Get the opportunity to earn a Luminari. But Issac always responded with the same tired look and words, 'I'm saving people from Demons. That's all that matters.'

"Do you want my coat? You're kinda turning into a popsicle," Issac offered, already flipping the hood off his head and moving to the zipper. She was quick to stop him.

"Thank you, but it's okay. We're almost there anyway."

He shrugged and didn't question it further.

Estelle looked up at the lavender sky, the color fading as the night crept closer. She could see the library up ahead. The vast walls stretched far in both directions, forming a perpendicular intersection with all the other spheres. As they drew near, she picked up her pace until they stood before the massive entryway and breathed a sigh of relief once they were out of the winter cold.

"He said level six, right?" her companion asked, shedding his coat.

"Yeah, but don't worry, I know where to find it. You go ahead and get that 'extra assignment,'" Estelle teased, smirking slightly.

Issac huffed out a laugh before they parted ways into the labyrinth of bookshelves.

24

Estelle paced down the aisles between the vast rows of books, though she paid them no mind, rereading the instructions on the scrap of paper, then turned her attention to the sparse furniture around her. She searched until she found a potted plant with silver-tipped leaves and rose-purple flowers on a long stalk. The girl looked around the study hall. It was surprisingly populated and looked like most of the Angels were from the second sphere.

There must be a test coming up for them, she thought, right as she saw something that made her eyes light up.

Not wanting to shout in the library, Estelle quickly walked through the crowd toward a familiar head of pure white hair. She put her hand on the other's shoulder, only to jump when half the books on the table snapped shut automatically from her being a lower level.

"Ah, I'm sorry, Lilith!" Estelle whispered loudly, meeting violet eyes. "I just wanted to say 'hi,'" she muttered, taking the vacant seat next to the Angel.

Lilith's mouth turned into a beautiful smile at the sight of her friend. "Well, hi! And don't worry about it. I was finished with most of those anyway."

The raven-haired girl smiled back. "Oh, I should probably call you 'Miss Audelaire' now that you're a higher level, huh?"

The teachers referred to everyone by their last names, more so out of respect than anything else, but it was common practice that once an Angel ascended, the lower levels would then formally address them. It was more heavily enforced for levels four and higher.

"I don't mind," Lilith said, waving her hand dismissively. "It seems a little weird to call you 'Amadea' after being on the same level for sixteen years."

Estelle chuckled softly. "So, how have you been?" she asked, leaning forward so they wouldn't disturb the others as they talked. "It feels like forever since I last saw you. How do you like tier three?"

"It's alright," Lilith replied with a shrug, patting one of the closed books. "Keeps me busy. But I wish they didn't make me live in the second circle; we would be able to see more of each other otherwise."

Estelle laughed lightly, agreeing with her statement. Her eyes darted over the closed books with a glowing three along the spine, and she couldn't help but ask, "What are you reading about?"

"Mostly battle strategies," she said as if it were the most boring thing she could have been doing at that moment. Estelle would die again to be able to read a higher-level book.

"Oh, are you going out soon?" Estelle questioned, positively beaming with euphoria.

"That's what they're telling me," Lilith answered with a look that made Estelle wonder if she was just nervous. "Within the next week, if I pass the exam."

"That's so exciting!" Estelle gushed, a wide grin stretching across her face. "I hope I can join you soon!"

"Yeah," Lilith replied, tone a little bit lower. "It'd be nice to see all of you again."

"Well, I'll be sure to work hard and ascend as soon as possible." Estelle got up to leave as Lilith smiled, averting her eyes.

Snow white hair fell before the girl's face as she returned to the books.

The dark-haired Angel weaved through the other Angels and back to the plant. After a glance over her shoulder, she reached into a nook behind it and pulled out a book stashed away there. It was heavy despite the thickness, but it was nothing she couldn't handle.

She shook her head nostalgically as she recalled the first time she was asked to retrieve a book for her mentor.

"*It's to keep other people from taking it,*" Antares had said. "*You'll understand when you're at my level, Amadea. Everyone does it!*"

She laughed softly, leaning back against one of the shelves, and examined the cover.

'Children's Fairy Tales'

Estelle blinked. *This was level six?* she thought as she turned the book over in her hands and tried to open it. Sure enough, the cover remained firmly closed, and on the spine, a large number six began to glow in response to her attempt. It was just another reason why they should ascend.

What kind of fairy tales are in here? she wondered before sliding the book into her bag. Glancing around the aisle, the Angel yawned as the exhaustion started to catch up to her again. *I should probably find Issac.* She sighed, leaning farther back onto the shelf, and allowed her gaze to wander lazily over the titles of the other books until a gleaming red script caught her eye. She leaned toward it and read the bold lettering on the hefty book.

'Demonic Powers: Codes Against the Godless'

Estelle's breath hitched. She reached for the book, looking around nervously, confirming no one was paying her any mind, before her fingers wrapped around the spine and pulled. It didn't move, as if it were a permanent fixture on the shelf. Then, a number illuminated the spine.

Nine.

She frowned. *Well, I guess I won't be reading that anytime soon, not until I receive a Luminari... if I get one.* She sighed, then nearly jumped out of her skin when someone called her name.

"Estelle?"

The girl quickly turned around and found Issac standing a few feet away.

"Oh, sorry," he said, holding up the hand not occupied by a stack of books. "I didn't mean to scare you."

"No, you're fine!" she replied, though her heart still pounded. "I was just in my head."

"Nothing out of the ordinary—did you find it?"

It took a second for Estelle to comprehend what he was talking about, but then she nodded, patting the bag at her hip.

"Yeah, I did," she said eventually. "I see you found your books."

"Yup. Ready to head out?"

Estelle nodded again.

The walk back to school was mostly quiet. Estelle shifted the bag several times from one shoulder to the other, trying to ease the burden. Issac offered to carry it for her, but she insisted it was alright and made it easier to ignore the cold, especially since the sun had gone down.

Eventually, against her better judgment, Estelle spoke. "Hey, I know this is kinda out of the blue, but... have you ever seen a Demon?"

He turned toward her and stared as if she had grown an extra head. "No," he said firmly. "I haven't gone on any missions in the Rapture Zone yet, so I'm not sure how I would anyway."

"Right, right. That makes sense," she said, looking away and internally punching herself for asking in the first place.

It had been two weeks since the encounter, but it was still fresh in her mind. She had many questions, but there was no one to talk to. Estelle had wanted to speak with her mentor, Antares, more about her encounter with the Demon since it happened, but their schedules never lined up. He was away doing a seminar in the second sphere for a few days, and then he was busy with meetings. He was scheduled for another class in the third sphere in two days.

After a few seconds of silence, Issac asked, "Have you?"

Estelle took a deep breath and watched the exhalation swirl in a flurry of mist, debating if she should tell him. She regretted saying anything at all.

"Once," she answered after a long pause.

"And you got away unscathed?" he asked incredulously.

She nodded, laughing nervously. "Yeah, it was... strange." Estelle didn't want to get him into more trouble than he already was, but she knew he wouldn't let it go.

"Strange how?"

"He didn't try to attack me."

"So, it saw you, too," he stated. "Must have been a close encounter."

She nodded but kept her eyes plastered to the ground.

"What was it like?"

"Uh..." Estelle hesitated, not expecting the question. "He was..." *Surprisingly decent* was what she wanted to say, but she stopped and went for "Crass."

Issac snorted. "Guess I'm not too surprised about that," he said, pausing before he continued. "Be careful, Estelle. Don't let it fool you. Even if it seems non-combative, don't turn your back on them."

"I'm always cautious, don't worry about me," she reassured him, looking up and smiling.

He visibly relaxed. "To think it even dared to speak to you," Issac scoffed, readjusting his hold on the pile of books he carried.

They passed by the gates to the third circle. The lanterns on either side automatically started to glow red in the darkness, denying them entry despite not seeking it. The lights returned to their natural, soft, golden glow after the two low-ranked Angels moved out of range.

4

Sisters

THERE WERE NEVER TOO MANY people inside the churches. Estelle often wondered where others would go if not inside chapels. Though she would like to think that other Angels were working efficiently, the simple truth was that the rate at which they were evacuating people couldn't account for the sheer level of desolation Estelle constantly found as she worked. Surely, there were more believers around than her missions would have one think—more outside the churches.

The Angel thought about it more as she wandered down a stone-paved road on the outskirts of the desolated city of Salford, England, late into the afternoon, gazing at the wreckage of a once lively area. She had finished clearing out the last assigned location of the day, but it didn't feel like her job was done.

She thought about taking to the skies and getting an aerial view, but decided against it. Much like the rule where Angels were not permitted to fly unless on the flight field, or going to and from the surface, the Apostles strongly enforced lower-level Angels not to fly unless absolutely necessary. To avoid drawing unwanted attention from a Demon.

Estelle sighed as she rounded a corner, pulled her hair over her shoulder, and braided it to have something to do with her hands. If she didn't find any more humans, she might be lucky enough to find a new movie to watch, just as long as the DVD wasn't too damaged. Her eyes roamed the streets, watching a breeze kick up some dust, when something caught her attention.

She heard movement.

Ahead of her was a large, dilapidated building with boarded-up windows. As she got closer, Estelle realized it was a small boarding school for girls. She had already finished her appointed rescues, and there were no rules stating she had to leave after the mission's completion, so there shouldn't be any harm in investigating. Or at least, that's what she was telling herself.

Projecting confidence, the Angel strode up to the front door, grabbed the heavy handle, and entered. She took a deep breath and opened her mouth, prepared to announce her presence, but in the end, all that came out was a shriek as someone spoke from behind her.

"Someone's breaking the rules."

Estelle bristled, raised her barrier, and quickly turned around to meet glowing red eyes. "You!"

"Me," the Demon said, lips curling up in amusement.

Estelle took a staggered step backward and looked him up and down. His horns and tail were gone. Had it not been for the luminescent eyes, he might have passed as human—he would have probably looked more like an Angel than she did if it weren't for the red eyes.

Do all Demons have red eyes? she thought as Antares' warning echoed inside her mind. *If you see wings, run.*

"What are you doing here?" she yelled, still suffering from being startled.

"I could ask you the same thing. Aren't you supposed to be at a church somewhere?" Zylis asked, grinning as he leaned back on the door.

Estelle heard the soft click as it closed.

"I was passing through—"

"Yeah?" Zylis quirked an eyebrow, and something about his tone grated on Estelle's nerves.

"*Yeah.*" She clenched her jaw. "I heard movement. I came to see if anyone needed help."

"Aw," he cooed, an amused smirk plastered across his face. "How altruistic of you."

"What do you think an Angel's job is, if not to help people?"

Zylis stilled and stared at her for a few seconds. He maintained the same grin, though it was noticeably strained, as if he was barely holding back laughter. Eventually, he slowly lowered his chin, brows raised. "Do you..." He took a breath, "Really want me to answer that?"

"What else—" Estelle started, only to stop abruptly, biting her tongue to keep herself from starting an argument with him. After a moment, she shook her head and took a staggered breath, forcing her curiosity to sit aside. "You're here for evacuation?"

"I'd hope that past experience would be enough for you to figure that out yourself," he said easily, gazing at Estelle with half-lidded eyes, tone shifting to condescension. "Come now, Star, think about it. Try not to hurt yourself, but do your best to crack the code."

Estelle had a sudden urge to flick his forehead as her wings twitched in irritation. If it hadn't been for every warning bell going off in her head, she probably would have done it, just as she would have if the Demon were Giovanna. Estelle mainly asked to see if he was explicitly following her, or if they ended up in the same area again by chance. She was betting on the former.

"Whatever," she muttered. "Just don't get in the way of my job, okay, Demon?"

"Your job?" he snorted. "Anything you do that's not inside a church isn't your job, Princess," he continued, smirking as he rolled his eyes. "Be careful; Daddy's gonna clip your wings."

"So kind of you to care about my well-being, but I'm not breaking any rules by being here," Estelle quipped.

"You're not following any instructions either," Zylis fired back, holding his gaze. "We both know that's just as bad."

"Are you going to tell on me, then?" she challenged, tilting her head to the side.

He seemed taken aback for a moment, but then he stood up straight and sighed.

"Nah, I'm not a snitch. Besides," he paused for a second, looking her up and down, glowing eyes roaming over her body in a way Estelle wasn't sure how to interpret. "Things are more interesting this way."

For several seconds, the Angel glared at the Demon. Golden eyes met crimson as she tried gathering her thoughts. *When we met, he told me his job wasn't transporting people.* Then her curiosity got the best of her, and she blurted out, "What do you do? If you can't transport more than a couple of people, what's the point of you being here?"

"Do you think it's a coincidence that the inferno hasn't burned this place to the ground?"

Estelle froze. Other Angels occasionally spoke about having close calls during evacuations when they traveled too close to the Combat Zone. They had come back with singed clothes and a sort of rattled demeanor one could only expect of a person who narrowly escaped the destruction of their soul. They had said that hellfire surged through the streets with all the vengeance of a flash flood, burning everything in its path indiscriminately. Estelle had always thought herself lucky to have never encountered it, but up until that moment, she had never asked why that was.

"So, you..."

"Redirect the flow of hellfire until a transport Demon can get here," he supplied. "You know, you should be thanking me. I make your job easy."

Estelle opened her mouth to ask more questions, but closed it before anything could escape her lips. She was oddly fascinated with the Demon and hated to acknowledge it. If she had been taught about them beforehand, she wouldn't need to get her information from the subject personally.

Estelle found herself thinking back on her conversation with Antares again. *You should work with him,* she thought, then sighed, activating Truth Seer. "Can you tell me where the girls are?"

"Oh, they're in the mess hall," Zylis said, gesturing toward a set of large double doors at the far end. "Probably would be in the dorms right now, but of course, you clumsy, overgrown chickens, blew that up."

She faltered for a moment, unsure of how to respond. Eventually, after working around the insult, she mumbled, *"I'm sorry."*

Estelle then turned and walked down the hall. Before she had turned around, she caught a glimpse of Zylis looking genuinely surprised, with his eyes widening slightly at the apology.

He trailed a few steps behind her as they approached the doors. Just as the Angel placed her hands on the door, he responded, his voice quiet, almost reverent. "Tell that to them."

Estelle didn't hesitate to push the doors open and enter a large group of girls, most sitting around the tables with books and a few on the floor in sleeping bags. They immediately looked up.

"This is Sta—"

"*Vegariel*," Estelle interjected, giving in to the urge and flapping her wings slightly so that the feathers would smack the Demon in the face. He must have made a face because some girls started giggling. Estelle did her best to ignore him afterward, going through her usual spiel before proceeding to each girl individually.

Distantly, she knew that it was possible that some of the girls might not have been true believers. Children were wildcards when it came to faith. On one hand, with them being so young, they weren't at the point where they'd begun to have doubts yet. On the other hand, considering they were from religious families, they could be merely riding on their parents' faith instead of their own.

On the off chance that neither of those was true and they don't believe at all, the child was forced to be left behind. It was a rough situation to be in, but it was incredibly uncommon. Angels received training on how to handle it gracefully, but no amount of instructions could prepare one to confront it in real life.

The girl was perhaps twelve years old, with long red hair and freckles decorating her face. Vegariel could already tell there was something wrong from the look on her face. Her voice quivered, and tears welled in her eyes as she repeated the five words and looked into the Angel's eyes.

"I-I'm a child of God."

It hit Estelle like a heavy boulder dropping into the pit of her stomach. Because the girl wasn't, or at least, she didn't believe she was.

Estelle offered a smile she hoped would be comforting, though her voice shook when she spoke. "S-sit tight for a moment. Everything is going to be okay," Estelle told her, then moved on to the next girl.

Estelle schooled her features as she carried out her duties, trying to look calm. But every once in a while, she'd glance over at the red-headed girl, only to find her in the same position time and time again: knees pulled up to her chest, and her head ducked down between them.

A few minutes later, she came across another girl with red hair, though this one couldn't have been older than seven. She repeated the exact phrase, and Estelle could tell she was a believer. So, the Angel started reaching out her hand, only to halt at the sound of a sudden, desperate cry across the room.

"No!" the other girl shouted, scrambling to stand and run toward them. She practically tackled the younger girl, wrapping her arms around her protectively. "P-please," she whimpered. "She's my little sister; please don't take her away!"

Estelle became tense and pale, at a loss for what to do. She hesitantly reached her hand toward the girl again, but they recoiled, heels squeaking against the floor as they frantically scooted back into the wall. The younger one began to cry into her sister's shirt while the older one barely held it together.

"P-please don't take her away, *please!* She's all I have!"

Estelle let her hand fall back to her side, stepping back as she stared at the sisters. What was she supposed to do?

"I can take them," Zylis said.

Estelle whipped her head around and was startled to see him a mere two feet away. She instinctively put up her shield. "You'll do *what?*"

"I can take them both with me." He shrugged. "If it's just them, it's not a big deal."

Estelle stared at him in shock for a few seconds while something hot bubbled up inside her until it burst. And suddenly, she was *furious.* In one quick movement, Estelle grabbed Zylis' wrist in a harsh grip and stormed out of the room, offering the girls a short "Be right back" as she dragged the Demon out of the room with her.

Once out, Zylis snatched his hand away right as Estelle slammed the door shut behind them. "The void, Star! What's your—"

She spun around sharply, opening her wings to their full length as a shield to the door.

"You're not taking them to Hell," she snarled.

"And why not?"

"*That* should be obvious."

The Demon stared at her for a moment, blinking slowly, before it seemed to dawn on him.

"Oh, for love of Concave—how brainwashed are you? I'm not going to toss them on a fire and use their flesh as fuel! If Hell were as terrible as you Hell-bells wished it was, we wouldn't live there."

"I don't care, it's not happening," she hissed.

"So, you're just going to separate them?" he shot back, taking quick strides toward her until they were only inches apart and he could glare down at her menacingly. "Send one to live peacefully while the other dies from hellfire?"

Estelle faltered. "No, I—"

"So what?" Zylis raked his hand through his hair in frustration.

Estelle noted that he appeared to be shifting, seemingly involuntarily, because when he pulled his hands out of his hair, the tips of his fingers had morphed into sharp, black claws, and horns peeked through the blonde hair.

"I take one, and you take the other?"

"No—I don't know!" Estelle shouted, looking away from his intense gaze. "I don't want to separate them, but I can't take anyone who's not a believer into Heaven, and I can't just leave them here or let you take them..." she trailed off, thinking about the man she almost let into Heaven because the 'system' deemed him worthy and overruled the terrible sins he had committed. *How is it that a child can't enter Heaven, but a scumbag can just because of belief?* Estelle sighed. "She's just a little girl. Her sins can't justify going to Hell."

For a long moment, Zylis didn't say anything. The Angel could feel his gaze fixated on her, and eventually, he spoke. "Kids can still sin a whole lot, Star." His tone almost sounded like a question.

"Is she a murderer? Is she abusive to her sister?" Estelle asked, meeting his eyes again.

He raised an eyebrow. "She forgot to feed her cat a couple of times." Zylis shrugged.

Estelle couldn't tell if he was joking or not. And even if he wasn't, that didn't justify a little girl going into eternal damnation.

Her training on the subject stated different approaches to the situation, but three options were heavily stressed for use. The first was to bless the child and leave them behind to fend for themselves. The second was to use the blessing of song to sing them to sleep. A peaceful end for them when the hellfire inevitably came. Lastly, the Angel was permitted to end their suffering themselves. It was considered a mercy compared to a soul being destroyed by the inferno.

Estelle slowly lowered her wings and folded them against her back as she considered her options, but none were good. She could either separate them, in one form or another or give them to a Demon. She felt defeated, but one option could be better than the others.

"What will happen to the girls," she began, slowly and steadily, "if I let you take them?"

The Demon held her gaze as he took a couple of steps backward and out of her personal space.

Estelle activated Truth Seer.

"Can't say for sure," Zylis replied. "But they'll be fine. I mean, the weather kinda sucks, but they'll have everything they need to live a happy existence."

Estelle released a breath she hadn't realized she was holding. Zylis was telling the truth. The sisters could stay together and not worry about what fate the other would be forced into. She still didn't like the idea of sending them to Hell, but believed they would live happily as long as they had each other.

"Okay," she said after a moment.

He stared at her for a few seconds longer, his eyes calculating. "You serious, Star?"

Estelle took a deep breath and resisted the urge to smack him. "You know, if you *insist* on not referring to me by my Holy name, the least you can do is call me by my real name."

"Oh?" Zylis laughed, his eyebrows nearly reaching his hairline. "Okay, no problem. What's your name, then? Gonna tell me?" he scoffed, his tone sarcastic. It was like he was laughing at a joke she wasn't getting.

"Estelle Amadea," she said calmly.

Zylis froze and stared at her briefly, eyes wide, mouth gaping in what seemed nothing short of pure, genuine shock. He stepped back further and sighed, dropping his head into his hands.

"You just—" he groaned, then laughed with a mixture of disdain and disbelief. "Y'know, I expected them to withhold some information to keep you pillocks in line, but this? Void, this is just going to get someone *killed*."

Estelle stared at him, sensing she had utterly screwed up. "What—"

"You're not supposed to tell me your stupid name, genius!" Zylis interjected, head snapping up. "Why do you think they make you choose Holy names in the first place?"

Her hand was against her mouth before he had finished talking. She felt physically ill, shaking from the realization of what she had done.

I didn't know. How could I have known? Then, the more rational part of her brain answered. *They weren't specific on why you needed a Holy name, only for a name to be called by the humans.*

"You're lucky I'm not out to kill you," Zylis continued. "Because if I were, you'd be dead the *second* that came out of your mouth."

At that, Estelle was a little offended. She wanted to tell him off, that she wouldn't go down without a fight, but feared she would throw up if her hand were removed from her mouth.

Zylis seemed to have read her mind. "There wouldn't *be* a fight," he deadpanned, walking back up to her. Estelle held her barrier up as he proceeded to poke her sternum, the tip of his claw pressing against her threateningly. "That pathetic little shield of yours—your spiritual condom? It's completely useless," he spat. "Your real name is more sacred than those 'Holy names' you come up with." His voice lowered into a dangerous cadence. "I'd slice through your chest and squeeze the life out of your heart before you even knew what was happening."

Estelle took a shuddering breath, the whole reality of her mistake setting in like a cold weight deep inside her. She slowly lowered her hand and forced herself to meet the Demon's gaze. "So, why haven't you?"

Zylis smiled—a mocking, borderline cruel smile. His claws retracted as he stepped back, shifting back into looking like a human. "Guess I don't feel like it, Princess."

5

Immutable Orchard

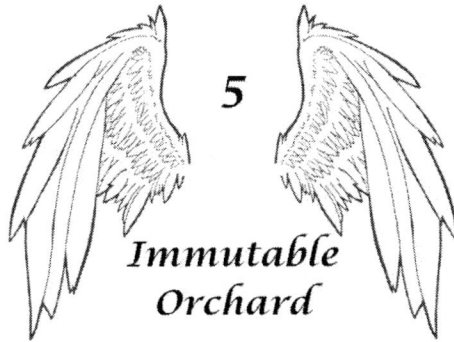

THE ANGEL SPENT THE NEXT few minutes sending the rest of the girls up to Heaven, watching clothes hit the floor before turning to the next child. Oddly enough, the Demon was with the red-headed sisters, speaking to them calmly with kindness in his eyes. Estelle wondered if the girls knew or could feel, in a way, that he wasn't human, even though he looked like one. As an Angel, she could feel the Demonic aura, an underlying feeling of danger that was dulled by his disguise, but still present.

Once the evacuation was finished, Estelle smiled and waved goodbye to the sisters before taking her leave. She would have liked to give them a blessing of some kind, but felt it would be best not to approach them, so she wouldn't scare them further.

She flew up, landed on a roof a couple of buildings away, and waited for the three of them to emerge. Estelle wouldn't be able to forgive herself if the Demon ended up harming the girls. After about twenty seconds of waiting, Estelle started to re-braid her hair, splitting it into two sections to make Dutch fishtail braids. She started at the top of her head and worked down one side, crossing the strands of hair to the ends before starting the other. Six minutes later, Zylis walked out with the two girls, and Estelle had two black braids.

The younger of the two sat propped up on his biceps; the older held his hand and walked beside him as he made his way down a cobblestone path. He took a left turn where the main road ended and started uphill, moving leisurely on a dirt path that stretched out to the horizon.

The Angel quietly moved from the rooftop and trailed after them beneath the violet light of the setting sun. If it weren't for Estelle's extreme concern for the girls, she would have thought that Zylis taking care of two frightened girls was incredibly cute and endearing.

At first, she had been content to observe from a distance, but when Zylis took a turn into what appeared to be a forest, Estelle found herself moving before she had consciously realized it. She hastily flapped her wings and took flight, gliding over the road she thought she had seen them take, and landed as silently as possible.

At the side of the road, there was a path paved with gravel and surrounded by trees. If Estelle held her breath, she could hear the soft footfalls and crunching of leaves in the distance. Cautiously, she stared down the path.

After about ten minutes, the trees began to thin out, and she saw, up ahead, a tall, black fence with an iron gate that had been left wide open. As the Angel drew closer, she realized that the road, more or less, faded away into the depths of... *An apple orchard?*

She blinked in confusion as she passed through the gate, looking back and forth and listening for footsteps, but there were none. The orchard was completely silent.

Estelle wandered between the trees, growing more confused as she went since they appeared to be flourishing despite the mayhem outside. The leaves were green, and blood-red apples hung from nearly every branch. It was as if the orchard, for whatever reason, had been suspended in its own little realm—as if the war didn't exist.

As the sky began to darken, the shade from the trees pushed the space surrounding her into a deeper night. Estelle wasn't sure when she had given up searching for Zylis, only that she had turned her attention to a tree and a low-hanging limb. She inched closer and reached up, fingers gently brushing against the shiny, red fruit as though it were some illusion. But it was real.

After a moment, Estelle sighed and stepped away. Her idle curiosity still buzzed in her mind, but the sky above had gone completely dark, casting everything, aside from herself, in the shadows. She walked out the same way she had entered and, with one last glance over her shoulder, took flight.

That night, Estelle lay awake in bed for what might have been a couple of hours, or just a few minutes. She stared at the ceiling as her mind darted from one subject to the next, some thoughts connecting while others strayed to something unrelated, but never quite settling into any particular idea. The Angel wondered what would happen to the girls, whether she had made the right choice. Estelle wondered what Zylis' motives were and if they genuinely aligned with hers. She wondered if Antares was right.

The orchard became a permanent fixture in her mind. She wondered what it meant and what Zylis was doing there. If he was passing through, or if there was a path to Hell within the orchard itself. Why the trees looked so well cared for, and why she couldn't hear anything outside the black gate. If the apples tasted as good as they looked—and at that moment, she realized that she couldn't remember what an apple tasted like.

She racked her brain, rolling flavorless saliva over her tongue as she tried to remember, but couldn't. For the first time in her afterlife, Estelle found herself longing for the memories she had forfeited. It was stupid and made no difference in terms of how she lived.

Estelle loved being an Angel. Angels were a rare breed; fewer than one out of two million believers were offered the chance to become one. It was a massive honor just to be selected, and despite the things she had left behind in favor of being an Angel, she couldn't imagine wanting to spend eternity any other way.

But she still wished she could remember what apples tasted like, and whether she liked the flavor or would still like it. The thought circulated inside her head, polluting her thoughts. In her heart, she knew that she wouldn't change her life for anything in the world, but she couldn't help but wonder.

Estelle wished she could remember the person she was back when she was human.

6

Demons

101

"I'm sorry, Antares. I didn't—"

"No, I'm the one who should apologize," he said, shaking his head. "As your mentor, it's my duty to teach you what you need to know in order to be safe. I didn't provide yo"u with adequate information, and that's a failure on my part, not yours." The older Angel sighed and leaned back in his armchair.

It was around seven in the evening the following day, and Estelle was wringing her hands, staring down at the hardwood floor of Antares' study in his home. She hadn't been able to focus during flight training and had received one of the worst scores of the day.

"Honestly, I just didn't expect you to run into him again so soon," Antares mumbled sheepishly.

"It surprised me too…" she trailed off.

"Well," Antares continued. "I suppose all I can say is we're lucky nothing bad happened."

Estelle merely nodded, eyes locked on her feet. Everything she had been told about the Demons wasn't necessarily wrong, but so much more didn't add up.

Time passed before her mentor continued. "Welp," he clapped his hands together, "I think it's time for a little 'Demons 101.' Wouldn't you agree?"

Estelle's head snapped up. "Wait, seriously?" she squeaked, waving her hands around meaninglessly. "I-I mean, are you sure? Wouldn't you be in some major trouble for that?"

"You're correct, but..." He smiled wanly and looked away. "I've already put you in unnecessary danger by withholding information." He met her eyes again. "I have my reasons for teaching you, but if risking a strongly-worded letter from the Apostles is what I need to do to protect you, then I'm more than happy to take that risk."

She stared back into his bright blue eyes for a few seconds; her brows pinched together in worry. Eventually, she relented. "If you're sure," she said, then smiled. "Thank you, Antares."

With a firm nod, the high-ranking Angel stood up and made his way to the far end of the room, opened a closet door, and retrieved a large blackboard. They both winced as the wheels squeaked. He apologized for the noise but continued to push it toward the girl. Once he had the board where he wanted it, Antares began.

"Alright," he said, grabbing a piece of chalk. "I suppose the first thing you should know is this: There are different *types* of Demons, but regardless of variety, there are five innate abilities that all share." Antares made a numbered list and continued to write as he spoke. "The first is Corruptive Touch, as I'm sure you're aware; it's why we need a barrier. The second is Vice Detection. Third: Sinful Feed. Fourth: a mild Hypnotic Gaze, at least for lower-level Demons." He turned and looked at his student. "Any questions so far?"

"Uh... am I allowed to write this down?"

"Oh well…" Antares hesitated. "I suppose that would be all right. I know it's a lot to take in. But understand you can't show it to anyone. What I'm teaching you is strictly for second sphere Angels and above."

"Right, of course." She nodded and quickly reached into her bag to pull out a notebook and pen, then leaned forward eagerly, poised and ready.

"Alright, let's address the elephant in the room." He turned back to the blackboard and wrote down the last Demonic ability before turning to face her again and stepping off to the side.

Number five was *Name Revoke*.

"The reason why you're not supposed to tell Demons your real name is because it opens up several offensive capabilities that wouldn't otherwise be available to them," he explained. "What you need to understand is that your real name is your human name. If a Demon learns an Angel's true name, the theory is that there are certain ways in which the Angel is rendered no different than humans, at least as far as their powers are concerned."

Estelle blinked, pausing in her note-taking. "What do you mean by 'theory'?"

"Well," he sighed. "Truthfully, there's a lot we still don't know about it because it just doesn't come up very much." He shrugged. "What we know is that if you give a Demon your name, the effectiveness of your barrier is more or less at their mercy. There's some evidence that it also makes you more susceptible to hypnosis, but the main issue concerns your barrier. If the Demon chooses to do so, they can break through it by just saying your name aloud."

Estelle felt her blood run cold, and Zylis' words suddenly rang in her ears. *That pathetic little shield of yours is completely useless. I'd slice through your chest and squeeze the life out of your heart before you even knew what was happening.* She released a shuddering breath. Her body felt numb with cold hands that shook slightly. Zylis could have killed her. But he didn't. He hadn't even tried to say her name.

"I take it you understand the gravity of the situation," Antares said, offering an empathetic smile.

The young Angel nodded.

"Now, what can you tell me about their corruptive touch?"

It took Estelle a second to recognize that he had asked her a question. Luckily, Antares was a patient man. "Uh... right, uhm, with direct skin contact and without my barrier, a Demon can corrupt my soul and force me to Fall," she answered confidently.

"Correct, though it won't happen immediately; it has to be done with prolonged contact." He nodded and turned his attention back to the board. "You already know about Vice Detection, so we'll move on to Hypnosis." Chalk in hand, he began to write. "For lower-level Demons, this ability can only be used with direct eye contact. After that, they can control you with simple commands. This doesn't usually come up in battle because they must maintain eye contact with you, but I'll explain more about that later. Sinful Feed is fairly self-explanatory—"

"They feed off of sinful desires?" Estelle guessed, pausing her penmanship to look up at the other.

"Yes, among sinful emotions and thoughts," he praised, facing her before continuing the lesson. "All of this is the basics. The next thing you ought to know is that, as alluded to earlier, there are different *types* of Demons. Generally speaking, Demons will fall into one of seven categories, each named after one of the seven deadly sins. When

I was still on Active Duty, we had long, arduous training sessions on this because knowing how to figure out what type of Demon you're up against is an essential skill. It gives you a framework for what sort of tactics you can expect from them," he explained, turning back around. "Types aren't set in stone. They're interconnected, like a clock, if it had only seven points."

Antares began to draw a circle on the board, placing a notch at the top and moving clockwise, placing six more notches at equidistant points on the circle.

Estelle did her best to replicate the depiction in her notes.

"Let's start with Envy," he said, labeling the first notch. "These are Demons whose abilities are primarily based around stealth-related things." On the second line, he wrote *Pride*. "Pride Demons are the most well-rounded, which makes them highly unpredictable and difficult to classify. They tend to fight in teams." On the third, he wrote *Greed*. "Greed Demons are the second most powerful in terms of raw strength. Their fighting style primarily relies on exploiting their environment." Next, he wrote *Sloth*. "In contrast, Sloth Demons are generally the weakest, at least from a brute force standpoint, but they make up for it through speed and are often sent in as a first line of attack, with hopes of wearing you down before a stronger Demon deals the final blow."

"Wait," Estelle interjected. "Their abilities are opposite to what they represent," she said. "Envy and Greed seem to make sense, but Pride working in teams, or Sloth Demons being *fast*?"

Antares let out a soft laugh. "It does seem backward, doesn't it?" he said. "So, depending on the type of Demon, they fall into one of two branches," he explained as he reached over to put a footnote on the

51

blackboard. "User, or *Attacker*. The difference is that a User will embody the sin, while an Attacker will use the sin against you. For example, Sloth Demons are Attackers; they have abilities that will affect *you*. Meanwhile, say, Envy Demons are Users and have abilities that will affect *them*."

Estelle's brows pinched together as she noted the information. "So, would that mean Pride and Greed Demons are... Users?"

"Yes. However, as I've said before, Pride is hard to classify. Part of this is because they tend to switch from User or Attacker abilities." He paused as he labeled the fifth notch. *Gluttony*. "Gluttony Demons aren't particularly strong physically, either. Similarly to Sloth Demons, they are Attackers. What they are known for are their traps. Most of their abilities are suited for lie-in-wait, so they'll usually be involved in ambushes, if anything."

Sixth was Lust. "Like Gluttony Demons, Lust Demons are also Attackers and a bit less common on the frontlines, though the more powerful ones can be extremely strong. They're capable of hypnosis far beyond that of any other type. Finally..." At the seventh tick mark, Antares wrote *Wrath*, thus completing the circle. "There are Wrath Demons, who are Users and by far the strongest among the Demons, as far as sheer physical power is concerned," he said, setting down the chalk before turning toward Estelle again. "Based on what you've told me so far, I would say you're probably dealing with a Wrath Demon."

The girl nearly dropped her pen, stumbling a little to catch it before it clattered to the floor. "Really?" she asked, eyes wide.

Antares nodded. "Repelling hellfire is a relatively advanced ability for Wrath Demons. It also means he can likely manipulate or manifest it to some degree."

"So what you're saying is..." She gulped, feeling a bead of sweat roll down her neck. "I wouldn't stand a chance if he chose to attack me because he knows my name *and* because he's the most powerful type of Demon."

"Well, yes, but—to be fair—as things stand, you probably wouldn't stand a chance against any Demon, regardless of type."

"I'm royally screwed," she said with a huff of air.

Her mentor sighed and moved to sit down in his chair once again. "Honestly, I don't feel you're in too much danger."

"Oh, please elaborate on that, because from where I'm sitting, I can't go back down to Earth ever again." Estelle buried her face in her hands, groaning softly.

"See, Wrath Demons... Well, yes, they're powerful. In terms of raw strength, they're unmatched. And I know that doesn't sound very reassuring, but what I'm trying to say is that if he wanted to kill you, I think he would've done it already. Though that's not to say there's nothing else worrisome he could do."

"What do you mean?" she asked, removing her hands from her face and slumping back in the chair.

"Well," he rubbed the back of his neck. "This is where the adjacency circle comes into play. Wrath Demons are positioned between Envy and Lust, which means they can also learn abilities from those classes. It also means they can use either Attacker or User abilities. I'm not sure if there's a limit on it, but in any case, it sounds like Zylis already has some cross-type abilities."

"Like...?"

"The night you said he snuck up behind you and then disappeared?" Antares said. "That, to me, sounds like an Envy trait. Moving in complete silence is a pretty basic ability for Envy Demons. It's the same with traveling through shadows, though I think that's considered more intermediate."

"Okay... but what's so worrisome about this?"

"Well, even if he's not planning to kill you, there are still bad things that could happen. If he's learned any Lust abilities, that could be problematic."

"How so?" Estelle leaned forward in her seat slightly.

"Lust Demons... Well, they're a special kind of dangerous because most of the time, they're not out to kill you," he said, lacing his fingers together and resting them on the desk.

"I don't think I understand," she said, eyebrows pinched together.

"Maybe an anecdote would explain things better," Antares said, pausing to take a deep breath before continuing. "Once, when I was younger, a couple of people from my squadron were involved in a fight against a powerful Lust Demon. They managed to win, but when they came back..." He hesitated for a moment. "Things weren't the same. It was like they weren't all there, mentally; they didn't talk much, just stared into the distance."

Estelle sucked in a breath.

"There were five of them, all level seven, but it was a close call against a Demon of that caliber." He looked down and rubbed the back of his neck. "At the time, we all just assumed they were a bit traumatized by the experience—understandably so, but four days later..." A beat of silence. "They Fell—every single one of them."

Estelle paled.

"Mass Falls are *extremely* uncommon, especially in the third sphere, so this was quite devastating. Things were never quite the same after that."

Estelle was frozen, her eyes blown wide. She was shaking and tried to take a deep breath to calm herself. She had one question on her mind: "How?" she asked, barely above a whisper.

"Lust Demons…" Antares sighed. "They specialize in a particularly insidious kind of psychological warfare. They can plant ideas in your head, little seeds of doubt—things so small you might not even be aware of it happening. But those seeds remain even when they're gone, even after they're *dead*. And they can sprout and grow into something you can't fight against," he explained. "We call it weaponized self-corruption."

Estelle didn't speak—couldn't speak. She just stared straight ahead, rattled and numb. She had never heard of anything that bad before. She hadn't even seen anyone Fall before.

"Honestly, when you first told me about this… Zylis fellow, I pegged him as a mid-ranged Envy Demon," Antares said, chuckling slightly. "Of course, all Demons can be dangerous, but Envy Demons, even ones who've learned attributes from their adjacent classes, are relatively harmless psychologically. I might not have been… quite so emphatic about this had I known he was a Wrath Demon earlier." After a second, he hastily waved his hands. "But let me be clear! I'm not saying this to deter you from working with him. I want you to be prepared. And frankly, the story I told you was an extreme case. As a Wrath Demon, it's very unlikely he'd be capable of anything more than a few mid-range Lust abilities. Again, I want you to be prepared."

Estelle nodded, though she was still tense. The room was nearly silent. The ticking of the clock above Antares' desk, which she had tuned out, came back into focus again, and for a few minutes, that was all Estelle could hear until her mentor cleared his throat. "If it would help you feel safer, we could do some private training."

The girl did a double-take. "What?"

"Probably not anything too in-depth," he clarified. "But I don't want you feeling defenseless."

"Are you sure?" Estelle would be overjoyed to learn some self-defense, but he was already risking quite a bit to teach her about Demons. Teaching her skills meant for tiers three through five Angels could be disastrous.

"I'm already breaking the rules," Antares said, laughing, seemingly reading her mind. "What's a few more? So long as you don't mention it to anyone, it should be all right. What do you say?"

"That would be incredible," she replied, nodding effusively. "Thank you so much!"

The older Angel smiled. "Then it's settled," he said. "We can start tonight. No time like the present." He stood up and held his hand out. Estelle took it, beaming, practically vibrating with excitement. "Oh, one last thing: when you get to the third tier and start learning this stuff officially, do your best to act surprised and pretend to be bad at the techniques for at least a few weeks."

"Alright, I'll be sure to do that, Antares." She laughed. But a second later, her smile faltered.

"Is something wrong?" he asked.

"It's just that all of this sounds good in theory, but..." She took a deep breath. "What if he doesn't want to work with me? I get an advantage in my application to ascend by avoiding temptation, but what incentive would Zylis even have to agree to this?"

He was quiet for a moment, then chuckled.

Estelle looked up at him, confused.

"Oh, Amadea," he said, shaking his head. "If anything, he has an even greater incentive to work with you than you do with him. The greatest incentive of all."

"Which is...?"

The high-ranking Angel smiled. "You. Don't forget, this is a test of strength on your part," he said. "Zylis has every reason to want to work with you. You're offering him a rare opportunity: The chance to corrupt an Angel."

7
Team Up

THE FOLLOWING MORNING, ESTELLE LEFT with jitters running through her limbs and nerves prickling the back of her neck as she took flight. The wind whipped through her hair as she soared across the sky, drawing closer to the source of the chaos. Antares had ensured that she wouldn't have nearly as much work to do that day. After all, she had a higher calling. She was going to convince Zylis to work with her.

Ascension was the goal, and teaming up with a Demon could speed up the process. On average, Angels ascended to the next level every ten years. Estelle had done it in eight and was on track to do it again until the war started, delaying nearly everything. But if resisting temptation directly from a Demon could help her get back on track—help her gain clearance to learn more and get on the front lines—it would be worth it.

She just needed to find him first.

From up above, the Combat Zone looked like hell on Earth. Vast billowing smoke stacks stretched out to the sky, dwarfing the buildings surrounding them as hellfire filled the streets, surging like white water rapids. The sight alone made Estelle uneasy.

She scanned the area for any disruption to the flow—places where the hellfire appeared unnaturally disrupted—but after half an hour of searching, she couldn't spot any signs of him. Estelle landed on the roof of an old shop and sighed. How could she be certain that he was in Manchester? For all she knew, he might not be in this country. He might not even be on Earth.

The thought gave her pause.

Wait—the orchard.

She took flight once again. It was a long shot, but it was better than nothing. Her heartbeat picked up as she glided across the morning sky until she came upon a familiar Victorian-style schoolhouse. From there, she retraced the path up the dirt road and landed at the turning point. Estelle entered the forest, making quick strides down the gravel path. But after fifteen minutes, the forest was still as dense as ever. She stubbornly continued, following the trail deeper and deeper, but slowed to a stop after another ten minutes.

The path split into two different directions.

I don't remember there being a fork in the road. Estelle peered down the two paths, confused. "Where did it go?"

"You're not going to find it."

She released a rather unbecoming shriek and spun around fast enough to smack herself with her hair, but didn't see anything.

There was a soft chuckle. "Up here, Princess," that rough voice called, directing the Angel to look up into a nearby tree.

Zylis was casually sitting on a thick branch, wearing a black leather jacket, his muddy combat boots dangling about ten feet over her head. He was holding something in his right hand, roughly the size of a grapefruit, but its skin was black-plum. Estelle wasn't sure what it was, and when the

Demon brought it up to his lips, she maintained eye contact with him as he sank his teeth into it. When he lowered his hand to chew, Estelle noticed his lips were covered in a strange, almost blood-like substance.

Zylis wiped his mouth on the back of his hand. "It's not here anymore," he continued. "Not right now, anyway."

"How do you keep finding me?" she blurted out.

"I don't have to answer that," Zylis replied, sounding bored. "But I will tell you that you make yourself very easy to find." He paused, taking another bite of his... Fruit?

Estelle watched the bob of his Adam's apple as he swallowed.

"It's pretty stupid. You should cut it out," he said, then amended, "Which is not to say I think you'd know how, but y'know..."

Estelle's eyes followed his movements as Zylis finished his snack, oddly entranced by the sight. The clawed tips of his fingers were left coated in the same bizarre carmine juice. The Demon maintained eye contact as he shoved each of them in his mouth, sucking the liquid from his fingers one by one. He then hopped down from the branch and landed gracefully, like a cat. He looked human, aside from the lightly glowing red eyes; there were no horns, claws, or a tail.

"So?" Zylis prompted, strolling toward her. "Ya gonna tell me what you want, or what?"

Estelle felt her face get warm for some incomprehensible reason, and it took her a moment to force her brain to focus. "I've been looking for you," she said lamely, physically winced, and pressed her lips into a hard line.

"That much is obvious," Zylis shot back, lips twitching up at the corners. He took another step toward her. "Even after insisting you were never going to be looking for a Demon. But the question is, why?"

"Well," the Angel started, taking in a breath. "I was going to ask if you would be interested in, uhm, working together?"

Zylis stared at her for a moment, then snorted. "*What?*" he laughed. "You're joking, right?"

"I'm not."

Zylis evidently didn't believe her, if the increased mirth of his laughter was any indicator.

"I'm serious!" Estelle shouted, suddenly furious. "I want to work with you! Why would I try to find you if I were joking?"

He chuckled a bit more, but it began to peter away when Estelle kept an insistent, imploring look on her face. Slowly, the amused grin faded away, and a distinctly guarded demeanor arose in its place. Zylis' relaxed aura gradually froze over, and he regarded Estelle with a cold, calculating expression.

"Why?" he spat.

"I think we could accomplish a lot; people can stay with their loved ones, and we don't taint Heaven with people who don't deserve—"

"Lying's a sin, Star," the Demon interjected, his tone patronizingly sweet, contrasting the relaxed look on his face.

"I'm not—"

"You *are*," Zylis clipped, his expression morphing into a disgusted sneer. "And frankly, I see no reason for me to trust you if you don't even have the decency to be transparent about it." He brushed past her, his shoulder bumping hard against Estelle's as he walked away.

The girl blinked before whirling around to follow him, her heart rate picking up as she did so. "Alright, I'm sorry!" she called out. "I'll tell you the truth!"

Zylis turned around but continued walking backward as he stared at Estelle with an expectant look on his face.

"I—" Estelle fumbled. "My mentor suggested it. He said it would look good to the Apostles—when they review me for ascension."

Zylis slowed to a stop and stared at her for a moment before snorting with a mixture of amusement and disdain. "Oh, so I'm your extracurricular?" He scoffed. "You think I'm your path to a promotion."

"I mean..." She looked away sheepishly, her wings drawing in. "Technically, yes."

"And what would I be getting out of this?" he asked, his expression disgusted. "What *exactly* do I stand to gain from helping you move up the hierarchy, Star?"

Estelle looked back into his eyes and stepped back, nearly tripping over her own feet at the proximity.

Zylis huffed a dry, humorless laugh and shoved his hands into his pockets. "Goodbye, Star," he spat, turning on his heel with a clear intent of making a swift escape.

Estelle could hear her heartbeat pounding in her ears and moved without thinking in her state of panic. "Wait!" she shouted, leaping forward, her wings opening in her haste, and closing the distance just enough for her to reach out and grab Zylis' hand.

She felt the Demon's skin against her own. The subtle, pleasant difference in the transfer of heat, and she immediately knew she had screwed up. She hastily put her shield up and yanked her hand away, but there was no reversing the damage she had already sustained. The look in Zylis' eyes told her he knew what had happened, too, as if he could somehow *feel* her slip up. Estelle quickly looked away, sinking back into a wall of white feathers, her face unbearably warm.

"You offered before. That night," she mumbled after a moment. Steeling herself, she looked into those eyes again, her wings rolling back to reveal herself. "You said, 'Let me know if you ever feel like taking a dive.'" Estelle watched as his expression grew even more incredulous as the words left her mouth. "I don't, but you could persuade me," she said, then quickly tacked on, "It won't work, of course, but you can still at least try to—"

"Make you Fall," Zylis finished, his voice resonant with some combination of disbelief and reverence.

She nodded, the smallest of movements, so she wasn't even sure she had moved at all.

As he stepped closer to her, the sound of gravel and leaves crunching was overwhelming. "You're telling me..." he began, circling her slowly, his shadow dancing across the ground from her halo's light. "That you want me to tempt you?"

Estelle swallowed. "It wouldn't say much about my ability to resist it if you didn't."

Zylis scoffed, laughing deep under his breath as he came to stand before her again, pinning her beneath a glowing gaze. He smirked. "You're weird," he said, his tone almost affectionate. "Who's your mentor?"

"I uh—I'm not sure you'd know him," Estelle hesitated, taken off guard by the question.

"Try me."

Estelle blinked. "Antares," she said, carefully observing Zylis' face. The Demon's eyebrows seemed to rise slightly, but apart from that, his expression betrayed little more than a vague recognition.

After a moment, he said, "Fine," before fixing her with a stern gaze. "But let's get one thing straight: *you*—" he poked Estelle in the sternum with his forefinger, "—don't know what you're doing." The statement was so direct and harsh that the Angel almost didn't know how to react. She opened her mouth to retort, but Zylis continued, "You *don't*. So if I tell you to do something, even if you don't exactly understand it, even if it makes absolutely no sense to you—if I say it's *important*—you do it and ask questions later. Got it?" He stared down at her, glowing, red eyes boring into gold as she looked back.

"What would you have me do?" Estelle asked, swatting his hand away.

"Depends on the situation."

"But what would be so 'important'—" she used air quotes, "—you would have me do it instead of yourself?"

Zylis glared at her.

Estelle stood her ground. "If I don't know what I'm doing, as you have stated, why would you have *me* do it?"

For a moment, they stared at each other. Estelle could see him evaluating her challenge, his face unchanging from a tense, calculating gaze. But then he cracked a smile.

"Breaking from the pack, Star?"

Estelle blinked, confused. "What are you talking about?"

Zylis shrugged, feigning innocence. "Never knew an Angel to ask so many questions."

"I do when it concerns my safety," she shot back.

He laughed. "Did you, or did you not, tell me your real name?" His smile grew colder, as if he could see straight to her soul.

Estelle opened her mouth, but no sound followed through with the movement. She needed to stay compliant as per the need of an Angel of God. Carry out orders when given and don't ask questions. But her duty was to protect humans and escort the believers to Heaven. And as a result, she worried about their safety. But if her questions revolved around their well-being, there would be no harm.

She swallowed roughly. "What would you have me do?" Estelle repeated. She didn't know about Name Revoke until the worst had happened, so in retrospect, her safety was at the mercy of Zylis. But that didn't mean she couldn't find the lies in his words.

Estelle activated Truth Seer.

"Tell you what," Zylis said, clicking his tongue. "I promise I won't tell you to do anything that would endanger the humans or yourself. "

Estelle sighed and opted to give a simple nod in agreement. "Alright."

He was telling the truth.

Zylis seemed to know more about what was going on than she did, and appeared to have some experience on the surface. Estelle just needed to be careful until her application was accepted.

The blonde seemed to relax slightly and, after a beat of silence, turned around and began to walk away, prompting her to follow with a tilt of his head. She walked a couple of paces behind.

"We're taking care of my stuff first," he muttered. "I'll talk to the others later and work something out, but at least for today, I think it's only fair that my job takes precedence."

"Of course," she quickly agreed. "I appreciate you humoring me."

Zylis sighed and proceeded to reach under his jacket, appearing to grab his upper left arm. "Hey, Cyrus. It's me," he grunted. "You're not going to believe this, but…"

8

Cyrus

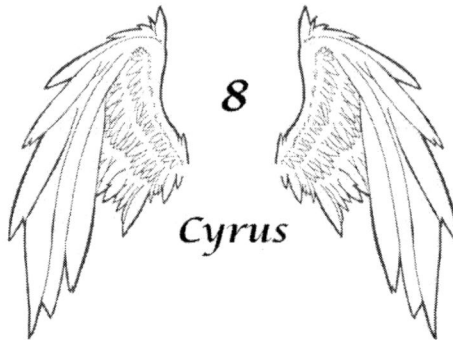

ESTELLE'S MIND HAD BEEN RACING the entire time as they walked. Out of the eighteen years of being an Angel, teaming up with a Demon was probably the single most reckless and idiotic thing she has ever done. There was a great possibility that Estelle would Fall before her application was accepted. If anyone were to figure out her extra-curricular activities and report them, she wouldn't be the only one being reprimanded.

Antares had said before that breaking the rules wouldn't give him more than a slap on the wrist, considering his rank, but that only made Estelle worry more. He could lose teaching privileges and be stripped of the ability to ever leave the first sphere. He would become stuck in one place, forever.

The risk was high, but the reward would be worth it. Estelle would ascend to level three and join the Holy Army on the front lines, attacking the Demons head-on. If the plan worked, everything would be better.

Estelle's thoughts didn't stop at the dangers of her secret mission as she wondered about everything Demon-related. In truth, she found this opportunity to be like the discovery of a new species that had yet to be explored. She wanted to know how Demons thought and differentiated from each other—if one *type* of Demon acted differently from another. If other animals could speak, people would be lined up to ask questions.

Estelle was sure there were multiple black strands out of place, as she hastily twirled, braided, and re-braided her hair during their walk. It was a nasty habit she had whenever she started overthinking something, begging for answers with unorganized thoughts, unnoticed by most.

It had been all of ten minutes before she broke the silence that had fallen between Zylis and her when the thought of meeting another one of them won the race, and she couldn't stop herself from asking, "Do all Demons have red eyes?"

"What the devil do they teach you up there?" Zylis asked, glancing back at the Angel and pausing slightly on his footing. "What the void happened to your hair?"

"Far too little," she admitted, ignoring his second question. She combed her hair with her fingers, her right hand tingling slightly. "But what better chance to learn all things Demon than from the subject itself?"

Zylis rolled his eyes before falling into step again to continue toward wherever they were going. "No. What we're born with tends to stay the same as we get older," he answered, voice overbearingly sweet.

The girl hardly picked up on it as something clicked in her mind. "I didn't know Demons could reproduce," she said. "In the history of The Three Realms, I was told that the Original Seven first created them.

Gradually, as people began to be corrupted and become truly wicked, they turned into one when they died."

"So first: How do you not know about *eye color* but know about the Originals?" Zylis asked as he brought a hand to rub his eyes with his forefinger and thumb. "Second: we can't reproduce; at least, the women can't. It's like natural birth control. And third: people get sent to Hell for four different reasons." The hand came down as he extended his middle finger, beginning a tally, though the Angel could have done without the crude sign. "They get rejected from entering Heaven, by either dying and not 'being worthy'—" he used air quotes with his other hand, "—enough to enter, or not ascending with a magical pelican." Another finger extended. "They really were just a scumbag and deserve everything that comes to them as a Demon takes them down." A third finger went up. "Or we escort people who can't go with Angels—like those two girls from a couple of days ago. And specialty cases." The hand fell to his side.

Estelle blinked, sorting all the new information away. "Okay, you realize that Angels are not birds, right?"

"Angels have wings and are just as stupid," he said, then quickly tacked on, "Wait, I shouldn't have said that. That's an insult to the birds."

Estelle clenched and unclenched her hands several times before deciding to leave it be.

"So, Demons are just anyone who dies and goes to Hell?"

Zylis nodded, putting his hands inside his pants pockets.

"But what stops the guys from impregnating human women?"

Zylis let out a short, humorless laugh. "Humans are fragile and could die if you even look at them funny," he said, turning around to face Estelle as he continued to walk backward. "Having sex with one would be no fun. Who in their right mind would want to go easy and worry about not killing them while having sex?"

Estelle felt her face get hot and her feathers ruffled before he had even finished talking. It didn't help that he was looking at her with a wicked grin.

After a moment, he stopped walking and directed her attention to their destination and his assigned spot: a large community center with boarded-up windows. They approached a set of double doors with a sign that said 'gymnasium.' Estelle could hear the rumble of chatter within.

Just before they entered, Zylis turned to her again, one eyebrow raised. "Well, since this was your idea," he said. "I'm assuming you've got some plan for how you think this should work. Tell me, and I'll let you know if it's actually good."

"Well..." Estelle hesitated. "I was thinking we could start by telling everyone to find their families so no one gets split up," she explained. "Then, I could start checking people, and maybe we could have a signal, for when you see someone you think is a bad person. You'll signal me, and I'll know not to send them up."

"Is that it?"

"Not quite," Estelle replied. "I mean, I don't know how long it will take for your *support* to get here, but depending on how long we'll need to wait, I could run out to some of my churches and bring them over here. It might be easier to process people that way."

Zylis hummed. "It usually doesn't take that long," he said, then shrugged. "The longest I've had to wait is an hour, but most of the time, it's about thirty minutes or so."

The Angel nodded as they meandered toward the entrance to the gymnasium.

He threw a glance over his shoulder. "Oh!" he said, as if he had just remembered something. "There's just one issue with your plan, Star."

"And what is that?" she asked, brow furrowed. Zylis turned toward her, his hand holding the handle, opening the door a sliver, just enough to let the noise out.

He grinned, putting sharp, white teeth on display. "It only works if you assume that my definition of a 'bad person' is the same as yours."

Estelle stared at him for a few seconds, processing. When the implication finally hit her, she felt a spike of cold air rush over her. "Wait, what do you—!"

"Let's do this," Zylis declared and opened the doors.

If Estelle had to guess, she'd estimate there had been around two hundred people inside the community center to start with. By the time they had gone through everyone, that number had fallen to about one hundred and twenty, or so. She didn't know how she felt about the whole predicament. Most of the humans were families, and because of that, when only ten percent of them couldn't ascend, the rest chose to go to Hell with them to stay together.

She could see why people would rather stay with family, but it didn't seem rational. When Estelle sent people to Heaven, they went to the Mainland, a separate area from where Angels lived, where they would live the rest of their existence. It was painless and peaceful. From what she understood, the journey to Hell was not a fun experience.

Estelle had only seen two instances, one with the two little girls, the other with the abusive man. Even though she didn't see the whole process, neither one looked peaceful or easy. And once they got to Hell, she was sure it was... well, hell.

It was around ten-thirty in the morning when Zylis suddenly seemed to tense, and his posture straightened as he reached under his jacket and grabbed his arm, much like before.

Estelle stared at him, wondering if he had a communication device attached to his arm, but it didn't seem like his jacket was stuffed with anything but the limb. Whatever it was, Zylis could talk to someone whom only he could hear.

"Yeah?" he grunted, then fell silent for a moment. "Alright."

The girl gave him a quizzical look as he ran his hand through his blonde hair.

"Big guy's here," he explained, then sighed. "Brace yourself."

Estelle didn't even have time to comprehend those words before the gymnasium doors suddenly burst open, and with them, the sound of a booming voice resounded throughout the room.

"Hello!" he shouted, grinning from ear to ear as he quickly strode up to them.

Estelle's eyes nearly popped out of her head. Zylis was tall, but the newcomer was *huge* and had short, fire-blue hair. Estelle barely had time to activate her barrier before the Demon suddenly grabbed her hand and proceeded to shake it with enough vigor to yank her shoulder up and down.

"You must be Star! It's nice to meet you! I've never met an Angel that wasn't trying to kill me!" He leaned toward her, and Estelle reflexively leaned away.

"Hey, Cyrus," Zylis growled. "Calm the concave down. You're gonna spook her."

"Right! Sorry!" he said without any loss of enthusiasm. The Demon stood up straight again. "My name's Traten."

"H-hello!" Estelle squeaked, gently extricating her hand from Traten's grip. "It's, uhm, nice to meet you, too?" She tried to glance over at Zylis from the corner of her eye.

He just snorted. "Don't worry. He's always like that," the blonde said, rolling his eyes. "Absolutely no concept of indoor voice."

"I'm still here, you know," Traten said, a little softer but loud enough to make the Angel jump.

"I'm *well* aware." Zylis scoffed. "Anyway, everyone's over there," he said, gesturing toward the large group. "Well, most of them. Some kids are playing across the hall. I'll round them up." He turned and started toward the entrance of the north hall. He threw one last glance over his shoulder. "Try not to scare the living void out of her while I'm gone, Cyrus."

"I'll try!" the other Demon shouted, his tone cheerful. The sound of the door closing echoed throughout the gym. Traten grinned, turning to face the Angel. "Zylis told me so much about you!"

Estelle did a double-take. "Really?"

He nodded enthusiastically.

A small, nervous smile played on her lips. "Good things, I hope...?"

"Totally! I mean, other than the part where he called you an idiot and guessed that you had at most three months before Falling. That's just how he is."

"I see." Estelle pursed her lips and straightened her back. "But I'm not going to Fall."

"That's what everyone says before they Fall."

"I'm sure that's what most Angels would say in general."

"You've got me there!"

Estelle paused when she thought she heard children laughing in the hall where Zylis went in.

Traten was certainly strange. Compared to Zylis, he seemed more relaxed. It was as if he thought they were all on vacation, enjoying exotic sights instead of trying to survive a war. With a smile and a cheery voice, Traten spoke as if they were long-lost friends.

Estelle's thoughts were put on pause as a young man walked up to her, his eyes watching the Demon wearily. He believed in God but chose to stay behind and go to Hell. From the heavy bags under his eyes and jittery manner, the Angel supposed the human did not feel worthy to enter His Kingdom. Though most humans these days looked similar, it was the smell of marijuana that called out to Estelle.

She smiled warmly and stretched out her hands toward him, palms up. He took hold, and Estelle recited a holy blessing meant to calm the soul and make the recipient feel rejuvenated.

"Better?" she asked.

The young man breathed in, his movements stilling. "Thank you." He made a low bow before retreating.

Traten whistled. "Never saw an Angel do anything but blow things up."

Estelle sighed. She couldn't imagine doing anything else with her existence—the opportunity to help and save people. There was no chance, in all of the Three Reams, she was going to Fall and give that up.

"How often do Angels Fall?" she eventually asked, looking back toward Traten, watching his eyebrows rise.

"Not very often," Traten answered, scratching his head. "They say it usually averages out around once every eighty years, but that's during times of peace when we don't have much contact with Angels." He shrugged.

"And I take it you think it'll happen more, now?" Estelle asked, then added, "Because of the war?"

"Well, yeah. I know it will," Traten replied. "Because it has."

The Angel exhaled a puff of air through her nose that could be interpreted as a laugh. "Well, it's not going to happen to me. I enjoy being an Angel. I get to help people." Estelle brushed her hands against the dress she was required to wear while on the surface, removing any dust that had gathered on the skirt. "It's hard work, but that's part of why I love it."

"I do respect you guys' passion," he said, smiling widely. "If nothing else, I'll give you that: you're passionate about what you do."

The girl smiled before hearing another bout of laughter. That time, she was sure she heard it.

"Can I ask you a weird question?"

Estelle hummed. "Um, sure?"

"Do you trust Leonhart?"

Estelle narrowed her eyes. She didn't know anyone by that name.

Seeing her confusion, Traten clarified. "Sorry, Zylis, I mean. Do you trust him?"

"Oh, I..." she fumbled. "I mean, I guess?" She paused before adding, "I can tell when he's lying."

"Would you trust him without the Truth Seer?"

Estelle blinked. "No."

Traten laughed. "Very blunt, I like that! You remind me of—" A muffled shout came across the hall, cutting him off.

The Angel jolted in alarm, looking in the direction with concern. "I should probably..."

"Yeah, no worries!" he agreed. "Go make sure dear old Zylis doesn't die!" He laughed again. "I should probably get things set up here, anyway."

Estelle nodded before she jogged over to the door and yanked it open, entering the north hall. She glanced in both directions, quickly zeroing in on one room a few doors down, from where a high-pitched screech appeared to originate. She quickly approached it and opened the door to the sound of shrill laughter and deep, aggravated groans.

9

Nicknames

THE SCENE NEARLY CAUSED ESTELLE'S eyes to pop out of her head.

A young boy, no older than four years old, was sitting on Zylis' shoulders. Zylis was partially shifted, and the boy had both hands on his horns, leaning back and pulling.

Estelle leaned against the door frame, her hand covering her mouth to prevent a burst of laughter as she watched.

"Hey, quit fu—*fudging* pulling on them!" Zylis shouted.

"Why do you have kitty ears?" the little boy asked. "Are you a cat?"

"*What?* No, they're clearly not—"

"He's got a tail, too!" a little girl exclaimed.

"Zylis is a kitty!" another boy giggled.

"Zitey!" the boy on Zylis' shoulders exclaimed.

"I just said—!"

"Zitey! Zitey! Zitey!" the kids chorused, drowning out the Demon's protests.

Estelle couldn't help but giggle along. After a moment, she cleared her throat. "Hey, kids?" she finally said, prompting Zylis to look up at her, wide-eyed. Estelle was grinning from ear to ear, barely holding back the urge to laugh outright. "Come on, give it a rest. It's time to go."

"Awww!" They seemed to cry collectively.

The boy on Zylis' shoulders frowned. "But—but—"

"It's not nice to pull on the kitty-cat's ears," she scolded, waving a finger. "You're going to make *Zitey* upset." She snorted, having to look away as the Demon glared at her rather intensely.

The children didn't notice, but seemed to get the message.

Estelle stepped to the side and ushered them all out into the hall, extending one of her wings as a guide, then propped open the door to the gym with her hand. It took a minute, but eventually, they managed to herd the children back inside.

"Epaitu, the lot of them," Zylis hissed, horns and tail receding as he entered.

"Aw, they're just kids," Estelle cooed, side-eyeing him. "You seem to be good with them."

"Oh, was that a compliment just now?" Zylis teased, looking down at her with a mischievous smirk.

"Don't get ahead of yourself," she countered, feeling her face get extremely hot. "Zitey."

"Oh, my—"

"What's wrong, *Zitey?*"

"You're never going to let that go, are you?"

"Nope," she said, popping the 'p.' "But I could be persuaded to call you Zye instead."

The blonde opened his mouth to retort, but before he could get a word out, Traten's booming voice filled the room. "Alright, everyone!" he shouted. "Since you're all here, let me introduce myself! My name is

77

Traten, and I'll be helping you evacuate today! If you would be so kind as to gather around the center of the room, it will make the trip much smoother! Thank you!"

There was a commotion as people shuffled around, doing their best to fit closely together in the center of the gymnasium.

Estelle couldn't believe how friendly a Demon could be. Zylis was not the best comparison, with his brash and unapologetic manner, but even he was surprisingly good with kids, and she was pretty sure Traten never dropped his smile. It was beyond strange.

After a couple of minutes, Traten spoke up again. "Ready, everyone?" he shouted as Estelle felt Zylis' hand grip the back of her dress, yanking her away from the crowd.

She sputtered indignantly, her wings failing lightly, as he dragged her to the edge of the room and pushed her against the wall.

The other Demon looked over at them and grinned. "It was nice meeting you, Star! I wish I could stay longer. If I'm around long enough to meet you again, I'd love to get to know you better!" Estelle furrowed her brow, but she didn't get a chance to say anything before he began yelling again. "All right! Here we go!"

The air inside began to swirl, slowly at first, but quickly picked up speed until what appeared to be a tornado formed at the center of the room. Estelle watched in half-terrified awe as the rapid winds became opaque and she heard a loud crack from within. That was when she noticed the tornado began to sink into the ground. It took about ten seconds before the winds started to slow and disperse. In their absence, there was a massive pit at the center of the gym, and Estelle's jaw dropped.

"Show off," Zylis muttered, then sighed and stretched his arms above his head. "Well, I guess we should head out. What's your closest place?"

Estelle didn't respond at first, still trying to understand what she had just witnessed.

"Hey, Earth to Star."

"Ah, sorry!" The Angel jolted, shaking her head, and went to follow the Demon as he opened the door to the hall. "It's just around two blocks east. But what did he mean about being around long enough to meet me again?"

"Oh, yeah." Zylis clicked his tongue. "He's on combat duty starting tomorrow," he said, then shrugged. "Not too concerned about him, though. You saw what he just did; he'll be fine. He'll be back to annoy me soon enough." He waved his hand dismissively.

"I see," Estelle muttered. She followed Zylis outside, and for a moment, neither of them spoke until he turned a corner to head east, and for whatever reason, something came back to her. "Hey, Zye..."

The Demon groaned at the name.

"What did you mean—earlier, before we went in—about you not having the same, uh..."

"Oh, the stuff about your plan?" Zylis asked. "What do I think defines a bad person?"

"Yeah." She nodded. "What do you mean by that, exactly?"

He shrugged. "I just think it's cute how you're assuming my definition of a bad person is the same as yours."

Estelle did her best to ignore that statement's 'cute' part. "Yes, but you wouldn't let me send up anyone dangerous, would you?"

"Depends on your definition of dangerous," Zylis replied. "If you mean people who have committed violent crimes, then no. My ability lets me see what humans don't want others to know about. That includes a lot of pretty benign stuff."

The Angel blinked. "Such as...?"

"Eh, drug addiction, usual fetishes, things like that," he said, then snorted. "I *honestly* couldn't care less about ninety percent of the secrets humans keep."

"So, you're not going to tell me about those people?"

"Absolutely not," he answered, his tone joyous. "Pretty sure Heaven would be near empty if I did, anyway. I mean, do you have any idea how many religious people are kinky? It's at least fifty percent."

"*Excuse me?*"

"You heard me," Zylis snorted. "It's all that repression, y'know? That 'leave room for the holy spirit when you slow dance' type of crap, or pamphlets saying you'll burn for all eternity if you jack off." He made a vulgar gesture, and all Estelle could do was stare at him, mortified, as he continued his rant. "It's just what happens when you attach feelings of shame to natural desires. The desires don't go away; they just get *weirder*. I mean, void, the day I met you, you sent up a woman who almost *exclusively* fantasized about having people watch her have sex with someone, and I just sat there and watched it happen because, frankly, 'what makes you horny' isn't my litmus test for moral character."

Estelle just gaped at him, eyes wide and cheeks burning. *How can he say things like that aloud?*

"So, you still want to work with me?" Zylis chuckled, clearly enjoying her expression.

It took her a second to reboot her brain before she spoke. "I-I mean, it's still better than nothing." She gathered her hair and pulled it over her shoulder before making tiny braids. "But there's nothing I could say to persuade you otherwise?"

"Not a devil-damn thing," Zylis said, grinning. "Sorry, Star. You're just gonna have to make peace with the fact that at least half the people you send up are gonna be into some things."

Estelle sighed, turning her head away, cheeks heating up again. "I guess... Some sins *are* worse than others."

"Damn right," he agreed. "And I mean, if Heaven is going to be full of people who've got a stick up their butt, might as well let in people who're already into that."

Estelle felt something bubble up inside her and burst out in the form of an abrupt laugh that surprised even her. She reflexively smacked a hand over her mouth to stifle it, but Zylis' grin let her know it was already too late.

By the end of the day, they had evacuated everyone with time to spare. As the last of the clothes hit the floor, Zylis breathed a sigh of relief and sat on the altar. Estelle watched and winced as the Demon leaned back on his hands and propped a foot up on the edge, his boots leaving dirty marks on the pristine, white fabric.

"Couldn't you at least try to show a little respect?" Estelle grumbled, flexing her right hand. It had bothered her all day, almost as if it were itchy.

"I've got none to give, Princess," Zylis shot back, staring vacantly at the ceiling.

Estelle's jaw clenched as she looked at the irreverent Demon, anger building up inside her.

She opened her mouth to retort, but the words died on her tongue as he spoke up again. "Okay, that was a little harsh," he admitted, grimacing as if the very act of doing so caused him physical pain. "It's... It's not *you*, I hate. It's just what you stand for."

The Angel's anger calmed, but only slightly. "Isn't that fundamentally the same thing as hating me?"

Zylis laughed, finally tearing his eyes from the ceiling to look at her. "You tell me, Star. I'm taking a page out of your book, after all. The phrase 'hate the sin, love the sinner' ring any bells?" he asked. "I can see why you would think that, but no, it's not."

She stared at him briefly, eyes narrowing as she tried to piece together what he had said, but fell short. "I'm failing to see your point."

"Let's put it like this," he said, sighing again. "I hate the things they make you do, Star. I hate that you help prop up their 'holier than thou' nonsense, and I hate that you're brainwashed into thinking it makes sense." He paused momentarily and said, "But I don't hate you. If I truly hated you, I wouldn't want you to Fall."

"So what you're saying is," Estelle maintained eye contact with him as she lowered her chin slightly. "You want me to Fall because you like me?"

"Not particularly." Zylis snorted. "It's kinda like dealing with a kid. You do dumb stuff because you don't know any better." He shrugged. "It's irritating, but I'm not mad at you 'cause of it."

"Sorry to break it to you, but Demons are not my type, Zitey," she said, raising an eyebrow.

"You know what, I take everything I said back. I hate you, and you're annoying, like a jantu."

She stared at him for a moment, unsure of what he was comparing her to. "I don't see how insulting me lends itself to your goal."

Zylis laughed again, pushing himself onto his feet. "Yeah, maybe it doesn't." He walked down the aisle until he stood a few feet away from her and smirked. "Then again, the last Angel I got this close to didn't make it out alive, so y'know..." He shrugged again. "Compared to my past interactions with you pillocks, I might as well be dragging my tongue across your body right now."

"Oh, my—" Estelle brought her wings forward to hide behind, cheeks heating up. "Would it kill you to tone down the vulgarity?"

He hummed, pursing his lips as if contemplating it. "No, maybe not," he finally replied. "But you're the one who wanted to be tempted. You signed up for this, Star."

The Angel groaned, closed her eyes, and nodded.

A couple of seconds later, Zylis spoke again. "Seriously, though, Star—think *really* carefully about whether this is what you truly want. 'Cause if I have to clear my schedule only for your wishy-washy birdbrain to back out, I swear I'll break your stupid halo over my knee. You're sure?"

Estelle lowered her wings and faced him, looking into his eyes without hesitation. "I'm sure."

For a long moment, they held eye contact, crimson eyes calculating.

There was a part of her that wondered if a goal of making her Fall was worth it. Then again, killing a Demon was regarded as a great deed in the name of God. Zylis was probably in it for a promotion of some kind—the exact reason for herself.

Eventually, the Demon sighed and brushed past her. "In that case, when are you scheduled next?"

"I, ahh—" The Angel fumbled as she moved to follow after him. "Wednesday."

"Alright," Zylis said, nodding as he opened the door, "guess I'll see you then." He started down the street.

"Wait!" Estelle called out. "How will I find you again?"

"Don't worry about it, I'll find you," he stated over his shoulder.

"How do you do that exactly?" she mumbled.

The Demon snorted and ducked into an alleyway cast in shadow. "Same way I always do."

"Which is...?" she asked, turning the corner as well, but Zylis was already gone, disappearing within the shadow itself.

10

Swears

ESTELLE WASN'T DREAMING, OR AT least nothing she could remember. But waking up to an odd pulsating sensation in her right hand was not how she wanted to start her morning. Sluggishly, Estelle pulled her arm out from under her pillow to look at it. She was still half asleep and her vision was blurry, but the vague, fuzzy sight of black markings on her hand was enough to shock her into cognizance.

Estelle shot upright in bed, her eyes quickly focusing in as she angled her hand in the light of her halo. For several seconds, she was dumbstruck. On her right hand was what looked to be a black, tree-like scar. It stemmed from her palm and wrapped around the back like vines, branching out in an intricate, almost fractal-like pattern. She traced the pattern as her heart rate picked up, recalling the day before when she had reached out and grabbed Zylis' hand.

Without a second thought, Estelle flung herself out of bed and ripped open the top drawer of her dresser. She pawed through it frantically, carelessly tossing hats and scarves over her shoulder until she found a pair of gloves. The Angel assembled the first vaguely presentable outfit before sliding the gloves on and walking out.

It was roughly six o'clock in the morning on a Saturday. Antares wouldn't be at school, but Estelle knew the path to his first sphere residence like the back of her hand. Well, it might not have been the best comparison. After all, she didn't exactly know the back of her hand anymore.

Estelle ran to Antares' doorstep and then proceeded to knock on the front door insistently and continuously until her knuckles met empty space.

"Miss Amadea?" Her mentor was still in his pajamas and looked like he had just rolled out of bed.

"Antares, I-I—" Estelle stammered, trying to catch her breath, "—I'm so sorry to bother you... so early, I just—"

"No, no." Antares shook his head and stepped aside. "Come in, please."

The young Angel interrupted her panicked expression with an appreciative, if strained, smile as she went in, toeing off her shoes as her mentor shut the door behind them. "I'm really, *really* sorry," she repeated.

"It's quite all right, Amadea," Antares said calmly. "Just tell me what's going on."

"I just—" Estelle quickly slid off the glove on her right hand, lifting it so he could see, "—woke up, and this was there, and I think it's because," she swallowed, voice wavering, "I accidentally touched him yesterday, w-without my shield up."

Antares placed a heavy hand on her shoulder. "Oh, Estelle, it's nothing to worry about," he laughed. "Just a stint of corruption damage is all. It'll go away on its own."

Estelle lowered her hand. "Oh..."

86

"I understand why you'd be alarmed, though," he said. "I know I was, the first time it happened to me."

She smiled weakly and nodded, leaning back against the door. "That's a relief. I was, um, pretty scared." The low-ranked Angel looked down at her hand. "So, how long will it take to go away?"

"It should start to fade in a few days," Antares said. "Might take a couple of weeks to disappear completely, though."

"*Weeks?*"

Her mentor nodded and smiled apologetically. "Your body needs time to clean itself up," he said.

"Can I use my blessed healing to make it go away faster?"

"If it's strong enough, yes."

Estelle perked up until Antares continued.

"But with your scores in that department, it wouldn't help. Besides, that's a skill only the most qualified medical Angels can perform, and even then it's tricky to get right."

Estelle looked down at her hand again.

"I do have something that should help, though. It's called rosebay tea. I believe I've got some left over from when I was on active duty..." he began to shuffle toward the kitchen.

"Thank you, Antares!" Estelle exclaimed, trailing behind him.

The older Angel waved his hand as if to say, 'Of course.' He opened the pantry and began searching, pushing various things aside until he found a large box near the back. "Ah, here we are," he said. "I can give you some to take with you, too, if you'd like."

"Really?" Estelle said. "That would be wonderful. Thank you so much!"

"It's no problem at all." Antares pulled out a kettle and filled it up before setting it on the stove. "Since you're already here, how about you tell me how yesterday went?" He grinned. "I want to hear every detail."

Estelle smiled back and pulled out a chair at the kitchen table. She told him everything, from when she tried to find the mystical apple orchard, to when the new Demon arrived to help transport the remaining humans, through a relatively uneventful day, and when she was to meet with Zylis next.

By the end of it, the tea kettle was empty, and they had both moved into Antares' study to work on her combat training.

"It's difficult to understand what he's talking about," Estelle said, grunting slightly as she kicked at her mentor's padded hands.

"It seems to me it might be a way to draw you in," her mentor provided. "Engage your core—keeping you guessing and wanting more information."

"It's not just that." Estelle switched her position and lifted her fists. "His language is confusing, and I'm not sure what he's talking about half the time." She swung at the high-ranked Angel, but he dodged and countered her attack. "He called the kids a—an epaitu, and referred to me as a jantu? I'm fairly certain it's nothing good, but I don't know what it means."

Antares chuckled softly. "That is nothing to be worried about, Amadea." He smiled. "Both of those are creatures that reside in Hell. A epaitu is a little furry animal, like a chinchilla. And I believe a jantu is some kind of insect." He crossed his arms, a signal for Estelle to stop.

The young Angel released her stance and plopped onto the floor to catch her breath.

"Amadea, do your stretches," Antares chided.

"Right, sorry." Estelle sat up straight and flexed her wings out to their full length. "Do you know what Zylis is talking about when he says 'concave' or 'void'?"

"Those are places within Hell," the older Angel said, placing the palm of his hand on her back between the white wings. "A couple of the most dangerous places to be." He pressed down, helping Estelle know where to move specific muscles and stretch more fully. "'Void' is used similarly to how humans use 'go to hell,' but since Demons are already there, they substitute it with a place within Hell."

Estelle hummed in understanding. After a moment, her exercise was done, and they both exited the study.

"If it wasn't already apparent," Antares started. "You can't find this information in level two books, so don't mention it to your friends."

11

Misty Light

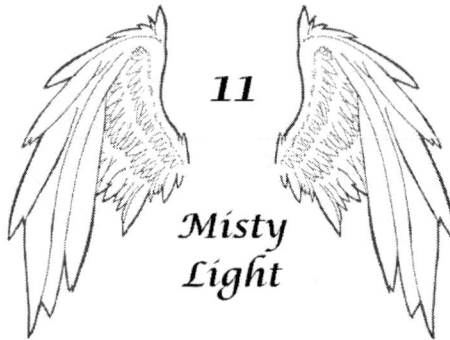

Estelle landed near her first destination and looked around, half expecting Zylis to materialize in front of her. After a minute, she sighed and began walking down the sidewalk. The surface on Wednesday morning was primarily quiet, apart from birds chirping and the rumble of the ongoing battle a couple of miles out. The smell of burning, accompanied by the sight of flashing lights and flickering fires, which she had long since learned to tune out.

Zylis hadn't given her much information on how he intended to find her, if she could do anything to make it easier, or even how long it would take. It was aggravating when she thought about it. The Demon was almost pathologically cryptic when it came to things like that.

Estelle meandered into an alley, stopping to lean against an old dumpster. She was sure it would have been overflowing with trash if not for it littering the ground, the wind playing its part, or people desperate enough to find food and anything they could use to survive. It was rare to find anyone running the streets where she was stationed, with the battle raging only a few short miles away.

She closed her eyes and wondered if it'd be petty of her to count the minutes until Zylis got there. Her lips turned up at the thought.

"Hey."

Estelle shrieked, the feathers on her wings ruffling as she leaped forward and turned around. He was sitting on the dumpster lid, his legs spread out and tail flicking around behind him. "Why do you always do that?" she shouted, placing a gloved hand on her chest above her heart.

"Do what?" he deadpanned.

Estelle stared into his glowing eyes, glaring.

After a drawn-out moment, Zylis' expression morphed into one of performative realization. "Oh, you mean sneaking up on you?" he asked, leaning forward. "Yeah, see, the thing about that is... It's undoubtedly funny."

"Hilarious." She rolled her eyes.

"Yeah." He grinned and hopped off the dumpster, brushing off the back of his pants.

Estelle took quick strides out of the alley.

Zylis trailed behind her. "Talked it over with the others," he said conversationally. "As of today, I'm on 'special assignment.'"

Estelle slowed and looked over her shoulder. "What does that mean?"

The Demon shrugged. "Whatever we want it to mean," he said. "But in this case, it means we've decided you're worth the effort of trying to tempt."

The girl blinked a few times. "Good...?" She glanced away. "I'm, uh, not sure how to feel about that."

Zylis snickered as they approached the front entrance to the church.

By the time they had finished everything, it was an hour before sunset. The odd duo decided to check some buildings in the surrounding area for any remaining stragglers. Estelle was peering through a dark, dusty window of a dilapidated motel when Zylis spoke.

"What happens if a bug flies into your halo?"

Estelle was so bewildered by the question that her instincts somehow bypassed an entire spectrum of confused reactions, and she wound up defaulting to something mundane. She turned and looked at Zylis over her shoulder. "Sorry, *what?*"

The Demon shrugged, his gaze drifting off as if bored. "Just wondering. Like, does it get zapped? Become a little bug Angel?" he asked, smirking. "Does it go to bug-heaven?"

It took her a moment to respond as her mind tried to follow his thinking. "Where did this even come from?"

"Just crossed my mind a couple of times. So?"

"Well…" Estelle started, tilting her head slightly. "I don't know. As far as I'm aware, nothing happens." She shuffled over to try the door. It seemed to be jammed, and her voice was straining as she kept trying to open it. "Which makes sense if you think about it. Our halos aren't things you can physically touch; they're more like a misty light."

At that moment, she felt a tingling sensation above her head as the Demon's hand went to grab the floating crown of light. She instantly raised her shield and focused on not shivering at the touch and making her feathers stay still.

"Huh, would not have guessed that," he said, twisting his hand a couple of times through the small light, watching as the halo moved and warped around his clawed hand before retracting it.

The halo resumed its natural state a second later.

The Angel's muscles tensed and cramped as she continued to fight with the door, wiggling the knob and muttering under her breath. After a second, she spotted Zylis' approach in her peripheral vision and took it as a cue to step aside. Taking her place, Zylis grabbed the doorknob and, without so much as a grunt, shoved the door open in one sharp, efficient movement.

"Oh," Estelle said, surprised and unsure how to react when he took his hand off, and she could see the doorknob was deformed, as though partially melted. "Wow."

The Demon grinned. "And for the low price of your soul, you too could have powers with actual practical applications, Star."

Estelle rolled her eyes and brushed past him, trying to hide the smile that crept up on her lips. Only after she stepped inside did she realize the door had been boarded shut from the inside, though all that remained were splintered planks and loose nails. The room appeared to be the hotel's lobby, but as far as she could tell, it was vacant. Most of the furniture was hidden beneath dusty sheets as though it had been abandoned months ago.

"I guess we should check the rooms," Estelle said.

Zylis hummed in agreement and went ahead of her. One by one, they knocked on doors, and one by one, Zylis forced them open with unsettling ease that had Antares' words echoing inside the Angel's mind.

Wrath Demons—by far the strongest among the Demons, as far as sheer physical power is concerned.

Estelle felt uneasy; her pulse picked up each time Zylis showed her the proof of that fact. Whether or not the Demon was doing so as a deliberate show of strength, she couldn't tell, but if he was, he had certainly achieved his goal. She watched as Zylis took his hand off one of the doorknobs, and in the dim light, she could see that the metal was glowing slightly.

She swallowed.

Estelle always knew Zylis was stronger than she was. And there wasn't even anything unique about Zylis; most Demons on the surface were stronger than her. But it was one thing to be passively aware of the power imbalance and quite another to observe the consequences of it. To watch the man, the Demon, and be viscerally aware that if he wanted to kill her, he could. Estelle was at his mercy.

Zylis could do *anything* to her. It was a terrifying yet strangely entrancing thought, like a tornado wreaking havoc on a city or hellfire swallowing a skyscraper. She felt the desire to keep watching out of morbid fascination and curiosity.

"Hey, Star. Star!"

The Angel jumped, her wings doing a single flap.

"Finally." Zylis clicked his tongue. "Been trying to get your attention for a thousand years, Princess."

She blinked, eyes wide. They were back in the lobby again, she realized.

Zylis was leaning against the edge of the front desk, looking at her like she had grown a second head. "What's up with you?"

"I uh..." Estelle's eyes darted around. Her mind felt scattered, and she didn't want to tell him what she was actually thinking at that moment. She opened her mouth and blurted out the first thing that came to mind. "Can you pick things up with your tail?"

"What?" Zylis seemed dumbfounded for a moment, but quickly recovered and snorted. Estelle took that as a sign that the diversion had worked, and the tension melted away as Zylis continued, "Well, duh. Of course, I can." He demonstrated by wrapping the tip of his tail around a nearby lamp and flinging it across the room. It hit the wall, and the glass base shattered upon impact. "What would even be the point if I couldn't?"

"Are they not usually used for balance?" She shrugged, looking away. Her eyes landed on a DVD case left behind on the desk. Without looking at which movie it was, she stashed it away in her shoulder bag.

Zylis hummed. "Yeah, I guess so." He wandered over to the shattered lamp and began idly kicking the shards of glass. After a second, he looked back over to his partner. "But I mean, strictly speaking, if you want to know the *real* reasons why Demons have tails, then I'm pretty sure it's 'cause God wanted us to be repulsive or something, so He gave us traits He thought would achieve that." Zylis paused, then smirked with all sharp teeth on display and hooded eyes. His pitch dropped. "But obviously, that plan backfired pretty substantially since most humans associate us with sex to some degree."

Estelle had no idea how to respond to a statement like that. She opened her mouth, closed it, and then tried again. And by a miracle, she managed to keep her voice even when she said, "Well, lust is a sin, so it kind of makes sense for people to associate you with it."

Zylis laughed, low and breathy. "I think it's a bit deeper than that, but sure." After a pause, he added, "Don't worry, plenty of people out there wanna do it with Angels, too." He winked.

"O-okay...?" she said, covering her face with her wings as her cheeks burned. "I wasn't worried before, but now I kind of am."

"Oh yeah?" Zylis asked.

Estelle heard his footfalls as the Demon approached her, stopping just short of a foot away, leaning against the front desk again.

"Why? Afraid someone might try and make a pass at you?"

The Angel shuddered as she continued to stare at the white fathers. She mumbled, "I don't understand why they would even..."

"Want to?" he finished, letting the question hang in the air before pressing on. "It's not that hard to figure out, Star. You seriously don't know?"

"I don't *want* to know," Estelle said firmly, finally looking up to meet his eyes.

Zylis snickered, the corner of his lips curling up as he looked her up and down. "Uh-huh. Sure—"

"I already know that I'm allowing people who think that way into Heaven," she cut in. "And I've made my peace with that. But I would rather not know how they fantasize about... me."

The Demon rolled his eyes, his mischievous expression fading to boredom.

"What did you mean earlier?" Estelle asked. "About me being 'worthy to tempt.'"

He sighed. "What d'you mean?"

"I mean, is there..." She waved her hand around meaninglessly. "I don't know. Is there some sort of criteria for that?"

"Not exactly. It's not a common enough occurrence for there to be a standard way to do things," he answered, looking up in thought. "As things are, we mostly judge it on a case-by-case basis. Like, 'does this Angel seem like they can be swayed morally?' stuff like that."

"You think I can be convinced to give up my morals?" she asked, more than a little incensed at the thought.

"What? No," Zylis spat, looking back at her again with a scowl. "That's the *opposite* of what I was trying to say. Some Angels are loyal to God above all else. It's like…" He gestured vaguely. "They don't have coherent ethical principles. They just do what they're told. And yeah, they think they're doing the right thing, but it's very dogmatic, 'this is right because God says so,' and that's the end of it." He stopped to take a breath before continuing, "But there are some Angels who do have strong morals. They usually follow God because they think that's the best way to uphold their value system. So, in theory, if someone could convince them there's a more effective way to do that…" he trailed off. After a moment, he shrugged. "Anyway, those are the ones worth trying to tempt: the ones who actually want to do good."

"So… you think I have a moral imperative to join you?"

"I *know* you do."

Estelle scoffed. "I find that very hard to believe."

And then Zylis smiled slowly, in an off-color way that immediately put the Angel on guard. "Oh, but there's one other type, though," he said. "Sometimes, once in a blue moon, you'll meet an Angel who just really wants to sin. And like, it's painfully obvious."

Estelle swallowed. "Ah."

"Yeah, not a lot of them, but they're out there." He drummed his fingers on the countertop. "So, once we've decided that someone's worth trying to tempt, we next have to ask who's up for the task. Usually, if we're dealing with someone who could be swayed if you present them with the right information in the right way, we'll ask someone who's particularly good at rhetoric. If it's someone who wants to sin or some combination of the two, it gets more personal."

"I'm guessing you've done this a lot, then," Estelle said, taking a deep breath as the Demon grinned.

"Nope." He shook his head. "Not once. It's not even remotely close to my area of expertise." With his elbow on the counter, Zylis tucked his chin into his palm, staring at Estelle with a smug, knowing look in his eyes. "Frankly, I'm not the talking type. I'm more..." He trailed off and hummed. "*Physical*, you could say. If someone calls me in to help deal with an Angel..." He laughed darkly, his tail swishing behind him. "Well, let's just say they're not trying to de-escalate things." Zylis stood up straight and turned to face Estelle directly. "But despite that, everyone thought I'd be a good fit for you." He leaned forward a little into the Angel's personal space, pinning her with hypnotic, glowing red eyes.

Estelle took a staggering breath. "For someone who's not the talkative type, you sure do love the sound of your own voice."

"For someone who doesn't want to know things, you ask a lot of questions."

Estelle was sure she had stopped breathing.

Eventually, his eyes widened slightly, and his demeanor shifted as he broke contact. "Ah, that reminds me..." He opened his rucksack and pulled out a thick, leather-bound book. "I've also got this." He handed it to Estelle.

"What..." Estelle trailed off as she accepted and opened it, flipping through the pages. They were all blank. "Zye, is this just a blank book?"

"It's a sallvie," he said. "You know, a sallbokvie."

"A what?"

Zylis gave her an odd look. "Wait, seriously? You don't know?" The Angel shrugged and shook her head. He groaned and rolled his eyes. "Guess I shouldn't be too surprised."

"What is it?" Estelle pressed, flipping through the pages again.

"It's a type of communication device."

She closed the book again and made a face, prompting him to explain further.

Zylis sighed. "Do you know about the double agent defector incident?"

"Oh!" Estelle chirped. "The Faux-Fallen Angels, Alsphere and Ventiel, right? The spies who rejected God?"

"They didn't re—" Zylis stopped and took a breath, "—historical inaccuracy aside, yeah," he replied. "When they were still trying to keep tabs on us, they needed a way to communicate. So, they made these." He gestured toward the book. "The trick is that the sallvie has a twin. It's basically like a two-way diary. Whenever one person writes in their book, it will also appear in the other."

"So..." Estelle said. "You're giving me this to communicate with you?"

"What? No," he said, swiping the book out of her hands. "This one's mine. You've gotta find your own."

Again, Estelle had confusion written all over her face, prompting him to continue.

"Now that you've touched it, its twin should be in Heaven somewhere."

"That's not very specific."

"It doesn't have to be," the Demon said, shrugged, and turned away, walking toward a more defined patch of shadows. "Just trust me, Star; it might take a few days, but if you're patient, it'll find its way to you."

Estelle blinked, and he was gone, leaving her with more questions unanswered, and bathed in a soft, misty light.

12

The
Navitas

"WHAT'S UP WITH YOU?" GIOVANNA asked suddenly. The three of them—Estelle, Issac, and Giovanna—were sitting on the stone wall that framed the flying field, enjoying a well-earned break.

"What do you mean?" Estelle asked, sitting up a little straighter. She had been commenting on one of their classmates' forms—their wing not quite making it through the final hoop—when the other changed the subject.

The girl shrugged. "You just seem happy."

"Do I usually seem *un*happy to you?" she asked, a small smile pulling at her lips.

"It depends on the day," Giovanna said, earning a chuckle from Issac. "Most of the time, you just seem focused on something—"

"You've been smiling this whole time," Issac interjected with his low, monotonous voice.

Estelle reflexively looked at him when he spoke, though his eyes were still focused on the flight field, watching as one Angel took their turn. "Well, I guess it shouldn't be that surprising," she said, tucking a stray black strand of hair behind her ear. "I just beat my record again. Isn't that incentive enough?"

It was all thanks to Antares that she had improved her physical skills. She didn't think learning combat tactics and self-defense would improve her flying, but she could clear the last three rings within one week of private training. However, her time stayed the same.

"Issac beat his record by a landslide," Giovanna added, turning on the lilac-haired Angel, somewhat irritated. "You got through forty out of fifty rings and got twenty-three seconds faster. But I would have appreciated it if you hadn't lied about your scores in the first place."

The Angel in question rubbed the back of his neck. "The books helped out, I guess." He glanced at Estelle with the last words, making her blush. "And I wasn't lying about anything," he said, looking away from a nasty landing from a level one Angel. "It's hard to keep track of all the information the teachers have been pouring into each lesson."

"Please, they've been doing that since the war started two years ago. You should be used to it already—and no one gets that good in a couple of weeks from just reading a few books," Giovanna said, frowning. "And you're your worst critic." She gestured toward Estelle. "No matter how fast you go, you're never enough."

"Like you're one to talk," Estelle sneered, keeping her voice low and even. "Unlike us, you can't get through that last ring and throw a fit every time you get off the field." She scoffed. "From what I can see, Issac has more potential. Especially since he actually studies."

"Like he could beat my time before the application submission deadline," Giovanna said, rolling her eyes. But then she added, in a softer tone, "I've already submitted mine. You guys should start calling me by Rūnnel, just to get into the habit."

Issac and Estelle gaped at her with unmistakable smiles creeping onto their faces as a whistle blew, signaling the new round of practiced flying. Issac shoved the tall Angel in the shoulder, nearly pushing her over the edge.

Sometimes, Estelle wondered why she was friends with Giovanna. The girl was brash, rude, and a slacker in every subject except flying. But she was honest, brutally so, which Estelle guessed made up for what was lacking.

"How are things with your missions, Estelle?" Giovanna asked, doing a complete one-eighty, smiling warmly at the girl once she had regained her balance on the wall. It was dropped shortly after when she began watching the practice field.

"Fine!" Estelle replied, perhaps a bit too quickly. She looked onto the field. "I-I mean, it's challenging but rewarding. Last week, I forgot about not using my real name while working on the surface."

"What's so bad about that?" Giovanna asked.

Collectively, they all curled in on themselves, breath hissing between their teeth. An Angel's wing smacked against a ring, sending them spiraling. Luckily, they were able to correct themselves before crashing to the ground.

Issac sighed. "If the enemy learns your name, you're dead."

"Which is why they had us choose Holy names before going on our first mission." Estelle continued. "Unfortunately, I forgot about that detail."

Giovanna shrugged. "Well, you're not dead, so you should be fine. Besides, it's impossible to keep all the little details straight."

"Wait a minute—" Issac started.

Estelle laughed weakly. She couldn't tell them the whole story. If they reported that she had been encountering the same Demon multiple times, it would jeopardize the partnership and put her and Antares in a lot of trouble. It was better not to say anything at all.

"That Demon hasn't given you any more trouble than?" Issac asked.

"What?" Estelle's eyes darted between him and Giovanna.

"The Demon." Issac side-eyed her. "The one you said you met."

"You met a *Demon*?" Giovanna exclaimed.

"Wait, you didn't tell her?" Issac frowned, turning to face Estelle fully.

Estelle rubbed the back of her neck sheepishly, letting her long black hair fall over her face. "It didn't come up," she replied.

The tall Angel snorted. "Didn't come up?" she repeated incredulously. "*Estelle.*"

"Okay, I'm sorry," she shot back, raising her wings to somewhat hide from their sight. "I didn't think it was such a big deal. I mean, nothing *bad* happened!"

"So you haven't seen it again?" Issac probed.

Estelle hesitated, gripping the stone wall until her knuckles turned white.

"Estelle?"

"Ah, no," she fumbled. "If I did, I would have told you guys. Meeting the same Demon twice would be a cause for concern." She could feel Issac's eyes on her, but she kept her gaze fixed on her shoes.

"Really?"

Estelle tasted a foul, sour flavor bloom on her tongue, and she tried to swallow it before saying another lie. "I promise."

"You better," Giovanna added. "My gosh, I nearly had a heart attack."

The girl continued to express her relief and then moved on to a different topic, but Estelle never heard a response from her best friend, as his eyes seemed to be calculating something.

Antares entered his study with one hand wrapped around the handle of a large bucket. He set it down beside the blackboard before turning toward Estelle. "So, tell me, how much do you know about the soul?"

The girl hesitated, caught off guard by the question.

"Don't worry, it's not a pop quiz—just tell me anything."

Estelle relaxed as she tried remembering everything she had been told about the subject. "Well... I know that when I put up my barrier, what I'm actually doing is hardening my soul so that it can't be corrupted through touch," she said, then shrugged. "But that's all I've been explicitly told. Everything else is sort of just a jumble of contradictory rumors."

"Yes, that's fairly typical for someone at your level," Antares said. "I should say, though, the part about barriers isn't quite right. It'd be more accurate to say you're *flexing* it."

"Huh, interesting," Estelle mumbled. "I wonder why they didn't tell us that to begin with."

"As you mentioned before, there are a lot of misconceptions floating around," he said. "But that is what's technically happening. You're just flexing the outer layer of your soul, so it's impermeable."

"Wait, 'outer layer?'" Estelle asked, tilting her head to the side. "I didn't know souls *had* layers."

"Oh?" Antares genuinely looked surprised. "That's interesting. I think I knew that at your level, but perhaps things have gotten stricter." He paused for a moment, rubbing his chin. "Well, to give you the abridged version—essentially, your soul has two main parts." He held up one finger. "The outer shell." He raised a second finger. "And a fluid-like substance contained within."

"Fluid?"

"Yes," he answered. "It's called Navitas; it generates the power Angels use to fight, and the outer shell protects it."

"So, the... Navitas is the source of our power?"

"No. Almost, but not quite. It *generates* power," Antares explained as Estelle scribbled away in her notebook. "It's important to be precise about this because although an Angel can temporarily run out of power, the Navitas remains the same in form and volume, at least under typical circumstances."

"Okay..." Estelle replied, brows pinched together. "So, wait, there are times when it wouldn't stay the same?"

Antares smiled. "Well, sure. What do you think corruption does?"

The young Angel glanced down at her hand, where the dark, tree-like scar remained, albeit faded.

Seeing her hesitation, he continued, "The main difference between Angels and Demons, at least on a physiological level, is the resting state of their soul."

She looked up at that moment. "Demons have souls?"

"Oh, yes. Corrupted ones, but souls nonetheless," he replied. "Essentially, when an Angel sustains corruption damage, the Navitas becomes partially coagulated. In those cases, given time, the Navitas will circulate and return to its liquid state. But if an Angel's Navitas completely thickens, there's no going back. That's what happens when an Angel Falls."

Estelle's eyes fell onto her hand again as she hummed and nodded reverently. Absentmindedly, she rubbed the spot where the mark was more prominent. She didn't notice anything different, other than her hand feeling itchy when it happened. *Maybe it's because I don't know what to look for.*

"There are other circumstances where things can happen to the Navitas," he continued. "But for now, let's focus on how one utilizes this power."

Estelle looked up, her golden eyes sparkling excitedly as her mentor turned around. He pulled open a drawer on the far side of the room, taking out something Estelle couldn't quite see. He dusted it off with his hands and then turned toward his student again.

"If you want to use your power, you'll need a vessel to channel it through. That's where these come in." Antares handed her something that Estelle quickly recognized as a pair of gloves.

They were off-white, and the embroidery on the back formed a large, golden sun, with the rays extending toward the fingertips.

"These are technically gauntlets," he explained. "I wish I could offer you a more substantial weapon, like a sword or a bow, once you've got the hang of the basics, but that would attract too much attention. You can still pack a punch with these, though."

Estelle smiled. "Well, hopefully, I'll be up for ascension by then."

"Oh, I'm sure you will be," Antares said. "I've already submitted your application."

"Wait, really?" the girl squealed, practically jumping up and down where she stood.

"Really," he replied, just as enthusiastically. "It'll be a few weeks before the Apostles review it, and then a couple more for the process to be complete, but... fingers crossed!" He grinned, holding up a hand with said superstition. "Now then, shall we get started?"

The other Angel nodded, eagerly slipping on the gauntlets, pleased to find that they fit her well.

"Ah." Antares held up a finger. "One last thing you should know—actually, two things," he said. "Firstly, there is generally a pretty steep learning curve. I want you to know that you probably won't figure everything out on the first try."

Estelle hummed. "I guess that's to be expected. What's the other thing?"

"This is probably going to hurt."

She blinked. "Sorry, what?"

The older Angel shrugged, offering a tight, sympathetic smile. "It's just something every Angel has to deal with in the beginning, unfortunately," he explained. "Although these powers are innate, your body isn't accustomed to using them yet. The damage won't be irreparable, of course, but..." His eyes drifted toward the floor. "Well, there's a chance you might throw up."

"So... that's what the bucket is for," she said, looking down at the object.

"Just be prepared," her mentor said, grabbing the bucket and setting it a little closer to his student. "Are you ready?"

"I hope so."

Antares laughed. "In that case, close your eyes."

13

Angelic Powers

ESTELLE CLOSED HER EYES, TAKING a deep breath to try and wash out the nervousness suddenly swarming her. She was prepared for the outcome she was submitting herself to, but that didn't stop her from praying she was the exception to the rule.

"Now, harden your soul slowly, and pay attention to how it feels," Antares instructed her.

Estelle did just that. She gradually raised her shield, noting the familiar feeling of her chest filling, as if she had taken a breath, and expanding outward until it reached her toes and fingertips. Typically, the process would have taken less than a second, but Estelle forcefully slowed it to around five seconds.

"Did you notice anything different?" her mentor asked.

"I don't think so," Estelle said, eyes pinched closed. "It all feels normal."

"Then start again. And try to focus on any subtle changes you feel within your soul."

The student nodded and lowered the barrier. After taking another breath, she repeated the process. Her chest slowly became full, and as the feeling extended outward, Estelle realized that something felt as if it was being squeezed. Without being told, she stopped and started again, trying to pinpoint the sensation. It was almost as if her heart—no, something *surrounding* her heart was tightening.

"My soul," Estelle started, "it's constricting." She opened her eyes and looked at Antares as what she was feeling dawned on her. "It's as if I feel scared."

He smiled and nodded. "That is exactly right. When you are taught how to flex your soul, they tell you the penalties and dangers of not doing so, using fear to teach you the vital technique."

"I remember that. But I thought it was my heart tightening from fear."

"Your heart plays a part because the key component of controlling your Navitas is emotion," Antares explained. "Like fear, you unintentionally trained your soul to react and protect itself when you're scared."

"But I have to actively think about raising—or, uh, flexing my soul," Estelle countered.

"That's because it's not second nature for you yet," he said softly. "Until a couple of years ago, before the war started affecting the mortals, Angels were not permitted to leave Heaven until level four, after they had mastered the basics and begun training for higher-level skills. Even then, their job was essentially what you are doing now. Administering blessings when needed and saving people from destruction."

Estelle had been an Angel for the past eighteen years. It had taken only eight years for her to ascend to level two, and she remembered being ready for ascension shortly before the surface became a battlefield and all Angels needed to learn more.

"They moved up the curriculum," she said, then asked. "But how did the Apostles know the war would get worse?"

"No war happens without warning, Amadea."

The two Angels looked at each other for a long moment, golden eyes trying to understand what was behind the older blue eyes.

"So, the Navitas reacts to emotion?" Estelle asked after a while.

Antares nodded. "Whether good or bad, it will activate the Navitas and generate the power needed for defense or an attack," he further explained. "Since the Navitas is powered by emotion, the strength of the attack depends on the feeling of the Angel, focused into the output of power using a vessel." He gestured to the gauntlets on Estelle's hands.

The young Angel looked down at the gloves and turned her hands over to look at the delicate sun design on the back. "And how do I do that, exactly?" she asked, looking up to meet his eyes again.

He gave a strained smile. "That's where it gets difficult. First, you must focus on a strong enough emotion to activate the Navitas and then guide the power through the vessel. It will feel similar to hardening your soul but far more intense." Antares took a step back. "The best place to start is remembering something positive."

Estelle nodded and closed her eyes as she searched her memories. *Something positive. I'm excited to search for the Sallbokvie—but I might be more anxious than anything. I saw Lilith again, but maybe that's not strong enough. Is it okay to just think of my friends?*

The girl huffed a sigh, reaching up to brush through her hair, but her hair stuck to the fabric, making it more frustrating. She opened her eyes. "What do you think about, Antares?"

Her mentor seemed taken aback by the question, eyes widening slightly and brows pinched. "I can't choose the memory for you," he said.

"No, I know. I'm just having trouble finding one strong enough."

Antares' expression softened. "The strength of emotion is based on yourself. A memory can be more vivid for one than it is for another," he said, and after seeing Estelle deflate slightly, he continued, "but I tend to lean toward the time I spent on the surface a few weeks before I was permanently stationed in Heaven. I met someone sitting on a roof, and our conversation stuck with me."

Estelle couldn't help but smile. She'd heard a few of his stories and learned that he liked to compare them to fairy tales as they watched clouds drift by. But most of his retellings didn't involve meeting humans or them having a big enough impact on him to bring it up. She loved learning more about her mentor.

"Okay. I know what to do now," the student said, shutting her eyes again.

Estelle's first thought was when she became an Angel, accepting the duty and forfeiting her human memories. It was an incredible honor to become a servant of God. But the feeling of peace was replaced with harmony as her memories shifted.

A week before she was to start going on missions to Earth alone, the higher-ranked Angels in charge wanted to test Estelle and sent her into a chapel within a broken-down hospital. As was expected, there were several there who were injured, all praying for mercy and deliverance.

But what set that memory to the forefront of Estelle's mind was a mother singing a lullaby to all in the room, a song that was foreign to the Angel's ears. Her voice was clear, even with the tears that streamed down her cheeks, and she didn't stop when the Angel entered. It made Estelle wonder if the woman had been blessed with the gift of song.

The young Angel carried out her duties, quickly learning the lyrics and merry melody she wouldn't be permitted to use because it was not of the Holy Hymns. Estelle guessed that if the woman sang one of the holy melodies, it would have had a greater calming effect on the others; even so, the emotions she felt while listening were real.

Tranquility. Happiness. Curiosity.

Estelle felt something stir within her, and as she focused harder on the memory, the feeling grew. Just as Antares had said, it was almost as if her soul was preparing to harden, but at the same time, it was not. If she had to describe it, Estelle would compare it to stored adrenaline, as if waiting to be released into her veins. It continued to grow.

What am I supposed to do? she thought as her breathing picked up.

As if reading her mind, the older Angel replied, "Now, channel the energy toward the gauntlets."

She was not sure how she was supposed to do that, but the pressure in her chest almost became unbearable as a sense of panic set in. The very next second, her eyes opened, and gloved hands clutched her chest as if she had been shot.

Estelle stumbled back, hunching over, and for a moment, she couldn't breathe.

"That's a good start," Antares praised.

She gasped for air, wincing in pain. "What happened?" she wheezed, looking up at him.

"From what I can tell, you hardened your soul when you began to panic, thus making it backfire." He gave a sympathetic smile and offered his hand.

The girl accepted the help, slowly returning to her original position. "Wouldn't that just make my defense better, not hurt me?" Estelle asked as she straightened out.

"If you know how to expel the energy correctly," Antares corrected. "That technique is usually taught among level five and six Angels."

"I don't understand. How could I have done so badly?"

"No, Amadea, you did well for it being your first time activating the Navitas." He looked up in thought and hummed slightly. "It's hard to explain what went wrong, but I might be able to, in a way, *show* you what's happening. Give me a moment." He turned on his heel and walked out of the study.

Estelle stood there for a moment, wondering if she was meant to follow him or stay where she was. Ultimately, she jogged after him into the kitchen, trying not to pay attention to how her chest ached with every other breath.

Her mentor was standing by the sink and holding two equally sized, tapered cups in his hands. Antares motioned her over without looking.

Estelle walked over to stand beside him.

"This cup will represent your soul," he said, holding out one of the glass cups toward her. "Will you hold it over the sink, please?"

Estelle blinked and accepted the glass, positioning her hands over the sink.

"Thank you. And *this*—" Antares turned on the faucet for a brief moment, a small amount of water landing inside the cup she held, "—is the Navitas within your soul."

"Okay, I'm with you so far."

"When you flex your soul, you harden the outer layer to protect the Navitas inside, and when you do that, figuratively speaking, you create a lid." He gently placed the second cup inside the first, the bottom just touching the surface of the water.

Estelle nodded in understanding, and he continued, taking the second glass out.

"But when you activate Angelic power…" Antares filled her cup the rest of the way with water. "And then raise the shield, powered by negative emotions—" he dropped his glass inside her full glass, forcing the water out with a splash, spilling out onto her hands and the sink below, "—the energy has an explosive effect on the Angel. Now, this isn't technically accurate with what's actually happening, because the Navitas never changes in volume, but you get the idea."

Estelle nodded again, then gasped when the glass slipped from her fingers and shattered upon impact with the ceramic sink. "I am so sorry!" she said, starting to reach down toward the broken glass before Antares grabbed her wrist.

"No, it's quite all right, Miss Amadea." He moved her hand away from the sink. "Just don't cut yourself on a little accident." Antares smiled.

Estelle returned the gesture, looking back at the broken cups. Surprisingly, only the outer one shattered while the one sitting inside was perfectly fine. Just then, something occurred to the girl as Antares retrieved the interacted cup. "Wait, you said that both positive and negative emotions can activate the Navitas," she said.

"That's correct, but let me explain," he said calmly, opening the appropriate cupboards to put the item away. "Negative emotions are generally used to power attacks, while positive emotions are used to maintain control." He turned to face her. "However, the use of the Navitas is stronger if an Angel seethes with anger or other intense emotions at the moment, while using happier memories from the past to control their anger. Without proper training to balance the two, you end up injuring yourself."

The lower-ranked Angel continued to follow the other back into the study. "Could you show me how to do it? Like, use your powers?"

"I can't." His answer was immediate.

Shocked, Estelle paused short of entering Antares' study, staring at the three sets of wings on his back.

The following second, the older Angel turned to look at her and continued. "Rather, it would be of no use to you." He beckoned her to enter the room, and she obeyed. "The only way to understand is to experience it yourself."

Estelle nodded. All she needed to do was trust her power and not get overwhelmed by the pressure and fast-flowing energy begging to be released. She needed to focus on the positive and push out any negative thoughts that might end up backfiring.

Easier said than done.

Estelle returned to her room that night with the taste of bile on her tongue and an ache deep inside her chest. Generating power with the Navitas proved to be more challenging than she had initially hoped, with several attempts backfiring before she got it right, resulting in a slight glow emanating from her hands and gauntlets.

As she took off her clothes and prepared to step under the shower spray, the sight of her reflection gave her pause. She stood there for a while, eyes fixated on her chest. Bruises like nebulas bloomed from her sternum and sprawled out across her upper body. They stretched out to her shoulders and the bottom of her rib cage, and colors gradually blended into her natural complexion like watercolors.

Estelle partially wondered if it was worth it to remove minor corruption damage if the Angel performing the blessing would receive a bruised rib in return.

14

Sallbokvie

ESTELLE WAS NEVER ONE TO give up, but even she had to admit that searching for the sallvie was trying her patience. She had spent almost every waking moment searching.

It had been four days.

Four days since Zylis first introduced her to the concept of a sallbokvie, before flippantly sending her on her way without so much as a hint about where she ought to be looking. She had spent more time at the library in the past few days than she had in almost her entire afterlife, spending most of the new year looking over books. The longer her search continued, the more questions people asked.

Estelle knew it was a long shot to find the sallvie in the library of all places since it was initially made and used by high-ranking Angels to spy on the Demons of Hell. But aside from her dorm room and her small collection of books—which she had checked with no success—it was her only chance at finding the twin book.

One day, she nearly jumped out of her skin, feathers standing on end as she reflexively extended her wings like a cornered animal, all because someone tapped her on the shoulder at some intermediate point during her tireless search.

"Woah, hey," Issac said, putting his hands up. "It's just me."

Estelle relaxed slightly. "Issac," she breathed out, trying to settle her heart.

"Yeah." He blinked. "What's gotten into you? Are you alright?"

Estelle's mouth opened, and no sound came out for a moment. Eventually, she offered a small, shaky, "What do you mean...?"

He arched an eyebrow. "How long have you been here?"

"I, uh..." she paused, glancing out the window. She had arrived a little before noon, and it appeared to be early evening. "A while," she replied honestly.

"I figured," Issac deadpanned. "I've been here twice in the past week, and both times, you've been here," he said, frowning. "I know we don't have an exam coming up."

Estelle bit her lip, averting her gaze. She had known this would happen. Her friend was far too perceptive for his own good. Estelle had spent a considerable amount of time over those few days contemplating ways she could respond to such questions without outright lying again. But she couldn't gather her thoughts to form a strategic response in her exhausted state.

After a length of silence, she sighed. "I'm sorry," Estelle mumbled, staring at the pile of books she had been looking through as her wing drooped. "It's just..." she glanced up at Issac's face, which showed green eyes narrowed in a mixture of concern and suspicion. "Just something I'm working on. Nothing's wrong, I just kind of lost track of time."

The other Angel stared back at her for a while. Beneath the weight of his gaze, Estelle felt naked, the cool air creating pinpricks on her exposed flesh.

"I suppose that would be in character for you," Issac said eventually.

She snickered, offering a small smile to her friend. Issac was never one to voice his concerns, but Estelle had known him long enough to recognize them when they appeared.

"So, what's your obsession this time?" he asked.

Estelle froze. She was known for going a little overboard in research when she learned something new, especially if she was genuinely curious about it. She typically went down the rabbit hole to learn everything about the subject. The last time it happened—during the beginning of her training on the surface as two upper-ranked Angels watched over her and three others—it was about different species of birds after she had saved some from an abandoned pet store.

But she couldn't tell him the truth—he could get into a lot of trouble if she did.

"Ah... It's more of an extra assignment," Estelle said, tucking a hair behind her ear.

Issac blinked. "An extra assignment?"

"Yeah, Antares is preparing me for ascension and sent me on this wild goose chase to find, uh, information."

Her friend stared at her, concern evident on his face.

Estelle opened and closed her mouth several times, trying to find the words to explain. She sighed. "I'd tell you if something was seriously wrong," she said softly, her brows pinched together. "You know that, right?"

Issac blinked a few times, tensed slightly, and then relaxed. "Yeah," he said. "Yeah, that's—I know."

"I appreciate you worrying about me, though," Estelle said. "It's sweet of you."

Issac's eyes widened slightly, and he quickly turned around and moved toward the door. "It's getting late. I should probably get back," he muttered, but then, in a slightly more stern tone, he added, "So should you. Settle down and watch a movie, or something."

Estelle took a deep breath. "You're right," she sighed, hastily returning the pile of books to the shelf, moving as quickly as she could while keeping things in order because Issac was waiting for her. She didn't ask him to, but he was.

After a minute, she stood up and jogged over to Issac, who held the door open for her. "Hey, um. I mean it," she said as they started returning to campus. "I do appreciate it. It's very kind of you to be concerned about me."

The other Angel sighed, stuffing his hands into his pockets. Estelle wasn't sure, but as she trailed behind her friend in the cold, rapidly deepening night, she could have sworn she heard him reply: "*You say that as though it was a decision I made.*"

Five days of searching, with no luck.

Zylis stood on the roof of an old schoolhouse, leaning back against the railing, devouring another one of those fruits he liked—the ones that evoked some disconcerting image of violence. Estelle had just finished lamenting her struggles to find the sallvie.

"What the void?" he said, speaking with a full mouth, his tail seeming agitated. "Star, what part of *'be patient and* wait' did you not understand?"

"*Excuse* me?"

"What, you don't remember?" he said, licking his lips. "I said it would find its way to *you*, pillock."

Estelle stared at him for a moment, mouth agape, blinking rapidly. "You could have been clearer about it!"

Zylis laughed mirthlessly. "Would it have helped if I gave you a checklist of what *not* to do?"

"Would it help if I gave you a book on how to give proper instructions?"

The Demon glowered as he licked the blood-red juice off his fingers, one by one. "All you had to do was go about your daily routine or whatever," he said, lips stained red. "Don't know how you managed to screw up doing nothing. It's almost impressive."

Estelle frowned, her face beginning to feel very hot. Zylis' attitude certainly didn't make her feel less embarrassed. "How was I supposed to know any of that, when I hardly know anything about Demons as it is?" she asked, rubbing her eyes and looking away. "I just wanted to make sure I found it before someone else did... Give me a break."

Zylis' expression softened slightly, and the tail stilled. He shuffled closer, exhaling. "That's not something you need to worry about."

"What makes you so sure?"

He shrugged. "I've never heard of it happening before."

"Zye..." Estelle sighed and, in her sleep-deprived state, spoke without forethought. "I don't think you understand how much trouble I could get in if the wrong person finds it," she said, anxiety saturating her tone. "I-I mean, it would have been nice if you could've told me what it was before you had me touch it, and—"

"Hey."

Estelle could feel the heat of Zylis' hand. The fingers partially shifted into claws and hovered just beneath her chin, as close as possible, without touching her. She put up her barrier and held her breath.

"Look at me, Star."

The Angel released a shuddering breath and turned her head, surprised to see Zylis was much closer than she had expected. His red eyes glowed like a second sunset against the orange sky.

"You've been staying up late for this, haven't you?"

Estelle's face heated up slightly. "Sometimes..." She hadn't slept properly for almost a week. She was exhausted with all the Angelic training, bruises, and searching—to say the least.

Zylis scoffed. "Idiot, you look like Hell."

Despite herself, Estelle smiled at the irony of the statement.

After a moment, his tail resumed its normal sway, and he sighed. "Look, you're right. I should have told you what it was first."

Estelle blinked. She hadn't expected the Demon to admit fault so readily.

"But..." he continued, his tone firm. "I mean it when I say this isn't something you should freak out over," he said, the tips of his claws still a phantom presence against her skin. "I have it on good authority that what you're worried about is, at the very least, rare. Even if someone does find it, odds are they won't know what it is."

"Okay, but—"

"I'm not finished," he interjected, claws finally making contact with her skin. "Listen, on the off chance that whoever finds it does know what it is, finding out who it's linked to is not a trivial thing to do, Star. It's possible, but it'll take a while." His fingers lightly tapped against the underside of her chin. Zylis smirked. "And here's the kicker: if someone else opens it, I'll know. And all I need to do is sever the connection. Past that point, there's nothing they can do. Got it?"

Estelle swallowed. The movement of her throat made the Demon's knuckle brush up against it. "And you're sure you can do that in time?"

Zylis grinned. "All I gotta do is destroy my own," he said, and out of the corner of Estelle's eye, she spotted his other hand resting on the metal railing.

She watched as his fingers gradually started to sink into the bar, with the surrounding metal glowing red as it collapsed, liquifying beneath his touch. Estelle didn't move, not wanting to receive more injuries on top of the bruises she had been getting from her extra lessons.

Zylis licked his lips. "I'm pretty good at destroying things."

The girl could feel the heat radiating off the molten metal as Zylis slowly pulled away, his hands sliding into his pockets.

"Don't overthink it," he said, walking away.

He approached a spot behind where the school's stairwell would've been—the only part of the roof cast in shadow.

He threw one last look over his shoulder. "Oh, and get some sleep while you're at it." After that, he stepped into the shadows and dissipated into the darkness.

Estelle spent a few minutes just standing there, staring at the place where the Demon used to be, before sitting down.

How was she not supposed to overthink it? What if she couldn't find it because it was a higher-level book, and she couldn't open it even if she did find it? How would he know if it was her or someone else opening the book?

Why would he care about me getting sleep?

Estelle stayed there for half an hour before finally gathering the will to fly home.

It had been two days since Estelle had stopped her search. A full week since the whole thing had started, and though she felt better physically, it would have been a lie to say that the anxiety hadn't gotten to her. It wasn't that she didn't believe Zylis. She knew for a fact that the Demon was telling the truth, at least to the best of his knowledge. Still, the waiting game fostered a strong sense of unease that she couldn't shake.

Estelle decided to get up after around two hours spent lying awake in her bed. She paced for another few minutes, silently warring with the temptation to return to the library and continue her search. There were only a few sections she hadn't been through, so it wouldn't take her more than a couple of hours.

Eventually, the memory of Zylis' words echoing inside her mind won out, and with a sigh, she forced herself to sit at her desk. She just needed to distract herself. One option was to go down to the common room and watch whatever new movie one of the other Angels had found on their trip to Earth.

Movies were not against any rules set by the Apostles. Everyone knew that they were all fabricated by the imaginations of humans— even 'historically accurate' movies tended to stretch the truth to make a more compelling story—so, whenever they could, they would pick up a DVD from the surface and bring it back. Angels did the same thing to books made by human authors.

Or, what better way to distract myself than an assignment that's due in a couple of days? Estelle grabbed her notebook and the assigned text—some book called The Economics of Faith that she had admittedly been putting off reading for a while due to lack of interest. With another sigh, the Angel opened it.

But there was nothing there—literally nothing. The page was completely blank. Curious, Estelle flipped to the next page, but it was also blank. And the next one. And the next—she thumbed through the book, but it was completely bare.

A glance at the cover told her she had grabbed the correct book, but then a flash of something irregular caught her eye. She turned to a page near the beginning and felt as though her entire world had just clicked into place.

There, she found a single sentence in a surprisingly elegant script:

Looks like you found it, Princess.

She stared at it for several seconds, her hands shaking. The ink was so red it almost looked as though the words had been cut into the flesh of something living. Eventually, she shook herself out of her trance long enough to pick up a pen.

Zye, I need this book for an assignment!

Writing in the book felt different, somehow. As though her pen sank deeper into the parchment, transcending a barrier she never knew existed. After a second, she added: *It's due in two days, what am I supposed to do?!*

After that, she forced herself to put the pen down. A minute passed before the book warmed up in her hands, the pages bowing outward before relaxing again, almost as though it were a living, breathing thing. She watched as the words appeared right before her eyes, stroke by stroke, until the book went cold in her hands, reverting into its inanimate state as if to signal the message's end.

Not my fault you left that to the last minute, idiot.

Despite the insult, Estelle found herself smiling. She was going to need to get a new copy of the book, but in the end, she supposed it would be worth it.

She imagined Zylis somewhere far away, where the skies were dark and the environment unforgiving. A place where ash fell like snow and embers drifted across the sky in a parody of starlight. Somewhere in the vast expanse, Zylis' long, clawed fingers wrapped around the book's spine as he walked alone, his glowing, red eyes as passing lanterns in the perpetual night.

15

Not
Normal

THOUGH THE SALLBOKVIE WAS INITIALLY intended for the Angel and Demon to coordinate meeting locations, it wasn't long before it became something more. She couldn't resist the urge to ask Zylis questions, knowing the answers were right at her fingertips.

Do Demons still make contracts with humans?

No. Not for like 1,500 years.

Oh, what happened 1,500 years ago?

Lots of stuff happened, like the Hagia Sophia cathedral burning down because of a deal. But the main thing is we figured out how to make agriculture work for us.

Agriculture? Don't Demons feed off of sinful emotions?

That's what I meant about making it work for us. Basically, we figured out how to grow food enriched with sin.

Wow. Is that what the fruit you're always eating is? The black one with the red juice.

Yep. It's called an embrite. They're full of Wrath. And Gluttony, but all of our food has some amount of that in there. Go figure.

That's really interesting! But I'm curious. What do they taste like?

Spicy. Very spicy, like the kind that would make you want to rip your tongue out.

And you... ENJOY that??

Hell yeah, I do.

Is that all you ever eat?

Nah, that's just what I like to eat around you.

Why?

I can tell it makes you unsettled. And that is extremely funny to me.

That's weird. Do you go out of your way to make EVERYONE you interact with uncomfortable?

No. Only the ones I'm trying to tempt.

It was around an hour before sunset. Estelle found herself standing on the roof of an old, abandoned convenience store, her gaze skybound. She watched as the Ophanims, with their interconnecting spheres that looked as if they were made of diamond and their many eyes, led the Holy Army. Smoke billowed in the distance as they blasted away swaths of Demons in their path. Screams were drowned out by the explosive attacks from the Demons as hellfire raged through the streets. Its direction changed long before it would have reached her.

"So, that's your dream, huh?" Zylis spoke up, his voice monotone, and came from somewhere behind her. "You want to be a weird ring of fire covered in eyes?"

Estelle glanced over her shoulder, lowering her wing slightly. "Well, no, I mean—it would be an honor, of course! But I'm just working on getting to the second sphere right now. I want to be on the front lines, maybe even get a Luminari—"

"A what?" Zylis interjected, coming to stand beside her.

"A Luminari. It's when an Angel performs a great deed in the name of God and receives the name of a star, usually forgoing their given name during the ritual," she explained while playing with a strand of black hair. "My Holy name—Vegariel—I chose it because of the star Vega and its story..."

"The Star-weaver Girl," Zylis concluded. "A princess who fell in love with a lowly servant, and because of the forbidden love, they were banished to either side of the Milky Way. She then weaved the stars together and made the constellations so that they could be reunited."

The reason for his specific nicknames made sense within the confines of Estelle's mind. He had known all along what her Holy name meant.

"Yeah," she said, almost breathlessly. "Uh, most Angels above level seven have a Luminari, but it's not unheard of to get one at a lower level," Estelle continued. "So it just seems more attainable. I can't imagine being as powerful as the third sphere Angels."

Zylis hummed and raised an eyebrow as he looked out at the horizon. "So, overall, Angels get creepier as they become stronger?" he asked. "That's weird, Demons just get sexier."

"Wha—really?"

"Yeah, I mean, have you seen Lucifer?" Zylis whistled. "Dude's like, the personification of sex."

Estelle hesitated. "Well, I guess it helps to tempt people if you're, uh, sexy." She instantly regretted her words as the Demon turned toward her with a wicked smile and hooded eyes.

"Oh, and you think I'm sexy?" He stepped closer, his tail waved side to side in large movements, beckoning her to get closer.

The Angel stepped backward, stumbling slightly. "I, uh..." she trailed off, blinking rapidly, trying to get her brain to work correctly. She watched as Zylis tilted his head to the side and leaned down as he waited for an answer. Subconsciously, her eyes looked him up and down as her cheeks became impossibly warm.

The Demon's smile grew.

"I mean, you look... Ah, okay?"

Zylis chuckled, low and deep. "I'm 'okay'?" he repeated, stepping into her space again, catching the light of her halo on his face.

It took every fiber in her being not to step away.

"Alright, who, out of all the magical pelicans—because I know you've never met another Demon aside from me and Cyrus—is better looking than me?"

Estelle was looking at everything except Zylis, her wings extended as if ready to take flight. When she caught sight of the thrones off in the distance again, she blurted out the first Angel that came to mind.

"Reclerstin!" In a panic, Estelle physically slapped a hand over her mouth.

She didn't know why she had said *Issac Sterling's* Holy name, but she wished she hadn't. Over the past month, Estelle hadn't even mentioned her friends to Zylis, and vice versa. Most of their conversations were her asking questions about his world, and him mocking her education.

Zylis' smile faltered. "And who's that?" he asked, standing up to his full height. The tail was moving faster as if agitated.

"He's in my class," the Angel answered, folding her wings against her back.

Zylis looked uneasy, as if her answer was unexpected. "You know," the Demon started, taking a couple of steps back, extending his right hand out to the side. "Temptation isn't inherently bad. I can easily find him and make it so he's not so pretty."

Estelle watched as his palm began to glow bright orange before a small explosion erupted. It was beautifully frightening as the embers flickered to life, and the heat brushed against her face.

"That seems pretty tempting to me." Zylis let the fire die in his hand.

Estelle stared at him for a long moment, attempting to understand if there was an underlying argument he was trying to make, but to no avail. "I'm sorry, are you trying to frame bullying someone for being *prettier* than you..." she said, articulating each syllable carefully, "as some sort of roundabout way of *altruism*?" She shook her head. "I don't know how to tell you how fundamentally bizarre that is."

Zylis hesitated. "Okay, yeah. I'll give you that."

"Is this your way of trying to tempt me?"

"Well, it's not exactly my department, *Princess*," he spat, glaring at her with a light blush on his cheeks.

Estelle started laughing. "But I don't—" she snorted, shoulders shaking, "—I don't even know what *point* you're trying to make!"

"Void you!" Zylis shouted back, face turning redder. "I don't need that from you. Your entire belief system is incoherent!"

Estelle merely laughed harder, clutching at her sides.

"Okay," she wheezed after a moment. "Okay, I'm sorry, but what were you trying to argue just now?"

The Demon sighed, closing his eyes and clenching his fists as the Angel wiped tears from her eyes. "Look, honestly? It's not all about lust or the other six sins, and temptation isn't even the right word for it," he said, raking a hand through his blonde hair. "It's not like some carnal process where the only thing pulling you in is the promise of frivolous pleasure. I mean—" he threw his hands up, "—*are* there things like that I can capitalize on? Absolutely. But it's far more effective to convince you my side's better, and there's more than enough evidence to back that up."

Estelle raised an eyebrow. "Such as?"

Zylis stared at her for a second, looking her up and down as he crossed his arms in front of his chest and smirked. "Do you really want to know?"

The Angel sucked in a breath. It was a bad idea. She knew it was, but at the same time, his goal was to get her to Fall, so the whole thing was inevitable anyway.

"Sure, why not?" she sighed.

But then Zylis gave her one of his *smiles*—the slow-spreading, mischievous ones that always seemed to precede dangerous interactions.

Estelle's stomach instantly filled with regret.

"Well, in that case…" Zylis proceeded to reach into his rucksack and pulled out a thick book with dozens of tabs in various colors sticking out from the pages.

"What is that?"

"Just something I picked up a few weeks ago," he replied, shrugging casually, his tail returning to its normal speed. "Been tempted for a while, but I finally caved a couple of days after I had to explain to you what a sallbokvie was."

Estelle squinted, trying to read the cover, but Zylis' hands were in the way. "Okay…?" she said. "But what is it?"

"Oh, you know—just a brief little synopsis of the sociopolitical concave you call Heaven," he replied as he began to flip through the tabbed pages. After a moment, the Demon grinned as he had found what he was looking for. "Alright, so here's what we'll do," he said, "As far as I know, this book is still up-to-date, but I'm not positive. So, I'm gonna read off an excerpt, and when I'm done, you'll tell me whether or not it's still true. Got it?"

"I'm not sure what you're getting at," Estelle said. "But go ahead."

Zylis smiled curtly and began reading aloud. "An Angel's ability to obtain accurate information is contingent on their position within the hierarchy. Depending on the level of their students, instructors may be forbidden from teaching specific subjects, and curious Angels are barred from so much as opening books covering topics deemed to be inappropriate for an Angel of their status.

"Most telling, however, are the places where the lines are drawn. Books covering combat, Angelic powers, and Angel physiology are almost entirely forbidden in the first sphere, which encompasses Angels from levels one and two. While these are allowed in the second sphere, which includes levels three through six, in most cases, books covering the history of Heaven and Hell's conflict are still off-limits. Books which look at Demonic culture and government, to the extent that they exist in Heaven, are only available to level nine Angels." Zylis stopped and looked up at her expectantly.

After a second, Estelle nodded. "That's true."

He closed the book with a *snap*. "Do you know how I got this book?" he asked, enunciating each word slowly and deliberately. When Estelle didn't respond right away, he took it as a cue to continue. "I walked into the library and asked the librarian where I could find current information about the structure of your overgrown chickens' society. She recommended this book, I checked it out, and I went home." He pinched the bridge of his nose. "I mean, concave, Star—you do realize this—" Zylis held out the book, "—isn't normal, right?"

The Angel rolled her eyes. "And who made you the judge of what is and isn't normal?"

Zylis groaned and shoved the book back into his bag. He closed his eyes and rubbed his temples in small circles.

When he finally opened them again, he looked at Estelle and began to speak in a patronizingly sweet voice. "Star, *baby*, you're getting voided," he said. "You're getting voided by some pillock you've never even spoken to—" he suddenly pointed at her as if to preemptively rebut some response he had anticipated, "—because yes, the book mentioned that too, Star. I know that the vast majority of Angels never even get the chance to speak to God."

Estelle scoffed. "Well, when's the last time you spoke to Lucifer?"

"Last week, in a public bathroom." Zylis shot back with a wide grin. "He asked about the recipe for a dish I brought to a mutual friend's birthday party last month. About a week after you got the sallvie."

She stared back at him for a while, unsure of how to respond. That was far from the response she had been expecting. "We're talking about the same person, right?" she finally asked. "Lucifer, as in...?"

"The so-called 'Prince of Darkness'?" Zylis snorted. "Yeah, Star. That Lucifer."

The Angel blinked several times, trying to recalibrate her brain. She was beginning to wonder whether the Demon had found a way to lie to her undetected. But then, out of nowhere, it suddenly occurred to her that, although she had always known that Zylis was powerful, she had never actually stopped to ask where exactly he sat within the hierarchy.

The epiphany sent a cold shock through her, and without really meaning to, her stance shifted to something a bit more defensive, wings flexing.

"Zye..." she cautiously said. "Just how high-ranking are you?"

Zylis stared at her for a split second before bursting out into a fit of laughter. He clutched his sides and looked at Estelle as though she had said something absurd.

"Star!" he wheezed. "Holy devil!"

"What?" Estelle demanded, suddenly embarrassed for reasons she couldn't understand.

Her face felt hotter the longer the Demon's fit went on, but eventually, he calmed down enough to speak normally. "Star, that's not how this works."

"How *what* works?"

"*Our* society," he said. "This might come as a shock to you, but not every society is like a totalitarian surveillance state. Lucifer's just a guy." Zylis kicked a can off the rooftop. "A strong guy? Absolutely. Arguably the strongest—but he's just a guy.

"Don't get me wrong, his strength is no joke. Being so ancient, he's had time to master just about every type of Demonic power that exists. Occasionally, that expertise might give him opinions more weighted— you know, when it's relevant—but he's not categorically *important*."

Estelle frowned. "But he's one of the Original Demons, isn't he?"

"Yeah, but who the void cares?" Zylis snorted. "I don't know about you, Princess, but 'finders keepers' doesn't seem like a very logical idea to build an entire society off of."

"Well, a lot of human societies were created like that."

"And the vast majority of people were miserable."

Estelle stared at him for a long time, her mouth opening slightly. She wasn't sure what she was feeling. There was a part of her that was angry, and on an instinctual level, she felt like she knew why. But for whatever reason, Estelle just had no idea what to do with the feeling. It was there, churning deep inside her—she just didn't have the vocabulary to express it.

After what felt like an eternity, the Angel tore her eyes away and went to sit on the edge, looking down at the vacant street below. A moment later, Zylis sighed and sat next to her.

"Star, what are you doing?" he asked, tone soft, almost affectionate.

"What do you mean?"

"I mean…" He gestured to the skyline, where the war raged on. "Why do you want to be like *them*?"

After a moment of thought, Estelle exhaled. "Zye, there is a finite number of people on Earth." She pulled her knees to her chest. "Eventually, our job here will be done. I want to keep helping, even after that time comes."

"And you think fighting in the war will... *help* people?" he asked, cocking his head with a frown. "Have you considered just, like..." He gestured vaguely. "Maybe starting a community garden or something?"

Estelle laughed softly under her breath, but shook her head. "Zylis, that's not enough. I want to be able to protect people."

"From what?" the Demon asked, and for a moment, neither of them said anything. Then, with a soft voice, he added, "People like me?"

Estelle's breath caught, and she couldn't respond. She could feel Zylis' eyes on her, pinning her in place. The silence stretched between them, only interrupted by the muffled sound of explosions and impact in the distance that both had long since learned to tune out.

"Maybe I'm just the exception," he added after a moment.

The girl smiled, despite herself. "The exception that proves the rule."

He sighed and looked out on the horizon. "You know, I've never really understood that phrase..."

16

Educational Purpose

"I JUST FEEL... STRANGE," ESTELLE said, staring down at her cup of rosebay tea, stirring it idly. "I don't know. I feel like I've gotten too comfortable around him. I keep trying to remind myself how easily he could hurt me if he felt like it," she paused, releasing the spoon.

The Angel watched the amber liquid gradually settle; her murky reflection gently rippled in the mug.

"Maybe that's *why* I feel this way. Because he could do it, but chooses not to." When Estelle finally looked up from her tea, she found Antares seated across from her, elbows on the table, fingers laced together beneath the chin of a frowning face. "Sorry, maybe I said too—"

"No, no," Antares reassured her, waving his hands. "Apologies—this is just my thinking face."

Estelle relaxed a bit. He was the only person she could honestly talk to about what happened on her missions with Zylis. She couldn't tell the other teachers, because the fewer people who knew, the better. Telling her friends was out of the question because it could get them in serious trouble, like what she'd been finding herself in.

She nodded as she looked down at her lap, where her hands were folded. Her gloves sat discarded on the table. The corruption mark was barely noticeable after seven weeks, but she still wore it around others to be safe.

Estelle had finally gotten the hang of her Angelic powers, at least to the point where she was no longer receiving bruises along her chest and abdomen, which had mainly faded.

"However," Antares continued with a sigh. "I'd be lying if I said this wasn't an issue. Frankly, based on some of the ways you've described him, I didn't expect this to be a major concern, but perhaps the boy is more charming than I gave him credit for." He chuckled softly, and Estelle smiled.

"Charming is definitely not the word I would use to describe him," she lightly replied, carefully lifting the mug to her lips and blowing on it before taking a sip. "Half the time, he's insulting me, and the other half, he's just excessively crude—probably on purpose, to try and make me feel unsettled." She glanced up, and the grave look on her mentor's face made her pause. "Antares?"

The older Angel took a deep breath, regarding her carefully. "Amadea... are you certain he hasn't been using his abilities on you?"

"Um..." She blinked a couple of times. "What do you mean, exactly?" Estelle frowned. "He hasn't hurt me or anything—"

"Not with his Wrath abilities, Amadea," Antares interrupted, shaking his head slightly. "I'm talking about Lust abilities. Are you certain he hasn't been hypnotizing you?"

Estelle paled, mouth falling open. "I mean... would I know it if he did?"

Antares hesitated, lowering his chin slightly. "Given that he's a Wrath Demon primarily, I would say probably, but not necessarily."

"Well, great."

The high-ranking Angel stood up. "You need to ask him," he said, pushing his chair in. "And be sure to get a straight answer; don't allow him to dodge the question. Understand? This is very important."

Estelle nodded silently, then nearly jumped out of her skin when the kettle began to scream.

The sunset filtered through the stained glass windows at around five in the afternoon, stretching colorful lights over the altar and pews. After Estelle sent the last human to Heaven and the clothes fell to the floor, Zylis sighed, shoved his hands into his pockets, and wandered down the aisle. Estelle braced herself, trying not to look as nervous as she was.

She had tried to bring it up before, but Zylis was too busy talking about the current human holiday, Valentine's Day. He questioned why they needed a designated day to celebrate being in a relationship. The Angel wasn't paying attention, mainly because they didn't celebrate it in Heaven, or at least, the Angels didn't. The humans on the Mainland probably still held on to the long-established holiday.

Estelle cleared her throat, catching the Demon's attention as he looked at her. "Zye, are you..." she winced, looking away from Zylis' glowing eyes. "Doing something to me?"

When he didn't respond immediately, Estelle glanced back and found Zylis staring at her with his head cocked to the side, a bewildered look on his face.

"*Doing something?*" he repeated. "The void are you talking about?"

"I mean, like..." She gestured vaguely, her cheeks growing redder under his attention. She took a deep breath. "Look, you're a Wrath Demon, right?"

Zylis blinked a couple of times before throwing her a slight smirk. "I don't have to answer that."

"I'll take that as a yes," Estelle said, reaching up to play with her hair. "My mentor told me about Demon types." She watched Zylis' realization through her explanation as she spoke faster with each word, almost as if trying to outrun the Demon's comprehension. "He said that every type falls under a different category and has two adjacent classes. Meaning that you can also specialize in—"

"Oh, I get it," Zylis cut in, suddenly stepping closer to her. He loomed over Estelle; his grin was downright predatory. "You think I'm pulling some kinda Lust magic on you, huh?" He began circling her with a particular spring in his step that made Estelle want to take it all back.

She instinctively hardened her soul.

"What if I told you I'm not?" he asked playfully, hot breath wafting against her right ear. "What if I told you it's all just you, huh?" Zylis laughed, circling to speak into Estelle's other ear. "Would you believe me?"

The Angel found herself unable to speak, suffocated by the way he moved around her like a predator playing with its food before the kill.

"What's wrong? Tongue-tied?"

Estelle could have sworn she felt the timbre of his voice reverberating inside her as Zylis looped around to her right. She took a decisive step to her left to put space between them.

"Would I know if you did?" she asked, forcing herself to look up and meet the Demon's eyes, activating Truth Seer.

Some of the playfulness melted away as Zylis frowned, looking her up and down with an eyebrow arched. Estelle held her ground, fists clenched behind her back.

The Demon scoffed. "Look, it's adorable that you think I'm doing something with your feelings right now, but I'm not."

The keyword 'right now,' Estelle's brain supplied. *What if Truth Seer doesn't work because of hypnotism? He could be lying.* She narrowed her eyes. "I'm not sure if I—"

"Believe me?" Zylis completed, tilting his head with both eyebrows raised. After a moment, he sighed and took a step closer, forcing the Angel to look up to keep eye contact as he loomed over her again. "How about I just show you how it feels?"

She blinked a few times, her mind going blank. "I don't follow."

He rolled his eyes. "I'm saying, instead of speculating about whether or not I've found some clever way to hack your lie detector, how about I just settle this by *showing* you how it feels when those abilities get used on you," Zylis said, shrugging. "Probably save us both a concave amount of time."

Estelle froze, her whole body tensing up. To say that the idea made her nervous was a gross understatement.

"I won't do anything bad, Star. Promise. It's purely so you can see how it feels."

He was telling the truth; she checked. *But still...* "I don't know, Zye," she said, laughing anxiously.

"You wanna be on the battlefield someday, right?" Zylis said, red eyes studying her carefully. "Don'tcha think knowing how it feels beforehand might be useful?"

The Angel opened her mouth for a second and then closed it again.

The Demon leaned in closer. "Y'know, the next time this happens to you, it ain't gonna be for educational purposes, Princess."

Estelle swallowed, eyes downcast. She hated admitting it, but the Demon made a good point. And really, how many Angels got to experience the effect of a Demon's powers in a non-hostile setting?

She smothered the doubt within herself. It had been a long time since it had done her any good. With a sigh, Estelle nodded. "Okay, fine... but you promise you won't do anything bad? As in my definition of bad?"

"Promise."

She released a shuddering breath and nodded again.

"In that case, look into my eyes."

Estelle did as she was told, turning to meet the Demon's gaze. The innate, enchanting quality of his eyes made it all too easy to get lost in them—a feeling she was well accustomed to. But after a moment, she felt something new. Something clicked inside her head, like a door she never knew existed. Then, her mind felt heavier all at once, and her vision grew hazy.

Zylis smirked, slow and dangerous. "Get on your knees."

Estelle's body moved before the words even reached her consciousness. Everything was slow, muted, like she was immersed in warm molasses. Before she even knew what was happening, Estelle's knees were on the floor, pressed into the faded red carpet. But just as quickly as it had happened, she felt the extra weight leave, exiting her mind with a second click, as though locking the door behind it.

The Angel blinked a few times to clear the fog as she stared at Zylis' black combat boots, mere inches from where her knees were situated. Estelle remembered Antares saying that the hypnotic gaze only works with direct eye contact. She looked up at Zylis and found the Demon staring back down at her, an amused look on his face.

He offered her a hand, but she stood up on her own.

"You get it now?" Zylis asked.

Estelle brushed off the front of her dress, her mind still feeling slightly off-balance. "Yeah, it's..." she hesitated, trying to find the right words, but nothing particularly descriptive came to mind. "Pretty distinctive."

He hummed low. "So, you believe me now?"

She nodded quietly.

"Good," Zylis said. He slid his hands into his pockets and began to walk in circles around her again. "So... what exactly did you think I was making you feel, anyway?"

Oh, dear.

"I-I mean—" Estelle sputtered. "Antares—ah, my mentor's the one who wanted me to ask. It's not what you think."

Zylis snorted. "Yeah? And what do I think, Star?"

"I don't know!" she exclaimed, voice rising in pitch. "But I'm sure it's very inappropriate!"

He cackled. "*Inappropriate?* Come on, Star, we're both adults and—" He suddenly stopped before her, turning to face her with narrowed eyes. "Wait, they let you guys have sex, right?"

Estelle's hands shot up to cover her face along with her wings, when the words left his mouth, turning sharply on her heel. "Oh my—Zylis!"

"But they do, right?" Zylis asked, matching her movements to stay in front of her. "*Right?*"

The Angel's feathers ruffled as she tried to use her wings to push him away. She was on the verge of screaming.

"Void, they *don't*," he said, a grim realization evident in his tone. "What's even the point of—"

Estelle covered her ears. "La la la la la—!"

The Demon knocked her hands away from her ears with his wrists, using the sleeves of his leather jacket as a buffer. "What are you, five?"

Estelle stuck her tongue out at him, only for Zylis to suddenly reach up and try to grab it. She lurched back, barely dodging his fingers. Somehow, her cheeks burned brighter. "What the—Zye! What's wrong with you?"

"What's the point of going to Heaven if you can't even indulge in all the stuff you weren't allowed to do when you were alive?" He threw his hands up.

The girl threw her hands up higher. "Why did you try to grab my tongue just now?"

"You were acting like a child, and I figured you'd lost tongue privileges!"

"What does that even mean?"

"Whatever the void I decide it means!"

"Why are you yelling?"

"I don't know, why are you—!" Zylis suddenly tensed, and a sour expression overtook his features. "Seriously, *now*?" he grumbled, unzipping the front of his jacket. "This better be concave important."

Estelle looked at him in confusion, shuffling back as the Demon proceeded to shed his leather jacket. Underneath, he wore a simple black tank top.

The first thing that caught Estelle's attention was the size of his biceps—physical proof of the strength the Demon had demonstrated many times over. The second thing she noticed was the intricate tattoo adorning his upper left arm and shoulder, depicting what looked to be fire. Or maybe it was a bird, or perhaps it was someone?

Zylis put his hand over it, and it began to glow—the black ink lighting up orange.

"What do you want?" he said, speaking through gritted teeth, though the irritation faded as time passed, with Zylis remaining silent. After a minute, he said, "Okay, but why are you telling me this?" Another minute went by, and he sighed. "Void. Alright, fine, I'll meet you there, I guess." His hand fell away from the marking, and he seemed to deflate.

"Is everything okay?" Estelle asked, with several new questions swirling inside her head.

"Yeah, it's fine," Zylis muttered, raking a hand through his hair. "Apparently, Cyrus got into some trouble on the front lines, though."

"Traten?" She frowned. "Is he okay?"

"Terminally stupid, but he'll be fine."

"Well, that's good."

He raised an eyebrow. "You're glad your enemy made it home alive?"

Estelle sputtered for an answer. He was right. But Traten was so friendly when she met him. It was easy to forget he was a Demon. "Are you not happy he's alive?" she accused.

Zylis shrugged, projecting apathy, but Estelle could sense he was relieved. She wondered when exactly she had learned to read the Demon so well.

"I should probably head back, anyway," she eventually said, tucking a stray hair behind her ear. "Um, tell him I said 'hi,' I guess."

Zylis gave a brief nod in response, throwing his jacket back on.

Estelle's eyes followed the movement.

The unlikely pair parted ways beneath a cloudy, pink sky.

17

Vostarist

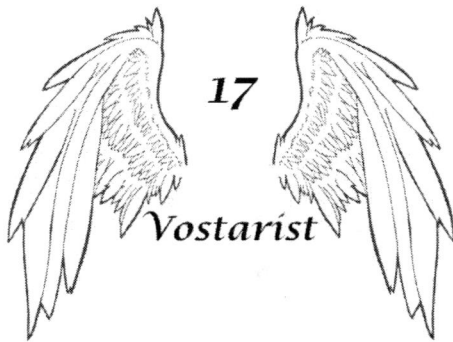

JUST BEYOND THE GATE OF Heaven, there was a dispatch station. The station contained six platforms serviced by a shuttle with four cars, each designed to take passengers to one distinct, unchanging location on the tracks.

The first platform was the largest, as its shuttle was bound for the most populous portion of God's Kingdom: the Mainland, where virtuous humans spent their afterlife. The car had been temporarily disabled to keep the civilians safe. It had been a long time since Estelle had last seen it running.

It had become scarce for humans to die naturally because of the war. The only way to get into the Mainland would be for an Angel to escort them. As far as she knew, Angelic attacks couldn't hurt mortals directly, but Demonic attacks could. Because of its nature, if hit with Demonic abilities, a human soul would become tainted, resulting in them going to Hell.

The most dangerous attack was that of hellfire. When engulfed in its flames, the human soul would be destroyed, with no chance of an afterlife in either Heaven or Hell. The same effect happened with ethereal beings, wiping them from existence.

The following three platforms were entry points for the inner circles, where working Angels, like Estelle, lived. Of the remaining two platforms, one went directly to the hospital, mainly used for injuries sustained from battle. Very rarely did Angels get sick, if ever. The last platform went to the High Temple, where God resided, along with His council. That platform was hardly used, as the only ones authorized to use it were the Apostles, their Vostarists, and theoretically, God himself—though the idea of God needing to rely on shuttle transport seemed almost laughable to Estelle.

In all her years, Estelle had never seen anyone use that shuttle. Perhaps that was why it caught her attention when she noticed a tall figure standing alone on the platform, waiting. But then again, it was also generally difficult not to notice when one was in the presence of such a person.

The Apostle's Vostarist was an odd sight, standing just fifteen feet away in his white and gold robes, which flowed and billowed out around him unusually as if hiding some writhing mass within. Only one set of wings was visible, though Estelle was sure he had more hidden beneath the robe. The strangest part was the crimson scarf that covered his eyes and wrapped around the entire upper portion of his head, mostly hidden beneath a white cowl. Estelle wasn't exactly sure why the Vostarists wore blindfolds, or how they managed to see despite them.

She didn't mean to stare. It was just difficult not to. The few times she had seen Vostarists before, they always seemed to have a bizarre gravitational pull about them, as though thousands of souls lived within their bodies. All high-level Angels felt like that to some extent, but even among them, the Vostarists were in a league of their own—a de facto tenth level beyond the normal ninth.

From what she could remember, the next ninth-level Angel on track to become a Vostarist was Regulus. He had ascended the ranks in record time, much like Antares, earning a Luminari at level five and proving a great asset in the Holy Army. If it weren't for a life-threatening injury that Antares sustained, causing him to retire from active duty, Regulus would probably be second in line for ascension.

Her vision went out of focus as she continued to gaze at the man, and it wasn't until the Vostarist turned toward her that Estelle became aware of what she was doing. His head turned slowly and tilted to the side. Somehow, Estelle knew he was watching her despite the blindfold.

She felt a cold rush travel down her spine as she hastily turned away. A moment later, the shuttle car arrived, and Estelle boarded alongside a couple of others, her heart racing. She had to be more careful. The powers of the Vostarist were not fully understood. She had heard rumors that they could see into the minds of Angels.

As the shuttle car doors closed, Estelle worked up the nerve to give the Vostarist one last glance. She was relieved to find the man standing in the same spot as before, his head facing forward, remaining so as the car began to move.

Her heart continued to pound in her ears for the duration of the trip, only allowing herself to breathe once she set foot on the familiar ground of the first sphere. It struck her as strange that she would rather interact with a Demon than be in the same vicinity as an extremely high-ranking Angel.

Estelle knew something had happened before she set foot inside the dorm building. Through the window, she saw Giovanna in the common area, pacing as she spoke. Issac, who seldom hung around the common room, stood, leaning back against the wall, listening and occasionally nodding. Estelle's heart immediately jumped into her throat.

When she opened the door, Giovanna stopped and looked at her. "Estelle!" she shouted.

"Yes...?" the raven-haired Angel said, eyes darting between the two. "What's going on?"

"Lilith's hurt!" she said.

Issac nodded. "She's in the hospital. We only just found out."

"What?" Estelle said as a cold weight settled in her stomach. "What happened? Is Lilith going to be okay? How bad is it?"

"We don't know," Issac replied.

Giovanna shook her head. "They haven't told us anything else. We tried to figure out more, but that's all they would say. Just that she's been admitted."

That was not a good sign. If they weren't given information about Lilith's condition, it could be life-threatening.

"We were about to head over there," the lilac-haired Angel said. "See if maybe they'll let us see her." Estelle nodded, already making her way back out the door. "Don't you want to change out of your uniform first?" Issac called after her as they all scrambled out the door.

"I'm not wasting time changing," Estelle said, feeling the sting of tears in her eyes.

The three sat in the waiting room for what felt like several hours but was probably around twenty minutes. Estelle zoned out, staring at the 'No Talking' sign as she waited, listening to the steady sound of the clock ticking above her head. The coincidence of Lilith and Traten getting sent to the hospital on the same day seemed odd. Was it possible they had been attacking each other? Most likely not. Battles were happening in all corners of the Earth, some worse than others; realistically, they had nothing to do with each other's injuries.

Eventually, the door to the emergency wing opened, and a single nurse emerged. She greeted them pleasantly before she gestured for them to follow her. They all stood up, thanked her, and hastily trailed behind, barely avoiding stepping on each other's ankles on the way down the hall.

A minute later, they arrived at a door near the end of the hall, at which point the nurse bade them farewell. The three Angels didn't waste any time and piled inside. Estelle braced herself for the worst.

There, Lilith Audelaire sat upright in bed, a cast on her left arm and gauze wrapped around her left shoulder and across her neck. Estelle felt the tension inside her melt away almost instantly.

"Oh," Lilith said, looking up at them. "Hello. I wasn't expecting you guys."

Giovanna was the first to speak. "We were worried when we heard you were injured, but didn't know how bad it was! Did you think we wouldn't show up?"

"Come now, Giovanna, I wouldn't go down without breaking a record first," Lilith joked. She had ascended right after breaking the class record for fast flying.

"Are you feeling alright?" Estelle finally asked.

Lilith gestured toward her left arm and shoulder. "Not in ideal condition, but nothing they won't be able to heal in a few days."

"Oh, thank goodness," Giovanna sighed. "We were terrified!"

"Sorry to make you worry."

"No, no!" the tall Angel waved her hands. "It's not your fault, Lilith—ah, Miss Audelaire."

"We're just glad you're alright," Issac said, speaking for the first time since they left the dormitories.

The snow-white-haired Angel smiled. "I was lucky. It could have been a lot worse."

"If you don't mind me asking, what happened?" Giovanna asked.

"Just had a close run-in with a Demon." Lilith shrugged. "It was my fault, I guess. I let hi—" She cleared her throat. "It caught me off guard. I need to learn not to let... that happen."

"You need to be more vigilant," Giovanna said, smiling. "I don't know what I would do if you never returned."

"I imagine everyone slips up sometimes," Estelle said. "Don't be too hard on yourself. It was only your..." she trailed off. "Uh, third battle, was it?"

"Second, actually," Lilith supplied.

"That just makes my point stronger," Estelle said. "You're new at this, Lilith. You're bound to make some mistakes."

"Hopefully, none of them will be fatal," she said, momentarily making the room fall silent.

It was extremely difficult for an Angel to 'die' again. Still, the chances of Falling and becoming a Demon increased significantly when they'd been badly injured, elevating the risk of corruption damage.

"Well, you must be tired, and we don't want to stunt your healing progress," Giovanna said, actively urging the others to follow her lead. "So we should probably head out."

Issac cleared his throat as the taller Angel not so subtly pushed him out the door. "I'm relieved you're alright, Lili—Ow!" He reached up and rubbed his upper arm where Giovanna had punched him. "What was that for?"

"*Audelaire* is a higher rank than us."

Issac rolled his eyes.

"Please stay safe out there," Giovanna added.

"Will do," Lilith said, slightly confused. "And I don't mind you using my—"

"It's the proper way to address you until we ascend," Giovanna chirped as she headed out the door, with Issac trailing behind. Estelle, however, remained in place.

"Estelle?" Issac called, looking over his shoulder.

"You guys go on ahead," she said. "I think I'll stay a few more minutes." She looked over at the patient. "If that's okay with you, I mean."

Lilith nodded.

Issac paused for a moment before shrugging. "Alright. Well, I guess I'll see you later, then." The door clicked quietly behind him, muffling the sound of their footsteps as the two Angels walked away.

Estelle supposed the lock on the door would need to be replaced, as it wobbled slightly when the door shut. Though considering the locks were only used by the Vostarists, the need to fix them was minor.

With no one else around, Estelle opted to sit in the chair beside Lilith's bed—it had been left vacant until then; Estelle figured no one wanted to be the person who sat while all the others had to stand.

"So…" the black-haired girl said, fidgeting with the hem of her right glove that hid what remained of the corruption damage. "Are those physical injuries?"

Lilith was surprised by the question, only noticeable by the minuscule rise of her eyebrows. After a second of hesitation, she gestured toward her left arm. "It's a mix. My arm is broken, and I have some bruises, but the rest is corruption damage."

Estelle nodded, chewing on her lip. "I guess that's pretty common to get corruption damage."

"Yeah, I'd say so. It seems to happen less often, the more experienced you are." She blinked. "Holding a barrier while fighting is harder than you might think. I don't even remember when it slipped. A lot was going on." After a moment of silence, Lilith added, "And even for the more experienced Angels, there are some Demons who can get around barriers."

Lust Demons, Estelle's mind supplied. She swallowed. "Do you think it was one of those?"

"No. They teach us to determine that based on how Demons fight. This one didn't match what you'd expect from a Demon like that."

"So, it was just one, then."

"Yeah. Just one."

The lower-level Angel hesitated before asking, "Did the Demon survive?"

"Yes," she said. "And I don't think I could've beaten this one. Too strong. But I did get in a few good hits."

Estelle hummed before silence fell between them.

Both of them, Estelle assumed, knew what the other was doing, carefully structuring sentences designed to avoid referencing Demons with any particular pronoun. It wasn't something Estelle usually thought about. She didn't even bat an eye when others called Demons 'it.' Most of the books she read that mentioned them did the same. Likewise, most Angels didn't care when she referred to Demons with words like 'he' or 'she.' Depending on the context, many switched back and forth between the two modes.

But at that moment, when she sat beside Lilith in that sterile hospital room, it seemed to matter, for whatever reason. The avoidance felt like a signal of some kind, though Estelle couldn't say whether it was to be between the two of them or something else.

"That's where most of the corruption damage came from," the white-haired girl said, interrupting the quiet atmosphere. "The broken arm is embarrassing because it's unrelated to the fighting. I was flying and dove down, but I didn't stop my decent fast enough, and well," she gestured to her broken arm, "I broke my fall with it on a large rock." She smiled softly. "Next time I go down there, I'm wearing bracers."

Estelle giggled. "That sounds like something I'd probably do."

"I still remember when you fractured a wing on one of the hoops in the flying field."

"It was dark!"

"Which is why they don't have us practice after sunset."

"Yeah, I learned that lesson the hard way. But I still think we should have training on night flying," Estelle said, smiling. She had made the same argument back then, too.

"They start teaching that at level three," Lilith added as they laughed at the memory.

After a moment, Estelle asked, "Did they say how long they plan to keep you?"

"Just a couple more hours, thankfully." Lilith smiled, rolling her eyes slightly. "I have to come back every morning for the next few days for treatment, but after that, I should be fine."

"That's good news," Estelle said. "You should drop by the dorms sometime soon, Lilith. We all miss you."

The girl's cheeks were lightly dusted with blush at the comment. "I know. It's been hard to get away, but maybe they'll give me more free time after what happened."

The other Angel hummed. "We'll all understand if you can't make it."

"No, I'll figure something out." After another long stretch of silence, as Estelle prepared to excuse herself, Lilith spoke up again, speaking quietly with eyes seeming far away. "It's funny..."

Estelle blinked and leaned in closer to hear her better. "What is?"

Lilith hesitated for a moment as her eyes refocused. She looked away and stared at her hands. "Just that..." she frowned. "I'm still unsure if the Demon was... trying to *kill* me."

"Why do you say that?" Estelle asked, furrowing her brow.

"It was weird. The Demon didn't really try to hurt me, just grabbed my arm and wouldn't let go."

"Was the Demon trying to force a Fall?"

Snow white hair shifted as the girl shook her head. "The Demon let me go after a minute."

"That's... very strange." Estelle leaned in a bit further. "Any guesses as to what..." she trailed off.

"I think..." Lilith said, voice barely above a whisper. "I think he just wanted my attention."

He. Somehow, hearing her utter that word held a sort of reverence in the quiet room. "Did he say anything to you?"

Lilith nodded. "I think so, but it was too loud, so I couldn't hear anything."

"Are you sure it wasn't some kind of trap?"

"It wasn't."

Estelle blinked, momentarily shocked at the immediacy of her answer. After a beat, she asked, "What makes you so sure?"

Lilith didn't say anything at first. For a moment, the only response was the steady beeping of the heart monitor, the muted sounds of footsteps outside, and the subtle creaking of the walls as the wind blew against them. But then the Angel spoke once more. "I don't know," she murmured. "That's what I'm trying to figure out."

18

McKelle

On a typical day with Zylis, Estelle would meet up with him in the morning at the first church she was assigned to. As one might expect of humans who gather in a church amid a global catastrophe, the vast majority of them were true believers. Once in a while, Zylis would discover a bad apple or two in the bunch, but most people were decent.

On the occasions when stragglers remained, their numbers were almost always under five. At that point, Zylis would take over, escorting them to Hell personally before meeting up with Estelle once again at the next church. But for the first time since their partnership, there were too many non-believers for Zylis to handle on his own.

The two of them sat at the front of a large cathedral near the center of what used to be a major city. After a moment of silent deliberation, Zylis groaned, shed his jacket, and activated whatever was on his arm, allowing him to communicate with other Demons.

"Hey, McKelle. It's me. Need some backup over here." After a moment of silence, he side-eyed Estelle. "Yeah... she's here," he cautiously said, narrowing his eyes. "Why?" A few more seconds passed before he took his hand off the tattoo. "Void, she's closer than I thought."

"Who is?"

"Our transport Demon," he replied, standing up straight and heading toward the door. "Come on, it's probably best if you meet her somewhere..." He gestured vaguely toward the group of stragglers. "Y'know, not in front of fifteen people."

Estelle furrowed her eyebrows as more questions flooded her mind. She hesitantly followed the Demon, and as the ornate door closed behind them, Zylis tensed as if he remembered something and smacked a hand over the mark, making it glow again.

"Me again," he barked. "Listen, I shouldn't need to tell you this, but do not touch her without warning." He paused. "I *know* you know. I'm telling you so you won't forget." He dropped his hand, and the tattoo returned to its normal, black state.

To say Estelle was nervous would be an understatement.

"Devil, she's close. I can feel it," Zylis muttered, turning to look at the Angel for the first time. "Whoa, hey, calm down, Star. It's okay."

"Are you sure?" Estelle shot back. "Because everything you've said and done these past few minutes seems to imply the opposite."

"Star, I mean it." The Demon rolled his eyes. "Like, yeah, she's weird but harmless."

"And that's where the problem lies." The Angel pointed at him. "You've said it yourself. I don't think your definition of harmless is the same as mine."

"Anything McKelle could do to you is nothing a little therapy couldn't fix—"

"This is the *opposite* of reassurance!"

"Hey, hey!" a feminine voice called out.

Estelle jumped, suddenly seeing her standing ten feet away with a wide grin. She had glowing blue irises that seemed more intense with her wild, light pink hair. Like Zylis, she was partially shifted, a tail swaying lightly behind her, and though Estelle could see her horns through her hair, she was sure they were there.

"Leonhart, babe, didn't anyone ever teach you it's not nice to talk about people behind their backs?"

"I could kill you with my bare hands, McKelle," he deadpanned.

"Thanks, but I'm already seeing someone." She winked, grinning from ear to ear as she jogged up the steps. She came to a stop a couple of feet from the Angel. "And who's this?"

"You already know that."

She rested her head in her hand with a finger against her cheek. Estelle was sure she was flipping the other off. "Humor me."

Zylis sighed and stepped closer, wrapping an arm around the Angel. Estelle stiffened, her wings rising slightly as his hand fell on her hip and his tail curled around her leg. She could feel the heat of his touch through the fabric of her dress.

In a sarcastically sweet tone, Zylis said, "This is Star; she's my pet Angel. Y'know, one of those weird bird things that fear God."

"Zye, what—"

"Zye!" McKelle interjected.

"Void," Zylis groaned, removing his tail and hand. It brushed along Estelle's lower back as he moved it.

The Angel suppressed a shiver.

"That's so cute!" she exclaimed, jumping up and down. "You guys have pet names!"

"They're not pet names." Zylis glared at her. "They're insults we got used to somehow."

Estelle laughed at that. When she thought about it, she didn't know why Zylis warned her about Melody. She seemed like any other nice person. So far, every Demon Estelle has ever met was normal. Quirky, but normal.

McKelle gasped, freezing as she looked at her. The Angel reflexively put up her shield. "I'm gonna pinch your cheeks," she said.

Estelle blinked. "You're going—wait—" But it was far too late, as McKelle was already in her space. She winced as the Demon did just as she had said she would.

"You sound just like a bell; that's so precious!" she said, tugging Estelle's cheeks. She winked at Zylis. "You picked a good one, Leonhart."

The other Demon sighed. "I think Star would like you to stop touching her face, McKelle."

"Ah, right." Her expression morphed into faux-seriousness. She dropped her hands and cleared her throat performatively as she took a step back. "Of course. Nice to meet you, Star. You can call me Melody, my first name. McKelle is too formal." She held out her hand.

It took Estelle's brain a second to catch up, but she eventually reached out and accepted the handshake, careful to maintain her barrier.

Afterward, the Demon took another step back and looked her up and down with a discerning gaze. "You look like you'd make a great Pride Demon."

Zylis snorted. "You're just saying that because that's what you are."

"Nah, she looks like the type who'd want to go for something well-rounded," Melody said. "Unlike *someone* I know." She winked at Estelle. "I could teach you some sick moves."

"You just want an excuse to harass her more." Zylis rolled his eyes. "Pride doesn't fit her, anyway."

She frowned. "Well, what does she look like to you?"

Zylis paused as he looked the Angel up and down in a way that made her feel oddly exposed. Estelle wasn't even sure what was happening at that moment. Were they really trying to guess what kind of Demon she would make? She flushed and looked away from the glowing red eyes.

"Greed?" Melody offered. "I can see her being Envy, maybe."

"Nah." Zylis shook his head. "She sucks at lying. The playing-with-her-hair would give her away, and she's not one to be stealthy."

"So, uh..." Estelle finally piped up. "Is this, like, something Demons are born with?"

"What? No." Zylis shook his head again. "You can pick any path you want. We're just trying to figure out what you'd be good at."

"Gluttony?" Melody said, continuing.

"I could see that," he replied, nodding thoughtfully. "Gluttony, or..." he paused, tilted his head, and hummed. "Lust."

"Oh, really?" Melody asked, grinning.

"Yeah, the more I think about it, the more sense it makes."

"Fallen Angels do tend to take faster to Lust abilities."

Zylis shrugged. "Sure, but even without the advantage, it seems... right, somehow."

Estelle felt as if she had been hit by lightning. They agreed on Lust—they hadn't even discussed the others—spent less than a minute debating the voiced options, before landing on Lust. From what she knew about it, it wasn't anything she wanted to be, and Estelle didn't want to be any of the others—didn't want to be a Demon in general.

The Angel swallowed. "You think I'd be a Lust Demon?"

Melody waved her hand. "Oh, calm down, sweetheart," she said. "It's just a name. Lust Demons aren't any hornier than other Demons."

"I dunno, McKelle," Zylis said, snickering. "They can be pretty horny." The other Demon jabbed him in the ribs with her elbow. "Ow! What the—"

"I'm trying to make her feel better!" she shouted. "She looks like she's about to explode!"

Zylis' eyes darted up to Estelle's face and studied her momentarily before shrugging. "Eh, I've seen redder."

"*Leonhart.*"

He rolled his eyes. "Look, it doesn't matter, anyway. Whatever Star picks is what she picks."

Estelle frowned. "You both are far too confident about me Falling," she said, flexing her wings, a movement similar to how someone would roll their shoulders. "Last time I checked, it's been three full months since Zye has actively started trying to tempt me, and four months since we first met. Your odds don't look good."

"I absolutely adore you!" Melody squealed, actually spinning around once in her excitement. "Good luck to you, Leonhart. She's the cutest paklen I've ever met."

The Angel blinked. "Paklen...?"

"Oh, sorry!" she said. "It's slang—a little bat-like creature that bursts into flames. Basically, it means an Angel who's expected to Fall."

"Wow, okay..." Estelle blinked. "I'm not sure what to make of that."

"I won't call you that if you don't like it," she said, shrugging. "There's also 'Hell-bell', it is one of the, uh... kinder words for Angels, though." Zylis snorted, and Melody side-eyed him. "I'm sure Leonhart could tell you about the others."

"Where would I even start?" he asked, grinning.

"I would prefer that you didn't," Estelle replied.

Her partner rolled his eyes playfully. "Anyway, there are about fifteen people inside."

Melody nodded. "Right. Guess it's time to get this show on the road!"

The three of them filed back inside. Estelle and Zylis stood back as the humans gathered around Melody.

Once everyone was accounted for, Melody jumped up from within the center of the small crowd and waved at Estelle. "Nice meeting you, Star!"

"You too." She awkwardly waved. And then, Estelle watched in awe as the floor began to cave in beneath the group's feet, as though melting.

It was slow at first, but soon picked up speed; before long, all that remained was a gaping chasm, toward which all furniture deformed like a surrealist painting. After a moment, Estelle carefully inched over to it, peered over the edge, and gulped when she realized she couldn't see the bottom. For the first time, Estelle wished she could grab her halo and use it as a practical light source.

"You'll probably want to back away from that," Zylis said.

"Why?" Estelle asked, but then she heard it.

A rumbling noise that quickly got louder. The Angel hastily backed away as the chasm rapidly decreased in depth until the floor snapped

164

back into place like a trampoline. Estelle was thrown off balance, landing on her butt a good five feet away as the floor settled. If she had been any closer, it likely would have shot her straight into the ceiling.

She turned and looked at Zylis, her eyes blown wide.

He just grinned. "Hey, don't say I didn't warn ya."

Estelle walked into her room around seven that night. Her missions had become easier to manage since working with Zylis. They were getting done faster, and even after spending another couple of hours searching other buildings for stragglers, she was still getting back earlier than before.

The Angel dropped her bag by her desk and picked up the sallbokvie, writing a question she hadn't asked earlier.

What would happen if someone jumped into that pit?

She placed the book on her bed, setting the pen between the pages as she took off her shoes.

That was another thing. Before the partnership, Estelle would sleep in her uniform, not bothering to change before collapsing from exhaustion.

Estelle grabbed an oversized shirt and a pair of sweatpants from the dresser and laid them out on the bed. Before she began to change into the pajamas, Zylis wrote his reply.

Presumably death.
Zye.

If you're asking whether they'd end up in Hell, then no. Other than dying, the only way to get to Hell, if you're not a Demon, is to have a Demon take you there—one who knows how to expand their soul.

Expand their soul?

Yep. That's what Gluttony Demons do. Just expand their souls until they engulf everyone and everything around them. It's how they're able to transport large groups.

Didn't Melody say she was a Pride Demon?

Pride is a jack of all trades, able to do a lot of abilities that others can, but not as powerful. Traten is Gluttony and was able to transport 150 people easily, while Melody could, at most, do around 30.

Estelle hummed to herself as she unlaced her dress and read. Then something occurred to her, and once her hands were free, she picked up the pen.

Wait, how do YOU transport people?

We all learn the basics of each branch before we specialize. I can expand my soul, too, just not to the size of a concave gymnasium.

I see. Then, can the opposite be true? If some Demons can make their souls big, does that mean some can make them small?

166

The closest thing to what you're thinking of is compression, and it's about half of what I do. Wrath is compression + heat.

Wow! Why did you choose that?

Have you ever looked at someone and thought to yourself, "I want to hit them, but I also want to set them on fire"? Wrath Demons don't have to choose. We can do both simultaneously.

I'm quietly pathologizing this.

That's weird, considering you can't seem to shut the void up.

It just seems like an oddly specific reason.

That wasn't the only thing, pillock. If you want the real reason, it's because I was stubborn. I went with Wrath because everyone told me not to.

Yeah, that sounds like you. But why were they telling you that?

Estelle slipped on the shirt and pants, settling herself down on her bed as she waited for his full reply before reading.

Wrath usually has the steepest learning curve because it's really hard on your body. Other branches are challenging in different ways, I guess. Envy and Greed are very technical, and Pride takes sustained concentration. Those are all challenging in some way, but Wrath is the only one that HURTS.

So they didn't want you to do it because it was painful?

No. It's particularly bad for someone like me. I learn faster, but the physical consequences are worse. People kept saying I'd be lucky not to end up passed out in a puddle of my vomit after each session, which turned out to be true. I got through it, but it sucked for a while.

You're actually pretty lucky, Star. Fallen Angels have it easy.
What do you mean?

Fallen Angels tend to pick up on Demonic abilities quickly but without much backlash. Not to say it won't still be challenging, but it will be easier for you.

That's pretty interesting. But what do you mean by "someone like me," though? You're different somehow?

Yes.
In what way?

Estelle waited, but Zylis never responded.

19
From Level One

It first happened in a dream.

Estelle walked down the gravel path inside the apple orchard in the dream, admiring the impossibly red fruits. The sun beat down on her skin, and her shoes kicked pebbles around on the ground. Then she blinked, and suddenly, a woman appeared before her.

She wore a white-silver floor-length ball gown with an intricate gold pattern on the skirt. The bodice was a shining corset that looked almost like body armor, with gold gems reaching her collarbone. The sleeves were long and looked like wings as the glistening fabric folded and swayed in a nonexistent wind.

It was beautiful.

She was beautiful. The woman looked human, aside from the snow-white hair one would expect an Angel to have and glowing crystal blue eyes like a Demon, but something about her told Estelle that the stranger was so much more.

"Who are you?" Estelle asked.

The woman extended her hand but said nothing, yet it was as if her voice was present, soft and as clear as a bell, asking for help.

Estelle was hesitant, stepping a bit closer, but eventually, she returned the gesture, reaching for the other. But then, an apple fell from the tree beside them and landed at the mystery woman's feet. In an instant, the ground swallowed the fruit and began to sprout up with the makings of a tree.

The Angel jumped back at the rate of growth. It was entangling the woman, who still had her arm outstretched for Estelle. At that moment, the girl saw tears sliding down the other's face and turned to find her training gloves on the ground nearby, as if they had been there the entire time.

She quickly retrieved and slid them on, turning back to see only glowing blue eyes peeking through a tree trunk before disappearing within. Estelle felt the familiar surge of power through her, like electricity in her veins. She swung her fist at the tree. She heard it crack and—

Estelle opened her eyes just as she tumbled out of bed, hitting the wooden floor in a way that had her gasping in shock and pain. She sat up quickly and looked around her room, disoriented. She stayed there, eyes wide and panting for a few moments before her brain fully adjusted to reality again. It was only then that she noticed the pain radiating from her right hand. She looked down, doing a double-take at her bloodied, discolored knuckles.

"What the..." she mumbled. *What happened?* Estelle carefully stood up and looked around, and that's when she saw it. The headboard of her bed was broken, the wood splintered. *Did I...?* She looked at her hand and then back at the headboard.

After the initial shock wore off, the Angel padded to her bathroom. Her body moved on autopilot, turning on the light and faucet, and she washed her knuckles under the cold water. It was only then, as she watched the blood wash down the drain, that the true realization hit her.

There's no way I could've done that on my own, she thought. *Did I use power while I was sleeping?* She tensed, and her blood ran cold. *Without a vessel.*

"I need to talk to Antares," she said aloud, turning off the sink. *But... I can't.* She remembered that her mentor was teaching in the third sphere and wouldn't be back until the next day. She'd have to wait.

Estelle gripped the edge of the sink with her uninjured hand. Her vision swirled like the water going down the drain, and an overwhelming sense of dread settled within her.

This is going to be a very long day.

The Angel grabbed the hand towel to gently wipe her hand off before bandaging the knuckles. She briefly considered going back to sleep, but worried that if she did, it would happen again. And even if she wanted to sleep, she doubted she'd be able to. So, with nothing left to do, the Angel sat at her desk.

She wasn't sure if it was a good or bad thing, but based on what Antares had said before, Estelle could deduce that it was, at the very least, a strange thing.

What was even more unusual, and that added to her growing anxiety, was her dream. Did it mean anything that it was about a strange, regal woman that she had never met before, or that it was placed in the apple orchard? One thing she knew for sure was that whatever caused her to use Angelic powers must not be good.

Estelle released a shuddering breath and glanced at the clock on the wall that forever played a soft ticking. It was half past four in the morning. *The library opens at five,* she thought, already putting on her shoes.

As April approached, the temperature was getting warmer, but it was still chilly enough in the early morning to warrant a jacket. The girl, however, only had enough brain power to put on shoes before stepping out into the cold—a welcome distraction from the overpowering thoughts that swarmed her mind. She walked slowly.

At five in the morning, the library was a vacant chasm, save for the lone librarian who dozed behind her desk. Estelle shut the door quietly behind her and gripped the strap of her bag as she scurried over to the medical section. After confirming that she was out of sight, she set her bag down with a sigh and started at the top.

Estelle wasn't entirely sure what she was looking for. All she had to go by was a vague hope that she'd know the right book when she saw it. The Angel scanned the spines of over a hundred books before something finally caught her eye.

'Abnormal Souls'

She pulled it from the shelf. It opened for her, to her relief, but as she began flipping through the pages, her hope quickly waned. The book wasn't a medical book. It wasn't even non-fiction. It was a novel that had evidently been misplaced. Estelle considered notifying the librarian of their mistake, but she didn't want to call attention to herself. She put the book back where she had found it.

Her search continued, and after another hundred titles, she again came across one that caught her attention.

'Conditions of the Soul: Common and Rare'

The girl's pulse picked up as she reached for it, but as soon as her fingers grazed the spine, it began to glow. Her heart dropped into her stomach.

Eight.

"Of course," Estelle said under her breath, her tone cynical. *Maybe Antares could transcribe it,* she thought. *He peaked at level eight. He might still have clearance. Perhaps if I can just...*

She grabbed the book by the spine, testing the weight. It wasn't moving, so she took hold of it with both hands and pulled as hard as she could. She clenched her jaw, muscles straining in protest. But the book didn't move, as though it had been cemented in place as a permanent fixture on the shelf.

Estelle sighed, exasperated. Adjusting her grip and looking around, ensuring she was alone, she put one foot up on a lower shelf, using it as leverage as she tried again.

Still, nothing.

She put her other foot on the lower shelf and tried to use her body weight to drag it out. But in the struggle, her hands began to get sweaty, and it was only a matter of time before her grip would slip.

The girl landed on her butt, wincing as her tailbone hit the edge of the shelf behind her. The impact caused a couple of books to come loose and fall, hitting her over the head. Estelle sat there silently for a moment, her body tense. She stared up at the book, the glowing 'eight' still illuminating the spine, and scowled. It was like it glowed brighter to spite her.

And then, out of nowhere, a thought entered her mind, like a cold weight in the pit of her stomach. *What if I'm sick? Was generating Angelic power without a vessel a symptom? Is it harder to control the*

Navitas when sick? Angels didn't get sick very often, and when they did, it was usually relatively minor. Severe illnesses were rare but not completely unheard of.

She recalled her first training days when one of her classmates fell ill. Nobody took it seriously at the time, but in retrospect, Estelle could trace the path of his decline. He grew increasingly lethargic over the course of a few days. She should have noticed it; the rate at which it progressed was quite alarming, but it wasn't until they found him under the stairwell, his halo nearly blinking out of existence, that they realized their mistake. She never found out what happened to the boy from level one and never saw him again.

There had been other instances, as well. Though she could count the number of times a classmate had fallen seriously ill on one hand, they all followed that basic pattern.

An Angel's work was necessary, and as such, they seldom took sick days or even reported their symptoms at all. Part of it, Estelle supposed, was due to the social expectations. The other part was failing to recognize when something was wrong. Besides obvious things like pain and discomfort, Angels were not taught to watch for warning signs of developing conditions.

As Estelle sat there, zoning out at the glowing book, she imagined the Angel from level one. She could almost see the phantom image of him sifting through the same aisles, searching for answers, yet finding most of them inaccessible. Estelle's eyes panned across the vast wealth of knowledge sitting uselessly before her. She wondered if any of it could have saved him.

She caught herself, squeezing her eyes shut as she banished the thought from her head. In its absence, however, a heavy sense of unease fell, like a shadow of a panic attack, because Estelle didn't usually think like that.

"Estelle?"

The Angel jolted, heart pounding in her chest as she bit down on her lip hard to prevent herself from screaming. Her head snapped up, and she saw Lilith standing a couple of feet away with a frown and slightly widened eyes betraying her surprise.

"Whoa. Are you okay?" she asked.

"Y-yeah!" Estelle scrambled to her feet, brushing off the back of her pants, before dropping into a squat to gather up the fallen books, shoving them onto the shelf randomly. "Sorry, I was just—"

"That?"

"Huh?" Estelle looked back at the other. Lilith was pointing at the book she had tried to pick up, the spine still glowing. "Oh, um…" To her surprise, the older Angel reached up and grabbed the book and gave it a try herself

Lilith grunted slightly, her body straining as it began to tip outward slightly, only to snap back into place. "Well, I tried," she sighed, shrugging. "Even if we could get it off the shelf, we probably wouldn't be able to carry it out of here."

Estelle stood there for a moment, her fingertips cold and body tense. *Why would Lilith try to help me with this? Shouldn't she be getting the librarian to kick me out or, at the very least, lecture me?* She cleared her throat. "Uh, thanks anyway."

Lilith turned toward her, concern evident on her face. "You're sure you're alright?" When Estelle didn't respond right away, she added, "We could talk outside if you want."

After another second of hesitation, Estelle nodded, stood up straight, and followed her out the door. It was still dark out, but it wouldn't be for much longer. Estelle quietly cursed herself for losing track of time. She needed to go to the surface soon.

Lilith led them to an oak tree before turning to look at her again with a raised eyebrow. "You can tell me if you're sick, you know," she said. "I wouldn't tell anyone else."

The black-haired Angel smiled and laughed nervously. "Thanks, but I..." she sighed. "I don't know. I feel fine. Physically, that is."

"Well, I assume there's a reason you wanted a book about conditions of the soul."

"Yes..."

Lilith tucked a strand of white hair behind her ear, maintaining eye contact with Estelle. She seemed to have made a full recovery. Even the corruption damage appeared to be a faint shadow on her skin. Estelle wondered if the black marks disappeared faster when given proper medical attention.

After an uncomfortably long minute, Lilith tilted her head. "Are you doing something you aren't supposed to?"

Estelle's body tensed, freezing in place. She couldn't drag her eyes away from the higher-ranked Angel's face despite every instinct inside her telling her she should.

When Estelle didn't answer, Lilith sighed. "You know I wouldn't judge you if you were," she stated. "I wouldn't tell anyone either. I'm not *that* desperate to ascend—"

"Sorry, I just..." Estelle said, voice cracking. She wiped her sweaty palms on her pants. *Why am I so... scared?*

"This is big, isn't it?" Lilith asked quietly. Estelle gulped. In lieu of a verbal response, she nodded. "Is it something that could get you killed?"

Estelle froze. She had never thought about it in those terms before. Angels can't die—not in a normal sense. They could be destroyed, their souls obliterated by hellfire or some other unholy force. But beyond that, the only alternative was...

The face of the boy from level one barged into her mind again. The memory of his vacant eyes, as he lay catatonic beneath the stairwell, sent shivers down her spine.

"Estelle?" Lilith probed, her tone becoming increasingly worried.

"No, it's..." the raven-haired Angel stumbled, "I—I don't think I'm in danger."

The older Angel stared at her for a while, frowning and searching her eyes, but eventually, her expression melted back into neutrality. "Well, if you ever feel like talking about it, let me know," she said with a small sigh.

"Thank you," Estelle replied, her smile genuine.

They said their goodbyes, and the younger returned to her dorm room, hands shaking as she packed her bag and prepared to head down to the surface.

20

Any
Other Option

ESTELLE WAITED UNTIL THE FIRST church was cleared before broaching the subject, but hesitated nonetheless. Whenever she would ask Zylis questions, she did so through the sallvie. And generally, the things she would ask about were nothing more than little inane curiosities—the sort of things Zylis wouldn't have much incentive to lie about. That was primarily because Estelle couldn't detect whether he was lying through writing, but it still created a precedent.

The Angel wouldn't usually ask the Demon to answer something so important, but paradoxically, it was the importance that meant she couldn't afford not to.

Zylis stood with his back turned toward her, facing a stained-glass window depicting the Garden of Eden. The light from outside created a halo around his body. Estelle cleared her throat; the sound echoed in the large, decadent chamber. Zylis turned his head slightly.

"There's something I... wanted to ask you," Estelle said. "I don't know if you'll know, but..." She exhaled. "Well, I don't have any other options right now."

Her unlikely partner fully turned around to face her, his curiosity evidently piqued. "Okay." He raised an eyebrow. "Shoot."

The Angel explained what had happened a couple of hours prior, aside from the dream, which didn't matter. When she had finished, Zylis looked almost as bewildered as she felt.

"So, you used power, as in *angelic abilities*, while you were asleep?" Zylis narrowed his eyes. "I'm assuming you don't sleep in enchanted gloves."

Estelle frowned. "Of course not."

He took a deep breath. "Well, that's definitely not normal."

"I know that," she snapped. "I'm asking if you have any idea *how* this could happen."

"Okay, first of all, chill."

The Angel looked away sheepishly.

Zylis sighed and moved closer. "Here's the thing, Star," he said. "For the most part, I know about stuff that's useful for me to know about. If you're looking for a diagnosis, I'm not the guy to go to."

"But you're the only—"

"I'm not concave finished," he interjected, exasperated. "Look, I'll cut to the chase: I don't know what's happening to you, Star. I *don't*. The only explanation I can think of would be if you had something like a divinity implant put in, but that'd raise way more questions than it would answer."

Estelle cocked her head. "Divinity implant?"

"Back in the day, they used to give Angels these implants that let them use power without any special equipment," he explained. "They stopped using them around three hundred years ago."

"Why?"

"I don't know. I wasn't around back then. From what I've heard, they never actually explained it." Zylis shrugged. "If you wanna know what Demons believe, most of us assume it was 'cause having an armed populace made them nervous, so they switched to enchanted weapons and armor because they were easier to control."

"Oh." She frowned. "Is that what you think?"

"Well, yeah. I mean, I think it was a bit more complicated," he muttered, scratching the back of his head. "Probably a combination of that and the fact that the implants made their soldiers too vulnerable. If a Demon figured out where the implant was, all they'd have to do is rip it out, and then that Angel's useless. Having layers of enchanted armor and weapons is just more practical."

"I guess that makes sense..." Estelle mumbled. "But, I feel like I'd know if something like that happened to me."

"Most likely," Zylis agreed. "I didn't bring it up because I thought it was plausible; it was just all I could think of. Y'know, just 'cause I know more than you doesn't mean I've got all the answers. Especially when it comes to things God would have a strong incentive to keep secret." He shoved his hands into his pockets and meandered down the aisle. "I'm sure there's like ten other possible explanations buried in the secret archives of the Almighty's sex dungeon." The Demon opened the door with his back, allowing golden light to spill into the church. "Anyway, are you coming or what?"

His last comment made Estelle burst into flames, though she was grateful for his transparency. However, without actually knowing what was happening to her, she feared the worst possible option.

The following day, Antares came back to the first sphere, and Estelle was finally able to speak with him. She sat in front of him, wringing her hands as she fumbled through the explanation a second time about her using Angelic powers without the gauntlets.

When she finally got through it, she paused; a cold sweat clung to her neck. "Antares... Am I going to die?"

"No, no! Of course not," he replied in earnest. Estelle relaxed slightly until— "You can't die, because you're already dead."

She blinked, and her mouth hung open slightly. "Antares," she said, taking a deep, shaky breath. "With all due respect, I'm not in the mood for jokes."

"I apologize," Antares said with a sigh. "I was just trying to lighten the mood. I mean it, though—you're going to be fine." Estelle nodded, releasing a breath she had been holding. "However, this is highly irregular," he continued. "And I'm afraid I don't have an answer."

"I see..." Estelle frowned. "Well, maybe there's a book about this somewhere?"

"It's... possible, I suppose. But I highly doubt it."

The young Angel cocked her head to the side. "But I found a book about soul irregularities in the library yesterday. It was level eight. You could—"

"Amadea," he interjected, putting a hand up. "I guess now is the part where I need to tell you that some of the information I gave you regarding the soul was... well, not exactly *standard*."

"What do you mean?"

"Put simply, you won't find any information about your situation because what you're experiencing presupposes that your soul generates power independently."

Estelle blinked. "But... Doesn't it? That's what you told me."

"But that's not what the textbooks will tell you," Antares replied. "The accepted narrative is that souls can't generate power, but rather God endows Angels with it."

"So, you lied?"

"No," her mentor was quick to say. "What I told you is accurate to the best of my knowledge. More accurate than the official facts, anyway." He shrugged. "After all, if what the Apostles said was true, you wouldn't have been able to use power at all."

"But why would they lie about something like that?"

"The Apostles lie about quite a lot of things."

Estelle's mouth fell open. "Antares, that's—"

"Not as blasphemous as you think," he cut in, chuckling slightly. "The Apostles lie, but they have real reasons to do it."

"What reasons?" Estelle couldn't believe the words she was hearing. She always got a bad taste in her mouth whenever she lied, and avoided it at all costs. Wasn't it a sin to lie?

"Well, you have to understand that Heaven is at a large disadvantage when it comes to keeping secrets," Antares explained. "A Demon can never become an Angel, but an Angel can quite easily become a Demon. The Apostles disseminate misinformation about certain things in order to protect sensitive information when Angels inevitably Fall."

"So, they lie to protect us?"

"In a sense, yes."

For a while, Estelle remained silent. She could understand the rationale. It seemed like a reasonable decision to her, at least in the abstract, but somehow, it didn't sit right with her. Why lie when it could be explained *why* they can't know the information?

It doesn't have to make sense to you, Estelle reminded herself. *So long as it makes sense to God.* "Well..." She bit her lip. "I'm sure God and His Apostles know best." After a moment, she shook her head, her attention shifting back to the issue at hand. "But I'm worried. How am I able to use power? What if I use power in my sleep again, and someone hears it? Or what if I accidentally use it in public and hurt someone?"

The older Angel hummed. "That is the main concern, I would agree," he said, rubbing his chin. "I believe you are using Angelic powers because it was too soon for you to learn. There's a reason why you don't learn it until level three. As for not having it happen again, I may be able to find something that will help you keep that from happening, but it will take a few days."

Estelle paled.

The thought of going multiple nights without some safeguard was frightening. Although nothing really had happened the night before, she didn't want a repeat.

"But as for the next few nights..." Antares continued. "Well, I can offer you a short-term solution, but you won't like it."

She shook her head. "I'll do whatever I need to do."

Her mentor nodded, stood up, and left the room. He returned a few minutes later, holding a pair of handcuffs and ankle shackles. Estelle's heart sank. "It won't be comfortable, but it should prevent you from destroying the dorm building."

21
Bite, Chew, Swallow

FOUR.

Estelle had spent four nights sleeping—trying to, anyway—in shackles. Five nights since she had gotten any decent sleep, and it was taking a toll on her, to put it lightly.

It was like a perpetual fog in her head, obscuring and blurring all sensory information into one indistinguishable experience blob. If someone had asked Estelle to elaborate on what that meant, she wouldn't have responded, but she felt it deep in her bones.

On the morning of day four, she woke up to discover fresh bruises on her wrists, evidence of her straining against the cuffs in her sleep. It was a bittersweet realization. It proved that the shackles had been working, but it also proved that they were necessary.

She wasn't the only one who had noticed the bruises. Zylis commented on them when they met on the surface that morning.

"What happened there?"

"Oh," Estelle said, eyes glazed over as she stared down at her wrists and shrugged. "I've been wearing hand and ankle cuffs to bed these past few days so I won't destroy anything in my sleep by accident."

Zylis hummed. "Huh. That's kinda kinky, Star."

Estelle barely registered the comment. For most of the day, she was moving through space, carrying out her duties like an emotionless automaton. All her reactions were delayed as she weakly fought against the haze of sleep deprivation and emotional exhaustion. At one point, Zylis even asked if she needed to go home and rest. But she couldn't bring herself to leave early.

Things went on that way for the rest of the day until the last stop.

The two of them had temporarily parted after the last church so Zylis could escort the three remaining stragglers to Hell, and when Estelle entered the church, she was surprised to find it empty—well, almost empty.

"I think this one got cleared out by one of our people about a week ago."

Estelle didn't see him at first. She spun around, looking in all directions before she thought of looking up. That's where she found him: leaning over the railing of an indoor balcony. He had foregone the leather jacket for his return, wearing just a dark tank top. Zylis hopped over the railing a second later, landing in front of the Angel. Only then did she realize, with slight confusion, that Zylis was holding an apple.

"I actually like this one alright," he said, gesturing at their surroundings. "Usually, I find church architecture kinda obnoxious, but this one's decent. Clear color scheme, not too over-the-top. I don't think there's a single cross in here." Zylis took a bite out of the apple, sharp teeth cutting through its red skin.

"Is that... a regular apple?" Estelle asked, shaking her head slightly to clear the fog from it. The movement only made her head spin.

The Demon looked at her. "Yeah," he said. "Never said I couldn't eat human food, just that I don't need to. I still like it sometimes." He took another bite, the sound sharp in the otherwise quiet space.

"What does it taste like?"

Zylis blinked, staring at her blankly. "Like an apple, Star."

Estelle averted her eyes. "Sorry," she mumbled. "I was just asking..."

There was a beat of silence before Zylis spoke again. "Wait, do you..." He paused. "Do you not know what an apple tastes like?"

The Angel laughed nervously. "I don't know what a lot of things taste like, uh... you know. Because I don't remember anything from when I was human, Zye."

"Okay..." Zylis narrowed his eyes. "But you can still eat, can't you?"

Estelle nodded. "Sure, I mean, technically. I usually don't, though."

"Why not?"

"No one mentions it out loud, but it's sort of frowned upon." She shrugged. "Angels are supposed to be above human desire. There's not a stigma around drinking water or herbal teas, but eating... Well, no one wants to look like a glutton, I guess." Estelle wasn't sure why she had decided to tell him all of that. It felt like she had just opened her mouth and dumped her thoughts out into her tongue, but she was too mentally worn out to think about it.

"That's so stupid," Zylis said flatly.

Estelle just shrugged again. "It is what it is."

"And what it is, is dumb," he said, taking a step toward her. "I mean, what's the point of existing if you can't even enjoy it?"

The girl sighed and rubbed her eyes with her hands, feeling her wings droop slightly. For several seconds, she was quiet, racking her brain for a response, but the fog was too thick. "You know, maybe if I weren't so tired, I'd be able to answer that question," she said, removing her hands from her face. "But at least for now, all I can say is... I don't know. But there's probably a reason."

For a long moment, Zylis just stood there, staring at her silently. But eventually, he spoke up. "Do you want to try it?" he asked.

Estelle looked up, meeting his eyes. Red, entrancing, glowing in the dim light.

He took a step toward her, his tail lightly waving behind him.

She took a step back. "You mean...?"

"Yeah. There's no one else here." Zylis shrugged. "No one is around to judge you for doing something that doesn't affect them."

He took another step toward her. Estelle tried to copy the movement backward, but her foot hit the wall instead. She found herself backed up against a frosted-glass window. Her eyes darted back and forth between Zylis' face and the apple in his hand.

But it was strange.

Zye should be smiling, Estelle thought. *He should be smirking at me and speaking in that condescending tone of voice.* Everything about the situation matched up with the times Zylis had teased her before, except for the way the Demon was acting.

With Zylis, everything was loaded until proven otherwise. Estelle had gotten better at recognizing when he made a statement with strings attached, but at that moment, the Demon's demeanor revealed nothing. He just looked at her, regarding her casually. Zylis was in her space, but it wasn't like the other times. It didn't feel like he was trying to invoke a reaction. It felt almost normal somehow.

"One bite can't hurt," Zylis said, his tone calm, conversational. "Aren't you curious?"

She was. But Estelle didn't trust her voice. So, instead, she just nodded slowly.

Bracing one hand against the wall beside her head, Zylis leaned in a bit closer, his face catching the light of the halo, raising the apple to her lips. He quirked an eyebrow. "Well, go on then. Open."

She did and felt her teeth graze the skin with a firm resistance. The aroma was subtle, floral, and inviting.

"Bite."

Estelle tried, tentatively at first—not sure how solid it would be, but the flesh gave away easily enough. There was a satisfying snap that echoed softly in the stillness.

"Chew."

She did, and immediately, a burst of cool, sweet juice flooded her mouth. Her tongue welcomed the vibrant, tangy flavor—delicate yet bold—a perfect balance of sweetness and tartness. The taste was unlike anything she'd known before. She closed her eyes, savoring the flavor.

After a couple of seconds, Zylis said, "Swallow."

And like the times before, Estelle did as she was told. The crispness left behind a lingering, fresh aftertaste that seemed to dance on her palate. It felt as if she uncovered a secret, something pure, simple, and wonderfully alive, already longing for another bite.

"There you go," he said, voice low and rumbly; she could almost feel it in her chest.

Estelle's knees felt weak. She glanced down at the ground and noticed that one of Zylis' shoes was positioned between her own. But soon enough, her vision started darkening around the edges. She looked up, and—

Ah, there it is, the Angel thought, almost relieved. Zylis' signature smirk was back, coupled with a dangerous glint in his eye that suggested he knew something Estelle didn't. The air between them felt hot.

Estelle's eyes followed the movement of his tongue as Zylis licked his lips. "How was it?" he asked.

"Tastes... sweet," she said in a daze.

"Do you like sweet things?"

After a second, the girl nodded slightly. "Yeah," she said. "I... I do."

"Good," the Demon whispered, raising the apple to his lips and taking a bite. Estelle watched, transfixed, as his sharp, white teeth sank into the flesh.

He licked the juice off his lips and chewed slowly, his Adam's apple bobbing as he swallowed, and then raised the fruit to Estelle's lips again. With her eyes locked with Zylis', she followed his example.

Bite.

Chew.

Swallow.

Zylis' smile grew slightly as if to congratulate her for getting it right on her own. It was intoxicating, somehow. Estelle felt as though she were floating in space, and all that existed was the man in front of her.

Zylis gazed down at her. His eyes were half-lidded, cat-like pupils blown wide. "You know, you look good when you do that," he whispered, warm breath wafting against her face.

Estelle shuddered, feathers standing on end. It took a second for her brain to catch up. "Do what?" she asked.

The Angel held her breath as the Demon leaned in closer, their faces just millimeters apart. He reached up, his hand hovering over her neck, radiating heat but never quite touching.

And then Estelle leaned into it. For a brief moment, she felt Zylis' fingers caress her neck. Her eyes fluttered.

Zylis grinned, sharp and dangerous. "Take what you want."

22

Broken Mirror

ESTELLE COULDN'T MOVE. WHEN SHE opened her eyes, she saw nothing but darkness. A spotlight shone down on her, and as she looked around herself, her mind sluggishly put together the pieces that spelled out her predicament. Estelle was trapped, strung up at the center of a vast web, her body ensnared in spider silk. She pulled at the restraints, but they would not give.

The Angel squinted, searching for shapes in the darkness, but it was far too dark. Estelle gulped. "H-hello?" she called out. "Is there anybody out there?"

Estelle heard a voice say before the void shifted, and a form materialized before her.

"Oh, you're awake."

Zylis.

He looked different somehow, but Estelle couldn't quite discern why. "Zye, what's going on?"

Zylis shrugged, walking closer. "Your guess is as good as mine."

Estelle frowned, looking around in vain. "Where are we?"

"If I knew, I'd tell you."

"Well, can you help me out here?" she asked, wriggling against the bonds.

"Sure," he replied. "That's kinda why I'm here. Probably gonna take a while, though."

"That's fine," Estelle said, sighing. And then she glanced down at her body and gasped. As things were, the spider silk wasn't wrapped around her like a cocoon but rather in a strange, complex network of knots that exposed much of her skin in a rather... unbecoming way. "W-wait!" she squeaked, her face burning.

"What?"

"I didn't realize th-that I was..."

Zylis rolled his eyes. "Look, do you want me to untie you or not?"

Estelle whined, her blush only intensifying as she reluctantly nodded. With that, Zylis got to work, starting on her right arm and moving up from her hand. The girl's breath caught at the sensation of his fingers brushing against her skin, dipping beneath the ropes to test their tightness. Estelle's eyes darted around, looking at everything except Zylis.

"Did you put me here?" she asked. Estelle saw him shake his head out of the corner of her eye.

"Think you've always been here."

"Oh..." Estelle frowned. "What does that mean?"

Zylis exhaled, working his claws into one of the knots and carefully massaging it loose. "Who knows," he said. "Seems like there are many others in the same boat, though."

"Really?"

He nodded. "You're one of the lucky ones, I think. There are a couple whose bonds aren't as bad, but there are many tied up way worse. Sometimes it's so bad you can't even see them."

Estelle's brows pinched together. "Can't we help them?"

Zylis hummed. "Maybe." He shrugged. "But you gotta be careful. Some are wrapped up in so many layers they can't even see. If you're not careful, they'll get scared."

That didn't make sense to Estelle, but her mind was too scattered to ponder it for long. She felt the rope around her wrist loosen and sighed as it fell away. She rotated the joint as Zylis moved up her arm.

They both fell silent for a while. Estelle relaxed beneath the careful attention of Zylis' fingers. So much so that, when she spoke next, she didn't realize she had said anything until she saw Zylis' reaction.

"Your hands feel... nice," Estelle said, her right arm finally freed.

Zylis smirked, looking at her beneath his lashes. "Oh, yeah?"

The girl's cheeks lit up again, and she sputtered. "S-sorry, that was—"

"It's okay," Zylis purred, sliding his hands up to her cheeks, forcing Estelle to look at him as he leaned in close. "Don't be afraid of what you feel, Estelle."

She wrapped her arms around his neck.

Wait. Arms? When did my left arm—her thoughts stopped when Zylis ran his hands down her body and started working on one of the knots on her legs.

"Zye?"

"Yeah?"

Estelle hesitated, her mind foggy. "What happens after this?"

"What do you mean?"

She chewed on her lip, not quite sure herself. "Just... where do we go from here?"

Zylis slid his hand up to her inner thigh, working his fingers beneath a knot tied there, and stood up straight. He leaned in close, pressed his lips against her ear, and whispered something deep and rumbling that Estelle felt thrumming beneath her skin like a second pulse.

She opened her mouth and—

Estelle sat up in bed with a start, gasping for breath as she looked around frantically, her body drenched in sweat. However, the familiar environment of her dorm room eventually grounded her in reality. It took much longer than usual as she tried to convince herself that it was just a dream.

With a sigh, Estelle shifted on the mattress, moving to sit on the edge. She reached over and grabbed the keys on her bedside table and groggily unlocked the handcuffs before leaning over to do the ankle cuffs. That's when she saw something white at the edge of her field of vision. She turned her head to look just as it settled on the hardwood floor.

A single, white feather.

The Angel stared at it for a moment, frozen with the key in the lock. Was she still dreaming? Was she imagining it? She hastily removed the restraints and stood, leaning over to grab the feather.

The events from the dream rapidly dissipated as the previous night gradually began to return. Estelle sat down on her bed again, and two more feathers fell out, drifting elegantly to the floor. Her throat tightened, a rush of cold swallowing her entire body. Her heart lurched against the wall of her chest.

"No," she whispered.

Suddenly, the specifics of the encounter rushed back into her consciousness in full, vivid detail. The taste of the apple. Zylis' closeness. The sensation of his warm fingertips on her neck...

Estelle sprang out of bed and nearly slipped on the wood floor as she scrambled to the bathroom, wincing as she turned on the light and looked in the mirror. She froze at what she saw. On the side of her neck was a vine-like formation roughly an inch in diameter, stemming from the spot where Zylis had touched her.

Where I let him touch me.

The girl gripped the edge of the sink as she stared at the mark. Her breathing began to pick up, her chest rose and fell almost painfully as she leaned in, tentatively running her fingers over the mark, swallowing the metallic taste on her tongue.

Just as quickly as she had entered the bathroom, she spun around and marched over to her shower, sharply turning it on, and barely managed to get her clothes off before she climbed inside, cold water cutting into her like shards of ice.

The Angel planted her hands against the tile wall for stability, but before long, she started to slip down. Slowly, Estelle's palms slid down the wall, and she fell to her knees, curling up into a ball as her wings fell limply at her side. The freezing water continued to beat down on her head, soaking her hair and dripping into her eyes, the sound of it hitting her drowned out by the ringing in her ears.

This wasn't happening to her. It couldn't be, not to her, not to Estelle. These were problems that occurred to other people. Angels of different levels, in various classes—people who existed at the fringes of Estelle's awareness. Those were stories that Estelle heard in passing. Things people would speak of in the spaces between small talk and the main conversation. Estelle would hear about them, and her heart would ache for them, but she was always able to move on from it. It was a footnote in her life and nothing more.

She shivered beneath the onslaught of freezing water, the tips of her fingers turning blue and her muscles growing stiff as her body temperature dropped. It took her five minutes before she finally gathered the will to shut off the water, and ten more before she moved.

She stumbled out of the shower, sluggishly pulled her towel off the rack, and dried her hair before patting off the remaining water from her body and shaking her wings to remove excess water.

Another feather fell out.

Estelle tensed for a moment before picking it up off the floor. She leaned against the sink and stared at it for a minute, then closed her fist around it and squeezed. She slowly looked at her reflection in the mirror. At the black mark on her neck.

And then the mirror shattered from the force of her punch. Estelle dug her knuckles deeper into the broken mirror, gold lightning crackling around her arm. It didn't fully register with her that she had used Angelic powers until the pain caught up with her. But she didn't have time to think about that as there was a knock on her door.

"Estelle?" a muffled voice called.

Issac.

"Are you alright in there?"

The girl rushed to grab her bathrobe, dropping the feather as she hastily threw it on and tied it around her waist. She nearly tripped over her feet on her way to the door. There was another knock just before it was ripped open, finding a very concerned-looking Issac standing on the other side, his knuckles hovering right over where the door had been.

His expression only grew more shocked as he took in her appearance. Issac looked her up and down, frowning as his eyes settled on— "Estelle, your hand."

The girl blinked and looked down. Her knuckles were bloodied. *Of course.*

"What happened to your hand—and your wrist?" Issac asked, carefully taking her injured hand and pushing the fluffy sleeve up to fully reveal the bruising the handcuffs had left.

Estelle's heart raced as she racked her mind for an explanation, only to come back empty-handed. As things were, she probably wouldn't even be able to articulate the truth—how in the Three Realms would she be expected to craft anything resembling an excuse?

She didn't respond. For half a minute, she just stood there, eyes glued to her bloody knuckles as her friend gingerly inspected the injuries, while her other hand was still clutching the doorknob, her palm slipping as it became sweaty.

"Um... Can I come in?"

Estelle nodded mutely, and Issac took a step forward, but then she remembered—*The feathers.*

"Wait!" Estelle shouted, removing her hand from his grasp and holding it up. He stopped in his tracks, brow furrowed. "I'm... I'm s-sorry," she stammered, her voice squeaky. "I can't... can't..." she hesitated, squeezing her eyes shut. "Just wait!" She slammed the door and lunged to the floor, grabbing the three feathers near her bed before heading to the bathroom to retrieve the other. All the while, Issac pounded at the door.

"Estelle! Hey!" he shouted. "What's going on? *Please* open the door!"

Estelle yanked open the drawer under the sink, shoved the feathers to the back, turned on the sink, and hastily rinsed her hands off. She gently patted it dry until she was hardly bleeding.

Estelle took a deep breath and went to check her reflection, only to be reminded that the mirror was broken. She muttered under her breath, squinting as she leaned to the side, awkwardly looking into one of the larger shards. She sighed in relief when she confirmed that the mark on her neck was hidden by the robe, as long as she didn't move around too much.

She took a couple more measured breaths, schooled her features, and left the bathroom before opening the door again. When she got there, Issac was joined by Giovanna. Issac still looked worried, but Giovanna just seemed confused.

"What's going on?" the taller Angel asked with a yawn. "You guys woke me up."

"I'm sorry," Estelle said, trying her best to look them in the eyes. She was still trembling slightly. She was grateful that Giovanna was not a morning person and probably wouldn't notice anything out of the ordinary. Issac, on the other hand, was wide awake. "It's not a big deal. I overreacted. Uh, sorry for making you worry."

Giovanna shrugged. "Okay, but try to keep it down, would ya?"

"R-right, of course," Estelle said hastily as Giovanna walked back to her room.

"But what *happened*?" Issac asked in a softer tone.

"I..." Estelle hesitated. "I had a nightmare. I've been having them a lot lately, and this one just shook me up, and—"

"How does that relate to your hand and wrists being injured?" Issac interjected.

"It's nothing, really," the raven-haired girl said, subconsciously pulling down the sleeve to hide the evidence. But her friend snatched her hand, lifting it to look at it in the darkness. Estelle sucked in a breath from the pain.

"Estelle, this is *not* nothing," Issac said, his eyes roaming over the cuts in full alertness. "You're still bleeding—"

"It's fine," Estelle said as she yanked her hand away. "Please don't make a fuss over this." She let out a breath before making eye contact with her best friend.

He quirked an eyebrow as a silent question, '*Are you going to let me come in?*'

She didn't want him in, considering the state of her bathroom, let alone her bed, with the broken headboard and restraints.

For a long moment, they stood there exchanging looks until Issac asked again, "Estelle, what happened?"

"I..." A pause. "I have a problem with moving around too much while I sleep," she blurted out. "I've been sleeping with handcuffs to limit it, so I won't knock things over and break stuff. This morning, though, I wound up falling out of bed, and because of the nightmare, I freaked out and ended up pulling my hand free by force, which is how it got all cut up like this." As soon as she said it, she realized how many holes there were in the story. But she forced herself to stay relatively calm while explaining the lie.

Issac frowned. "Then why is your hair wet?"

"I took a shower." Thankfully, she didn't need to lie about that.

Issac still looked uncertain. "Alright, well... at least let me help you bandage that before it gets worse."

Estelle hesitated a second longer before nodding and stepping aside to let him through. He, in turn, went straight for the bookshelf where she kept the medical kit. It might not have been the best place to keep it, but at that moment, Estelle was glad she didn't leave it in the bathroom like most. She was also glad Issac knew her well enough that he didn't have to ask where it was.

Once Issac retrieved the bandages, they both sat on the edge of her bed. It was quiet, uncomfortably so. Estelle was glad that Issac didn't question anything further, and she didn't try to start any small talk, but the tension in the room was palpable.

He worked efficiently, gently wrapping her hand in the bandages. After he finished his work, he muttered something under his breath, and a soft glow came from her hand.

Estelle could feel her hand sewing itself up just enough to stop the bleeding. Issac recited the prayer of healing.

"Let me know if there's anything you want to talk about, I guess," he said, standing up.

"O-of course!" Estelle stuttered as she watched him walk out of her room. The door closed with a soft *click*, and she allowed herself to breathe out a sigh.

She padded over to the closet, grabbed the box of rosebay tea Antares had given her, and collected her electric kettle. Once it started brewing, she went into the bathroom to clean up the broken glass, then poured herself a cup that she started drinking too soon.

Still, it calmed her and helped her think more clearly. Four feathers wasn't the end of the world, but it was disconcerting in a way that regular corruption marks were not. She remembered her mentor had talked about it in the past, albeit not in great detail.

Contact-based corruption damage always appeared at the site where the contact occurred. It would take extensive tactile contact before feathers began to fall out, so given Estelle's situation, the fact that her feathers were falling out pointed to a deeper issue. Something in her heart and mind translated into her soul.

It wasn't the result of some accidental contact. It was Zylis' plan working.

I need to talk to Antares.

Estelle sighed, finishing off the tea. She dressed, picked a shirt with a high collar, and slipped on her shoes. But before she left, she paused and slowly reached back toward her wings. Though she was terrified of discovering more loose fathers, it would have been so much worse if they fell out in public. Estelle carefully tested each one, pulling gently to ensure they were secure. She sighed in relief when none of them came loose.

23

Helpful Items

ESTELLE LEFT THE DORMITORIES AND ran to her destination, reaching Antares' house in record time. It was a weekday, so this time around, she didn't wake him up with her insistent knocking.

Antares ushered her inside and offered her a cup of the special tea before leaving to retrieve something. Estelle gladly took the cup, letting the warm, mild, somewhat sweet, floral taste calm her nerves.

Her mentor returned with an unmarked, black jar and what looked like a paintbrush. He set them down on the kitchen table before Estelle.

She stared at them over the steaming cup before looking up at the older Angel. "What is it?"

"It's glue."

Estelle furrowed her brow, staring at Antares for a second. Then it hit her. "Wait, you're serious?"

Antares chuckled, sitting down across from her. "I am! Well, it's more like a sealant. They have this at the hospital, but one doesn't make it to the third sphere without at some point acquiring a supply of their own," he said, grinning. "Feathers can fall out for internal reasons, but they can also fall out due to just normal corruption damage caused by a Demon touching one's wings. Naturally, because the wings are one of the least armored spots on Angels, they're also one of the most common places for corruption. And since soldiers can't have our feathers falling out willy-nilly..." He gestured to the jar. "Well, feather glue!"

The young Angel laughed slightly. It was such a simple solution she hadn't even considered. But after a moment, her face fell. "But in my case, it wasn't normal corruption damage," she said quietly.

Antares exhaled. "Yes."

Estelle put her face in her hands. "I'm such an idiot," she said, muffled. "I mean, I was tired. I haven't been sleeping well, so I guess I was more susceptible, but... still. I should have never let him get that close." She wasn't sure whether she was referring to physical or emotional proximity.

"All things considered, I think you've been doing quite well up to this point." Estelle gave a mirthless laugh. "No, I mean it!" her mentor assured. "I know third-tier Angels who would've crumbled in under a month, and you've been at this for nearly four."

Estelle flushed and looked at him through the gaps in her fingers. "You're just saying that to make me feel better."

"If I may be frank, Amadea," Antares sighed. "I wouldn't have put myself in such a... risky situation for a student I didn't consider to be extraordinary."

The girl was quiet for a while, looking away as she fought back tears that threatened to spill from her eyes. She cleared her throat. "Just... Would you still feel that way if I *did* Fall?"

The high-ranking Angel hesitated for a split second. Estelle was too scared to check his expression. "It's no use worrying over things like that."

She looked up at him at that moment. "But I'm *scared*."

"I understand that," he said soothingly. "But, Amadea... Falling is the result of a lapse in faith."

"Yes, but lately—"

Antares reached across the table and placed his hand over Estelle's injured one, causing her to go silent. "Faith doesn't just mean faith in God," he said. "You also need to have faith in yourself. This is just a trial. You can make it through, but you need to trust yourself."

After a long moment, Estelle nodded. "Okay," she said softly. "I'll... I'll do my best."

Her mentor smiled, stood up, and reached for the glue jar. "Now, let me show you how to do this before classes start. There's a bit of a trick to it."

Antares proceeded to explain, in detail, how to apply the feather sealant. She needed to make sure she did it in front of a mirror, especially when doing the back feathers. If she put too much on, they would get gunked up, but if she put too little, it would wash off easily. The most significant part was to avoid getting the glue on the vane and focus on the shaft, painting each feather's base closest to the skin.

Once her mentor was done explaining and each feather had sealant, he left the room. Estelle extended her wings and brought them around to examine them. They looked nicer. Granted, from the first day an Angel arrives in Heaven, they're taught how to clean and maintain their wings, so they always look nice. But this was different; her wings reminded her of higher-ranked Angels.

She looked closer at the feathers, moving them aside to see the shaft. Then she realized why higher-level Angels' wings always seemed so nice. Because of the glue, the afterfeather was smoothed down to make a sleeker finish to the wings.

Antares walked back in then, and Estelle folded her wings against her back once again. He handed her a small box that fit perfectly in her palm.

"What's this?" she asked.

"Well, I'm pleased to inform you that you'll no longer need to sleep in handcuffs," he said, gesturing to the box.

Estelle perked up. She could almost feel the dark circles under her eyes fading at the thought. She glanced up at him, quietly asking for permission. He nodded, and Estelle opened the box. Inside, she found what looked like two rings made from a black stone.

"Obsidian rings," Antares provided. "So long as you wear them, they should prevent you from using power in your sleep."

"Wow." Estelle picked up one of the rings and examined it. It was incredibly smooth inside, but the outside had ridges and bumps. She couldn't tell if it was because of use or if it was crafted that way. "How do they work?"

"It's..." Antares cringed. "It's complicated," he said. "It's sort of like a distraction."

"A distraction?"

"Yes. The rings themselves are harmless, but the material is similar to laniesthole," he explained. "Your body falsely anticipates harm and prepares to allocate power toward counteracting it. Does that make sense?"

Estelle hesitated. "What's lan-thole?"

"Oh, right, sorry." He smiled sheepishly. "Laniesthole is a metal that Greed Demons use. It's one of the primary attacks they like to use against Angels. The material is harvested in Hell and can very well kill if they embed it inside."

"Ah, so is there any sort of danger in wearing these for long periods?" Estelle asked.

"Not that I'm aware of, but..." he trailed off momentarily. "Well, I'd advise against wearing them outside of sleeping, just to be safe." He paused and looked around the messy room with a frown. "You know, I have a note from the supplier that talks about all of this somewhere around here, but I can't seem to find it..."

"Supplier?" she questioned, carefully putting the ring back in the box.

"Perhaps that's too official a term," Antares said, chuckling. "I called in a favor from an old friend. Let's leave it at that."

The girl hummed, nodded slightly, picked up her bag, and stood up. "Well, thank you, Antares," she said, putting on her best smile.

The older Angel rose as well, leading the way out the front door.

They walked silently for a while, headed toward the school.

Estelle found herself unable to focus on a single thought. The idea of finally getting a night's sleep made her want to collapse right there, making it challenging to stay on one subject in her head.

"How do you conceal your presence on Earth?" she found herself asking, not fully registering she had said it aloud until Antares spoke.

"That type of ability isn't taught until level four," he said. "Mainly because it takes a great deal of training with your Navitas to achieve it effectively."

Estelle hummed. "Can you teach me?"

He looked at her meeting her eyes for a moment before glancing around. "The things I've been teaching you are within your skill level. Once you ascend, you'll have everything you need to know." He paused as they rounded a corner, the school in sight. "It was relatively hard for me to grasp the technique when I was taught."

Estelle looked up at him, brows furrowed.

Antares smiled, his eyes looking distant as if he was seeing something she couldn't. "I could grasp the idea, but executing it was a whole other story," he continued. "It's a matter of shrinking in on yourself. And though negative emotions are generally avoided, to conceal yourself from humans, there's no other way. At least, for beginners." He looked at her, pausing in his footsteps. "It's a shame you'll have to wait."

Estelle's eyes widened slightly, and she nodded. "I'll see you later in class." With that, they parted ways.

Estelle stumbled through her classes, floating between daydreaming and staring blankly at the books before her. Even after the sealant was applied, Estelle worried about people bumping into her and having a feather fall out.

As remarkable a mentor as Antares was, there were limits to the things Estelle felt comfortable telling him. Despite how much she trusted the man, some things were just too awkward to discuss. Like the specific things Zylis had said to her. Or the particular *feelings* Zylis had dug up in her.

She flushed, clutching the strap of her bag as she hurried back to the dormitories. She entered as discreetly as possible and took the stairs to her room. Once inside, she locked the door behind her and dropped her bag next to the door before collapsing onto the bed.

Antares was like a father to her, in a sense. She trusted him a great deal, and they were pretty close. But no matter how close one was with one's father, there were certain things one did not talk about. Unfortunately, the volume of things Estelle couldn't tell him seemed to be increasing with each passing day.

Estelle sometimes wondered if her mentor might not have been so optimistic had he known the extent to which she had fallen for Zylis'... charms.

She frowned against the pillow.

That word didn't seem right. Zylis was not charming. In many ways, he seemed to embody the antithesis of charm. He had his moments sometimes, in his unconventional way, but it was far from being enough to categorize him as charming on the whole.

No, Zylis was not charming. In fact, he was quite rude. Obnoxious. Arrogant. But the arrogance seemed backed up by genuine skill, at least from what Estelle had seen. It was justified arrogance. Maybe that made it confidence. But it seemed to carry over into everything he did.

Estelle rolled over on the mattress and sighed, staring up at the ceiling.

Zylis' looks probably helped, she supposed. Say what you will about his demeanor, but it was hard to deny that he was, in fact, quite handsome.

She shook herself. *Why am I thinking about this?*

Estelle never used to pay attention to Zylis' looks. She was aware, on some level, that most people would probably consider him quite attractive. However, the same could have been said about Issac or Giovanna, and she never caught herself ruminating about that.

The Angel groaned, restlessly turning over onto her side, and stared at the wall. The more she thought of Zylis, the more unstable her heart became. It felt like she was moving toward something she couldn't control, and though she suppressed the feeling as best she could, moments like those hit her, shaking her to her core. It was terrifying.

She glanced at the sallvie, sitting innocently atop her dresser, and then closed her eyes.

Maybe it would be best if she kept her distance for a while.

24

Found

Estelle made a strict schedule for herself: Wake up, get dressed, go to class and private lessons—or the surface, whichever she was scheduled for that day—return to the dorms, lock the door, and be alone.

It had been twelve days since Estelle had last opened the sallbokvie. She didn't know if Zylis had tried contacting her, though she assumed he must have. After all, they would have met up four times in that time frame under normal circumstances.

Estelle did her best to keep a low profile on the surface, and it worked. Antares had been teaching her to suppress her presence so her soul wouldn't be so easily detected, at least beyond a one-mile radius. It was a relatively simple trick for her to perform, considering she had already been getting familiar with the specific emotion needed for it.

Shame.

Apart from Angelic lessons and her missions, Estelle spent most of her time locked up in her room. The rings had helped her sleep better, but the anxiety was still very much present.

Every day, Issac would knock on her door. And every day, Estelle would make excuses not to come out until she stopped responding altogether and pretended to be asleep.

She couldn't take it. She couldn't face the questions—couldn't keep lying to her friends. It was tearing her up almost as much as her feelings for Zylis. Estelle found it easier to stay away from them altogether and be alone. But it was harder to pretend that everything was okay.

It was late at night as she sat awake at her desk, staring at the sallbokvie as it began to collect dust on her dresser. With a sigh, Estelle stood up and headed over to the closet to grab her stash of rosebay tea, along with the kettle, only to find that the thing wouldn't turn on. She frowned and tried turning it off and on again, but nothing seemed to be working.

She glanced at the clock—three in the morning. *Now's probably a safe time*, she figured. No one would be waiting to ambush her. She took off the obsidian rings, grabbed the tea, and headed downstairs quietly.

The kitchen was empty, like it usually was.

She found the kettle above the stove, dropped the tea infuser inside, and filled it with water. She turned on the stove and set it down with a sigh, wandering into the common area.

"Estelle?"

The girl jumped and looked to her right. There, she saw the person she least wanted to see—after Zylis, anyway. The thought made her feel ashamed. Why did she have to avoid her friends like that?

"Issac..." Estelle said, blushing. He was sitting in a chair near the corner, his feet up on an ottoman, reading a book that Estelle was supposed to be reading for class, but had not yet started.

"I wasn't sure if I'd ever see you come out of your room again, aside from classes," he said, laying the open book across his lap.

Estelle laughed nervously. "Yeah... um, sorry about that."

Issac blinked. "Giovanna is worried," he said, then looked away. "I've been worried for a while."

"I'm... really sorry," she awkwardly mumbled. "I didn't want to make anyone worry about me."

He shrugged. "It's not something you can control. Just something that happens when you have people who care about you."

Estelle frowned, her shoulders hunching. She wanted nothing more than to disappear. She felt so vile. So unbelievably inconsiderate. But she didn't know what to tell him—didn't know what she could say that would make things better.

Estelle slunk over and sat in the chair beside him. Issac still didn't look at her, but hadn't returned to his book. For a minute, they just sat there; the silence stretched uncomfortably between them. Estelle was afraid to speak. She didn't know if she could keep it together, not with the growing tightness in her throat.

"Please forgive me," she managed to say.

That got Issac to look at her. "What is there to forgive?"

Estelle shook her head, her lip quivering. "I've... I've been a bad friend," she said, barely hanging on.

Her best friend set the book on a side table and leaned forward. "No, you haven't," he said. "If anything, I have because I haven't been able to help you."

"Only because I haven't been honest with you," the girl said, voice breaking.

Issac looked at her for a while, his brow furrowed. He looked so worried. "Estelle, please don't cry." But, of course, that set her off.

A sob broke free from her throat, and Estelle keeled over, trying to hide her face in her hands. She felt the chair dip beside her and stiffened when she felt an arm wrap around her.

"Is this okay?" he asked.

Estelle nodded, leaning into his embrace slightly, trying to control her tears.

Issac sighed and began to rub her shoulder. "Is there anything I can do to help?"

Estelle sniffled. "I don't know... Probably not."

They sat there for a while until she stopped crying. Eventually, Issac broke the silence. "Is there anything you can tell me?"

Estelle didn't know what to say. Anything she wanted to say was knowledge beyond their level or had something to do with Zylis. She turned into Issac's chest, trying to get as small as possible.

He stiffened as she got closer. "Something's going on with you," he said, relaxing into her. "What's strange is that you usually tell me about what's bothering you." Issac sighed. "You've been acting off ever since your first mission alone. Since you met that Demon."

She tensed.

"Estelle?"

"That's..." She swallowed. "I—" The kettle whistled, and Estelle jumped up, her posture ramrod straight. "Sorry," she said, wiping her nose on her sleeve before rushing to the kitchen, turning off the stove, and pouring herself a cup of tea. When she returned to the common room, Issac was in the same place. Estelle couldn't meet his gaze. "I should go to bed."

He didn't say anything at first. "You're scheduled for tomorrow morning, right?"

The girl nodded. "Technically, this morning..." she weakly joked. Issac didn't acknowledge it. He didn't say anything at all. "Well, um... Goodnight, Issac," Estelle said, returning to her room.

She didn't hear him say it back.

The Angel strolled down an alleyway beneath a cloudy sky, lazily playing with the strings of her cloak, something to cover up the corruption mark on her neck while she was on duty. Thankfully, the one on her hand was gone. Puddles from the previous night's rain splashed beneath her feet when she saw it, a flash of luminescent red from the corner of her eye. Deep down, Estelle had always known she wouldn't have been able to avoid Zylis forever.

"Well, if it isn't God's favorite little liar."

Estelle spun around. Experience taught her to look for the Demon in the shadows first. She found him leaning against a nearby wall, his fiery eyes glowing in the relative darkness, his tail unnaturally calm.

"Z-Zye!" Estelle said, stumbling back.

"S-Star," he mocked, stepping toward her and into the light. His eyes were cold.

The Angel swallowed the lump in her throat, immediately raising her shield. "Sorry, I was just..." she sputtered. "I just didn't—"

"What?" Zylis interjected, tilting his head. "Didn't think I'd find you? Thought you could get away with avoiding me forever?"

"Zye, it's not what you think."

"Oh yeah?" Zylis snarled and, in a flash, grabbed the front of her cloak in his fists. Estelle backed up against a brick wall and pulled her wings close against her back. "Do you have any concave idea what it looks like when you pull a stunt like this? Huh? For void's sake, Star, I thought you'd gotten black-bagged!"

"I'm sorry!" Estelle cried. "I didn't—I wasn't—"

"What, try to make it look like your stupid government *disappeared* you?" he yelled, tightening his grip and shaking her slightly. "I thought you were dead, but now here you are, just walking down the street like nothing happened!" Something in his tone suggested pain, but then it shifted into fury.

"That's quite enough, Demon."

Estelle froze, and a shock of icy fear rushed through her. She'd know that voice anywhere.

No...

It felt as if time had slowed down. Estelle turned her head, and all the dust, litter, and mysterious stains on the ground became sharply detailed as they traveled through her field of vision. Still, her perception narrowed as her gaze fell upon the figure standing at the center of the alley, just ten feet away.

Issac.

He stared at Zylis with a stone-cold look, his fists clenched at his sides and wings stretched out like a wall. "Let her go," he said.

Estelle's mind was screaming at her to do something—Issac didn't have any weapons or armor, didn't know about Demonic abilities, or fully understand the danger he was in—but her body was still trying to regain feeling. All she could do was watch.

"Who the void are you?" Zylis hissed, throwing the Angel an incredulous look as his tail flicked side to side.

Issac slowly moved closer.

The Demon looked him up and down with a derisive sneer. "Devil, you look like you haven't slept since you died."

"Who I am is none of your concern, Demon," Issac said.

"And this is none of your concave business, Slumberlord," Zylis quipped.

"Iss—Reclerstin," Estelle stuttered, catching herself before the mistake.

Zylis side-eyed her, brows furrowing slightly.

"You followed me here?"

The other Angel averted his eyes. "I'm sorry. I was worried. You wouldn't say anything," he sighed. "I wouldn't have done this if I had any other choice."

Zylis snorted.

Issac glared at him. "Something funny, Demon?"

"No other choice, you say." Zylis rolled his eyes. "You could've made the choice to stay out of other people's business, but I guess you pillocks have always struggled with that."

Issac narrowed his eyes. "She's my best friend. I'm not going to stand by and let some pathetic creature like you hurt her."

Zylis tensed, and Estelle's breath caught in her throat.

After a second, Zylis finally released the front of Estelle's cloak and slowly turned to face Issac fully, casually sliding his hands into his pockets. They stood about five feet apart, and Zylis seemed to loom over him despite only being a few inches taller than Issac.

"Star," Zylis said, his tone eerily calm, almost sweet. "Is that true? This emu is your friend?"

Estelle nodded at first, before remembering he wasn't looking at her anymore. She cleared her throat. "Y-yes, he is."

Zylis hummed, cocking his head. "Well, you're devilishly lucky, *Slumberlord*," he said. "'Cause if it weren't for that, I would have killed you where you stand." He laughed, short and harsh. "*This* is the guy you thought was more attractive than me?" he asked, glancing over to the girl to see her blush before turning back to the other Angel.

Issac's jaw clenched. "Just leave her alone."

"Hmm, no." Zylis narrowed his eyes. "No, I don't think I will. But you'll leave *us* alone if you know what's good for you."

"I'm not asking, Demon."

"No," Estelle said softly. Her eyes met Issac's, and she shook her head quickly. "Please don't. *Please*, it's not worth it."

Issac seemed to ponder it for a moment before stealing his gaze. "Okay, well, if it won't leave—" Zylis' eye twitched, "—then you can just come with me."

After a moment of hesitation, her mind going a million miles a second, Estelle nodded, moving to follow him. As she passed Zylis, she brushed her hand against his arm, hoping it would help subside his anger, but the Demon only took the chance to grab her by the wrist and pull her back.

"Oh, no, you don't," Zylis said, his tone low and dark. "You're not going anywhere, Star. Not 'til you give me a devil-damn explanation."

"Release her," Issac hissed.

"Void off before my goodwill runs out, Slumberlord."

Issac snorted, crossing his arms. "*Goodwill?* That's a good one."

Zylis quirked an eyebrow. "Do you want me to kill you?"

"I just think it's funny how you're trying to act as though you have any morals at all."

"How's that cognitive dissonance workin' out for ya?" Zylis rolled his eyes.

"Let her go, or else," Issac spat.

The Demon laughed sharply. "Or else what?"

"Issac," Estelle said, pleading. "Please, I'll be okay. Just go. I don't want you to get hurt." She knew it was a bad idea to say his real name, but she needed to get his attention somehow.

Issac's expression softened momentarily, his wings lowering as he seemed to consider it, but then he shook his head. "I can't. I'm not leaving you alone here."

Zylis looked back and forth between the two Angels and then grinned. "Oh, I get it," he said, releasing his hold on Estelle with a shove.

She stumbled a few feet behind him.

The Demon took a few steps forward and loomed over Issac. "It all makes sense now. Star's not just a friend to you, is she? Not in your head, at least."

"I don't need you telling—"

"You want her, don'tcha?" Zylis said, leaning forward. "That's what this is really about. You want her all to yourself, huh?" His grin grew wider. "Perfectly understandable, of course—but do you really think Star would go for someone like you? Think she's gonna spread her legs for some pathetic little—"

Issac's fist cracked against Zylis' jaw.

25

Five
Seconds

Issac punched Zylis in the jaw. The force turned Zylis' head to the side. Estelle held her breath, paralyzed, as she watched him slowly turn back toward Issac. The hit must have caused him to accidentally bite down on his lip, as it had started bleeding.

"Aw, void," Zylis said, touching his bloody lip and looking at his fingers to confirm that it was bleeding. He started laughing, but Estelle could see the anger in his eyes. "Oh, man. You really are a pillock. You know, you can't screw Star if I kill y—"

Issac swung again, but this time, Zylis dodged easily, stepping back and into a shadow, only to emerge from another just behind the attacking Angel.

"They don't teach you Hell-bells *any* survival skills, do they? Almost like they see you as a disposable little—"

Issac spun around and swung again, but yet again, the Demon dodged easily, vanishing and reappearing from another shadow, like a game of whack-a-mole.

"Y'know, I think there's a nuanced conversation to have there," Zylis said.

"I am not concerned with the thoughts of disgusting things like you."

Zylis stilled and stood in front of Issac. He threw Estelle a glance. "See, this is why I prefer to kill Angels before they get a chance to speak."

Issac swung again.

Zylis grabbed his wrist midair and held it in a tight grip. "Look, let me be blunt," he said, grabbing Issac's other wrist before he could try anything. "You've got two options right now. You either get the void out of my sight right this second, or you end up hospitalized for the next six months, minimum. It's your choice."

Issac sputtered, fear evident in his eyes. "Y-you expect me to just leave you alone with her?"

"I'm not gonna do anything to Star," Zylis said. "Well," he side-eyed Estelle, smirking. "Nothing she won't enjoy, anyway."

The captured Angel tried to knee the Demon in the crotch, but Zylis let go and leaped back just in time, landing atop a dumpster a couple of feet away. "Oh, for void's sake," he groaned. "Y'know, I'm not exactly dressed for this jantu, but if you insist on being a pillock..." Zylis reached for the hem of his tank top, sighing. "You've got five seconds, Slumberlord." He proceeded to pull it over his head. "Five."

The garment hit the asphalt.

Estelle's vision darkened around the edges as the Demon rolled his shoulders, muscles flexing beneath the morning sun. In any other context, she might have thought the sight incredible, but in that moment, it just left a sinking feeling in the pit of her stomach. She could sense where it was headed, even before Zylis' body began to change.

"Four." His horns began to elongate, claws appearing on his fingertips, and Estelle's throat tightened.

"Issac, *go*."

"Three." As his horns grew, they began to twist and curve like the horns of a ram. At the same time, Zylis' hands enlarged, and the obsidian black of his claws began to spread up his fingers, hands, and arms.

Pure panic kicked in. "Issac, go!" Estelle clenched her jaw. "Now, please!"

"Two." Zylis' hands were black; the color continued up his forearm in a gradient that ended right around his elbows.

Estelle watched the roll of his shoulder blades as they began to stick out, the skin darkening. Antares' words from many months ago came to her then.

If you see wings...

Estelle tasted blood as she turned to her friend and looked at him with wild eyes. "*Run!*" she screamed.

The Demon jumped off the dumpster, and as he landed in front of Issac, large bat-like wings extended outward, blocking the Angel from view for a moment before he folded them against his back.

"One."

Estelle had always wondered what Zylis would look like if he were entirely shifted. She only wished she could have found out under different circumstances. Issac's eyes were wide with panic, and his body was paralyzed. While Estelle's attention was solely on Issac, Issac couldn't look away from the Demon.

"You're a real concave idiot, you know that?" Zylis' tail snapped like the crack of a whip.

Issac scowled, but Estelle could see his hands shaking. "I-I said I don't care what you—"

Zylis' fist connected against the Angel's sternum and sent him flying about twenty feet back into a wall. Issac slid down to the ground, clutching his chest and coughing.

"*Issac!*" Estelle cried out, launching toward her friend, only to be caught by the back of her cloak. Zylis shoved her away. "Zye, stop!"

"Just stay out of my way, Star," he said, shooting her a stern look before walking up to Issac leisurely.

The Angel stood up at his approach, wincing.

"What do you think, Slumberlord? Still think you're a knight in shining armor?"

Issac glared, wheezing as he took in a deep breath. Then he lunged, swinging his leg out to kick the Demon in the stomach. Zylis side-stepped it and grabbed the leg to knock him off balance before kneeing him in the gut. Issac hit the ground and rolled, stopping a few feet from the girl.

"Issac!" Estelle ran up to his side as he shakily forced himself up on his hands and knees, hacking and heaving as drops of blood hit the asphalt. She looked up and saw Zylis approaching again. Estelle stood up and placed herself between them as quickly as she could manage with shaking limbs, spreading her wings to shield the Angel more. "Zylis, stop!" she cried. "*Please*, you'll kill him!"

Holding her barrier, the girl grabbed Zylis' shoulders, shaking him slightly as tears began to blur her vision.

The Demon clicked his tongue, taking Estelle's wrists in the large, inhuman hands.

"He's fine, see?" he said, gently pushing Estelle aside as Issac shakily stood up. Zylis looked him up and down. "You devils are much more durable than you look, unfortunately."

Time seemed to slow down as the Demon reared back for another hit, aiming for Issac's jaw. As his fist came closer to its target, Estelle felt a surge of adrenaline through her veins and crackling electricity on her skin as she grabbed his fist, stopping him just in time.

Zylis looked at her, one eyebrow raised, then promptly gathered both of her wrists into a single hand and shoved Estelle against the wall, pinning them above her head. The girl squirmed in his grip; even with the silver lightning lapping over her body, Zylis' hold was like steel.

"Zylis, please, just stop!"

He groaned. "I'm not going to kill him, Princess. I'm just teaching him about consequences."

"But he means well!"

"Most people do."

"Get away from her," Issac said, still wheezing.

Zylis turned and looked over his shoulder, raising an eyebrow, unimpressed.

"Don't touch her with your filthy hands, you monster," the Angel hissed.

Zylis' hand tightened around Estelle's wrists, turning back to her.

She winced and repressed the urge to gasp.

He gave a mirthless laugh. "You think I'm a monster, huh?" he said quietly.

"You're *all* monsters. All of you," Issac said, grinding his teeth. "You're a plague. Vermin infesting the Earth." The Angel grabbed Zylis' wrist. Zylis didn't move or even look at him; he kept his eyes locked with

Estelle's. "Now get your filthy hands off of her and crawl back into whatever hole you came from, you subhuman freak."

With every word, Estelle watched Zylis' eyes grow increasingly cold. For a moment, it looked as if the glow had extinguished and lost all sense of life. He wasn't hypnotizing her, but she could feel and see inside him through the hollow eyes.

And then it hit her like a bullet carving through her chest. *Issac's going to die,* she thought.

Suddenly, Zylis released her wrists, stepped back, and laughed. It was quiet at first, but quickly gained momentum until he bent over and clutched his stomach.

"Ah... You know, it's pretty funny, in a concave sort of way—the way you pillocks talk about my people," Zylis said, wiping away fake tears. "It's the absurdity of it, I guess. I mean, devil, it feels like I'm looking at a carbon copy of the worst parts of human history here."

Issac scowled, adopting a defensive stance as the Demon turned fully to face him again.

"*Filthy. Vermin. Subhuman. Monster. Freak,*" he spat each word. "You say that so easily. You either don't know the history of words like that, or you do but don't care. I actually can't tell which one it is."

"What the hell are you—"

In a flash, Zylis had the Angel by the neck, holding him in the air, claws biting into his skin. "The enemy is not like us. The enemy is subhuman."

Issac gasped—or tried to—and clawed at the Demon's hand as his wings flapped uselessly.

"The enemy is weak, but the enemy is strong, and the enemy will getcha unless you do as our *perfect leader* says." Zylis tightened his grip, claws drawing blood. "We are pure; they are filthy. We are superior; they are inferior. The enemy will destroy us, so we *must destroy them first.*" Zylis threw him against the wall. His tail stilled.

Issac fell to the ground, clutching at his throat, heaving.

Estelle dropped to the ground beside him, tentatively placing her hands on him, hoping it would comfort the Angel, as Zylis went into a squat beside them. He didn't look at her.

"Y'know, humans had a name for this particular phenomenon," he drawled. "They've seen this happen many times. But at least humanity had the decency to feel ashamed each time and treat it like a stain on their history." Zylis slowly stood, turned on his heel, and began to walk away. After a few paces, he stopped and looked over his shoulder. "You're probably gonna wanna take him to the hospital."

Estelle blinked, still shaking. "R-right..."

He continued walking, but this time, he didn't look back. Estelle stared after him until he rounded the corner and was out of sight. In an instant, she began trying to heal her friend. But the best she could do was numb the pain a little and heal the scratches along his neck.

Estelle cursed herself for not working harder on her blessed healing as she worked on getting Issac in a position where she could support his weight. She placed one arm around his waist. Issac winced, hissing in pain.

"I'm sorry, I'm sorry!" Estelle said, holding back tears. "But I need help getting you to the hospital. He didn't hurt your wings for the most part, so I need you to help me."

Issac's breathing was labored, and with every movement he made, he hissed through the pain. One arm was broken with a large bruise emanating from the break. His forehead was bleeding, but Estelle couldn't tell where the cut was because of all the blood. She was sure there were a couple of broken ribs, too.

Issac slowly extended his wings but cried out as one bent at an awkward angle. "Ah—I can't!"

"It's okay, I'll do the flying," Estelle said, adjusting her grip. She counted down from three, then used her strong wings to carry them both into the air and flew back to the dispatch station in Heaven.

Issac was in and out of consciousness the entire way.

The trip was challenging, but when they finally made it back, they were able to board the hospital shuttle and attracted the attention of several nurses on duty. Upon arrival, Issac was placed on a gurney, and Estelle took a moment to breathe after explaining what caused her friend to end up in his current state.

"Estelle..." Issac said, his voice hoarse.

"Yes?" she answered, leaning down and angling her ear toward him.

The Angel looked away from her, his eyes sorrowful. "I saw the way you looked at him."

Estelle tensed. She opened her mouth to respond, but the words didn't come. She just stood there, paralyzed, as the nurses wheeled Issac away. The doors to the emergency wing closed heavily behind them, and Estelle was alone.

26

Messages

It WAS ONLY THIRTY MINUTES before Estelle was allowed to go into his room.

The steady beeping of the heart monitor cut the silence in the small hospital room. It had been two hours since they arrived, though Issac was sedated due to his injuries. He had two broken ribs, a broken arm, and a fractured wing, along with several cuts and bruises across his entire body.

Being Angels, very few physical injuries were fatal. So long as their souls were not destroyed, Angels could generally recover, given time. But, of course, that didn't make the symptoms any less uncomfortable.

Estelle was sitting beside Issac's bed, thinking over everything that had happened in the last couple of hours. Everything Zylis had said sounded personal, as if it were all from experience, and Issac's words cut him to the bone.

"Dang it, Issac..." Estelle whispered, feeling the familiar prickle in her eyes. "Were you trying to get yourself killed?" She took hold of his hand, thinking over the words he had said to her. "What would I... if you..." She took in a shuddering breath, biting her lip as she lowered her head over the top of their hands.

Tears were about to flow when an odd sensation pulled her back to herself. It was unnerving, as though the air itself was pressing against her on all sides. She straightened up and looked toward the door seconds before the handle moved. Her heart thumped against her chest as her fight-or-flight instinct immediately kicked in.

The door opened, and there, standing in the doorway, was a single Vostarist. His hands were clasped behind his back, and his cloak billowed strangely as he entered the room.

Estelle found herself unable to tear her eyes away from the powerful figure, even as the pressure against her skin began to increase. Then the Vostarist turned and looked at her despite the red blindfold over his eyes.

"Estelle Amadea."

It wasn't a question, but the Angel nodded anyway. "Y-yes, that's me," she stammered, feeling a single tear trail down her cheek.

The Vostarist tilted his head. "And I take it this is Issac Sterling."

"Yes, sir," she replied. "How may I—I assist you?"

He turned toward Issac and sauntered around the bed, shoes clacking against the tile like a metronome. "I understand you and your colleague here had a confrontation with a Demon. I came to inquire about the circumstances under which two first-sphere Angels found themselves in such a predicament."

Estelle gulped. She knew this would happen. But that didn't make it any less terrifying. "I see. Of course, sir." She cleared her throat and took a second to wipe her cheek, removing all traces of water that had escaped its confinement. But before she started, Issac stirred in his sleep. "Issac!" Estelle gasped, leaning forward as the other Angel's eyes fluttered open.

"What's going on...?" he slurred, wincing as he looked around. His eyes soon settled on the Vostarist, who stood at the foot of the bed like a sleep paralysis hallucination.

The heart monitor instantly sped up.

The Vostarist smiled slowly. "Ah, you're awake," he said. "Good. I was asking your colleague about the circumstances leading up to your confrontation with the Demon." He gestured toward Estelle, giving her a short but clear view of his hands.

The ends of his fingers were white like fresh snow, as though all the color had been sucked out of them. The odd bleaching effect gradually faded into a more natural skin tone around his knuckles, though even that looked slightly off, as if he were affected with some human disease, like jaundice.

Estelle forced herself to look away, but she couldn't stop the thoughts from entering her mind.

It was normal for higher Angels to undergo a physical transformation of one kind or another. But there was usually some resemblance from one level to the next, like getting another set of wings at levels five and eight or receiving a Luminari and being blessed with even more Angelic powers. Vostarists didn't resemble anything closely, except for other Vostarists.

She felt a chill run down her spine. *What happens to them?*

A second later, Estelle shook herself and looked at Issac again. He was nodding, the hazy look in his eyes long gone. He cleared his throat. "W-well, I was attacked, essentially. If it weren't for Miss Amadea, I probably would not have survived, sir," he said, technically not lying.

The Vostarist hummed. "And where were you two scheduled today?"

Issac's breath caught as he looked down. "Florence, Italy."

The high official looked toward Estelle. "And you?"

"Ah, Versailles, France, sir."

"And where did this confrontation happen?"

Issac sighed. "Versailles."

"Interesting." The Vostarist leaned forward. "Might I ask *what* you were doing so far from your assigned area?" His voice didn't change in volume or tone, but something sent alarm bells going off in Estelle's mind, as if the question was a threat.

The lilac-haired Angel hesitated, glancing at his friend before he answered. "I... followed her."

"Why?"

"I was worried about her. I wanted to make sure she'd be safe."

"From what, exactly?"

"From the Demon, sir. I had reason to believe she might run into one."

"Paris is a War Zone, Issac Sterling. There is always a small chance of running into Demons when one works in the Rapture Zone. But Estelle Amadea has evacuated such areas plenty of times before." He cocked his head. "What was different this time?"

Issac opened his mouth but hesitated. Estelle dug her nails into her palm as a bead of sweat rolled down her neck. Every second felt like an eternity. She watched Issac's throat bob as he swallowed.

"Amadea has not been sleeping well, sir," he said. "As her friend, I was just concerned that she wouldn't be able to react in time if she did run into a Demon." He looked down. "I've heard rumors about Versailles being... particularly hazardous."

Estelle held her breath as she wondered if that was true. She knew parts of it were, at least, but if she had to make a guess, she'd say the statement on the whole was only half-true. But was it enough to deter the powerful being before them?

Calm down, Estelle told herself. *You don't know if he can detect lies from other Angels. That's just a rumor.*

Angels couldn't use Truth Seer on their kind—not even Demons had the ability to know about Angels' past sins. But as the seconds ticked by and the Vostarist remained standing there, still as a statue, Estelle's heart rate accelerated, as a horrible, ominous feeling crept beneath her skin.

He knows. He's caught Issac in a lie. He knows. Her vision darkened around the edges. *I need to say something!*

But right before the Angel could make a sound, the Vostarist spoke. "Very well." After a full minute of silence, the sound of his voice sent a shock through Estelle. "I take it that you did not complete your assignment in Florence, then?"

Issac visibly shuddered. "N-no, sir."

"It does not look like you will be able to do so anytime soon." He lowered his chin. "There will be consequences, of course."

Without thinking, Estelle blurted out. "But sir, Iss— Mister Sterling meant well. He was just trying to protect me!"

When the Vostarist slowly turned toward her, she immediately regretted saying anything.

After a moment of sustained staring, the Vostarist said. "I suggest you get going."

Estelle blinked. "Sir...?"

"I am assuming this disruption kept you from completing your assignment, as well."

"Yes." Estelle quietly stood from her seat. "Right—of course."

"While you are at it, see to it that Issac Sterling's assignment is also taken care of."

Estelle's heart dropped into the pit of her stomach. "You want me to do both?" she asked.

"The world does not stop turning when an Angel breaks," he said as the corners of his mouth tilted up. "If what Issac Sterling says about your insomnia is correct, you should have no issue completing both."

The raven-haired Angel clenched her fists behind her back, resisting the urge to protest. "Of course, sir." She chanced a glance at her friend and found him pale and wide-eyed.

"Estelle, I'm so—"

"You are excused, Estelle Amadea."

Estelle froze for a second, looking back and forth between the two of them, and swallowed. She didn't want to leave Issac alone with the Vostarist. But as her eyes settled on her best friend's face one last time, she watched him mouth the words, *'Just go, it's okay.'*

Her stomach was filled with despair.

"Yes, sir," she said, making a small bow before turning around and heading toward the door. As she twisted the knob, she paused for one last look over her shoulder. "I'll talk to you later, Issac," she told him as though it were a blessing.

A Prayer.

A Promise.

This is not the last time I'll see you, it said. This is not the last time we'll speak.

The deadbolt sounded the moment Estelle closed the door.

By the time Estelle had returned to the surface, it was nearly half-past eleven in the morning. She had decided to start with Issac's assignment since it was shorter. It still took her nearly seven hours to get through it all, though, and it was dark by the time she had made it to the west of Paris. She was pleasantly surprised that nearly half of her assigned locations had already been evacuated. It was a relief, but it still took until three in the morning for her to finish everything and arrive at the dispatch station.

She never did run into Zylis again. Perhaps that was deliberate, or perhaps Zylis wasn't around.

When she eventually returned to her room, she decided to forgo showering in favor of simply collapsing on the bed. In doing so, her eyes fell upon the sallbokvie, still sitting on her dresser, untouched. She wasn't sure why she decided to pick it up then, except that it was within arm's reach while the light switch was not.

She turned onto her side, opened the book, and thumbed through the pages until she found a note she hadn't read before. The sallvie wasn't equipped with a mechanism for indicating when the message had been written. All Estelle had to go on was the reasonable assumption that the messages were written chronologically.

When are you scheduled next?

Hey, Princess. Where are we meeting?

Star?

Is this about what happened last time?

Listen, I did not come this far with you so that you could lose your mind over something so stupid like that.

Estelle rolled her eyes and turned the page.

But you're okay, though, right?

Star, this isn't funny. Are you okay??

Answer me, coward!

Princess, I'm serious.

Okay, FINE. Maybe I was a little pushy. You seemed alright with it at the time. I'm sorry, okay? I'll tone it down with everything. Promise.

Star, I seriously need you to respond so I know you're not dead. Can you PLEASE stop ruminating on your weird purity angst, or whatever, for like two seconds? I just want to make sure you're alive.

Estelle frowned. Guilt was taking root inside her. She turned the page, where large letters covered most of the space.

Hey, I'm looking for you on Earth. If I find out you've been ignoring me this whole time, you're in for a world of hurt.

STAR!

Do you have any idea how worried this is making me?

What in all of Concave am I supposed to think?

I'm still looking for you.

WHERE ARE YOU?!

Estelle's brow furrowed. Zylis seemed to oscillate between worry, anger, and remorse.

Watering down the guilt inside her, she turned the page.

Hey Princess, I've never mentioned it before, but did you know there are actually two different kinds of hypnotism? Of course, you didn't. Your education on everything needs improvement.

Well, there's more, but there are two main kinds: active hypnotism and passive hypnotism. Care to guess which one I used on you?

Here, I'll throw you a bone; it was active. It means I was controlling you without really messing with your head. Want to guess what passive hypnosis does?

Well?

Well, that's different, Estelle noted. It's like he's trying to see if he can bait me into answering.

The following line only confirmed it.

Here, I'll tell you a bit more about Wrath abilities. Maybe that'll get you to respond.

I mentioned in the past about it being compression + heat, but that's just part of it. It's also about movement. I compress my soul into a dense ball and use that density to hit harder by throwing it with my movement. That's why Wrath is so hard at the beginning. For a while, it feels like having a cannon fired at your insides all the time. Then, when you think you're getting used to it, you finally figure out how to superheat it, and then you've got the same issue, except now the cannonball is a small, condensed star.

Despite her exhausted state, the part of Estelle's mind that craved knowledge lit up as she absorbed the information. She turned the page, eager for more.

The only good part is that it cauterizes the wound it creates.

I bet you would cry. Fallen Angels still struggle with it, you know. Just not as much as regular Demons. Or Demons like me.

So, there you have it.

Any questions?

Comments?

Concerns?

Any last words before I kick your sorry little void of a Hell-bell?

Estelle did have questions. But it was probably too late to ask them. A little deflated, she continued, reading the last note on the page.

You're either dead or not reading these, and honestly, I don't know which one pisses me off more.

She turned the page and was met with a giant "GO VOID YOURSELF!" spread across two pages. She turned the page again.

Let me tell you a story.

I fought off an Angel once. They were probably a level seven, or something around that. Needless to say, much stronger than you. They had three pairs of wings when the fight began. Want to guess how many they had by the time I was through with them?

Zero.

I repeat: They were level seven. What are you again?

Estelle winced slightly. She was only a level two Angel, still living within the first sphere. Whoever went up against Zylis resided in the third sphere and most likely had earned a Luminari, far beyond her skill level at probably everything.

Now, you may be thinking to yourself, 'Gosh, Zye, that sounds like a threat.' And you'd be correct. I am absolutely threatening you.

So, you better RESPOND!!

If you're not already dead, I'll kill you myself.

You know, this is really messing me up. I actually want to hurt you now. Which isn't exactly new, but most of the time, when I want to hurt you, it's because I'm horny or something.

I hope you spend the next few days ruminating on the implications of that statement, and I sincerely hope that it causes you great distress.

But right now, I want to beat you up for the sake of doing it.

Any thoughts you want to share?

Nothing?

Really?

You don't have anything going on in that pretty little head of yours?

Star, if I ever see you again, someone's not leaving the hospital for at least three months, and it won't be me.

Well, he was right about that, Estelle thought. Probably not in the way he was expecting, though. She turned the page and read the last message. At the very top, there were only two words.

Estelle, please.

For some reason, Estelle's breath caught in her throat, and her heart ached more than anything else. With a sigh, she reached for a pen. She didn't have time to respond to all the things Zylis had said, but she had time for the last one.

I'm sorry, Zye, I messed up. I was wrong. And I'm really sorry.

She was just about to close the sallvie when suddenly it grew warm in her hands. She watched as new letters formed, bleeding through the page.

Void you. You're such a Seexana! Holy devil!
VOID YOU.

For a moment, that's all there was. Estelle's heart sped up as she prepared to write something else, but before her pen touched the page, more words started to appear and put her mind at ease.

When are you scheduled next?

27

Inherently Evil

ESTELLE WOKE UP THE FOLLOWING morning to someone knocking on her door. She groaned, rolled over onto her stomach, and covered her ears with the pillow. Couldn't they have waited until a more reasonable hour? Though she wasn't sure what time it actually was, she only hoped it gave her reason not to get up yet.

"Not now, Issac..." she grumbled into the pillow, half asleep. She didn't plan on responding. She just wanted the knocking to stop. But it didn't.

Estelle frowned. Issac usually gave up somewhere around the third set of knocks. What was making him so persistent? And then she remembered. Issac was in the hospital. Her body tensed, and she forced herself out of bed and shuffled over to the door. The only question that entered her mind was who it was.

She opened it slightly and peered through the crack, only to fully open the door a second later. "Lilith?"

The girl looked Estelle up and down. "Sorry, did I wake you?"

"What? No..." Estelle reflexively said, but then glanced down at her pajamas and faltered. "Well... maybe, but I probably needed to get up anyway." She laughed sheepishly, slipping off the rings on either hand and putting them in her pockets.

"It is strange for you to sleep in, even if it's the weekend," Lilith replied, shifting her weight from one foot to the other. "But it's understandable, considering what happened yesterday."

"Oh. Uh, would you like to come in?"

"If that's alright?"

Estelle nodded and stepped aside. The other Angel entered and stood awkwardly near the corner. The host pulled out her desk chair. "Here, you can sit."

Lilith muttered a soft 'thanks' before sitting. As she looked around, Estelle sat cross-legged on her bed, brushing her hair out with her fingers.

"So... you know?" Estelle asked, subconsciously touching the small, flesh-colored bandage on her neck.

"Half of it was guesswork," she said conversationally. "I didn't know you were the Angel that was punished with doing double the work, but after you didn't wake up until eleven in the morning, it seemed to fit in with Issac getting into a fight with a Demon and you being there."

Estelle blinked. "Well, that's... true."

"I also heard that you somehow protected him."

The younger Angel tugged on a lock of hair. "I guess so, sure."

Lilith tilted her head. "With all due respect, Estelle, that seems very far-fetched."

"I..." she hesitated. "What makes you say that?"

"Even the weakest Demons on the surface are still stronger than a lot of level four Angels. It takes a certain amount of skill to travel

241

between Hell and Earth, and Demons tend not to send out anyone who wouldn't be able to return on their own if they need to," Lilith explained as she drummed her fingers on the desk's surface. "That's what I've been taught, anyway."

Estelle stared back at her for a moment, then slowly looked away. "Well, maybe this one wasn't there to fight."

Lilith arched an eyebrow, disappearing beneath the white bangs. "What other reason would a Demon have to be on Earth?"

Estelle's black hair slipped from her fingers as she opened her mouth, but stopped short of actually speaking. *I have to be careful*, she reminded herself. *She'll have more questions if I tell her the Demons evacuate people, too.*

When Estelle looked up, she noticed Lilith looking around the room again. "Does anyone else have access to this room?

Estelle frowned. "Um. No, not that I know of. Why?"

"Just want to make sure this conversation is private."

"Oh..." Estelle swallowed nervously, joining her friend in checking their surroundings. It was a relatively sparse room. There were not many places to hide any recording device, at least not as far as Estelle could tell. "I mean, is there a way to check?"

Lilith shook her head. "If anyone at my level could detect something like that so easily, they wouldn't use it."

"Right," she said, continuing her search for anything out of the ordinary. "Well, for what it's worth, I don't see anything I don't recognize." There was no response. "If it would make you feel better, we could talk in the bathroom?" Estelle offered.

"Good idea," Lilith said, standing up. Estelle followed behind, but by the time she remembered the state of her bathroom, it was too late. "Estelle, what happened to your mirror?"

"Oh, that," Estelle said, her voice two octaves higher than usual. She cleared her throat. "The thing is, uh..." She thought about it for a second and genuinely didn't have the energy to come up with a lie. "Honestly, I'd rather not talk about it."

To her relief, Lilith seemed completely unbothered, shrugging without a word. Estelle closed the door behind them and sat on the bathtub's edge. Lilith sat on the toilet. For a moment, it was silent.

"Estelle, can I be blunt?"

"Are you ever not?" Estelle said with a soft smile, getting a smirk in reply before Lilith began.

"Even together, you and Issac would not survive a hostile encounter with a Demon on the surface, even with every other variable in your favor," she said. "Fighting a Demon without using Angelic powers is like trying to win a fistfight against someone standing fifteen feet away with an assault rifle."

Estelle winced. "We weren't trying to fight him, though. We just needed to escape."

"The idea that you could get away from a fully shifted Demon while carrying someone else without any use of powers is patently ridiculous," she shot back. "You can't hide from them without training, either."

"Sure, but—" Estelle hesitated, her mouth hanging open for a moment before she closed it. She had very few options, but eventually, she sighed. "Okay, I lied. We got away because the Demon allowed us to. Because he didn't want to kill us." Estelle observed

Lilith's face, searching for any signs of disbelief or hostility, but her expression remained neutral.

"Alright. That makes a lot more sense."

Estelle did a double-take. "*Really?*"

Lilith shrugged. "Demons are not mindless killing machines," she said. "I guess it's a bit weird to imagine a situation where a Demon would be hostile enough to attack you but not want to kill you. It's not that absurd, though. And people can change their minds."

Estelle's heart rate picked up a little. The higher-ranked Angel had mentioned Demons being more than a 'thing' or 'it' before, but to hear her refer to them as people just made the other happy. *This is the time to ask.*

"Lilith," Estelle started. "What exactly do you think of Demons?"

The girl blinked. "They're our opponents in the war. That's it," she replied. "If you're asking whether I think they're all inherently evil, then the answer would be no. I'm fairly certain they just tell us that so we'll feel more comfortable killing them."

For several seconds, Estelle was dumbstruck. Lilith never minced words, but somehow, it still came out as a shock to hear her put it so bluntly. But despite her normally calm exterior, as the silence stretched on, Lilith seemed to grow increasingly uncomfortable, if the way she fidgeted was any indication.

"Sorry," Estelle said quickly, shaking her head a little. "I agree. I've just never heard someone say it..." she trailed off, gesturing meaninglessly.

Lilith relaxed. "Well, it's not the most admissible opinion."

Estelle could almost hear Zylis in her head, snorting at the notion of an 'admissible opinion.' "Have you always felt that way?"

"I've always been skeptical, I guess," she replied, shrugging. "I think most people who buy into it do it because it's simple, and I guess that makes them feel safer. For me, it's the opposite."

"You mean it makes you feel... *less* safe?" Estelle questioned. The other Angel nodded. "How so?"

The seconds ticked by at an agonizing pace. Lilith was silent and looked down at the floor. Her brows pinched together ever so slightly. "I... don't know," she admitted. "I like to think that most people's actions follow some kind of internal logic that can be understood, even if I don't agree." She paused, then sighed. "I guess, for me at least, the world becomes a much scarier place once I decide that there are large groups of people who are just categorically evil for no coherent reason. But I don't even know if that makes sense."

"No, no, it does... I think," Estelle said. "I can see where you're coming from, at least."

Lilith smiled slightly, looking back up to meet her eyes.

"So, ah, when are you headed back to the battlefield?" Estelle asked. "I mean, if you haven't already?"

"I haven't. If plans don't change, I think it'll be sometime next week." Lilith stood up then and stretched. "I guess I should get back soon. They're probably wondering where I am."

Estelle nodded, standing as well. "It was nice getting to talk to you."

Lilith gave a small smile and started heading for the door, but stopped short. "One more thing before I go, actually," she said. "I guess it's only fair that I come clean about something since you did, too." The raven-haired Angel raised her eyebrows. "The story I told you in the hospital, about how I got all that corruption damage... It wasn't entirely true." At that moment, snow-white hair flipped from one shoulder to the next, allowing the Angel to look at the other over her shoulder. "My shield never slipped. It was up the whole time; it just didn't matter. He bypassed it." Lilith reached for the doorknob, looking away. "The Demon knew my full name, Estelle."

Estelle blinked a few times, staring at her back. "That's... *wait*—!"

"Don't tell anyone," the higher-ranked Angel cut in. "I know you won't, but... don't."

Estelle faltered. "Of course. Your secret is safe with me, Lilith," she said. "But *please*, be careful out there."

"I will," she said. "If I see him again, I'll get out of there. After last time..." She paused, sighing. "Well, who knows what could happen?"

28

Look Both Ways

THE DAY AFTER SHE TALKED with Lilith, Estelle was called into Antares' office at the end of class. The room looked messier than the last time she had been there.

"What's this about?" Estelle asked, sitting in the chair in front of the desk. Antares shut the door and sighed. For a moment, he didn't speak. "Antares?"

"It's bad news, I'm afraid."

Estelle immediately tensed.

Her mentor shuffled to his desk and picked up a large, open envelope. "I'm sorry, but... your application for ascension was denied."

The girl's heart dropped into the pit of her stomach. Estelle looked down at the floor, her throat growing tight. "Oh..."

"But it's not the end of the world!" Antares was quick to say, but then hesitated. "Well, it's the rapture, so I suppose it technically is, but..."

Estelle was already sniffling, her vision was beginning to blur, and her wings slumped low on her back.

The older Angel sighed. "I'm sorry. Now's probably not the time for jokes, I suppose," he said sheepishly. "What I mean to say is, well, this is just a minor setback. I can resubmit your application once the waiting period is over."

"Right…" Estelle said. The reminder made her feel better, if only by a small margin. "How long is that, exactly?"

"One year."

The young Angel felt a churning sensation in her gut, nausea rising in her throat. A chill ran down her spine, leaving goose bumps across her body and ruffling her feathers. Memories of her bloody fist clenched around one of her white feathers came rushing to the surface, and she lost control of the trajectory of her thoughts.

Will I still be an Angel a year from now? She clenched her jaw. *I feel like I'm hanging by a thread already, and it's only been four and a half months since Zye and I partnered up.*

Her breathing became shallow, and an abrupt sound made her nearly jump out of her seat. Her eyes refocused, and she realized that Antares had snapped his fingers in front of her face.

"Amadea…?" he said, enunciating slowly, his brows knitted together.

Estelle swallowed. "S-sorry." She cleared her throat. "I… I understand."

After a pause, Antares exhaled and reached across the desk, placing his hand over Estelle's. "Amadea, please don't take this as a reflection of your abilities or potential."

"But isn't that *exactly* what it is?"

"That's what it's supposed to be, but that doesn't mean it's always fair," Antares replied. "Sometimes, whether an Angel gets approved or denied just depends on whose hands the application falls into and what sort of mood they're in that day."

"But that's so arbitrary."

Her mentor chuckled. "You'd be in good company feeling that way," he said. "Amadea, really—many students don't get accepted the first time they apply."

"You did."

He faltered. "Well... yes. But it was easier back then. How do you think I reached level eight in only forty-five years, when the average is ninety? The standards weren't as high."

Estelle huffed out a laugh, reaching up to wipe away the tears from her cheeks.

"Deep breaths," Antares murmured, squeezing her hand. "Stay strong. This too shall pass, Amadea."

Despite his comforting words, the darkness wormed its way inside Estelle—a vile weight that writhed just beneath the surface.

Estelle found out the next day who was chosen for ascension as she made her way to class. The wound of rejection was still fresh on her mind, but she put on a brave face and stuffed the emotions deep down inside her. It took her a while to even notice that something was happening, as the halls were abuzz with gossip, and based on bits and pieces she had gathered from various conversations, it wasn't too hard to piece together what happened.

Estelle didn't know who it was until she entered the classroom and found a crowd surrounding Giovanna Rūnnel.

"Congratulations, Giovanna!" a class member told her.

"Yeah, that's amazing!" another squealed, jumping up and down. "I hope we can all join you soon!"

Estelle stood frozen in the doorway, staring at the group in bewilderment.

Giovanna, she thought. *Wait, really?* Estelle wanted to be happy for her, but ignoring how strange it was was difficult. *She's not even in the top ten percent of our class. How did she get approved if I—*

—Someone tapped her on the shoulder, making her literally jump. She quickly apologized and moved out of the way, tucking her wings close to her body. She headed to her desk and set her bag down beside it. Then, forcing her uneasy thoughts to the back of her mind, Estelle approached Giovanna. "You're the one who got ascended?" she asked.

"Of course I did," Giovanna replied, grinning.

It took every bit of control for Estelle not to cringe. "Well, congratulations. I'm sure..." She took a deep breath. "I'm sure you must have worked very hard for this."

She shrugged. "It was long overdue. Honestly, did you think they would choose someone who looks like one of them?"

Distantly, Estelle heard others snicker at the comment or congratulate Giovanna, but the Angel couldn't comprehend anything over the sound of blood rushing through her veins. She clenched her fists at her sides, feeling the familiar surge of energy as her Navitas reacted to the negative emotion.

Be happy for her. Be happy for her, Estelle told herself. She knew jealousy was not an admirable trait to have, but it was hard to feel anything but a mixture of anger, sadness, and confusion. *There are a million reasons why your application might have been rejected, while hers wasn't.*

A second later, it all fell away as Estelle relaxed and put on a slow-spreading smile, one she knew looked deadly, similar to the ones Zylis would use on her.

Giovanna's smirk faltered as her eyes widened slightly.

"Y'know, I've seen a Demon fight firsthand. They're quick—can appear right behind you before you even finish blinking." Giovanna opened her mouth to retort, but Estelle beat her to it, continuing to talk in a sickening, sweet voice. "You're not faster. So again, congrats!" Her expression dropped the moment she spun around and hurried back to her seat.

Just be happy for her! She hid her face behind her arms, resting atop the desk. *Void, this shouldn't be difficult!*

No matter what she did, she couldn't rid herself of the foul taste on her tongue.

After classes, Estelle found herself walking toward Antares' office without really thinking about it. Perhaps in the back of her mind, she hoped her mentor could provide some form of explanation, but mostly, she just needed to vent to someone who wouldn't judge her.

Upon arrival, she was relieved to see the light was on inside. She knocked on the door and waited. And waited. Estelle frowned, knocking once again, but was met only with silence.

There were a couple of possibilities as to why he wouldn't be answering, one being that he just went to the bathroom. But he always turned off the light in the office when he left, even if it was only for a few minutes. A knot formed in her stomach as Estelle knocked once more, louder.

Finally, Antares answered.

The door cracked open, a sliver of light leaking into the hall. Then Antares poked his head out and looked both ways before quickly ushering the Angel inside. Looking around, she was baffled to find the room somehow even messier than the previous day.

"Antares, is everything okay?"

The high-ranking official shushed her as he closed the door. With his back still turned toward her, he took a couple of deep breaths before turning around. Estelle's brows pinched together. He looked disheveled, with precise dark circles under his blue eyes.

"Sorry, Amadea," he whispered.

"What's going on?"

"Nothing," Antares was quick to say, only to then tack on, "Nothing you need to worry about, at least."

That just made her even more concerned.

The older Angel sighed, trudged over to his desk, and sat down. "I meant to send you a note, but I got so busy I couldn't find the time."

Estelle gingerly sat down in the provided chair. "What's this about?"

For a few seconds, he was silent, staring down at his desk, his expression conflicted. "I... I really shouldn't tell you," he finally said. "Not here. Apologies."

The subtext of the situation was more than a little disconcerting, and Estelle's curiosity only increased, but out of respect, she nodded and stayed quiet.

After another pause, he spoke again. "Is there a reason for your visit?"

"I, uh…" Estelle said, wringing her hands, debating whether telling him her true feelings about Giovanna's ascension was a good idea. Antares already looked stressed out about something else. It probably wouldn't do him any good to hear her angry ramblings. "Sorry. It's nothing, really."

Antares took a deep breath. "Well, for your safety, I must ask that from here on out, you refrain from visiting unless it's a scheduled meeting or an emergency."

Estelle's stomach dropped. "What?"

"Sorry. I don't mean to be harsh. I don't want you to get mixed up in…" he trailed off, then exhaled. "I mean it when I say this is for your safety, Amadea."

The girl bit her lip. "I… see," she mumbled. "Well, in that case, I guess I'll see you in a few days?"

Antares nodded, standing to open the door. He paused as he turned the handle and threw Estelle another look. "Please try to stay out of trouble."

Estelle tensed. "This isn't…" she started. "This isn't about what happened with Issac, is it?"

He shook his head. "No, it's not. That much, at least, I can tell you."

She nodded slowly, some of the tension melting away, though only a little, as her mentor opened the door just enough to poke his head out. "What are you doing?" Estelle asked.

"Looking both ways," he replied before stepping aside and ushering the young Angel out of the small office.

The door shut behind her, resonating like a gunshot in the quiet hallway.

29

Twin

ESTELLE'S SLEEP SCHEDULE COULD HAVE been better. With dreams about the floor collapsing beneath her, she found herself waking up in the early hours of the morning, restless and with no desire to go back to bed. It was better than it had been when she slept in shackles, but it was not ideal.

She left for the surface earlier than usual the following morning, but Zylis didn't seem too interested in talking when she arrived at the first church. They went about their respective duties in relative silence, and it wasn't until the end of the day, when the last person's clothes hit the floor, that Zylis finally broached the subject.

He leaned against the altar, fidgeting with the white linen cloth draped over it. "So, how is he?" he asked. "Still in the hospital, I'm guessing?"

Estelle was so surprised by the question that it took her a moment to respond. "Yeah. He is," she said. "As part of his punishment, they're not using blessed healing to accelerate his recovery, so I think it'll probably be about a month, at least."

"Devil," Zylis sighed. "I was shooting for six. Guess I'm just not used to using restraint."

Estelle scowled. "If anything, you should've used more restraint."

The Demon arched a brow. "Star, sweetie, with all due respect—go void yourself. Considering the kind of things he was saying, you oughta be on your knees thanking me for not killing that pillock."

She grimaced. "Issac was wrong to say those things," she replied carefully, crossing her arms. "But that's what we're taught, Zye. You know that."

"Is that supposed to make me feel better?" he snorted. "Guy basically opens with, 'Hi, I think you're subhuman,' and you want me to take his concave, tragic backstory into account? Void that. I'm not tolerating it. Had enough of that before I died."

Estelle's brow pinched together. *What is that even supposed to mean?* She shook her head. "Well, fine, but that won't make him stop thinking of you that way."

Zylis scoffed. "Do you think my being polite would've changed his mind?" he rolled his eyes. "Hate to break it to you, Star, but that ain't how the world works. And anyway, none of this would've happened if you hadn't concave avoided me for two weeks. What the void was that about, huh? I still don't know."

"I was just—" the Angel faltered, looking down, "—I mean... I don't know."

"Bullsh—"

"It's complicated, okay?"

"More complicated than me shoving my hand down your throat, or less?"

Estelle winced, clenching her fists as her wings twitched. "Look, if you need to know, I was afraid. There's your answer. I was scared."

"Of what?"

She narrowed her eyes and scoffed. "Don't act like you don't remember, Zylis. You *know*."

"So, you went out of your way to avoid me over a stupid apple?" he spat, almost laughing. "That's it? Seriously?"

"Of course, that's not it!"

"Then what the void is it?"

"*My feathers started falling out!*" Estelle shouted, her wings shot up, tears pooling in her eyes. "I woke up the next day, and four feathers fell out, even though you never touched my wings," she rattled on, venom on her tongue. "So, there you have it, Zye. Your plan is working. Congratulations! I'm *terrified!* Is that what you wanted to hear?"

Zylis stared at her for a long moment, his eyes wide, speechless in the aftermath of her outburst. Estelle stood there, body tense, her chest rising and falling rapidly with heavy breathing. It was only after the first tear finally slipped down her cheek that Zylis broke eye contact.

"Oh," he said.

"I just..." Estelle's voice broke as more tears fell, her wings drooping. "I... What if this was all for nothing?"

Zylis frowned. "What are you talking about?"

"I got rejected, Zylis!" the Angel snapped. "Even after all these months with you, my application to ascend was still denied!"

The Demon stared at her a moment longer as his expression slowly morphed into incredulity. "Is that all you care about?" he asked with a mirthless laugh. "Concave, seriously, Star? After all this time?"

"Of course not, but that's the only thing that made this okay, Zye! Don't you understand that?" Estelle cried, forcefully wiping tears from her cheeks. "I've spent all these months with you, clinging to that one thing that made this whole thing acceptable, and now it's just—just gone!" She gritted her teeth painfully. "What the void am I supposed to do, now? I have to wait a year before I can reapply, and—and at this rate, by then, I don't even know if..." She choked on a sob, shaking her head. She couldn't bring herself to say it out loud.

Zylis was just a blurry form standing silently before her, and Estelle was too far gone to gauge his reactions.

"And I know I shouldn't have bet so much on getting approved the first time. I just..." She sniffled. "I thought this would work..." She wiped her nose on her sleeve. "But despite all this time I've spent with you," Estelle continued. "Despite how *hard* I've been working, I *still* got rejected, and—and *freaking Giovanna*, a person who barely even shows up to class, gets to ascend?" She tugged at the roots of her hair. "It doesn't make any sense! She's—!"

Estelle cut herself off with a frustrated scream that had Zylis staring at her, eyes wide and mouth open.

"You just don't get it!" she cried. "You have no *idea* what it's like to be in my position. I work so hard, and everything I do gets scrutinized. Everything! I'm doing everything I'm supposed to, but they still..." Estelle crumbled to the floor, curled up against the wall, and sobbed. Her white feathers brushed the ash-covered ground as they slumped behind her. She was exhausted, both physically and mentally. Her emotions felt too big for her body.

A minute later, she felt a hand brush against her back, moving her hair over one shoulder. She tensed, instinctively raising her shield. She hadn't heard Zylis' approach, but when she peeked over her arms, she found him sitting on the floor beside her, expression calm. Estelle relaxed slightly, letting Zylis' hand stay there, rubbing gentle circles on her back.

Several minutes went by before the Angel was calm enough to speak. "I'm... I'm sorry," she said softly, wiping her face off on her sleeve. "I-I know that one day my work will be recognized. Right? I'll eventually—but..." she trailed off and released a shuddering breath. "Maybe I'm wrong. Maybe I'm just not working hard enough." Estelle curled into herself further, ducking her head between her knees, wishing her halo would go out and leave her in complete darkness. She quietly whimpered, "Or maybe I'm just not good enough..."

After a long pause, Zylis sighed. "Star, can I tell you a story?"

After a second, Estelle raised her head slightly, confused, but nodded.

Zylis scooted a bit closer. "So, there's this preacher who lives in a tiny little forest town, okay? One night, a mysterious woman appeared in his dream. Nine months later, this screaming brat showed up on his doorstep."

Estelle frowned. *Where's he going with this?*

"He takes the kid in, raises him as his own," Zylis continued. "Teaches him all about God. He tells him what he's gotta do to get into Heaven, all that stuff. He lets him call him 'dad.' But..." he hesitated, the hand on Estelle's back going still. "But there's something wrong with the kid," he finally said. "He's just not normal. Both of them can sense it; they just don't know why. At that point, it's just a feeling, but things start to get weirder over time.

"The kid starts to feel it—I mean, really feel it—around the time when he starts hanging around the other kids. He just knew he wasn't like them. He's trying to keep it hidden 'cause it was scary, but it's hard to hide a problem when you can't pinpoint the source." Zylis took a breath. "But it bothers him—actively, y'know? He has weird dreams. And sometimes, he gets this... *feeling*, like everyone's hiding something from him. His dad's church is always too cold. He prays every night, but no one ever answers."

Estelle's brow furrowed. "Zye."

"And it just gets worse, 'cause, by the time he's seven, the townspeople have started to feel it, too," he said. "The adults are polite enough to try to hide it, but... the other kids don't wanna play with him anymore. They say his presence makes them feel weird. They don't like the way he looks at them. In the beginning, the kid lashes out, but that doesn't work out too well—just seems to prove them right." Zylis winced and paused for a moment. "So, he just does what his dad always told him to do. Pray. He prays his heart out every day, begging for some unseen power to make things normal. Whatever *that* would mean."

Estelle fully sat up and shifted toward him, completely enthralled by the tale, sensing it wasn't just a story. Her heartache had switched from focusing on her pain to Zylis'. Subconsciously, she wondered if it was something she was born with to worry about others before herself.

Her companion sighed. "It's not long before the whole town becomes pretty much openly afraid of him." He snorted. "Wild, huh? A whole bunch of so-called *adults* are concave terrified of some little kid just because he gives them weird vibes. Just pathetic," he spat. "But anyway, after a certain point, he just has to avoid going outside most of the time. Which sucks, 'cause it means he can't help his dad with errands, but..." He shrugged.

"He's just so isolated. He has no friends, except..." Zylis paused, taking a deep breath. "There's this stray cat that always comes to his window. A black cat. She..." he faltered, voice sounding tight. "She lets him pet her, and he feeds her sometimes when he can manage it. He starts calling her Twin 'cause, being a cat, he figured she was just like him, y'know? People were afraid of both of them for no reason." Zylis fell silent momentarily, fidgeting with the hem of his pants.

"Anyway, by the time he's, like," he squinted, "eh, twelve, I guess... he's got a pretty good idea of what might be wrong with him, but he's still too scared to think too much about it. He's in denial, so he doubles down on his studies, memorizing scripture, and praying because his dad always told him that's all he had to do. *Just keep praying; God loves you. God loves all his children; this is simply a test of faith. You'll get through it, and one day, you'll live in eternal bliss in God's kingdom. Just have faith.*" Zylis laughed bitterly.

"Some nights, he'll go out to fetch a pail of water when no one's around. He's thirteen years old when it happens. He goes out that night, minding his own business..." he hesitated. "But he hears something strange and goes to investigate. He rounds a corner and catches a boy about his age hunched over in the alley, but as soon as the devil realizes he's been caught, he *bolts*. He thinks about chasing after him, but then he sees..." Zylis grimaced. He didn't speak for several seconds, and all Estelle could do was sit there and stare.

The look on his face was weary, a mixture of exhaustion and numb sadness, as though he were trying to resurrect a part of himself long after coming to terms with its death.

Eventually, he sighed. "Twin's alive, but she won't be much longer if he can't find help," he mumbled. "So, he panics, rushes over, scoops her in his arms, and books it. Heads straight for the town clinic 'cause, y'know, what else is he supposed to do?" Zylis shrugged, his face a mix of pain and anger. "Anyway, he starts banging on the door, yelling for help. There's a light inside, but no one answers. And here's the kicker—a few seconds later, the light goes out."

"*What?*" Estelle whispered.

"Right?" Zylis scoffed. "And the kid just... concave loses it. He's never felt this way before. And he's screaming at them, *begging* for help, but no one listens. And it's too late, anyway. So, he sits on the doorstep, crying, still cradling her. It takes him a moment to realize that Twin isn't *there* anymore. She's gone, and he's alone again." He clenched his jaw, pausing for a moment. "It gets worse, though, because a few minutes later, he hears footsteps and a woman gasps. He looks up and sees her face, but it's cold. And she asks him, '*What did you do to it?*'"

Estelle tensed. Anger flared up inside her, but she could only stare back at Zylis, speechless.

"Yeah... So, by morning, the news has spread. *Oh, did ya hear the preacher's kid killed a cat? How screwed up is that?*" he said, his tone mocking. "'Course he tells his dad he didn't do it, and his dad says he believes him, but honestly? Who in the void knows what his dad thinks at that point? He sure doesn't. The kid doesn't leave the house after that. Not for a while, at least.

"But then, when he's seventeen, his dad goes out of town to visit his aunt and asks him to take care of things till he gets back. He's nervous but agrees. Y'know, it's been a few years. Figures, maybe it's time to try again. And he wants to *help*. He wants to do good and wants to get into

Heaven. So he does everything his dad tells him to, as best he can with the town turned against him."

The hand on Estelle's back began to move again, Zylis' fingers tracing patterns across her spine, his sleeves catching slightly on her feathers. She didn't even notice her wings had risen back into their natural position against her back.

"It's fine for a bit, but of course, it doesn't stay that way," he continued. "One night, just when he's starting to think things'll be okay, he returns and finds his dad's church on fire. He's so shocked he doesn't even know how to react. Eventually, he goes for help and tries to explain what's going on. You can probably guess how *that* goes," Zylis said, snorting. "They chase him out of town, and... well, that's it. He's gone. Never sees his dad again." He took a deep breath and exhaled.

"Anyway, for a few years, he wanders from place to place, doing whatever he can to survive. He still prays and tries to be a good person, even though almost everyone he meets assumes the worst of him. He kinda knows what he is, but he's still trying to overcome it. Every day, he gets a little less hopeful.

"And then one day... he runs into him again—the monster who killed her—and just *loses it*. He ends up on top of him, strangling the devil. 'Course, he's making a lot of noise, so he gets caught before he can kill the monster. A guy comes rushing over, swings an ax at him, misses, and then backs him into a corner. He screams, Go *back to Hell, devil!* And you know what his last thought is before he dies?" Zylis laughed mirthlessly. "I'm already there."

For a while, Zylis was silent. He stared into space as he traced lines across Estelle's back. "When he opens his eyes next, he's lying in a field, looking up at a red sky. He learns the whole truth about himself. Half-Demons."

Estelle held her breath and stared at him in shock. From what Zylis had told her a couple of months prior, she didn't think it was possible. Though he never explicitly said it was impossible to impregnate human women.

"They're ten times rarer than Fallen Angels, especially these days." Zylis continued. "It reminds him of a conversation he had with his dad once. He asked him if Demons could ever earn a way into Heaven. His dad said no. The souls of Demons are far too filthy, you see." He arched a brow. "Even if they're born that way—even if they never asked for it—that cannot change. There is no repentance strong enough to make their souls clean."

Estelle frowned and felt a pulling sensation in her chest and a tightness in her throat. "Zye..." she said softly, "that's... I'm so sorry."

Zylis looked at her then, his sharp, red eyes glowing in the low light. "It was two hundred years ago." He shrugged. "Point is, sometimes hard work just ain't enough. You don't live in a meritocracy, Star. That's just a lie they tell you to keep you subservient." Zylis sighed. "The first step to breaking those chains is to accept that they exist," he murmured, his voice a low rumble resonating in her bones.

Estelle held her breath as the Demon caught a rogue lock of hair between his fingers and carefully brushed it behind her ear.

"The next step's easy." He smirked. "*Get devilishly angry.*"

30

Golden Apple

THE APOSTLES MUST BE GOING against God's wishes, Estelle decided. And that's not blasphemous because God gave us free will. If those whom God trusted could never betray him, Lucifer and the other Originals would have never Fallen.

That was how Estelle was rationalizing things, anyway. Admittedly, even that felt a bit dangerous, but at that point, It was one of the few things she had left to cling to.

Estelle reapplied the glue on her feathers every few days and prayed that God would root out the false confidants among His inner group. She convinced herself that one day, things would get better. That one day, stories like Zylis' would no longer exist.

Zylis.

It had been two weeks since Estelle broke down in front of him, and he, in turn, told her about his past. Things had more or less returned to normal since then—better than normal. Or worse, depending on how one looked at the situation.

Estelle could never entirely escape the persistent feeling of unease as far as their relationship was concerned. It was a bit of a paradox.

Being comfortable with Zylis had made Estelle uncomfortable. But if nothing else, she enjoyed those easy-going moments when they happened. It was a welcome distraction from all the stress and uncertainty that seemed to saturate the rest of her existence.

Her willingness to trust Zylis alarmed her at times. She no longer regularly used Truth Seer on him. She just took it for granted. And she had gotten a little too comfortable venting to Zylis. Sometimes, she had to stop herself from saying too much, lest she give away sensitive information by mistake. However, a cynical voice in the back of her mind mocked the action. *As if there is anything useful you could tell him that he didn't already know about. Zye probably knows more about Heaven than you do.*

Perhaps the most alarming instance occurred during their last meeting when Estelle asked a simple question to satiate her curiosity. "Zye, is there anything hypnotism can't do?"

They had finished the main objective of the day early. They walked down an empty side road at sunset and checked for any signs of stragglers.

Zylis grunted in affirmation. "Couple of things," he said as he peered through a cracked window. "You can't manipulate emotions with it, at least not directly. And you can't use it to force someone to tell the truth. Those are the big ones."

"Oh," Estelle said. "That last one's a bit surprising." Having found no one, Zylis returned to her side, and they continued walking. "I kind of assumed hypnotism would be mostly used for interrogation."

"It still can be. There are a couple of ways to get around it." Zylis shrugged. "Like, you can't make someone tell the truth about something, but you can force them to talk continuously," he explained.

"If you give them enough time, the truth will probably come out eventually."

"Ah, I see." Estelle nodded.

Zylis peered around the corner, confirming that it was empty before proceeding. "'Course, if you ever get held up by a Lust Demon, I'd tell them not to bother," he said, smirking. "That hair-twiddling habit of yours has the same effect."

Estelle glared lightly and rolled her eyes, dropping her hands from the small braid in her hair she had been working on. She stopped as they approached a small, abandoned bakery, where the door had been left open. Glass crunched beneath her shoes as she stepped inside.

"Hello?" she called out, but after a couple of seconds with no reply, they continued.

"So, there aren't any physical limitations?" Estelle asked. "What would happen if you just told a random person to tap-dance?"

"Well, yeah. You're limited by what the target's capable of. It's mind control, not puppetry. If ya can't do it, ya can't do it."

"But is that all? As long as the person can do it, you can make them?"

"Well, technically." Zylis squinted. "It gets harder the more complex the task is. Some things are practically impossible. Like telling someone to kill themselves. As far as I know, the only Demon who's ever actually pulled that off was Asmodeus." He shrugged. "But he was the OG Lust Demon, and most of the time, it just depends on how skilled the Demon is in performing the hypnosis." After a moment, he added, "And what kind of hypnotism it is."

"Ah, that's right," Estelle said as her companion forced open a door to an old middle school, looking around before gesturing for her to follow. "You mentioned that there were different kinds."

Zylis grunted. "Active and passive," he said. "There are some other, kinda more niche hybrids, but those are the two major ones."

"What's the difference?"

"Essentially, during active hypnotism, you're being actively controlled. That's what I used on you a while back. It's what you'd expect hypnosis to be, as it removes your free will," he explained. "Under passive hypnotism, you're not being directly controlled, but the way you perceive the world is. So, it's like a type of illusion. You're making someone hallucinate."

"Huh," the Angel said, peeking into an empty classroom. Their footsteps echoed in the quiet hallway as they continued. "Is there a way to break out of it?"

Zylis snorted. "Well, for one thing, you could just not get hypnotized to begin with," he replied. "Just don't make eye contact with hostile Demons, full stop. And for the love of Concave, if you think you're dealing with a Lust Demon, don't let them *touch* you."

Estelle furrowed her brow. "I thought that needed eye contact...?"

The Demon shook his head. "Star, eye contact is a pretty high bar to clear if you're fighting an opponent who knows better," he said. "Sure, if you're a Wrath or Gluttony Demon, it's pretty unlikely you've delved deep enough into Lust magic to do it, but learning hypnotism without eye contact is, like, one of the main objectives for Lust. It's like hellfire manifestation for Wrath or light bending for Envy."

Estelle suppressed the urge to ask more about 'light bending' and how he could create hellfire—*one thing at a time.* "Okay, but—" Estelle held her hands up, "—let's say you've already been hypnotized. What could you do at that point?"

"Regret."

"Zye."

He rolled his eyes. "Again, it depends on the type of hypnotism. With active, it's a willpower thing." He gestured vaguely. "It's tough to break out of it if you're dealing with someone stronger, but that type of hypnosis is harder to maintain, anyway. Takes more focus," he explained. "Under passive hypnosis, you can always break out of it, even if you're much weaker than your opponent. At least in theory. You just have to figure out what's wrong with the illusion."

"What's wrong?"

Zylis nodded. "Have you ever had a dream where you saw something too jarring and realized it was a dream?" He arched an eyebrow. "Passive hypnosis can be broken similarly. There's no such thing as a perfect illusion. Find the thing that doesn't belong, and you'll break the spell."

He backed up into a door that led the two of them into the cafeteria. As far as Estelle could tell, there were chairs scattered around, but no humans in sight.

"Huh…" Estelle moved a stray hair behind her ear. "Can you do that?"

Zylis blinked a few times. "On you, sure. But you're an easy target."

The Angel raised an eyebrow. "Well, would you?"

At that, Zylis laughed. "You're asking me to hypnotize you?" He grinned. "Seriously, Princess?"

Estelle blinked and averted her eyes. "I mean… I want to know what it's like. I'm curious, and it's just like last time. For an educational purpose."

"I just think you should maybe think more critically about giving me the power to make you hallucinate literally anything I want," Zylis said, taking a couple of steps closer to her. "There's a lotta nasty jantu I could do with that power, Star."

The girl frowned. Looking back into his eyes. "But you *won't*... right?"

The Demon stared back at her for a moment, then looked away. "Well, no." After a second, he shrugged and turned back to the Angel, red eyes glowing brightly in the dimly lit room. "Alright," he said. "Look into my eyes, pillock."

Estelle scowled but did as she was told. Within seconds, she felt a familiar click within her mind, but instead of being followed by a sense of weight inside her head, her surroundings began to ripple, and she was no longer in the cafeteria. Her vision cleared, and she realized she was standing in an apple orchard.

The Angel spun around a couple of times. "Zye?" she called out, but there was no response.

After a moment, she began to walk around. Every direction looked the same.

"Could've been a bit more specific about what to look for," Estelle grumbled, frowning as she did her best to study her surroundings. *What doesn't fit here...?*

She was about to shout into the sky when she noticed something unusual out of the corner of her eye—a glint of something... *Gold?*

Estelle turned toward it and approached a nearby tree. Like all the others, it bore large, red apples except for one. A single golden apple hung on a low-hanging branch to her right. The girl put her hand beneath it and felt its weight in her palm. Unsure of what to do, she picked it.

Immediately, the trees around her started to dissolve, and she was back in the cafeteria again. She turned and looked at Zylis, glaring slightly. "You could've told me a bit more information."

"Whatever, Princess," he scoffed. "You get the idea. It's not always that easy to break out of, though. There's always an out, but it can be a real seexana to find, sometimes. Especially if you don't know it's an illusion." Zylis shrugged. "As always, the best way to deal with it is to avoid letting it happen." He cast one last look around the room and then turned on his heel. "Anyway, I think this one's empty."

"Yeah." Estelle nodded. "But first, what's a seexana?"

"Oh, it's a creature in Hell. It's one of the most aggressive and deadliest, actually. Why?"

"Just trying to understand the language you use." She started toward the door. "Let's move on."

31

Full Moon

THE ANGEL AND DEMON PARTED ways shortly after the sun had set, with no other humans saved, which was good. From what the two unlikely pair could tell, the area had been completely cleared out. Estelle would have been more relieved if they hadn't been so close to the Combat Zone. What if no one was there because they had already been killed, lost their souls to the raging inferno Zylis had kept back with his Demonic power?

Zylis pulled on her hair after she voiced her concerns out loud, chastising her for even thinking about the worst-case scenario. "We clear out areas before devastation hits, or protect those areas that are being affected until we can get people out. Stop being so depressing," he said.

Estelle rubbed that spot on her head, smiling slightly. She flew higher, clearing a thousand-foot building with the full moon in complete view before going into a nosedive, her body reacting before she could fully comprehend what had happened. It was a miracle in itself that she even heard it. A baby crying—screaming. The sound filled her senses as she redirected her flight, pulling up before landing on the ground and running toward the battle that raged on.

It was the closest she had ever gotten to actual warfare. The burning debris produced ash that polluted the air. The smell of smoke filled her lungs. Flashes of Angelic light exploded in the distance, mixed with the flickering of flames as screams from Demons and Angels alike sounded all around her. It was terrifying, haunting, as the girl ran toward it all, following the infant's cry.

Estelle rounded a corner and came to a stop, a wall of hellfire blocking her path. It was dark red with sparks of deep orange flickering from the bottom. The tips of the flame were an electric blue as black smoke trailed high into the night. The heat from it alone caused her to shield her face, even though it burned fifty yards away. The fire raged onward to her right as if it were alive, thrashing violently to find its next victim.

Another scream snapped her out of the stupor, but it wasn't from the child. A woman crying out in pain and fear. Estelle wheeled to the left, down a side street, as she pulled her training gauntlets out of her bag and slipped them on. She had started carrying them around since Zylis and Issac had fought, just as a precaution—along with the sallvie, though that was out of paranoia more than anything; she wasn't anywhere near as good at using her Angelic powers as a second sphere Angel. Still, it could help with anything that might attack.

The Angel veered right, down an alleyway where the continuous screaming came from both subjects. *Maybe I should tell Zye about this,* Estelle thought. *He wouldn't be home yet, so I couldn't just write a message. I could expand my soul to announce my presence.*

The idea came and went as soon as it appeared.

Estelle had been continually suppressing her soul from the time she first arrived on the surface until she met up with Zylis and again when she made the journey back to Heaven. She hadn't had any trouble with others finding her, even if they already knew she was there and hadn't deliberately sought her out, but it was good practice for controlling her powers. But if she stopped suppressing her soul and *amplified* it instead, Estelle would be a lighthouse for disaster.

I'll help them by myself, she told herself. Get in, send them to Heaven, and get out. Zye's probably not even on Earth anymore. I'll be quick.

After another ten seconds of running, Estelle turned again into a dead end, cornered by three buildings, and found her target. A baby was screaming, lying on the concrete, partially covered by a bloodied blanket. But what made the Angel stop in her tracks was the woman sitting in the corner, covered in blood, with hellfire consuming the left side of her body, creeping up her arm and leg, eating away at her soul.

"*Please!* Save my baby!" the woman pleaded. "Get her away! *Please save—*" Her words were cut off by another horrible scream, piercing through the night as she tried to scrape off the fire with her other hand.

The Angel rushed forward. She raised her barrier to try to protect herself from the flames, ripped her skirt at the knees, and projected her soul out like a beacon, praying to God that Zylis was still on the surface. All of it was done within the time it took her to blink.

"Don't touch the flames!" Estelle called out as she picked up the baby with care.

It was then she realized the child was a newborn, covered in dried blood, probably only a couple of hours old at best. Luckily, there weren't any injuries aside from some bruising around one of her arms and a small cut on the back of her head that no longer bled.

"Agh! Get out of here!" the woman cried, only it wasn't as loud.

Estelle glanced over at her and had to remind herself how to breathe. The hellfire had turned the left side of the woman's body black, with her right hand slowly looking the same.

She's disappearing, Estelle thought, swinging her bag off her shoulder and laying it on the ground. *Can Angels even dispel hellfire? Can I send her to Heaven before her soul is gone? What if the fire gets on me?* She gently set the baby on the bag, and her heart throbbed as the infant began to cry again. But the Angel couldn't worry about her; she needed to stop the mother from dying.

"What the void are you doing?" Zylis yelled, appearing a couple of feet in front of Estelle.

The Angel nearly burst out crying at the sight of him.

"Stop that before you—" He stopped as glowing irises scanned the area in quick and efficient movements. His cat-like pupils turned into slits as his tail waved harshly behind him.

Estelle didn't hesitate. "Get rid of the hellflame!" she shouted as she turned on her heel and headed toward the mother, quickly reverting to suppressing her presence.

Zylis was quicker, reaching the woman and physically grabbing the fire—like pulling off a piece of string—and swirling it in his palm until it turned into a small, burning ball. He closed his fist and snuffed it out with a puff of smoke rising to the sky.

The Angel quickly took his place and placed her gloved hands on the woman's chest, uttering the sacred prayer of healing before she commanded her Navitas to give her the power needed. Silver light illuminated the gauntlets as they transferred to the mother, quelling her cries of pain, but they did nothing for the burns to her skin.

Estelle couldn't breathe.

The woman looked at the Angel and smiled as tears slipped down her cheeks. Her mouth opened as the light dispersed, casting them back into darkness. She said something Estelle didn't catch. Leaning forward and angling her ear to the mother's mouth, she heard it the second time. Tears finally escaped her eyes when the woman let go of her last breath.

She had failed. A woman died—lost her very existence—because Estelle wasn't fast enough. *What did I do wrong? Should I have flown to them instead? But I'm not allowed to, especially so close to the fight. I've gotten better at healing; I should have been able to save her. Zye would have been able to save her if I hadn't worried about my safety instead of—*

It was then that Estelle realized that the baby had stopped crying. In a panic, she looked back at where she had laid her to find Zylis cradling the baby in his arms, fully shifted, his black arms making the white fabric almost glow in contrast. Her heart swelled at the sight, only to be constricted with grief, knowing the mother would never be able to hold her child again.

"Did she...?" Estelle couldn't complete the question, even though she already knew the answer, taking a shuddering breath to stop the sob stuck in her throat.

Luckily, Zylis knew what she was trying to say. "Her soul was too damaged. Even if I got here sooner, hellfire isn't so easily removed from the soul," he explained reverently.

Estelle nodded and turned back to the woman, letting the last of her tears fall. She wiped her face on her sleeve before she stood up and walked to the Demon's side.

"Here, I'll take her," she said, reaching for the child, who was fast asleep, but Zylis twisted the baby out of the way, his tail curling protectively around the infant. "Zye—"

"We need to get out of here," he said, flexing his wings slightly as if preparing to take flight. "You're lucky Cyrus is fighting here. He told me how astronomically *stupid* you were being." With each word, his volume grew, and his red eyes seemed to get brighter.

The Angel frowned and furrowed her brow. "I heard a baby crying. Did you expect me to ignore it?"

"Yes, if it means running headfirst into death itself—"

"I do not regret saving her life," Estelle said firmly, cutting him off. The child stirred, and both ethereal beings looked at her, but she did not wake. "I *do* regret not being fast enough to save her mother." Their eyes met again, red clashing with gold. "To watch a soul devoured while I have not the power to stop it." An explosion sounded to the west, making the Angel flinch. "Now give me the baby."

"I can't." He stepped back, keeping the baby from her reach, shifting to hold the child in one arm.

Estelle flared her wings and followed his movements. "Zye—"

The Demon held out his arm, pushing the Angel back. "Star, you can't take her to Heaven," he said, tone unwavering with a softness that Estelle very seldom heard.

She faltered. "What?"

Zylis' eyes flickered down to the baby and then back. "She's like me."

A *Half-Demon*, Estelle's mind completed as her heart skipped a beat. *How is this even possible? Wouldn't I have sensed her being different? No. Not with other Demons fighting nearby.*

"But she's not a Demon," Estelle said, tears blurring her vision, making the child blend into the makeshift blanket. "She's a baby. She hasn't done anything—she was only just born—how can she not go to Heaven?"

"Star—"

"She's an innocent!" she cried. "You were—" Estelle cut herself off and turned on her heel.

Her eyes landed on the burnt body as her hands reached up and pulled at the roots of black hair. Her breathing became irregular, and she struggled to inhale. The world began to spin. Then, everything stopped as Zylis grabbed her arm, using the thin fabric of the sleeve as a barrier against her skin, grounding her with his calming yet unnatural warmth.

"Let's get out of here, Star," he said quietly, though Estelle couldn't tell if the ringing in her ears or the chaos around them made it sound so soft.

The Angel didn't trust her voice, opting to nod.

Zylis bent down and scooped up her bag. Weirdly enough, he began to empty it and put everything inside his rucksack. Just before she asked why, it became clear as he placed the infant inside the empty bag and then secured it tightly to her chest. The next moment, the Demon led the way through the skies with the Angel trailing behind, holding the precious cargo.

Flying had always felt so freeing for Estelle. Before she had become a level two Angel and Mebsuta's—her flight instructor—training intensified, she often found herself swimming in the clouds to think through new information or clear her mind of unnecessary questions.

It was calming, and with Zylis there to protect her from threats, she felt at ease again, even if it only lasted a few minutes.

They landed a couple of miles out, far enough away that they didn't need to worry about the battle approaching them. It was then that Estelle could sense the infant's presence was unmistakably not human, though it wasn't completely Demon, either.

Zylis was the first to speak. "Are you okay?"

The Angel gave a tight smile and nodded.

He was not convinced. "Star, talk to me. Seeing something like that can really mess with your head if you let it." He began shifting back into his usual appearance, with horns peeking through his blonde hair and a tail swaying gently behind him. "You did everything you could—"

"Zye, I'm okay. Really," Estelle interjected, closing her eyes and taking a deep breath before opening them again and looking at the Demon. "We're in the middle of a war. It's going to happen, and I..." She hesitated, choking down the tightness that crept up her throat. "I'll be okay. I'm just tired."

Zylis opened his mouth but hesitated. He shook his head slightly and took off his rucksack. "She'll be fine, you know. I mean, I turned out great," he said, using his signature smirk on the girl.

A small smile crept up on Estelle's lips before fixing him with a worried glare. "You were able to grow up human—all Demons live a human life before turning into one," she said, carefully removing the baby from the bag to hold in her arms. "It's the same for Angels, and even though we don't remember our past life, she will never have those same opportunities. She doesn't have the choice to become an Angel."

Zylis raised an eyebrow. "You *choose* to be an Angel?" he asked, emptying her things from his bag.

"Yeah. I mean, I don't remember choosing, but before one becomes an Angel, they give you the choice to refuse," Estelle explained, slowly rocking back and forth, almost on instinct, as the baby stirred in her arms. "Though I'm pretty sure no one has ever refused the offer."

Zylis sighed. "We don't get a lot of infants in Hell. At most, the youngest kids are between four and six," he said, putting all her things back in her bag. "But the kid will have better opportunities than she would have had on Earth or Heaven."

Estelle hesitated, debating on arguing that statement, but asked a question instead. "Who will take care of her?"

"I have a couple of people in mind who might take the brat in; if not, we have things in place to take care of cases like hers." Zylis held out his hands toward the baby.

Estelle hesitated and then pressed her lips to the infant's head, bestowing as many blessings as possible, unsure if it would work on the baby since she was a Half-Demon.

"Her mother's last words were her name," she whispered before looking up to meet Zylis' eyes. "Chandra. For the full moon she was born under."

Reluctantly, Estelle raised her shield and, shifting between limbs, passed the little girl over to the Demon's waiting arms, still sleeping peacefully. The Angel stepped away, grabbed her things, and took to the air, back to Heaven with a heavy heart.

32

Maybe For Fun

I am sorry to have to do this twice in a row. I'm afraid I'll need to reschedule our regular meeting again. Things are rather hectic right now, and I'll need a few more days to settle things.

Would Thursday or Saturday next week work for you? I could perhaps do Sunday as well. Please write down your availability and slip this note under my office door when possible. Again, I apologize for pushing our meeting back again. I hope you are doing well.

Antares.

Estelle sighed and folded the note, placing her head on her desk. She received the note discreetly from him while class was still in session and had only been able to read it when he left the room. It had been two weeks since her last interaction with Antares, and her mentor's sudden flakiness was worrisome. She knew Antares wouldn't do something like that if he didn't believe it necessary, but she couldn't help but feel a bit of resentment over it.

Worse still, it was feeding into a conspiratorial part of her mind that, up until recently, Estelle hadn't even known existed. In her longing for answers, her brain had started to draw connections where there were none.

Giovanna's ascension, for example. Wasn't it curious how she got approved around the same time Antares began acting strangely? Estelle's impulses wanted her to believe that the two events were related, but her rational mind knew it was unlikely, at best. Giovanna, or now that she was superior to her, Rūnnel, didn't interact with Antares outside of class as Estelle did, and she wasn't the type to go searching for incriminating information. For every scenario she could conjure up in her head, there were a million more plausible scenarios in which Rūnnel could have been approved based on skill. Academic performance was not everything, after all.

Estelle unfolded the note, wrote down the word 'Saturday,' and then folded it again just as class ended. She veered off from the rest of the group and down the hallway before quickly slipping the note underneath Antares' door as discreetly as possible and continuing on her way.

Lessons had been increasing in difficulty. More memorization for certain aspects of Earth and more written assignments about every subject they had learned in the previous months. Her bag had gotten significantly heavier, prepping for the upcoming tests at the end of the month and the beginning of the next.

Estelle couldn't imagine Lilith had it any easier. She didn't know what classes were like for second-sphere Angels, but it was probably worse. There would be similarities, like human behavior studies and flight training. They also had battle strategies, combat training, Angelic power manifestation, and any other classes piled on for ascending.

Lilith was true to her promise of visiting the lower-ranked Angel. Ever since their talk three months ago, she had come back from the second circle about every other month, usually after she had returned from being on the front lines.

Estelle would have liked to see Issac, but after the first day, the hospital didn't allow him to have any visitors, as per his punishment, and the inability to check on him had left her with a persistent feeling of unease.

Luckily, from Estelle's point of view, Giovanna had opted not to visit her. She guessed that the strain of learning Angelic powers was difficult for her to manage. However, training could have just been worse than it was with Antares.

🦋 🦋 🦋

It was cloudy outside, and the sun had just dipped beneath the horizon, leaving the world a murky gray. Estelle sat in the frontmost pew and leaned forward, resting her chin in her hands. She stared straight ahead, looking at nothing in particular.

"What's up with you?" Zylis asked, his mouth full as he finished off the last of one of those disturbing fruits he liked—an embrite, if Estelle recalled correctly.

The Angel sighed. "I'm fine, really," she said. "I just have a lot on my mind, I guess."

She listened to the quiet sound of Zylis sucking the juice off his fingertips before he sat down beside her. The wood creaked, but Estelle kept her gaze locked in front of her.

"Okay...?" Zylis said as he threw an arm over the back of the bench. "Kind of seems like something's wrong."

Estelle finally managed to tear her eyes from the void before her. She sat back against the ruined plush backing and exhaled. "I'm just stressed out. It's complicated," she said, pausing for a moment. "My mentor postponed our meeting again. It's the second time he's done it."

"Oh. That sucks. He didn't tell you why?"

She shook her head. "He's been acting kind of strange lately, but that's..." Estelle bit her lip. "That's probably not worth delving into. There's too much I don't know. Speculating about it is useless." It was the same line Estelle had been telling herself for the past few weeks whenever her mind got too close to the deep end. Saying it aloud, the statement sounded canned, even to her.

Zylis drummed his fingertips on the back of the pew. "Huh," he said. "You're doing the whole training thing under the table, right?"

Estelle shrugged. "Guess that's one way to put it."

"How's it going?"

"I mean, it *was* going well," the Angel replied. "But I haven't been able to train for two weeks. I'm starting to worry I might forget what I've learned..."

Zylis frowned. "I'm pretty sure that's impossible for you. Anyway, is there no way for you to train on your own?"

Estelle shook her head. "My dorm room's too small for me to do much more than stretch. And it's risky, anyway. Thin walls."

"Devil," he muttered.

A moment passed before Zylis reached up, stretched his arms above his head, and sighed. "Well, if you want, I could help ya out."

Estelle glanced at him, blinked once, and did a double-take. "Wait, what?"

"You heard me," Zylis grunted. "I dunno, why not? I'm not an Angel, but I've fought a concave ton of 'em. Could probably give you some useful tips, at least." He stood up and walked over to the altar. "Nothing about magic, obviously, more just fighting in general."

Estelle stared at his back for a while. She wanted to say yes, but there were questions she needed to ask. "How do I know you won't give me bad advice on purpose to sabotage my progress?"

Zylis looked over his shoulder and scoffed. "That's the dumbest jantu I've ever heard."

"I think it's a reasonable concern," Estelle said, even though she wasn't sure whether she believed it.

Zylis turned around, holding a candle in one hand and deforming the soft wax like it was dough beneath his heated touch. "Star," he spoke to her in a condescending lilt, looking at her from underneath his lashes. "I wish there were a nicer way to put this, but frankly, I do not see your 'progress'—" he used air quotes, "—as a threat in any meaningful sense." He started rolling the warm candle wax between his palms, gradually molding it into a ball. "It doesn't even matter who you're training under. It could be The Man Upstairs Himself, for all I care. You're still not going to learn fast enough to become a problem for me, or probably any Demon, for that matter."

Zylis stopped molding the wax and set his sights on the large, stained glass window about twenty feet behind the altar. He chucked the deformed candle at it, striking the window right at the center, where it flattened like a pancake upon impact and stuck.

"Void," he muttered. "Should've waited for it to cool down, I guess."

He reached for another candle.

Estelle cleared her throat. "If I concede your point, will you stop doing..." She squinted, eyes fluttering between the Demon's face and the malformed candle in his hand. *"That?"*

Zylis snorted. "I could be persuaded to stop doing it where you can see. No promises, though." He returned the candle to the altar and brushed flakes of dried wax off his hands.

Estelle rolled her eyes and sighed. "Well... I mean, how would this work, then? Where would we start?"

The Demon hummed and looked up in thought. After a couple of seconds, he roughly picked up the altar and hauled it off to the side, causing several items to fall over in the process.

The sight made the Angel frown, but she held her tongue. *At least he didn't kick it over,* she thought. *This is probably his version of courtesy.*

After a moment, Zylis returned to the cleared area, stood in the center, and looked at Estelle. "Hit me with your best shot."

Estelle's mouth fell open. "Excuse me?"

"You voiding heard me," he said. "Just come at me with your best move—kick, punch, whatever—and we'll go from there."

The Angel continued to gape at him for a moment. "But why?"

Zylis shrugged. "I just want to get an idea of where your skills are," he said. "It'll help me figure out what you're good at and what you're not."

Estelle frowned. "I still haven't agreed to train with you."

"This isn't training, Star; it's a consultation," he replied, monotone. "Look, just do it. You've got nothing to lose."

"Well, okay... I guess," she said, standing up from the seat.

"And don't you dare go easy on me, Princess," Zylis snapped. "I want you to voiding hit me with everything you've got."

"Right," Estelle said, nodding. She took a few steps closer and paused, taking a couple of deep breaths, closing her eyes, allowing the power to run through her veins, and adjusting her stance. A familiar tingling of lightning danced across her skin, and then she charged.

Estelle went at him straight on, landing a clean punch at the center of his chest. Zylis slid back across the wooden floor with the slightest of grunts and came to a stop a couple of feet from where he started.

He raised an eyebrow. "Not bad."

"Zye, you barely even reacted."

"Star," he rolled his eyes. "I've been training more than a couple of lifetimes longer than you have. All things considered, that's pretty impressive," he said. "So shut the void up and quit whining."

Estelle blushed slightly. "Thanks, I guess?"

Zylis hummed as he slid his hand into his pockets and walked toward her leisurely. "Anyway, your form seems fine. No major complaints there, but in an actual fight, you probably wouldn't have the chance to throw a punch like that."

"Well, sure." Estelle blinked. "That's what you told me to do, though."

"I know what I said." Zylis scoffed. "I had to make sure you wouldn't do something stupid, like throw a punch with your thumb inside your fist."

Estelle crossed her arms. "Well, okay. But now what?"

The Demon was quiet for a moment before he sighed. "Here, how about this," he said, "you just attack me, and—" he shrugged, "—I dunno. We'll see how it goes, I guess."

Estelle's eyes widened. "Attack you?"

"Yup. And do it like you mean it, too." He scowled. "I'm not gonna fight back; I'll just block and dodge."

"Uh. Well…" She tried to think of a reason not to do it, but nothing came to mind. Estelle began gathering her hair. "Alright, I guess…?"

Zylis nodded. "Whenever you're ready."

Estelle tied her hair back in a low ponytail, pulled her wings against her back, took a deep breath, and lunged. Electricity danced across her skin as she aimed her first punch at Zylis' jaw, but the Demon blocked it with his forearm. At the same time, Estelle's other fist swung toward his ribs, but with a swift bump to her wrist, Zylis knocked the hit off course.

Clenching her jaw, Estelle went for the face again, her fist meeting air as her opponent sidestepped it. The Angel lifted her leg, intending to kick him in the side before he could set his foot down, but Zylis grabbed her ankle, flipped her leg, and knocked her entirely off balance, and she tumbled to the floor. She winced as her hands hit the hardwood floor first, her knees soon after. With a frustrated sigh, Estelle stood up again, looking up at Zylis with a mildly irritated expression.

The Demon hummed, stuffing his hands back inside his pockets. "Alright, so right off the bat, you're kind of bad at maintaining a steady center of gravity," he told her. "You know how to move in a controlled situation, but your form gets screwed up once you have to respond to a moving target." He cocked his head. "I'm guessing you've been training with a punching bag most of the time?"

"Mostly…" she answered. "My mentor has been focusing mainly on the power aspect."

"Figured," Zylis said. "Magic is fine, but it won't do you much good if you can't use it effectively in an actual fight. You need to get to a point where those movements feel natural."

Estelle nodded, brow furrowed.

"That said, you have pretty fast reflexes, and your instincts are decent," he continued. "I like that you tried to kick the top of my leg and knock me off balance. Of course, the problem there was you were already off balance, yourself."

"Yeah," Estelle said. "That makes sense."

"Anyway, I'd say your mentor gave you a pretty good foundation." He shrugged. "You just need more practice applying the stuff you already know."

The Angel bit her lip, quietly cataloging the critique. "I see..."

There was a beat of silence. "I can help you with that part if you want," Zylis said. "It's something to do, I guess." He walked over to the altar, picked up a candle, spun it around in his hand, and then began tossing it in the air, each time catching it with one hand.

She had to admit that Zylis gave pretty good advice. "Right..." Estelle's eyes instinctively followed the movement. "I just, um..."

The Demon caught the candle and looked at her. "What?"

The Angel laughed nervously. "It just seems a little strange," she said. "I mean, my mentor started training me specifically because I was going to be spending so much time around *you*. He didn't want me to feel defenseless if something happened." She reached back and pulled the hairband out of her black hair. "I'm not quite sure how I feel about you being the one to teach me how to stay safe from, well, *you*."

Zylis stared at her for a long time, one eyebrow raised.

Estelle resisted playing with her hair.

After a moment, he closed his eyes and exhaled. "Star, baby," he said, opening his eyes. "Put your shield up."

"Sorry?"

"Now." Then he was gone.

Estelle had barely managed to raise her barrier before she felt a warm body press against her back. Zylis' arms ensnared her, one locking Estelle's arms against her sides while the other held the candle to her neck as though it were a knife.

Estelle held her breath. She both heard and felt Zylis take a deep breath behind her, and then he leaned in, hot breath wafting against her neck.

"Don't let a couple of months of training go to your head, Star," Zylis whispered. "The reason I haven't killed you is because I don't want to. As things stand, my being around probably makes you *safer*, not less. You'd be surprised how much stuff out there could kill you."

The girl opened her wings with a scoff, making him release her. "I'm not some damsel in distress, Zye. I don't want other people to have to protect me."

"So train with me, then," he shot back. "I'll teach you how to fight for real. Like, using everything at your disposal." Zylis gestured to her wings. "Can't promise you'll be able to beat me anytime soon, but at least you'll know what the void you're doing."

Estelle sighed and gave in, twirling a strand of her hair. A *Demon teaching an Angel how to fight, huh?* It was such a bizarre concept to her. The same could have been said about their existing arrangement, though that was a bit different since it was set up to be mutual.

She tensed as it suddenly occurred to her. The only reason Zylis was working with her in the first place was so he could try to make her Fall.

Estelle narrowed her eyes. "Zye," she said slowly. "What *exactly* would you be getting out of this deal?"

Her companion stared at her for a moment, his face twisted up in confusion. "Not everything is a concave transaction, Star."

The Angel narrowed her eyes even further.

"Maybe I just think it'd be fun. You ever considered that?"

Estelle didn't waver.

Zylis groaned. "Oh my—" He glared. "Look, if you want an explanation that plays into this voiding weird marketplace mentality, *fine.*" He threw his hand up. "I guess you could argue that because I am betting on you Falling, the act of training you now is simply an investment in your future utility." Zylis' eyes widened, and he gave a tight smile. "I am offering my services now so that your skills will be stronger, your labor will be worth more, and your existence will matter more." His arms fell limp, hands smacking against his legs as they dropped. "There. Was that soulless enough for you? Do you need me to put on a top hat and monocle? Maybe crush your windpipe under my boot? *Holy devil.*"

"Okay, I get it," Estelle said, holding up her hands in surrender. "I'm sorry, it's just that this whole thing started with a transaction." She looked off to the side. "Though it's turning a little more one-sided with having to wait another year," she mumbled, lowering her hands.

Zylis made a sound of frustration before dragging a hand down his face. "Look, if you don't Fall before then, training with me for a year will give you an advantage against all the other magical pelicans," he said, causing the girl to look back at him. "I would even give you the promotion since you would be breaking all the records for longest-lasting paklen."

Estelle giggled lightly, shaking her head. "I'll ask Antares about training with you and see what he thinks about it, okay?"

Zylis blinked, cheeks dusted pink. "Whatever."

33

Smoothie

"ANTARES?" ESTELLE SAID, STARING AT her mentor's face, a faraway look in his eyes. She waved her hand in front of his face. "*Antares?*"

The older Angel jumped. "Yes! Sorry, um. What were you saying?"

Estelle tilted her head slightly. "I was telling you about Zye's offer," she said. "You know, his offer to help me learn how to fight." She frowned. "I... wanted your opinion on it?"

"Oh! Right, right. Sorry." He looked around nervously. "Yes... Yes, I think that should be alright. He's proven himself to be trustworthy enough."

The young Angel nodded slowly. "Are *you* alright?"

Antares blinked a few times. "Yes, of course; why wouldn't I be?"

Estelle gave him a *look*.

Her mentor turned his head away sheepishly. "Sorry. It's nothing you need to be concerned about."

Estelle sighed. "I'm *already* concerned, Antares," she said. "You... you haven't been acting like yourself recently, and... and all the cancellations..."

He was quiet, staring down at the floor.

Her throat felt tight. "Please don't tell me not to be concerned. Everything about these past few weeks has been nothing but concerning." Her voice broke a bit. "I'm... worried about you."

For several seconds, it was silent. Then, Antares softly laughed. "Ah, I've messed up, haven't I? Making my student worry about me."

Estelle's vision blurred as she waited.

He sighed. "I will tell you everything, Amadea," he murmured, "just not right now."

The girl blinked as tears escaped their confinement.

"Please, trust me. I know this is hard on you. It's hard on me, too. But I need you to trust me."

"Isn't there anything you can tell me?" Estelle asked. "Anything? Anything at all?"

Antares fell silent for a moment that seemed to stretch on for an eternity. But eventually, he took a deep breath and whispered, "Someone has gone missing."

The Angel paled. She opened her mouth to respond.

"No," Antares continued quickly. "No, it is not someone you know. I cannot tell you anything more than that." He leaned back in his chair, and the two of them just sat there for a couple of seconds, stewing in silence.

'Gone missing' could have meant a lot of things. Estelle yearned to ask for something more precise, but she didn't. She couldn't. The words hung in the air like a noose around someone's neck.

Estelle cleared her throat. "So, then..." She took a moment to breathe and get her emotions under control. "Um, Zye. Do you really think it's a good idea? I mean, *really?*"

292

Her mentor smiled. "I do. Zylis..." he trailed off, then took a deep breath. "Zylis is a good man, I believe. In his heart."

His student nearly choked on her saliva. "Antares!"

"Yes?"

"You—you just," she stammered. "I-I mean—"

The older Angel chuckled, but there was something melancholic about it, his eyes downcast. "Amadea, I'm old. I'm tired," he said. "There comes a time when one must say the quiet part out loud."

Estelle remained frozen in place, her mouth hanging open.

"Zylis knows your full name," Antares continued. "He could have forced you to Fall a long time ago, but chose not to. I think that says more than enough about his character."

After a long pause, he sighed. "I'm not defecting, of course. I still think you should be careful. 'The road to Hell is paved with good intentions,' as they say. Just be sure to wear protective gear if you're planning on anything more hands-on."

Estelle forced her jaw shut and nodded stiffly. "Got it." She knew all of that. Zylis was a good person. He had shown that side of himself more than once, even though it hid behind the overall Demon exterior.

Antares stood up slowly. "That reminds me. I got you something that might help you out with training." He walked over to the closet in the office, where he stored the backboard, and pulled out a neat pile of folded clothes. He handed them to Estelle. "It took a while to acquire these since you wouldn't normally get them until the next level."

Instantly, the young Angel knew what they were: the uniform for fighting Angels. It was a simple design. Long white fabric was sewn to a silver sash that wrapped and tied around the waist, resembling a skirt for a dress, with a matching pair of leggings. Despite the appearance, the uniform was specially woven together to help Angels channel energy from their soul into their vessels for an attack. However, as Estelle took a closer look at what she was given, she noted they were slightly modified to resemble her current working dress. The leggings were more like Capris, the skirt was longer, and the silver lining was thinner.

"Anyway. I believe next Thursday should work fine for me," he said. "I'm compiling some notes and things for you that I hope you'll find useful. I should be finished with it by then."

Estelle blinked, mind reeling. "Really? What are they about?"

"A number of things." He shrugged. "I can't tell you much right now, but I look forward to showing you."

Estelle forced a smile and thanked him despite the ominous feeling that grew in her gut.

Antares said it's okay for me to train with you.

Cool. I'll have my mentor call your mentor, and we'll schedule a playdate.

Zye. Oh! One thing, though, he said to make sure we use protection.

Suddenly, tiny droplets of some blood-red substance began appearing all over the page. Estelle was hesitant to ask.

What's happening?
Zye?? There's red stuff all over the page.

It's all sticky??! Zylis, what IS this?!

I was drinking a smoothie. I spat it all over the page.

Didn't expect that actually to go through, though. Interesting.

I wonder what else this thing could transfer.

Why did you spit your smoothie on the sallvie? Is it even safe for me to touch this?

Gross.

Not important. But on a related note, are you allergic to latex?

No, of course not. I don't think that's even a thing for Angels. Why?

Several minutes went by.

Zye?

34

Show
Me How

AFTER ESTELLE'S ASSIGNMENT WAS DONE, she followed Zylis down the street, having evacuated all the churches. "How's Chandra?" she asked, dusting off her feathers. "Was someone willing to take her in?"

Zylis hummed. "Yeah, McKelle volunteered to take the brat," he said. "She's generally good with kids. Though I'm not sure what her partner thinks of the new situation yet." At the street corner, the Demon walked into a building through the shattered glass door, ascended some stairs, and forced open a boarded-up door.

Estelle waited for the dust to settle before following him inside. It was only then that she realized where they were. It was an old, vacant gym. Most of the equipment was covered with sheets haphazardly, and whatever wasn't was coated in a layer of dust.

"I'm glad she's with someone I know, I suppose," Estelle said, trailing behind Zylis as he strode down the hallway and peered into each room until he seemed to find what he was looking for.

Entering the room, the girl recognized it as a training room of some kind, the floor cushioned with thin, squishy material that extended from wall to wall. Zylis set his bag down in the corner and started fumbling with it. Estelle still stood in the doorway. She knew why they were there: to train. She had unofficially agreed to it when she wrote to him, but the question remained.

"So, how are we going to do this?" Estelle asked, a bit skeptical.

"With these," Zylis said as he stood and turned toward her, showing the Angel what he was holding.

It was a pair of long gloves made from shiny black material, like vinyl or latex. Zylis slid one of the gloves on, the top of the garment ending around his upper arm. He pulled on the material and snapped it against his skin.

He looked at Estelle. "You know. *Protection.*" He smirked and began to slide the other one on.

Estelle blinked a couple of times. "Zye, are those..." She tilted her head. "I don't know... opera gloves?"

"No," Zylis scoffed. "I'll have you know these are *fetish* gloves, thank you very much."

The Angel's eyes widened slightly as heat crept up her neck.

Once both gloves were on, Zylis smoothed out the latex and tested the movement of his arms in them. "Honestly, I'm mad at myself for not thinking of this earlier."

As Estelle looked closer, she realized that metallic caps were on each of the fingers, solid and slightly pointed. *Probably so that the gloves won't get ruined if he starts to shift on accident,* Estelle's mind supplied. She gulped. "What..." Estelle played with the silver sash that wrapped around her waist. "What exactly are you planning?"

Zylis shrugged and walked toward her at a leisurely pace. "Nothing much. We're just gonna spar. And this way, you don't have to worry about accidental contact so much." He cracked his neck. "I won't use any Demonic powers, at least not today. This is more about teaching you how to move in an actual fight."

Estelle chewed her lip and looked the Demon up and down. "I... Okay." She finally entered the room, set her bag alongside his, and untied the sash. She dropped the skirt to the ground and stepped around it, looking up to catch Zylis staring at her with raised eyebrows. "What?" she asked.

He blinked several times and shook his head. "I didn't know you had legs."

Estelle raised an eyebrow. She couldn't tell if he was being serious or not. "Of... course I have legs...?"

Zylis laughed. "Could have fooled me. It's kinda hard to tell beneath—" he gestured vaguely at the white fabric on the ground, "—all that."

"I—you saw my legs two weeks ago. How—"

"Relax, Star," Zylis interjected. "I knew you had legs. I'm not an idiot. I just didn't realize that you had *legs*." His eyes left hers and flickered down before a smile spread across his face as if he was thinking of something she didn't want to know. "Were you always wearing pants?"

"Uh, no," she answered, feeling a little self-conscious. She joined the Demon on the mat. "We're not issued fighting uniforms until level three, so Antares got me some since it'll be difficult to fight in a dress." The Angel gathered her hair and began braiding.

Zylis raised an eyebrow. "You nervous?"

"A bit," she confessed, tying off her braid.

"Y'know, I'm not going to hurt ya, Princess," he said, then smirked, eyes darkening. "Unless you want me to."

Estelle frowned. She had heard him say things like that before, and she wasn't sure what he meant, but the look on his face gave enough information for her to know that asking for clarification probably wasn't a good idea.

Rolling her eyes, Estelle sighed. "Where do we start?"

"Wherever," he said. "Just get ready, and I'll start whenever you do." Zylis shifted into a fighting stance.

Estelle did the same. She locked eyes with him—he nodded—and after a deep breath, Estelle launched toward the Demon. It was over almost as soon as it had started.

With her right hand, Estelle threw a punch, and with his left hand, Zylis smacked the first away. The Demon's right arm came around, making contact with her stomach as he twisted. Briefly showing the Angel his back, then immediately launching her over his shoulder. Estelle choked on spit as her body hit the mat with a heavy smack. She landed on her side, coughing as she squirmed, her wrist locked in Zylis' grip. She tapped on the mat, and he released her.

"You said you weren't going to hurt me!"

"Oh, did that hurt?" he asked, feigning surprise, but Estelle could see the amusement in his eyes. "*Whoops.*"

She mumbled under her breath as Zylis fell into a squat beside her.

"You good?" he asked, offering his hand.

The Angel glared and stood up on her own, brushing off her clothes. "You mean apart from the whole right side of my body being bruised?" She scoffed. "*Sure.*"

The blonde rolled his eyes, rising to his full height again. "Star, we're sparring. Hate to break it to ya, but if you wanna improve, you'll have to get used to getting a little beat up. If you're not bruised, you're not trying hard enough."

Estelle scoffed, but she knew the Demon was right, even if he had a rather annoying way of proving his point. After a moment of silence, the raven-haired girl said, "Show me how you did that."

Zylis nodded and beckoned her closer. "So, let's say I'm throwing a punch with my right arm." He imitated the move in slow motion. "You're going to push it away with your left hand and jab your right elbow into my stomach."

Estelle did as he had said, hand squeaking slightly against the black latex. "Now what?"

"Grab onto my wrist and turn around, back to me."

Estelle twisted her hand until she had a hold of him, then started her turn.

"Widen your stance. If you're not balanced, you'll end up throwing yourself onto the floor with your opponent on top."

Estelle nodded, returning to the starting position to try again. She spun to her left, her wings making contact with Zylis' chest. She could feel the heat radiating off his body. She swallowed, but her throat was dry.

"From here, you wanna hold your arm up and then *sharply* pull down," he continued. "Simultaneously, you're bending forward to give yourself some extra force with your elbow."

The girl nodded, adjusting her grip.

"Don't do it from here. You need the turn to give yourself momentum."

She bit her lip. "Right."

"Wanna try it?"

"Sure..." Estelle released his wrist and turned around to face him again.

"Alright." Zylis took a few paces back. "Ready?"

"You're not going to do this at full speed, are you?"

The Demon shook his head. "No, but I'm not doing it in slow motion, either. Moves like this don't work if you do them too slow."

Estelle flipped her braid to her back. "Okay." She took a deep breath. "Ready."

35

Training With A Demon

ZYLIS WENT AT HER WITH a right-hand punch. Estelle blocked it with her left hand and stepped forward to jab her elbow into his stomach. Her fingers couldn't quite wrap all the way around his wrist, so it was awkward, but she did her best to compromise with a tight grip as she spun around. Her back bumped against Zylis' chest as she bent over and thrust his arm down. Zylis followed the movement, flipped over Estelle's shoulder, and smacked against the mat.

Despite weighing more, he didn't hit the floor as hard as she had. Estelle wondered if there was some technique behind it.

"Not bad," he said, wrist still locked in the Angel's hand.

Suddenly, Zylis wrapped his fingers around her wrist, which was holding his arm, and pulled her down. Estelle toppled to the floor and ended up face down, her right arm pinned behind her back while Zylis straddled her thighs. The girl hissed as he twisted her arm uncomfortably.

He then leaned forward, left hand wrapping lightly around her neck, and tilted her head. Zylis rasped, "And that's a particularly fun way to get out of it." His breath was hot against her ear, and Estelle could practically *hear* the smirk on his face.

She didn't even know what he did that ended with him on top of her.

Zylis lingered for a moment before he released her, and it wasn't until the heavy weight on her body was gone that Estelle realized she had forgotten entirely to tap out. After a moment, she stood up, dusted herself off, and prepared to go again.

For the next hour, it was essentially more of the same thing. Zylis had started going easier on her once he got over the sadistic joy of hitting Estelle with outlandish finishing moves that left her pinned before she could even process what had happened.

Estelle lost every match but found it difficult to be mad about it. She was learning, after all, every time Zylis pulled an interesting move—evading an attack with some novel footwork or unconventionally blocking a hit—he was more than happy to slow it down and show her just how it worked, and coached Estelle through her fumbled execution. He still laughed when Estelle tripped over her feet, but not as much as she had expected.

It was fun.

Estelle grinned as she wiped the sweat off her forehead. She ducked under a kick aimed at her head and managed to land a punch on Zylis' ribs. That resulted in her lying on the ground face down, Zylis twisting one arm painfully as she frantically tapped the mat with the other. In the end, she still enjoyed it, somehow. How Zylis moved so smoothly made the whole thing feel like a strange, elaborate dance.

Estelle wasn't sure what she was feeling until the very end.

It happened right as Zylis was preparing to flip her over his shoulder again, only this time Estelle knew what was coming. As the blonde turned around, the girl quickly jumped up and locked her free arm around his neck, causing him to release her other wrist. She went to tighten the chokehold, but before she could lock it in, Zylis spun back around, bent down slightly, and grabbed both of her legs in either hand as they both toppled to the floor.

Estelle pushed at his chest, but Zylis just grabbed her wrists, pinning them on either side of her head. With her hands immobilized, the girl tried to use her legs to flip them, but the man dropped his body into her harder, keeping Estelle's hips trapped against the mat, preventing her from gaining any momentum.

They stayed that way for a moment, panting, before Estelle groaned and hit her head lightly against the mat. "I thought that would work."

Zylis laughed. "It might've, but you gotta be faster than that, Star."

A couple of seconds went by. Zylis was still holding her wrists, preventing her from tapping out.

Estelle shifted against the mat. "Um...?"

"Yeah?"

"Are you going to let me up?"

He hummed. "I dunno." He smirked, leaning closer, their faces just inches apart. "I think I kinda like you like this."

Estelle frowned, momentarily confused. And then she looked down.

"Oh. *Oh.*" Her eyes widened, cheeks burning as she registered their position. Zylis' hips were pressed against her, Estelle's ankles hooked around his waist. The Angel sputtered, her voice going out an octave higher than usual as she let her legs fall to the side. "Um. R-right, uh, th-this is a little..."

"What?" Zylis leaned in a little closer as his hands tightened around her wrists.

Up close, he smelled a little like smoke, a little bit sweet. It filled Estelle's nose until she could taste it. She opened her mouth, but no sound came out.

Zylis hummed, and she felt the vibrations resonating through her body. "See, the nice thing about this is it gives me a lotta control," he murmured, eyes darkening.

He shifted Estelle's wrists into one hand above her head, and the girl shivered as he trailed the cool, metal tips of the glove up her neck, catching the light of her halo. Zylis traced his thumb across Estelle's bottom lip, the rounded point pressed lightly against it.

There was a voice somewhere in the Angel's mind screaming at her to struggle. But as she stared into Zylis' eyes, she felt herself being transported further away from it until it was just an unintelligible murmur in the distance.

Zye is very attractive, she realized. It was far from the first time she had noticed that fact, but it felt different somehow at that moment. *Close.* Zylis was at the center of everything, his body eclipsing the world around her.

"I mean, just think about it." His voice was hushed, deep. She could feel it in her bones. "From here, I could do all sorts of things to you, Star."

Estelle swallowed. She felt hot, and the immovable weight of Zylis' body against her own only made the feeling more pronounced. It was like something emerged from a place very deep inside her, rising to the surface. She couldn't say for certain what it was, but somehow, she knew it had always been there.

"Like what?" Estelle whispered. She wasn't sure what exactly compelled her to say that.

Clever.

The blonde's eyes widened slightly, his brows raising. As the initial surprise melted away, his signature smirk returned. He licked his lips, his eyes half-lidded, and hummed. Then, to Estelle's confusion, Zylis slid his hand over her mouth, sealing it shut. Estelle watched hazily as the Demon's face drew closer, misty light hitting his cheeks, and closer still until, finally, his lips met the back of the glove, right where Estelle's mouth would have been.

Handsome.

Estelle's eyes fluttered closed as Zylis lingered, lips moving against the black latex as though there were nothing in between. As though she was genuinely kissing him. Estelle arched up off the mat slightly, a small involuntary sound breaking free of her throat, her lips mindlessly moving against his palm.

It was the sound that did it, she thought. The subtle, slightly wet sound of Zylis' lips breaking away from the surface of the latex. Something clicked into place and sent a wave of heat through her system, leaving everything scorched.

Strong.

Zylis pulled back and placed a small amount of space between their bodies. He removed his hand from her mouth, and when he turned it over, he laughed softly at what he saw. Estelle knew, from how her face felt, that she was completely red, and it only increased when Zylis turned his palm toward her. There was a distinct wet mark that she had left.

Then, all the while maintaining eye contact, Zylis brought the hand to his lips and slowly dragged his tongue across his palm.

A soft, aborted sound escaped Estelle's mouth.

Holding her gaze, Zylis smirked in that slow, cocky, devious way of his, like he wanted to eat her alive.

Terrifying.

He sat back on his heels, glowing eyes roaming over her body slowly and taking stock of the wreckage. Zylis licked his lips. "I'd say that's a good place to start."

Gorgeous.

36

The Journal

OVER THE NEXT THREE DAYS, Estelle didn't think too much about the event after it had occurred. On the rare occasions when the memory crossed her mind, she was generally quick to shut it down. However, over time, the aggregate of all those tiny thoughts would still synthesize into something more because Estelle was not ignorant. Although she had never experienced feelings like that night with Zylis, she knew how to put two and two together.

She felt conflicted about it. A part of her wanted to make excuses, the most common of which was the general idea that, because she had nothing to compare it to, it was impossible for her to know what she had felt back then with certainty. But it was a shallow rationalization—a chair she could wedge against the door if ever the thought tried to break into her consciousness. It only worked because her concerns were un-processed and underdeveloped. It worked because they were weak, which was how they needed to remain.

So she didn't think about it. Thinking about it gave it strength. Thinking about it made it *real*. Thinking about it fed into that which already tainted her soul. She knew that to be true, even codified in conventional medical knowledge. When Angels sustained critical amounts of corruption damage, it was not uncommon for them to be sedated for prolonged periods to give their souls a chance to recover without the risk of blasphemous thoughts tipping the scales.

Estelle couldn't know where she fell on the continuum of corruption, but as long as she kept consistent with the feather sealant and kept her mind far from it, the consequences would not exist because she hadn't reached the point of no return.

Estelle wasn't sure whether she found that thought comforting or terrifying. It was just another thing she did not want to think about.

Antares' study was quiet, apart from the subtle squeaking of the ceiling fan spinning overhead. Estelle sat at the desk, braiding numerous strands of black hair as she waited for her mentor. After a minute, he returned with a tray with two cups of tea and a thick, leather-bound book between them. He set the tray down in front of the young Angel.

"What's that?" Estelle pointed at the book, letting her unfinished work fall and unravel.

"Notes on Angelic powers and battle strategies, for the most part," Antares said, shrugging. "It's what I wanted to give you. I've been compiling it for some time."

"Really?" She perked up. "Thank you!"

He smiled and nodded, but Estelle did not miss the tension in his shoulders. Antares pulled up a chair and sat down, resting his elbows on the edge of the desk. "This isn't a normal journal, however. There's a precise way it needs to be read." He gestured toward it. "Open it up. Take a look at the inside of the cover."

Estelle did as he said, feeling the smooth leather between her fingertips as she flipped it open. There, she found what looked to be a long list of dates. "I'm... confused."

"That's the schedule," he said. "The days when you'll be able to read each successive entry."

"Oh." Her brow furrowed as she scanned the list. "Why, though? What would happen if I didn't follow it?"

"That's not something you'll need to worry about."

The young Angel blinked a few times. "I don't understand."

"The book is enchanted," her mentor explained as he picked up his teacup and sipped it. "It's set on a progressive time-locked schedule. You wouldn't be able to read the entries prematurely, even if you wanted to."

That, for whatever reason, made Estelle's gut twist up in a rather unpleasant way.

Antares set his cup down. "It's not that I don't trust you, Amadea. It's just that this is..." he trailed off, his eyes drifting away. After a moment, he closed them and sighed. "Well, it's just too important for me to rely on trust alone." He looked at her. "Please try to understand."

Estelle nodded slowly. After a pause, she asked, "What would happen if—theoretically—I just waited until the last date and read the whole thing at once?"

Antares frowned. "Well, it's impossible to predict, but it certainly wouldn't be good." He chuckled softly. "I'm sort of banking on your insatiable curiosity preventing that from being an issue."

Estelle gave a small smile despite her anxiety. "But..." she hesitated. "Why would it be an issue at all?"

"Amadea," Antares exhaled. "You have to understand that—among other things—these notes contain a lot of information transcribed from books beyond your level. Information you would normally acquire over *decades* of training." He leaned forward, lacing his fingers together. "I'm just trying to be cautious here. I can't predict what will happen, but Angels have a history of responding poorly to sudden influxes of dense information. I don't want you to get overwhelmed."

You didn't seem too concerned about that when you were teaching me about anything else, she thought, narrowing her eyes slightly. "What sort of information is in here, exactly?"

Antares stared at her for a while and then raised an eyebrow. "You've been unusually obstinate lately."

Estelle tensed. *Have I?* she thought, opening and closing her mouth a few times as her mentor reached for his cup again, taking a small sip. "I'm sorry, Antares." She looked down, forcing her hands to stay still. "Maybe... I've gotten too used to having all my questions answered immediately."

"It's alright," the high-ranked Angel replied lightly. Then, his tone shifted to something more serious. "But you should be careful to remember where you are, Amadea. I'm sure you're already quite aware of this, but how you act around me at times could get you in a lot of trouble if you did it around anyone else."

"I apologize," Estelle said, her voice going out a bit higher. She swallowed. "I don't mean to be disrespectful."

Antares shook his head, offering a reassuring smile. "It's not about me, Amadea," he said. "We know each other, which inherently means things will be less formal between us." He shrugged. "I'm only saying something because I've been noticing this trend for a while now, and you must remain conscious of it." He paused to set his cup down. "Things like asking pressing questions, speaking out of turn, or back-talk may be alright with me, but those same behaviors could garner a lot of suspicion if you allowed them to slip out around, say, a Vostarist, for instance."

The young Angel tensed, her eyes widening as she stared down at her lap, memories rushing back to the surface. *But, sir, Sterling meant well. He was trying to protect me!* She felt the phantom weight of the Vostarist's attention, and a wave of nausea swept over her.

"Amadea?" Antares said, frowning. "Are you alright?"

"Y-yes," she stammered. "I'm alright. Sorry."

"Are you sure? You look ill."

Estelle forced herself to swallow the bile that rose into her throat and smiled at her mentor. "I'm sure. Don't worry."

He stared at her a while longer, his brows pinched together, though he eventually sighed. "Anyway, I'm sure that's nothing you weren't already aware of, but I figured it'd be good to remind you."

"Of course." Estelle nodded. "Thank you for that."

The older Angel regarded her quietly, a faint look of worry marring his features. After a moment, he stood. "Well then, shall we get on with your training?"

"Actually," Estelle said, holding up the journal. "Can I read the first entry before we start?"

Antares smiled and nodded.

She opened the book and flipped through the beginning pages before reaching the desired content.

Entry I:

Alsphere and Ventiel were righteous Angels who were chosen to infiltrate Hell, a mission that took three hundred and fifty years to complete. But Alsphere betrayed God and attacked her companion hours before the mission's completion, inflicting a fatal wound that, in the end, killed Ventiel, but not before she made it back to Heaven to deliver the package and the salvation of God.

In honor of her sacrifice, the Apostles named the Blessing of God after her true name, 'Luminari,' someone who radiates light, and gave her the name of 'Solis,' the first Angel to be granted the name of a star.

Estelle knew the story well. The Faux-Fallen Angels were taught almost every other year in class. But the journal told it differently. She had been told that Alsphere had Fallen before Ventiel, and she had tricked the other into following soon after. And there was no mention of a 'package.' It was a mission to learn and gather information about Demons and Hell, compiling it mostly into level seven books and higher. There was no mention of their true names, nor was the Luminari named after Ventiel. It didn't make sense. Why would they leave out those details?

Estelle looked up from the journal and stared at Antares. "Why is this different from what is taught?"

He gave a tight smile. "It'll make sense in later entries," he said, then quickly changed the subject. "Do you need a moment to finish your tea?"

The girl picked up the cup of tea and downed the whole thing in one go before setting the cup down with an 'Ahh.'

"I'm ready."

37

The Truth

On her way back to the dorm buildings from Antares' house, Estelle opened the journal to the next entry, reading as she walked.

Entry 2:

The two Angels worked tirelessly to create two main components for the mission. The sallbokvie and velnero each took one hundred and fifty years to perfect. Anything less than ideal would have caused the situation to fail before it started.

During their research, they discovered many other applications of Angelic abilities that are still used centuries later. Even after the betrayal, the work they did for God and Heaven was imperative for the survival of future Angels and the later creation of Vostarists.

Estelle squinted, rereading the final line. The Vostarists have been a relatively new addition to the ranks, the first Angel achieving it only about three hundred years ago. But according to this, becoming a Vostarist isn't as simple as attaining more sets of wings.

She put the journal inside her bag when she approached the dormitories. Classmates talked among themselves in the shared space. A couple of them watched a movie Estelle hadn't seen before.

Someone must have gotten it during one of their missions, she thought, and headed for the stairs. But then froze when she overheard someone say her best friend's name.

"Oh yeah, Issac got back from the hospital a couple of hours ago," a boy said, absentmindedly.

"Did you see him?" a girl asked. "I heard he wasn't able to heal properly because of it."

Estelle didn't stay to hear the rest of the conversation, bounding up the stairs. Issac was released from the hospital after nearly five weeks of treatment. Despite her exhaustion, she headed straight for Issac's room, not bothering to drop off her things.

She knew the real reason why he was there for so long. As part of his punishment, they didn't perform any sacred healing on him to speed up the process. Everyone else should have known that as well, but knowing the truth doesn't mean there won't be rumors that sprout from it.

Estelle knocked on the door, a tight feeling in her chest betraying excitement and worry.

After a moment, Issac opened the door. Estelle did not attempt subtlety as she looked him up and down, studying his condition. For the most part, he looked alright—his arm was in a sling, and there was a gash on his forehead that had been sewn shut with stitches. But all in all, he looked much better than when she had seen him last.

It was a relief, though it probably shouldn't have been. There was a part of her, something small and quiet in the back of her mind, that worried Issac would have looked much worse, somehow. She didn't want to think about what that could mean.

"Oh, Estelle," he said. "Hello."

"It's good to see you, Issac." The girl smiled. "I've missed you."

Issac blinked and averted his eyes. "Do you want to come in?"

Estelle nodded and thanked him, walking into the room and setting her bag down in the corner. His room was a bit dark. He always kept the blinds shut, and only a couple of small lamps were scattered around the room, most of which were off. The only other light source came from the halos above their heads.

"Sorry it's so messy," the lilac-haired Angel said. "I haven't had a chance to clean yet."

Estelle laughed softly, taking a seat at his cluttered desk. "It's okay. It almost makes it cozier."

Issac smiled slightly and sat at the edge of his bed, sighing.

"So... how are you doing?"

"Hmm? Oh." Issac straightened a little. "Alright, I guess. My arm still hurts, but they say I should be more or less back to normal within a month."

Estelle chewed on her lip, the guilt stirring up inside her. "I'm sorry." She swallowed. "About everything."

For a long moment, Issac didn't speak. Then he exhaled, shoulders slumped a bit. "It's not your fault," he murmured, shaking his head. "I was in over my head. I should've realized it, but..." He looked down, eyes fixated on Estelle's bag in the corner. "I just wasn't thinking straight."

"I know you did it because you care about me."

Issac blinked. "Yes. But still, I shouldn't have followed you. I knew that even before then. But..." he hesitated, closing his eyes and sighing. "I'm not sure what would have happened to you if I hadn't."

Estelle was quiet, turning his words over in her mind as she debated how to respond. It didn't take long for her to decide, but gathering the nerve to speak was another thing. Still, he deserved to know the truth.

"I mean," she started, "if you want the truth, probably nothing."

Shockingly, Issac didn't seem surprised. He didn't even visibly react at all.

For a while, the room was barren of all forms of communication, the air still and lifeless.

Estelle thought back to what he had said to her in the hospital. *I saw the way you looked at him.*

"He went overboard," she finally said, speaking quietly, eyes down at her feet. "If it makes you feel any better, I yelled at him about it." She laughed awkwardly.

When she looked up, Issac was staring at her.

"Estelle..." he murmured.

She could feel the weight of all the words left unsaid. She nodded slowly.

"Zye—um, Zylis," she stammered, blushing slightly. She took a deep breath. "Zylis is sort of like... my partner. It was Antares' idea."

At that, Issac's eyebrows shot up. "Your *mentor?*"

"Yeah," she said, resisting the urge to play with her hair. "After I ran into him around five months ago, Antares suggested I work with him as a..." She squinted. "An extracurricular, of sorts?"

A look of disbelief was on her friend's face.

Giving in, Estelle grabbed a handful of strands and began twirling them around her fingers. "His rationale was that spending time around a Demon would make my application stand out by showing that I can resist temptation. Essentially."

Issac was sitting stock-still, looking at her with an incredulous expression. "That seems..." He looked off to the side, then back to Estelle. "Unlikely."

The raven-haired Angel frowned. "I'm telling the truth! Antares, really—"

"Not that." He shook his head. "I'm not doubting you're telling me the truth about what your mentor said. I'm just skeptical about whether he'd be correct."

Estelle looked down at the floor, smiling sadly. "Well, you'd be right to think so," she said. "Almost immediately after you were admitted, I found out my application had been denied, and Rūnnel was accepted."

Issac faltered, his mouth hanging open. "I'm sorry to hear that," he said, his tone soft. "I know you've been working very hard."

The girl nodded, swallowing around the dull ache of sadness within her. She was glad that he didn't comment about Giovanna's ascension. "It's alright. I'm sure I'll get there eventually."

Another stretch of silence fell between them before Issac spoke again. "That wasn't really what I meant, though," he said. "I mean... I don't know. I'm sure Antares knows best, but..."

Estelle looked up, brow furrowed. "What?"

"I feel like what you're doing would be more likely to get you in trouble."

Claiming the thought hadn't crossed her mind would be a lie. Her trust in Antares' judgment had always quelled her concerns in the end, but there were times when she would wonder. And the more she learned about Demons, the more she questioned it.

"I've thought about that before," Estelle confessed. "But I guess if they were going to punish me, they would've done it when they read the application."

Her friend blinked. "Did you read the application?"

"Well, no. Antares submitted it on my behalf." She cocked her head. "Why?"

Issac held eye contact for a while before looking away. "No reason, I guess."

Estelle never gave it much thought. Antares gave her no reason to suspect that he didn't add everything they had discussed on her application. If what Issac said is true—if the Apostles had known about her partnership with Zylis—there is a possibility they would be in a lot of trouble. Even more so than not getting ascended. She made a mental note to look into her application further.

"So," Estelle began, "what happened after I left that day?"

The Angel tensed, his fingers clenched around the bed sheets. "You mean...?"

Estelle nodded.

"I..." he squinted. "He asked me questions, I think. He wanted a physical description of the Demon. I described it—" he hesitated, "—*him*, I mean, as best I could, and then... I don't know. I think he just left."

Him. A small sensation of warmth bloomed somewhere in Estelle's chest, though more pressing emotions overshadowed it.

"You sound unsure," she commented.

"Well, I was pretty heavily sedated. At some point, I think I fell asleep. But it was after he left, I think." After a moment, he quietly tacked on, "It *must've* been."

Estelle stared at him, a dark feeling burgeoning within her. Issac spoke as though he were trying to convince himself as much as Estelle, if not more.

"Falling asleep before wouldn't have made sense," Issac muttered, fidgeting with his arm sling. "His presence alone woke me up the first time."

"Issac..." she trailed off.

He looked up, meeting her concerned gaze, only to look away quickly.

"Sorry. I'm fine, I just..." he sighed. "I don't know. Vostarists are strange." He grimaced. "They don't act like normal Angels, you know?" He laughed awkwardly—tried to, at least. It didn't work; he wasn't smiling. "The whole thing made me feel nauseous. I had a lot of weird dreams afterward."

Estelle frowned. "You had nightmares?"

Issac hesitated. "Not really? I don't feel like they were strongly good or bad, just weird," he said, wincing. "I can't directly remember anything about them, though." He went silent, then shrugged.

"I suppose it's possible it could have been a side effect of whatever sedatives they had you on," Estelle offered.

"Oh." His eyes got minutely wider. "I hadn't thought about it, but now that you mention it, yeah, that would make more sense." Issac's lips turned up slightly, and the tension in his body seemed to melt away.

"Well, I'm glad nothing too traumatic happened," she said, giggling softly. "I was terrified to leave you there alone. Part of me was worried that..." she trailed off, but the other Angel seemed to understand where she was going as he nodded and gazed down at the floor, a kind look on his face.

"I'm glad, as well," he said, looking back up to meet her eyes. "Thanks... you know, for being..." he shifted on the mattress. "Well, you know."

"Of course," Estelle replied with a bright smile. "That's what friends are for."

Before she understood what she was doing, Estelle got up from the seat and took a few short steps to Issac before wrapping her arms around his shoulders. Mindful of his arm, she squeezed lightly. Eventually, Issac returned the hug and wrapped his good arm around her waist.

"So," Issac started after a moment, "can you talk to me about things again?"

Estelle pursed her lips together. They pulled apart, and she took a seat next to him on the bed. "I would, but it could land you in a lot of trouble again."

"Embellish it then."

She blinked, baffled at the idea. "You want me to continue to lie to you?"

He shook his head. "No, not lying. Just don't tell me every detail."

Estelle stared at him, counting the different shades of green in his eyes as she thought it over. She supposed it wasn't a terrible idea. It would get her thoughts out in the open instead of festering inside her mind.

"But, Issac, I don't want you to get hurt again," she said. "Most of everything I've learn the past couple of months is only granted to the second sphere, or more likely, the third sphere."

Issac shrugged. "I know how to keep my mouth shut."

"But—"

"This is the only way I can help you," he cut in, grabbing one of her hands that had started braiding. "If you don't talk to anyone but the Demon, your head's going to explode."

Estelle let out a short laugh. Zylis was her only outlet as of late, ever since Antares had stopped seeing her on the regular. And since she couldn't talk to Issac, Zylis was her only option. She was going to tell her friend as much when he spoke first.

"You don't go to the surface every day."

She opened and closed her mouth several times before she hung her head in defeat. It was dangerous, and they both knew it, but regardless, he still insisted on knowing what was happening. Issac probably wouldn't know what she was talking about most of the time if she embellished the truth a little. However, the idea of talking to someone else about the matters at hand was relieving. But if she was being honest with herself, she missed him.

"Okay," Estelle said after a moment. "What do you somewhat want to know about first?"

"What do you want to talk about?" Issac replied.

There was too much, and a couple of subjects Estelle knew she didn't want to discuss with her best friend. But there is one thing she's been wanting to ask him for a while.

"How, in the Three Realms, did Giovanna ascend before either of us?"

Issac laughed, shaking his head slightly. "You're guess is as good as mine."

38
Celestial Dates

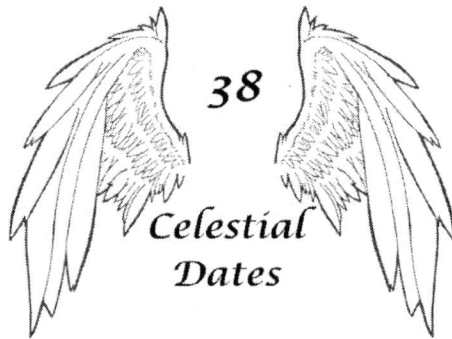

ESTELLE HAD A FEW THINGS weighing on her mind, each tugging at her in different ways. The first was a thought she'd rather not entertain. Still, it lingered at the back of her mind.

The second concern was her friend. Despite everything else, she couldn't help but focus on Issac's well-being. She knew how much he was behind in his classes and assignments and understood the struggle with keeping up on the demanding schedule.

And then there was her application. She started questioning what was written on her application—what had been said on her behalf. She knew Antares had filled out the paperwork for her and sent it in, but now she wondered if everything she'd wanted to say was truly reflected in those documents. Had Antares included all her intentions, or had he summarized her situation differently?

It seemed strange that none of the Apostles had questioned her about spending time with a Demon. No inquiries about how long she'd spent with him, what she'd discussed, or what she might have learned. It was as if her activities had been overlooked entirely, or perhaps deliberately ignored. But if they *knew*, if Estelle's interactions had been observed or recorded, then what did that mean? When all the books on the subject—beyond the prominent warnings—were classified as dangerous and meant for higher stations.

Did her application not explicitly state she was fraternizing with a Demon? And if her involvement with the Demon was hidden from her official record, what else might be concealed? Was it possible the records didn't reflect her true activities at all?

The implications chilled her. If her connection with Zylis was hidden from the official records, what else might be unspoken or overlooked? Perhaps her entire involvement was more secretive than she realized.

All these questions made her stomach tighten. Estelle understood that in a world governed by strict rules and veiled secrets, even the smallest omission could have serious consequences.

Estelle's thoughts swam with possibilities as she returned her things from the bag to their rightful place in her room. When she fished out the journal Antares had given her earlier that day, she pushed everything else aside mentally. The Angel sat down on her bed, slid an obsidian ring on each hand, and opened the journal up to the third entry.

It became apparent that not all segments were as if reading from a textbook, even if the story was different. Letters, or notes, written by one of the famous Angels with celestial dates, caught Estelle's attention, compelling her to reread them.

Entry 3: 3941.15.3.259

The task at hand is anything but simple. The experiments have been going smoothly, but we have yet to produce the result we were hoping for. If we can't communicate, the mission will fail before it even starts.

There are many risks, but we believe the final steps to making the sallbokvie are within reach. It must be something more than a blessed object to transcend both realms without being detected. The only question is, how can that be made possible?

The velnero seems to be more challenging to get correct. We might need to start over with our objective. There must be a way for it to work continually without any side effects, but dealing with laniesthole seems more complicated than the initial hypothesis.

Estelle recalled Zylis telling her about them—how they had made the sallvie—but she couldn't shake the question that kept nagging at her: what exactly was a 'velnero'? They didn't describe what it was or how it functioned. Granted, the note didn't go into much detail about the book either, but she knew enough about that particular object to piece together some facts.

From what she understood, the velnero was made from laniesthole—an incredibly deadly metal from hell that was infamous for its lethal properties. It could cause side effects that made Angels act more like Demons simply through contact.

Antares had told her about it before, describing it as a standard weapon used by Greed Demons against Angels. A weapon that poisons upon contact, capable of killing just by embedding it beneath the skin and letting its effects take hold. But if that was the case—if it could kill with just a scratch—why would an Angel make something with it? Why create something supposedly harmless but that has the potential to backfire and kill its wielder?

Estelle wished the entry had provided more details about the process, so, wanting to learn more, she tried to turn the page. But just as Antares had warned, it was stuck to the others, preventing her from reading more.

Well, he was right about my curiosity, Estelle thought as she turned back to the inside cover to look at the schedule. The first three entries she had read in a single day, their words flooding her mind, leaving her both exhilarated and overwhelmed. But the fourth entry was different— it was set to unlock four days later, a pause that felt agonizingly long and almost cruel, like waiting for a storm to break. Then, just four days after that, the fifth entry would be unlocked.

At closer inspection, she noticed something peculiar: the intervals between each entry weren't always consistent. Some openings seemed to happen with a predictable rhythm—every four days, every five days— yet others appeared with only a day or two in between. A few entries even arrived back-to-back.

The Angel wasn't sure what these irregular gaps meant. Was it a pattern, or simply a quirk of the mysterious process? Did the timing hold some hidden significance? The uncertainty gnawed at her, and her heart fluttered with a mixture of anticipation and trepidation. She was anxious to uncover what lay behind each new message, eager to piece together the puzzle, but also wary of what she might find lurking in the gaps of time. Whatever the reason behind the timing, she knew that these moments of waiting were as crucial as the entries themselves— each one bringing her closer to truths she might not be ready to face.

Entry 4: 4090.14.12.108

The side effects are manageable—headache and stomach pains with the need to eat. From our most recent observation of Demons, they still eat foods that humans provide, so it may be beneficial to act more like them, even if we must repent.

Operation 'Holy Devil' starts in three days. Goal: find and report back with information about the Demons—most importantly, a weakness.

As Estelle's gaze drifted across the delicate script, a shiver of realization prickled her spine. Her eyes paused on a faint, almost familiar phrase—one she'd heard on several occasions: "Holy Devil." The words were inscribed with a reverence that seemed out of place for such a vulgar exclamation, yet there was an unmistakable undertone of defiance. Her brow furrowed as she recalled the countless times Zylis had spat the phrase with disdain. 'Holy devil' wasn't just a curse. It was a reference—an ironic, provocative nod—to something far more clandestine.

But Estelle couldn't dwell on that for long. Her thoughts kept drifting back to the mounting pressure of her upcoming exams. The class assignments, already challenging, were now escalating in difficulty. She knew she'd have to explain that to her partner soon.

I'm scheduled for Friday.

Is that the only day?

Yeah, sorry. There's a test coming up, so they cut back my Earth visits.

Why would they do that? Isn't it your 'duty' to save the people you're killing?

Hellfire is doing most of the damage. Besides that, if we want to do better with our duty, we need to be tested on it.

That doesn't mean they should pull you away from it all.

39

Hell's Ideals

Estelle prepared to depart for the surface on Friday morning, but not without reading from the journal before she left.

> Entry 5: 4095.2.5.113
>
> Commander,
>
> We write to inform you that the Sinners have not been punished.
>
> It is quite bizarre, the 'society' these creatures have formed. When asked why they insist on subverting God's will, the Demons told us that His will 'serves no purpose.'
>
> Further investigation will be required, but the Apostles should be prepared to intervene in the near future.
>
> Regards,
>
> SA & LV

Estelle could accurately guess who was signing the message, though the initials were off from what she had gathered. 'LV' belonged to Luminari Ventiel, which makes the other Alsphere, but thus far, there had been no mention of her real name. Though now she knew it started with an 'S.'

This must be an excerpt from the original sallbokvie, she gathered, rereading the entry. *Why would Antares have this to begin with?*

'The sinners have not been punished.'

What exactly does that mean?

※　　※　　※

"Exactly what it sounds like, Princess." Zylis was leaning over the altar, his hands hovering above a small goblet filled with holy water. His brows were pinched together as he concentrated on heating it gradually, and a triumphant grin spread across his face when the water started to boil over.

Like most sacrilege, Zylis idly took part in, Estelle ignored it, if only to avoid getting sidctrackcd.

"So, you just have sinners wandering around unchecked?" she asked.

"Depends on what you mean by 'sinner.'" He rounded the altar, the goblet of steaming holy water forgotten as he hopped off the platform. "Most people in Hell didn't do anything bad while alive. The majority don't believe in God or didn't believe in the right God."

Estelle resisted the urge to point out that not believing in God was, in fact, a bad thing, at least by her standards. She sighed, pinching the bridge of her nose. "Okay, but what about the ones who did other bad things? You're telling me you just let them do whatever they want?"

Zylis scowled. "Never said that," he scoffed. "Star, I don't know if you realize this, but this is not an either-or situation. There are ways to handle this stuff that don't involve eternal concave torment."

At that, Estelle looked up. "Oh...?" she said, and after a second, followed, "Well, like what?"

Zylis shrugged. "It's a case-by-case sort of thing. A lot of human violence is pretty much just a byproduct of people's material conditions, which are, obviously, completely different in Hell." He paused, stretching his arms above his head, yawning. "Most of them don't end up being a real threat."

"So, you just don't punish those people? Like, at all?"

"Why would we?" Zylis asked, deadpan. "What purpose would that serve?"

Instead of responding, Estelle just stared at him, her mouth gaping.

Zylis groaned. "Star, y'know, punishment isn't the voiding end-all-be-all deal with stuff like this, right?" He raised an eyebrow. "I think we must be doing *something* right, given that Hell doesn't have much of a problem with antisocial behavior or whatever."

Estelle scoffed. "I find that very hard to believe."

"Oh, I'm sure you do," he snorted. "But fortunately, reality is not contingent on whether or not it fits into your worldview."

The Demon shoved his hands inside his pockets and strolled down the aisle, heading toward the chapel's front door. His tail wrapped around the handle and pulled it open slightly, allowing a slice of light to leak in.

"You coming?"

Estelle nodded and hurried over to him, shutting the door behind them.

As they walked side by side, Zylis spoke up again. "It's honestly not that weird if you think about it," he said, squinting at the sky. "Societies with weird conditions have to evolve to accommodate weird needs. Otherwise, they'll fall apart." He shrugged. "Hell gets a lot of violent people, at least compared to Heaven, which means we had two choices, we either—" he held up a finger, "—one, come to terms with the idea of having a permanently massive carceral class, or two—" he raised a second finger, "—figure out how to integrate those people into society. The second one aligned with the ideals we work toward."

"*Ideals?*" Estelle arched an eyebrow. "What ideals are those?"

Her companion hummed, pursing his lips. "I guess the simplest way I can think to put it is..." he trailed off momentarily. "Well, Hell, at least as it currently exists, was designed to function sort of like a scaled-up version of the way people already interact." After a second, he added, "Without the influence of any outside power, institutions, or whatever."

"What do you mean?"

"Remember how I told you that Lucifer is just another guy who just so happens to live in Hell?" The Angel nodded. "Well, that's just it. No one has power over anyone. They could be stronger, smarter, sexier beyond belief—" Estelle rolled her eyes, "—but they don't hold any more true authority than the new guy who showed up the day before. Everyone is equal." They turned a corner and made their way down a side road. "Sure, some people will be the *best* at something, but we don't hold them up on a pedestal so high that it makes them unattainable. They're ethereal beings, just as much as you or me."

Estelle nodded quietly before sighing and coming to a complete stop. "What's your point?"

"It's pretty straightforward; Hell is unlike Heaven," Zylis said, shrugging, "where whoever has the most power in whatever arbitrary metric system you have takes control of everything, and anyone who steps out of line is hauled down to the basement at gunpoint, where they will be waterboarded for an indeterminate amount of time."

Estelle cringed. "You didn't have to be that detailed."

"Yeah, but I wanted to be," he said, grinning.

Estelle rolled her eyes again, prompting Zylis to laugh. As it petered out, Zylis moved to walk beside her again. The Angel peered ahead, spotting the steeple of the next church on her list. For a moment, neither of them spoke.

"So," Estelle murmured, breaking the silence, "what about serious cases?" she asked, daring to look at him. "If they don't believe in your ideals or want to cause trouble?"

Zylis gazed at her and sighed. "Most of the time, people just go through a concave amount of therapy until they're ready to be integrated into society. But in *extreme* cases..." he hesitated for a moment as if searching for the words. When he spoke again, his tone shifted into reverence. "We call it 'Outer Darkness,' where they're sent to relive their worst regrets and sins while they were alive, on repeat."

Estelle couldn't help the slight intake of breath as she involuntarily imagined the experience.

"That's horrible," she said quietly, her wings curling around her body slightly. "Doesn't that mean you do punish them?"

He made a face. "Eh, not exactly. I mean, we put them in there, but they're the ones who essentially choose which memories to relive," he explained, raking a hand through blonde hair. "The door is always open. They can leave at any point, but usually, we have to stop the simulation to get them into therapy at different intervals. But if they're not ready, they go back in."

"You force them back into their worst nightmare?" the Angel said, louder than she had intended. "Who decides when they come out? And why—"

"Would you shut up and let me explain?" Zylis said, sighing loudly. "Holy devil."

For whatever reason, Estelle's eyes lit up at the usage of the swear word.

He rolled his eyes. "We force them in the first time, but they choose to go back every time after that. It's their choice whether or not to leave Outer Darkness. We make them feel worthy enough to do so."

Estelle frowned, looking up at him. "What if they can't change?"

Zylis exhaled quietly, shielding his eyes as he peered at the sky, where the sun peeked out behind the clouds.

"You know, humans have it pretty rough," he murmured. "When you're human, depending on how voided up you are, the time it takes to get better could be longer than you've got left to live." His lips quirked up a bit. "But I've been dead for two hundred years, and I'm sure as void not the same person I was when I died," he said and chuckled. "That's the great thing about eternity, Star. *Everyone* can change." Zylis rested his hands behind his head, interlocking his fingers. "Might take a thousand years, but immortality means you have all the time in the world to save yourself."

Estelle's breath caught as she stared up at him, taking in the softness of his expression. A few seconds later, she began to laugh.

Zylis blinked, glancing down at her. "What?"

"I don't know. It's just funny," Estelle said, smiling. They were approaching the front entrance of the last chapel. "You're framing a direct contradiction of God's wishes in a way that makes it sound... weirdly Christ-like."

Zylis shot her a look with raised eyebrows, then turned to look straight ahead and said, with absolutely no intonation, "We've also got this massive stadium called the Penjara where people can go to watch or participate in massive orgies twenty-four hours a day."

"What?"

"Yep. It's sort of a relic of the past, but it's still in use."

"Zye."

"Also, I live across the street from a sex dungeon. We've got a lot of those—really convenient—it's where I got those gloves. And oh man, Star, you would not *believe* the kinda *sounds* I've heard comin' outta that place. I could go on about it for concave—"

"Zylis!"

They visited all of Estelle's assigned churches and escorted the people within to their respective afterlives. There were more people than usual, and though most of them took the Angel's hand to go to Heaven, there were a few whom Zylis warned her about before offering her hand.

Later that day, Zylis led her to an abandoned workout studio. Estelle was lying on her back, wings spread out to either side, fingertips pressed against the mat. Zylis knelt at her side and held her right leg up at a ninety-degree angle, one hand wrapped around her ankle, the other resting on her thigh as he counted aloud, slowly pushing her leg back further. Once he counted to sixty, he switched to doing the same to her other leg.

"Twenty-one, twenty-two—keep your hips down—" he snapped as he proceeded to shove Estelle's hip back down against the mat with one hand before returning it to her thigh.

Estelle winced slightly before recollecting her breath and trying to release the tension in her muscles.

They had sparred earlier, but when it was all said and done, Zylis deemed her not flexible enough. Nothing too extreme had happened since the first time they had sparred, but it was always a bit tense, and Zylis seemed to have an affinity for pinning Estelle down in compromising positions, though Estelle might have read a bit too much into it.

Zylis' face hovered above her, red eyes glowing in the dim training room, soft lips forming around the syllables of numbers as he counted up to sixty. His latex-clad fingers shifted slightly as he eased her leg a little higher. Estelle straightened her head, fixing her gaze on the ceiling, her cheeks dusted red.

Fortunately, exertion was a decent enough excuse for that. But that was the least of her worries.

40
Falling Feathers

ESTELLE'S MIND WAS FOGGY FROM her time with Zylis, and she wasn't paying attention to her surroundings. As she approached the platform, she noticed an unfamiliar scuff mark on her skirt, and in her distraction, she wound up bumping right into someone's back.

"Oh my goodness, I'm so—" Estelle stopped, cutting herself off with a gasp. The sensation hit her like a ton of bricks, even before the stranger turned around. The Angel stumbled back a few feet, breaking out into a cold sweat as she registered the telltale pressure that seemed to weigh down the air itself.

The Vostarist turned around, a frown affixed to her face, and despite the presence of the typical scarlet blindfold, Estelle could feel the blunt force of the Vostarist's gaze on her. She felt like she was choking on her tongue.

"I-I'm—" she stammered, her voice two octaves higher. "I'm so sorry, ma'am. I was—wasn't looking where I was going. I'm sorry. I'm *really* sorry." She looked away as a jagged chill ran down her spine, with the eyes of the intimidating figure staring into her.

Estelle shuffled uncomfortably beneath her gaze, and it didn't stop for several seconds until the sound of someone shouting dragged her attention away.

Estelle looked up, and despite the darkness that lined the edges of her vision, her brain managed to make sense of the information. A gurney was being rushed down the breezeway. On its own, that would not have been particularly unusual; Angels got injured on the battlefield all the time. What set it apart was the brief flash of pure white hair showing for just seconds between the bodies and limbs of the surrounding medics.

In that instant, the spell was broken, and Estelle gasped, craning her neck to try and see over them.

She looked at the Vostarist, hands shaking. "E-excuse me, ma'am. That's my friend over there. I should..." Estelle hesitated but then shook her head. "Sorry!" she yelped and bolted toward the hospital platform, following the medics as they lifted the gurney over the lip.

"Who are you?" one of them snapped.

"I'm sorry!" She waved her hands. "She's my friend!"

The medic looked her up and down and then sighed. "Well, fine. But stay out of our way, okay?"

Estelle nodded quickly. "Of course!"

She boarded the shuttle after them and stood back on her tiptoes, trying to see over their shoulders without disrupting them. All she could see were scraps of bruised flesh and bandages. Estelle clenched her jaw and attempted to calm her breathing, but it was futile.

Upon arrival, they wheeled Lilith inside, Estelle trailing behind her. One of the medics shouted something too technical for her to grasp, but it made the on-duty nurses spring into action. The double doors of the emergency wing parted as they wheeled Lilith through, shutting heavily behind them.

And then she was alone.

The wait was well over four hours. During that time, Estelle would occasionally get up and pace around, maybe get a cup of water. But that was all she could do.

She contemplated returning to the dormitories and telling Issac—maybe even trying to contact Giovanna, too—but she didn't know the extent of Lilith's injuries. It wouldn't do them any good if she caused them to panic, like what she was doing now. It was also only a matter of time. Estelle didn't want to leave if there was a window of opportunity to see her friend. In reality, she would have had plenty of time to tell them.

The young Angel nearly jumped out of her skin at the sharp sound of a door handle turning, hinges creaking as a nurse emerged, with a clipboard in her hands and bags under her eyes.

"You're here for Lilith Audelaire?"

Estelle immediately stood, nodding.

"Well, she's stable. You're welcome to come and see her now if you'd like, but she probably won't be conscious."

"That's okay. Thank you." With that, Estelle followed her down the hall.

When they reached the room, the nurse opened the door for her, and Estelle thanked her once more before stepping inside. The door shut behind her, and Estelle gulped at what she saw.

Lilith was lying unconscious in bed, with her injuries much worse than before. Bandages covered her neck and arms, with patches of her wings wrapped tightly, red seeping through.

Estelle sat in the chair at the bedside and tried to calm her heart rate. But she couldn't help the tears that slipped free from her eyes. Then, as if on cue, the older Angel began to stir, her eyelids twitching until they fluttered open. Estelle held her breath. She remained still, quietly waiting for her friend to say something, but for a long while, Lilith just lay there, staring up at the ceiling.

Eventually, Estelle opened her mouth to speak, but Lilith beat her to it. "Estelle," she said, her gaze fixated on the ceiling.

Estelle felt something cold settle in the pit of her stomach, sending shivers down her spine. Her pulse quickened, a shot of adrenaline charging through her veins. She wasn't sure why, though. It wasn't a dire situation. It was just Lilith.

Estelle leaned in closer, swallowing despite the tightness in her throat. "Lilith, you're awake!" After a moment, she added, "Should I get the—?"

"No."

Estelle froze, her mouth still open. She blinked several times, trying to reset herself and correct the surly, misplaced feeling lurking within her. It didn't work.

"I... Why not?"

After a pause, Lilith moved to sit up. It was a difficult task, given her injuries, but she managed it eventually. She settled down with a sigh, still not looking at the other.

"They'll just put me to sleep again," she muttered.

Estelle frowned. *What's that supposed to mean?* Lilith's heart monitor was beeping at a steady, resting pace. She felt a cold bead of sweat roll down the back of her neck, a metallic taste polluting her mouth. *Something's wrong.*

"Well, if you need the rest, then maybe I should—"

Her head snapped toward Estelle. "No," Lilith spat, a wild look in her violet eyes. "I'm *fine*."

For several seconds, Estelle stared back into her eyes, paralyzed. Then she looked down at the ground, nodding quietly. Her hands started shaking in her lap. The room was cold. Bleach white. Sterile. Like they were the only living things that had ever been there.

"What happened?" Estelle finally asked. "What's going on?"

Lilith sighed, her gaze empty as she looked herself over. She glanced over her shoulder at the bandages around her wings and picked at them, just a little at first. But as she proceeded to grab the edge of one bandage and pull, all Estelle could do was watch, frozen in shock. Her mouth fell open, but she did not speak.

The older Angel began to unravel the bandages around her wings, occasionally wincing as she worked; gradually, what remained of her patchy wings became visible. With one sharp yank, she revealed a piece where a large chunk of feathers was missing, and Estelle finally found the nerve to speak up.

"I don't think you should be doing that—"

"It doesn't matter," Lilith interjected calmly. "Don't worry. It doesn't matter, anyway."

Estelle gripped the arms of the chair. "Lilith, I..." she hesitated. "I think I should get the—"

"No," the girl snapped, halting her movements to look at her with a stern glare that melted away a second later. "Please, Estelle."

Estelle's throat felt tight. She opened and closed her mouth a few times. "W-well, at least tell me why you're doing that."

Lilith looked away, exhaling, and moved on to her other wing. "It hurts," she mumbled. "They put the bandages on too tight." It sounded like a lie, but Estelle wasn't prepared to fight her on it.

The situation felt volatile in ways Estelle couldn't fully understand. So, she just sat there and watched uneasily as her friend continued to strip the bindings off her wings. The silence was filled with the sound of adhesive bandages being ripped away. Eventually, both wings were completely free of them.

Lilith rolled her shoulders and stretched her wings with a slight grimace.

Estelle bit the inside of her cheek as she took in the mangled state of them.

A decent number of feathers were missing from both—more than enough to impede flight—and there were a few places where the skin beneath was visible. Raw and still a bit bloody, like the feathers there had been ripped out.

Unconsciously, Estelle tucked her wings closer to her body.

After resting for a moment, Lilith moved onto her arms, beginning to work on the badges there as well. Estelle noticed that, as time went on, Lilith's movements became harsher and frantic. She was clenching her jaw, her facial muscles tight. Each bandage she tore away revealed more skin, showing the extent of the corruption damage she had sustained. For far too long, Estelle just sat there, paralyzed, her heart in her throat.

She stared at the black static scars that covered her arms, barely an inch of flesh left unmarred. "L-Lilith—"

"I figured it out, Estelle," she said, her tone void of affect.

Estelle's breath caught. "What?"

"I figured out what he wants," she paused, then her lips pulled up into a tight, cynical smile. "Or maybe it's more appropriate to say I *remembered*."

A chill shot down Estelle's spine. "What..." she hesitated, not wanting to ask. "What do you mean, exactly?"

Her friend's movements slowed, and she gradually came to a stop, allowing the last of the bandages to hang loosely off her upper arm. Lilith stared down at the hospital bed, her expression unreadable—more accurately, it was inconsistent.

As Estelle studied her, Lilith's sad expression remained constant, but the undertone seemed to shift. One moment, she looked grief-stricken; the next, she appeared almost nostalgic.

Estelle wasn't sure how much time had passed before a small, hoarse voice broke the silence. "We knew each other."

The raven-haired Angel tensed. "Sorry?"

Lilith swallowed audibly. "We knew each other, Estelle," she whispered, a faraway look in her eyes. "When we were alive, when we..." she paused. "When we were human."

Estelle gawked at her for a while, cold, shaking hands covering her mouth. "You're sure?"

Lilith nodded slowly. "I am," she murmured. "I remember, Estelle. I remember..." Her eyes grew a bit wider as she stared into space, gripping the thin hospital sheet between her injured fingers. "*Everything*," she finished.

Then, with a sharp intake of breath through her teeth, she ripped the rest of the bandage off, and with it, the temperature in the room dropped.

Estelle clasped her hands together and tried to make them stop shaking. Slowly, she began to register the shine in Lilith's eyes as she began to tear up, and wished, more than anything else, that she could have done something for her. That there was something she could say to Lilith at that moment that could have eased the pain of whatever unknown hell raged inside her mind. But there was nothing. Estelle was powerless.

Lilith slowly turned her head toward Estelle, her jaw tight and eyes unfocused. "It's all a lie, Estelle," she said, voice cracking as a tear slipped down her cheek. "Everything we've been taught. Every *unholy* thing."

The young Angel could hear threads popping as the older gripped and pulled at the sheets.

A single feather fell from Lilith's right wing.

41

A Just World

ESTELLE WATCHED THE WHITE FEATHER drift elegantly down, but her heart hit the floor first. It was a tiny event in the grand scheme of things, but at that moment, the implications were all-encompassing. Suffocating.

Estelle's chest clenched, a hollow ache spreading through her like a fist tightening around her heart. It wasn't the breathlessness that overwhelmed her, but a crushing weight—an unrelenting pressure that made her feel as if her ribs were collapsing inward.

Her pulse pounded in her ears as she stood up, the legs of the chair squealing as it slid back. She looked at Lilith, her vision darkening at the edges. "Lilith, you need to calm—"

"Lock the door."

"What?"

Estelle faltered. They could both get in serious trouble for even touching the lock. The locks were only to be used by the Vostarists to interrogate injured Angels without being interrupted by hospital staff, or otherwise.

"Lock the door," she repeated, teeth gritted, eyes hidden behind her bangs.

"Lilith, I can't just—"

"Lock the voiding door, Estelle!" Her head snapped up. Estelle saw the tail-end of her rage before her expression morphed into something far more desperate. "Please," she said, voice cracking. "*Please.*"

Estelle couldn't breathe. "Okay," she barely managed to say.

She stumbled over to the door, her joints locking, and turned the deadbolt, noticing a slight wobble. She ambled over to Lilith again just as another feather fell.

Estelle felt her throat close up, a painful knot that constricted her words and made each breath feel impossible. As if unseen hands were gripping her windpipe, but Lilith seemed less overtly panicked. Estelle sat back down and waited. It was all she could do. Just exist beside her.

Lilith closed her eyes, and more tears slipped free. "Your application was rejected, yes?" she said, voice hoarse.

There was a dull twinge of pain, but her mind was too far away for her to have truly felt it. "It... I was, yes."

"Well, you'll be relieved to know it had nothing to do with your abilities." The white-haired Angel forcefully wiped the tears from her cheeks. "Just like my acceptance had nothing to do with mine."

Estelle's brow furrowed. "What are you talking about? Lilith, you're very talent—"

"It doesn't matter!"

Another feather fell out.

"It doesn't *matter*, Estelle. It never mattered. All of this—" She started to gesture but seemed to give up partway through, her arms falling limply into her lap. She shook her head. "There are only two types of

Angels who ascend. Those willing to sell out their friends, and those with connections in high places."

After a moment of shock, Estelle pushed back. "Lilith, I don't think that's—"

"It's my voiding *father*, Estelle!" She ripped the IV needle out of her arm in a way that made the other cringe. "My void of a *father* is a level nine Angel. He's next in line to become a Vostarist. He's the *real* reason I ascended."

"How could you possibly know that's the reason?"

"I just *know*," she spat.

Another feather fell. *That makes four.*

"That's the secret to ascending. You either know someone important or prove yourself to be so mindlessly loyal that you'll keep all the Apostles' horrible secrets. And... and the Demon..."

A feather slipped free, and another followed a couple of seconds later. *It's getting faster,* Estelle realized with a wave of nausea.

"Lilith, please, you have to calm down!"

"He saved my life, Estelle," she said. "When I was human. That's how we met when I was about to..."

Another feather fell. Estelle's head was swimming.

"A-and now he's..." Her voice broke as she keeled over in the bed, tears staining the hospital sheets. "It doesn't make sense!"

Estelle's chest felt painfully tight. "P-please, Lilith. *Please*, we—we can figure this out, we can—"

"I *loved* him!" she shouted. Her voice was mangled, so far from anything she had heard from Lilith before. And it shattered the veil of isolation they had enjoyed up to that moment.

There was a knock on the door, followed by a muffled voice. "Miss, are you alright?"

Estelle's blood ran cold, but Lilith seemed unfazed, as though she hadn't even noticed. She sat there, tears slipping down her stained cheeks, shoulders shaking. Estelle heard the door handle jiggle, followed by more muffled voices outside.

Her heart hammered violently in her chest, each beat echoing the growing panic that had never before touched her as an Angel. The crushing weight settled deep, as if her very wings were being torn from her back, leaving her hollow and vulnerable. A suffocating panic gripped her, tight and relentless—something raw and primal that Estelle had never known in her life as an Angel. It strangled her voice, making it impossible to cry out.

Lilith harshly wiped her cheeks with her palms and wiped her nose on the hospital gown sleeve. By then, the feathers were falling steadily. Lilith's wings were mostly bare; less than half of her feathers remained.

"He was better than me," Lilith whispered. "But he went to Hell. I went to Heaven. My voiding *father* went to Heaven, but he went to *Hell*." Her lips were tight, her brow furrowed. "I *don't* get it. In what reality does that make sense?"

Feathers cascaded like snow onto the cold hospital floor. Estelle opened and closed her mouth like a fish out of water. What could she possibly tell her? What could she say that would make any of it better?

"I just... What the void are we even doing? What am I doing?" she said, shaky hands gravitating toward her head to grip the roots of her hair. "What am I even fighting for? This isn't justice!" she shouted. "If someone like my monster of a father can get into Heaven, but he *can't*—what—?"

348

The last feather fell, leaving her wings naked, trembling with her sobs.

The banging on the door became more insistent.

Estelle raised a shaky hand, reaching out toward her. But then, all the feathers on the floor abruptly turned black. Seconds later, they all burst into flames, burning rapidly, leaving only ash behind. Estelle looked up at Lilith and noticed that two bumps were beginning to appear on her head, growing until they emerged through her hair.

Horns. No... This isn't happening.

The girl's hands, cradling her face, grew longer, the skin becoming darker as her nails morphed into something resembling claws. As her naked wings began to shrink, the horns on the sides of her head started to twist. Finalizing their form, it tore through the halo until it dissipated, shattering like a prism. Lilith's shoulders continued to shake as she cried, though her voice began to sound distorted.

No, God—please, Estelle prayed.

The banging on the door became louder.

"Lilith!"

In a last-ditch effort to put a stop to it all, Estelle clambered onto the bed, tears streaming down her face as she desperately called out her name. Her hands were on Lilith's knees, her fingers digging in as she cried frantic, hollow words of placation, garbled promises, and reassuring lies that likely didn't make sense. It was all she had left.

And it wasn't enough.

Suddenly, two large, black, feathered wings shot out from her back, curling protectively around her body, casting them both in relative darkness. Estelle could hear the sound of the wooden door creaking and people screaming in the hall. And then, Lilith lifted her head. She looked at Estelle. Her violet eyes were glowing, highlighting the red, puffy skin around them.

"Lilith," Estelle sobbed.

Begging.

Pleading for a lost cause.

Lilith just gazed at her, quiet despair etched into her features as though she had already accepted it and had already given up.

"*Lilith!*" Estelle cried, grabbing her shoulders and shaking her.

She shook her head as she looked mournfully into Estelle's eyes. Then, Lilith whispered, "What just God would allow this to happen?"

The mattress began to dip inward, forcing Estelle to scramble away as it caved in. She stumbled back, tripping over her own feet and falling. The tile beneath the bed creaked and cracked seconds before it crumbled, and the space collapsed inward, taking Lilith with it.

And then it was over. She was gone.

"No," Estelle whispered. "No, please."

The door burst open, and several doctors and nurses piled in. "What's going—!" one shouted, but they all froze as they witnessed the scene before them.

The gaping chasm in the floor remained briefly before it began to reverse itself, the bed returning as the tiles flew back into place, solidifying. Everything was as it was before.

Except Lilith was no longer there.

"Oh... oh my—" one of the nurses whispered, placing her hands over her mouth. Estelle was still slumped on the floor, sobbing. The nurse turned toward the girl, a look of concern on her face. "Hey, are you—"

The nurse addressing her set her off. Estelle tensed, shook her head, and bolted. She rushed past them into the hallway, hastily wiping her tears away. They just kept coming.

She needed to get out. She needed to be somewhere she could scream.

It was nearing midnight as Estelle burst out beneath a starry sky. She looked around anxiously, searching for a place to hide, but the hospital exterior was far too sparse. She didn't think too much about it when she ducked back into a vacant hospital shuttle and sat down in the darkest corner before reaching into her bag and grabbing the spine of a familiar book.

Can you meet me on the surface?

It took Zylis a minute to respond.

What? Star, I'm at home right now. I'm about to go to BED. Please. I'm sorry. PLEASE.
What's wrong?

There was a sharp, mechanical sound as the hospital shuttle began to move. Estelle's fist clenched around the pen, teardrops falling onto the page. She wrote her reply: *I just watched my friend Fall*

More tears fell, staining the parchment. She wondered if Zylis would receive those, too. She figured he must have because no sooner after the sallvie breathed to life did she see his response appear.

I'm on my way.

42

What If

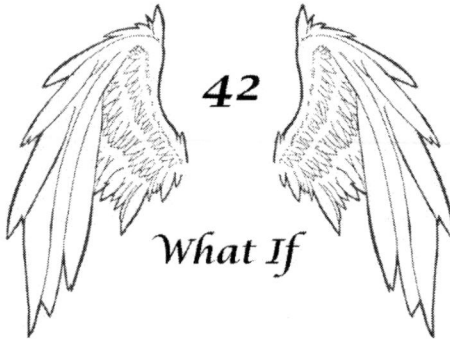

ZYLIS STOOD BESIDE AN OLD, dried-up fountain at the center of what used to be a vibrant city, and based on the way he was dressed, Estelle could tell he meant it when he said he was about to go to bed. He was wearing a simple, gray hoodie and what looked to be a pair of black pajama pants, haphazardly stuffed into the tops of his boots. His hair even had a disheveled appearance beyond his usual ruffled look.

As Estelle approached, Zylis turned, his posture straightening, and his tail swayed gently behind him. He looked her up and down, and Estelle could tell from his expression that she looked like a mess.

"Star," he murmured.

For whatever reason that set her off, the tears began welling up again as the tightness in her throat mounted. Estelle sniffled, eyes downcast as her wings began to wilt. Zylis closed the distance, removing his hands from his pockets.

In the face of her distress, she still felt the passing shadow of something warm when she noted that, despite his chaotic state of dress, he still remembered to wear gloves.

Zylis wrapped his arm and tail around her as her sniffles devolved into sobs, tears soaking into his hoodie. Estelle's shoulders shook, and Zylis' gloved hands patted and rubbed her back with a gentleness she had seldom seen in him before. They stayed that way for a while until Estelle's cries began to wane, and she started to pull back.

"What happened?" he quietly asked.

Estelle wiped her eyes on her sleeve. She took deep breaths until she could get herself under control. It took a few tries before she could explain the event entirely, and all the while, the Demon kept his hands on her shoulders, gently soothing up and down her arms.

When she finally got through the whole story, Zylis exhaled softly. "What's her name?"

"Lilith." Estelle swallowed. "Lilith Audelaire."

The hands on her arms went still. "Wait, you're serious?"

Estelle frowned. "Yeah?" she said. "Why?"

"Cyrus has been moaning about that girl for *months*, Star."

She blinked a few times, brows pinched together. "*Traten?*"

Zylis nodded. "He's been moping around *constantly*, crying about how the 'love of his life' doesn't remember him. He's been voiding insufferable." He grinned. "I guess he'll be happy to hear about this."

Estelle felt a spark of anger inside her and clenched her jaw. "Well, that makes one of us."

Zylis looked back at her again, and his smile disappeared. He opened his mouth but hesitated as though he were trying to choose his words very carefully. After a moment, he sighed, taking Estelle's hand and coaxing her to sit beside him on the fountain's ledge.

"Listen, Star," he began. "I know what you just experienced was pretty ~~concave~~ upsetting, but it's not like she's dead; she's just..." He shrugged. "In a different place. She's safe, if that's what you're worried about."

"But how do you *know*?" Then, a horrible thought entered her mind. "What if she's sent into Outer Darkness?"

"That's not possible," he said quickly. "In all of our history, only one Angel has *decided* to go there. All the others, well, Hell has a system for dealing with Fallen Angels," he replied. "People don't just spawn randomly in Hell. Not anymore, at least. When an Angel Falls from Heaven, they can end up in a few places, but they're all well-equipped to handle them."

"What do you mean, though?" Estelle asked. "*Handle them.*"

"It depends on the person," he said. "Therapy, usually. But overall, it's mostly just a place for support and re-education."

The Angel tensed. "Re-*what*?"

Zylis gave her an odd look. "Re-education?"

"So, you're brainwashing her?"

"What? No." He glared, hand tightening around Estelle's. "It's deprogramming, Star. Literally the *opposite* of brainwashing. You're kinda in the middle of the process since I started answering your never-ending questions."

Estelle maintained her scowl.

"Star, I know this might be difficult for you to comprehend, but Fallen Angels are kind of a concave disaster when they first arrive," he deadpanned. "We used not to do anything, but after a certain number of attempted coups, we realized we kinda had to."

"Coups?"

"If they can even be called that." He scoffed. Estelle frowned, and Zylis sighed. "See, the thing about Hell is..." he squinted and gestured vaguely.

"Well, how things are set up in Hell doesn't leave room for individuals to gain the upper hand over the rest of us. I died after the system was already in place. Still, according to our records, most of those 'coups' were just self-righteous Hell-bells standing on rooftops and loudly declaring themselves god-emperor, as though people were supposed to care, or something?"

"Why's that an issue?" she asked, tilting her head slightly. "How you're describing it just makes it seem like a minor annoyance."

"It wasn't an issue, but it could have become one," he said. "Star, this mindset is not an isolated thing. A lot of Angels have some bizarre ideas about power. You have to deal with it at some point—preferably *before* enough of them pose an actual threat."

Estelle pursed her lips, staring back at Zylis. Eventually, she dragged her eyes away. She didn't want to say it out loud, but she could see where he was coming from. She took a deep breath. "Just tell me how long she'll be there."

"I can't. It varies. I mean, she can technically leave whenever she wants, but..." Zylis shrugged. "Well, if what Cyrus says about their past is true, it probably won't be long. It's generally easier for Fallen Angels to adjust if they have someone they care about in Hell." His tone softened. "Star, trust me. She's going to be okay."

"I..." Estelle opened and closed her mouth a few times. "Well, even if that's true..." She bit her lip. "Still..." She swallowed around the lump in her throat, eyes beginning to water again.

Estelle wanted to believe that Lilith would be alright; she really did. But there was a writhing, jagged feeling in her chest, a weight on her heart that would not give up. No matter what she did, she couldn't force herself to believe that it was good.

Zylis sighed, roughly throwing an arm over her shoulder. "Star, y'know you're allowed to be upset, right?" he grumbled. "You don't have to introduce ethics or value judgments. You can *feel* sad."

Estelle froze for a second before curling further into his chest. "But... but it's..."

"I know."

"It's—"

"I *know*," he repeated, pulling her closer as his tail rested around her waist.

A small sob escaped from Estelle's throat, feathers rising, somewhat counseling both of them from the world. She gripped the fabric of Zylis' hoodie like it was the only thing that kept her grounded.

After several minutes, she spoke, her voice muffled. "Zye, I'll never see her again."

Zylis was silent for a moment. "You don't know that."

The Angel tensed and, after a second, pulled away, wings returning to their normal position. She glared at the Demon.

"Zye, I'm *not* going to Fall," she spoke through gritted teeth. "And I'm not in the mood to hear how much you think I will."

"You don't have to Fall to see her."

Estelle was briefly puzzled, and then it hit her. "You mean... bring her to the surface?"

"Well, no. Not exactly," he said, looking away. "I was thinking more about bringing *you* to see *her*." He sat up straight and stretched his arms above his head. "As in, bring you to Hell."

The girl stared at him for a long moment, her eyes wide. "*Excuse me?*"

"You heard me." Zylis scoffed, side-eyeing her. "Are there any laws forbidding you from visiting Hell?"

"I-I don't think so, but—"

"Then why not?"

Estelle faltered. "Why can't you just bring her to the surface?"

Zylis paused and licked his lips. "Well, I could pull that off, sure," he admitted. "But if I'm being completely honest, I have other motives here."

She narrowed her eyes. "Such as...?"

"Such as showing you what Hell is actually like, Star," he said, turning to look at her fully. "I know you still have a concave load of internalized ideas about it. You should see for yourself why you're wrong."

Estelle scoffed and mumbled. "Of course."

"*Of course*, what?" he snapped. "Of course, I want to show you that my *home*, which you seem to be so fond of making unsubstantiated assumptions about, isn't what you think it is?"

Estelle winced and averted her eyes. "I just..." She paused, feeling the pressure of guilt. "I don't know if I..."

"What?"

Estelle shook her head and didn't respond.

Zylis exhaled and stood up. "Look, just..." He raked a hand through his messy hair. "Just think about it, alright?"

Estelle stared down at the ground, gripping the fabric of her cloak. It would have been a lie to say she wasn't at least curious. Just like it would have been a lie to say the thought didn't terrify her. In her exhausted state, she couldn't tell which feeling outweighed the other.

After a moment, she gathered the will to reply. "Alright," Estelle quietly told him. "I'll think about it."

Estelle returned to her room in a daze. She collapsed on her bed and stared at the ceiling, her mind paradoxically both numb and anxious. Sometimes, she wondered if free will actually existed.

Although she did her best not to think about it too much, she could never quite rid herself of that persistent sense of inevitability. It was like she was on a conveyor belt, slowly but surely carrying her toward a singular end.

Because there were two different, irreconcilable images of Hell inside her mind: the version she had been taught, and the version Zylis' words had constructed. On some level, she had convinced herself that those were separate places. It wasn't rational, of course, but it was something she could get behind emotionally.

The fact of the matter was that there were specific fundamental ideas she had been taught early on—ideas about the way the realms worked and what was right and wrong. And just like all people, Estelle built her belief system from that groundwork.

There were times when talking with Zylis made her worldview feel like a game of Jenga. *Demons are capable of altruism.* It was the first block that was pulled. *Individual Demons can be good people,* was the second. *Demons, like humans, are probably primarily decent,* was the third.

None of those were critical. Groups of mostly well-meaning people could enact evil. Humanity had proven that fact many times over. She knew that what Zylis said about Hell was true to him, but that didn't make it real.

Zylis was real. His relationship with Estelle was real. Despite knowing her real name, Zylis never actually used it against her, never told the other Demons, never forced her to Fall, even though Estelle Falling was his ultimate goal—all of that was real because she had seen it. She had experienced it.

But Hell wasn't real. Or at least, it didn't *have* to be. Her concept of Hell wasn't strictly *foundational*, but it was deep enough in her hierarchy of beliefs to have the potential to destabilize things. Hell was the place where she stored her reservations. It represented the ideas she was too afraid to examine and too scared to give up. It was both the place where Zylis lived and wasn't. Hell was the evil built from billions of shards of good, an abstract structure that kept Estelle oriented in a world of ethical ambiguity.

Heaven never needed to be perfect. It didn't even need to be *good*. It just needed to be *better*. And as long as Estelle didn't have to see it, she could convince herself that somehow, in some way, Hell was worse.

But then there was that fear again. That relentless inevitability underscored Estelle's existence like an ominous rumble emanating from the tectonics of her reality. Because sooner or later, Zylis would lay it all out for her. Drag her down to Hell and make her look, make it *real*.

Estelle didn't know if she would be the same person afterward.

43

Regulus

THE KNOCKING ON HER DOOR startled Estelle from her dream, taking a few seconds to remember she was safe inside her room. She glanced at the clock on the wall and groaned upon seeing it was only seven-thirty in the morning. She hadn't returned to Heaven until two the previous night. After her talk with Zylis, her tears continued to flow whenever her mind wandered too close to the memory created only a couple of hours prior. Through that time, Zylis comforted and held her close, only letting go when Estelle pulled away.

Without any motivation to get up aside from the insistent knocking, the Angel rolled over and pulled her pillow over her ears, trying to tune the sound out. Then the door opened, revealing a startled Issac with one hand on the doorknob.

"Amadea—"

"What are you—?" They spoke simultaneously, but Estelle sat up in bed, fully awake, at the mention of her surname. "What's wrong?" she asked.

"The Vostarists are calling upon us," he said in a hushed tone. "They want to take us in for questioning."

The girl was off her bed before he had finished speaking, grabbing a couple of articles of clothing, and moved to go into her bathroom until Issac caught her wrist in his hand, stopping her. She didn't realize he had moved closer.

"It's not just us," he said. "Our entire class is being taken. And they want us now."

Estelle couldn't breathe. Why would they want all of them? As far as she knew, only the two of them had broken any rules or had been punished for interacting with a Demon. What would be the cause of a mass gathering? The Angel didn't voice her concerns but merely dropped everything and let her friend lead her out of the room, down the hall, and descend the stairs to where the other Angels had been waiting. She still wore the obsidian rings.

The formidable figure standing at the front of the room caught Estelle's attention when they joined the group.

Regulus was tall with broad shoulders, three sets of wings, and cold gray eyes that stared down at them with an unreadable expression. His hair was chestnut colored, pulled back into a low, short ponytail. But what caught her eye was the black scar spanning from the top of his right eye down to his chin. A scar that could have only been made by hellfire.

Regulus' gray eyes landed on the two Angels when they entered. He made contact with Estelle's gold irises before he addressed them all in a voice that one would only assume could come out of a frightening man. "Now that we are all here, follow me," he said. "I'll explain once we join the others." With that, he turned and exited the dormitories with twenty-four second-tier Angels in tow.

Estelle and Issac walked alongside the others to their unknown destination. Luckily, with it being a Saturday and early enough in the morning, there were very few Angels out and about. No one dared to speak, which did not bode well in Estelle's mind.

Where are we going? We couldn't go anywhere aside from the first sphere and the surface—and why do the Vostarists want to speak with all of us? Estelle thought as she walked hand in hand with Issac. *Why was Regulus charged with retrieving us?*

The only thing she could think of was Lilith's words. *Her father was next in line to become a Vostarist.* It was clear she was talking about Regulus, but was it true?

Estelle stared at Regulus' three wings folded neatly against his back. From what she could tell, they didn't hold much of a resemblance to each other. She supposed their eyes were similar, their facial shape, and they shared the same serious look.

It only took a few minutes for them to arrive at their destination. A meeting house, usually reserved for the teachers, with several adjacent rooms. Once inside, everyone froze. In front of each of the rooms stood a Vostarist.

Other Angels had been gathered from the second circle, including Giovanna. Estelle and Issac gravitated toward her as Regulus addressed the crowd of Angels.

"Many of you have already guessed why you are all here," he said, speaking in a commanding voice that grabbed everyone's attention away from the six Vostarists. "This is a mandatory questioning for those close to an Angel who has Fallen."

Several lower-ranked Angels gasped, looking around at the others, trying to see who was missing.

Regulus made eye contact with Estelle. "One of you experienced the Fall personally." He looked away. "You are all here because, at one point in your existence, you closely interacted with Lilith Audelaire, who Fell last night. This is to gauge how likely the rest of you are to follow. When I call your name, go to a waiting Vostarist for questioning."

There would have been an outburst of tears and shouts if the Vostarists hadn't moved from their spots. Estelle stole a glance around her. Issac's breathing was irregular as his chest rose and fell in fast intervals. Giovanna looked to be in shock, standing still and possibly not breathing at all.

Estelle reached forward and grabbed her hand. Giovanna released a breath, and a tear rolled down her cheek. She wiped it away quickly before the level nine Angel spoke her name and Issac's. They all stole a look at each other before walking forward and into separate rooms alone, with three other Angels in tow.

"Estelle Amadea," Regulus said, looking at the young Angel.

Estelle did her best not to look away from him.

"I'll be questioning you. This way."

"Y-Yes, sir," she said, stepping out from the crowd and following him into an empty room.

It was a decently sized room, with a rectangular table and chairs surrounding it, an ample light overhead dissipating any shadows. If Estelle hadn't been terrified, she might have looked closer at the pictures on the wall or how one chair was made from a darker wood than the rest. But all her attention was drawn to her superior—the tall, intimidating Angel.

He gestured for her to sit across from him. She did so, putting her hands in her lap to stop the temptation to reach up and twirl a strand of black hair. Instead, she fiddled with the rings on her fingers.

And then it began.

"What was your relationship with Lilith Audelaire?" Regulus asked, sitting down in his chair.

Estelle took a breath. "She's my friend."

He raised an eyebrow. "Is?"

She hesitated, blinking a couple of times. "Was."

"Why do you hesitate?" he asked, leaning forward slightly.

"We grew close in our years as level one Angels, sir," Estelle said, looking off to the side before returning to the gray eyes. "Forgive me, I didn't sleep well last night, and I—" she stopped and bit her lip, the tightness in her throat returning.

Her tears had run dry the night before, and she desperately wanted to believe that Lilith was okay, or would be. But the event was still fresh in her mind, down to the last detail and white feather.

After a moment of no further response, Regulus continued. "Do you believe the Fallen can still do work in the name of God?"

Estelle furrowed her brow. "I-I believe that they are..." She paused, searching her words. "Not inherently evil the moment they leave Heaven," she said, then quickly added, "Not until the Demons get a hold of them. But, uh, shouldn't we still have faith in them?"

"That is a lot of wishful thinking, Estelle Amadea," he said, face unreadable. "The reason behind a Fall is the betrayal of God."

The young Angel nodded, her eyes downcast.

He continued. "Did you witness any signs of Lilith Audelaire's corruption before it overcame her?"

"Not at first."

"Elaborate."

Estelle exhaled a shaky breath. "I didn't notice anything out of the ordinary until she Fell," she said. "But now, I'm remembering... little details."

She looked up and met his eyes again. It was clear from how long he stared at her that he was waiting for more specific details on the matter, but Estelle couldn't help that her mind went back to Lilith's words about him.

"Did you know her?" She remembered too late that it was not her place to ask.

His eyes widened slightly.

Her hands went up and waved meaninglessly in the air. "I'm sorry, sir! It's not my place—"

"Your mentor," Regulus interjected, "is Antares, yes?" he asked, placing his arms on the table and intertwining his fingers.

Estelle nodded, mimicking his movements with her hands.

"Please, speak freely," he said, making the young Angel do a double-take. "But no, I did not know her on a personal level. Why do you ask?"

Estelle swallowed, pushing back more questions her mind had come up with. "Sir, I apologize in advance for my forwardness."

Regulus tilted his head toward her slightly, indicating that she should continue.

"Would it not have been more productive to have someone who knew her personally ask the questions? I only ask because those who didn't know her wouldn't think such little things would be out of the ordinary for Lilith."

He did not hesitate with the answer. "The information we gather from you and the others is important. It helps us see similar signs in others and prevents them from suffering the same fate. They're given a second chance to serve God in..." he paused, looking off to the side before looking back to her, "more efficient ways."

Estelle cocked her head to the side, but before she could ask any further questions, Regulus continued with his questioning. "How do you feel about God?"

Estelle blinked, sitting up straighter. "I'm sorry?"

"Are you having second thoughts because of Miss Audelaire's Fall?" he reiterated.

"No," she replied. "I never want that to happen to anyone else."

Regulus nodded. "Do you know anyone who has the potential to Fall because of her Fall?"

"No, sir," Estelle answered without hesitation, even though in that instant, one name popped into her head.

Giovanna Rūnnel. From her reaction alone, Estelle wondered if she had placed any blame on herself for the event that would have been wrongfully attributed to her.

"According to the hospital staff, Lilith Audelaire locked you in the room with her. What did you two discuss in the hospital room while the door was locked?"

She bit her lip. She couldn't very well tell him what Lilith told her. After a moment's pause, Estelle breathed in and said, "Lilith was telling me that a Demon she had fought before was someone she knew during her human life. There wasn't much else before she... Fell."

"Very well," Regulus said, standing up. "Estelle Amadea, that is all. You may leave and go about your daily business."

Estelle stood up and impulsively bowed awkwardly in her pajamas. "Thank you, sir. But may I ask?" She looked up and met his eyes. She paused for a moment more, just in case, before she continued. "How do you know Antares?"

His eye flickered down to her hands, and his lips tugged upward for a split second before returning to his neutral facial expression. "He's an old friend." With that, he opened the door and escorted her out before calling the next Angel in.

Estelle quickly left the building, stepping out into the morning light and staying just far enough not to feel the presence of the Vostarists, but close enough to spot her friends when they *finally* emerged from the impromptu interrogation center one by one. She only had to wait around five minutes before both of them walked out, but Estelle could have said it took two hours, considering how time seemed to stop.

Giovanna had tear stains on her cheeks and blotchy eyes. Issac looked as though his mind was somewhere far away and didn't come back to reality until the raven-haired Angel pulled him and Giovanna into a hug, letting a couple of droplets fall from her eyes in the process.

"Are you guys okay?" Estelle asked, barely above a whisper. They both nodded. "Let's get out of here." She pulled away from the embrace. "I don't want to be anywhere near the Vostarists."

Estelle led them back to the dormitories, seemingly the only one who could make decisions, and gave them some of her rosebay tea. She had stopped using it for corruption damage at the beginning of the month. Still, she made a cup occasionally because she found it calmed her more than any others, though it was probably because of the sweet, almost minty taste and the fruity aroma that drew her in.

None of them spoke. It wasn't until Estelle had sat down, after serving the tea, that Giovanna broke the dreadful silence. "You saw her Fall, didn't you?"

Estelle inhaled sharply through her nose at the exact moment Issac asked, "Who?" A second later, both of their eyes were on her. Estelle looked away and stared down at the warm cup in her hands, steam rising before disappearing.

"You watched Lilith Fall?" Issac clarified, shifting in his seat to face her more fully.

Estelle swore at herself as the sting of tears and tightness of her throat began. She was tired of crying. Sick of replaying the image of falling feathers. But she owed it to them to tell them what happened. Right? Lilith wasn't just her friend. She wasn't the only one missing the Fallen Angel—

A gentle hand rested atop Estelle's forearm, making her refocus on the cup in her hands. Her vision was blurry with unshed tears.

"You don't have to talk about it if you don't want to," Issac reverently said, giving her arm a reassuring squeeze.

Estelle blinked away the salty water, a couple of drops rippling the tea, before looking up to meet Issac's green eyes. "I... I'm sorry." She looked at Giovanna, who sat in the armchair. "I can't."

For the rest of the day, no one dared break away from the others, in fear of not seeing them again. The three Angels stayed in the common area, drinking one cup of tea after another, and not talking aside from the occasional comment about the movies they watched that no one was paying attention to. In the end, they fell asleep huddled together in a mass of feathers and blankets, highlighted by the three halos that softly gleamed above their heads.

44

Lyra
Strix

ESTELLE'S EYES FLUTTERED OPEN AS she slowly woke up, and the first thing she saw was Issac's sleeping face in front of her. His lilac hair fell softly over his cheek as he breathed evenly. He was cute.

Shifting her weight onto her arm, she sat up, feeling her bones creak as a side effect of sleeping on the hardwood floor of the common room. She stretched, allowing her joints to release with a pop, before sliding out of her place, standing up, gathering discarded mugs, and walking into the kitchen. It wasn't until she turned on the water in the sink to start another round of tea that she realized she wasn't the only one awake.

"Did Lilith say anything to you?" Giovanna asked, making the girl jump slightly at her sudden appearance.

"Gosh!" Estelle exclaimed quietly, looking over to the Angel. "You know, I may look like a Demon, but at least I don't act like one. Goodness."

She laughed. "You just need to get better at spatial awareness."

Estelle rolled her eyes before turning off the water, setting the kettle on the stove, and turning on the burner. Giovanna passed an unmarked container to her—her stash of rosebay tea leaves—and then spoke again.

"I'm sorry for... everything."

Estelle quirked an eyebrow. "Why are you sorry?" she asked, leaning against the counter. "You were not the reason why she Fell."

The tall Angel looked off to the side and rubbed the back of her neck, her expression sorrowful.

"Giovanna, you know that, right?"

Giovanna hesitated, and with every second that ticked by, Estelle felt a foreboding pressure on her chest that only got worse as Giovanna spoke. "How would you know that?" Her breath caught in her throat. "How do you know I wasn't—"

"Stop," Estelle said, breathing deeply as she tried to choke down the chill that ran through her. "Don't blame yourself. You were not the reason."

Giovanna looked away and didn't speak for a while. "I haven't been the... best of friends to you, Estelle," she said. "And I'm sorry for everything." She sighed. "I need to get back. They'll be expecting my return to the second sphere today. I'm glad you were there for her final moments," she said, meeting Estelle's eyes before she left, almost bumping into Issac in the process.

"Did I just witness you two being somewhat nice to each other?" Issac commented with a yawn.

Estelle glared playfully, turning her attention back to preparing the tea.

For the rest of the day, Issac and Estelle stayed close to each other, reveling in each other's company and talking about lighthearted topics that, in the grand scheme of things, had no real value aside from filling the silence between them.

Estelle didn't retreat to her room until later that night.

She was lying on her bed, holding the journal up in both hands. The overhead light backlit the book, making it a challenge to read, but Estelle was too tired to do anything about it. She stayed still, squinted, and dealt with it.

Entry 6: 6102.11.10.1902

I'm not sure how to describe it. I think it's just one of those "know it when you feel it" sort of things. All I can say is that one moment, I was doubled over in pain with a laniesthole spear impaling me through my abdomen, and the next moment, I couldn't feel it at all.

I don't mean that in the sense that it was numb. It felt like the wound had healed somehow. I vaguely recall a sort of rush of relief, but after that, it gets fuzzy. I do remember Lyra looking very scared when she saw me. She had to pull the spear out of me before the wound could heal around it. I didn't even realize it was closing up until then.

I'm still not certain how she knew. I never got a chance to ask since... well, you know.

Anyway, I suppose I'm one of the lucky ones. It certainly doesn't feel like it, but I acknowledge that it could have been much worse. Please, be careful out there. If you have any reason to suspect soul bleed, get yourself to a medic immediately, consequences be damned.

It's taken me a few months, but I've come to terms with the fact that I won't be able to fight anymore. I'm looking into teaching and feeling a bit more optimistic these days. Perhaps, in some ways, this was for the best.

Estelle frowned and stared at the page, reading over it again. *Soul bleed? What's that supposed to mean?*

A firm knock on the door nearly made her jump out of her skin. After a minute of deliberation, Estelle forced herself out of bed and shuffled over to answer. She slowly opened the door and peered through the crack. To say she was surprised at who she found would have been a massive understatement.

"Antares?" She opened the door further.

"May I come in?"

Estelle nodded and stepped aside. "Oh, sorry, it's so messy, I've been..." she trailed off.

Antares laughed. "My office looks like this on a good day," he said. "If this is how your room looks on a bad day, I think you're doing just fine, Amadea."

A *bad day.* "Is that what this is about?"

He smiled. "I wanted to check to make sure you're doing alright."

"I'm fine." Estelle winced as the words left her mouth. She averted her eyes and began fidgeting with the hems of her sleeves. "I thought we couldn't see each other outside of scheduled times, though."

Antares opened his mouth to respond, but hesitated. "Well, when I heard what had happened, I figured I ought to make an exception," he said.

"But what if you get in trouble?"

He shrugged. "If I do, then it's my fault. Nothing for you to worry yourself over, Amadea."

Estelle's brows pinched together, and she looked down at the ground. As seconds ticked by, her eyes began to tear up, which surprised even herself. "But... how can I not? Antares, I—" her voice broke, "—I can't lose you, too."

She wiped her tears away and covered her face. She didn't want to cry. She had cried so much already that it was starting to annoy her.

The older Angel didn't say anything for a while. When Estelle glanced up at him, she found him standing there with his mouth open, an odd, almost pained look on his face. She looked down at the floor.

"I don't... want you to have to bear the burden of thoughts like that," he eventually said. "I know it's not a moot point, but a student shouldn't have to worry about their teacher's safety."

"But you're not just a teacher, Antares. You're..." Estelle trailed off, sniffling.

The older Angel gently pulled her into a hug. "I know," he murmured. "I know."

Estelle tried to get herself under control, but her shoulders shook.

"Deep breaths."

She nodded and tried to comply, taking deep, shuddering inhalations and slow, shaky exhalations. After a few minutes, she managed to rein herself in enough to pull back.

"I'm sorry," the young Angel murmured.

"Please, don't apologize," he said softly. "I understand completely. It's normal for you to feel this way."

Estelle nodded and finally summoned the courage to look him in the eyes again.

Antares sighed. "I'm sorry for getting you wrapped up in all this."

Estelle blinked. "What do you mean?"

"Well, uh..." he gestured meaninglessly. After a pause, he shook his head and chuckled softly. "I wish I knew how to answer that. Lately, it's felt like being caught up in a maelstrom."

Estelle offered a weak smile, sitting on the edge of her bed.

Antares pulled the desk chair closer and sat in it backwards, resting his arms on the back. "Have you been keeping up with the journal entries?"

"I have," she said, her brow furrowed. "It's... Antares, what is soul bleed?"

"Ah." His posture strengthened. "Right, yes. That was a part of a letter I wrote to a friend a while back after I retired."

Estelle tensed. "Wait, that was you?" she frowned. "Antares, I thought your injuries came from hellfire."

"Some of them did!" he quickly clarified. "But that's... well, it's not the real reason I retired. It was..." A pause.

"Soul bleed," Estelle quietly finished. "What is that?"

He scratched his head, brows pinched together. "Well, you know how Angels are generally considered to be indestructible? At least when it comes to regular physical damage."

Estelle nodded.

"That's not exactly true," he stated. "There is a limit to how much physical damage one can sustain."

"What's the limit?"

"It's..." He squinted. "Well, I can't give you an exact answer. As I mentioned in the letter, it's more of a 'know it when you feel it' sort of thing."

"I don't understand. What do you *feel*?" Estelle asked.

"Let me just start at the beginning," he sighed. "Essentially, when an Angel crosses a certain threshold of physical damage, the Navitas—the fluid inside your soul— begins to leak out into the rest of your body, where it's used to heal your injuries. This is called soul bleed.

"It's a physiological phenomenon. A last-resort sort of defense mechanism." He drummed his fingers on the back of the chair. "The point of this is supposed to allow you to escape an aggressor when your injuries would otherwise prevent you from doing so. In theory, at least."

"I mean, that sounds like it would be useful," Estelle mumbled.

Antares made a face. "Well, in some ways, I suppose it is," he said. "But there are issues. For one, it's unclear what conditions need to be met to initiate it. Not all severe injuries result in immobilization, but soul bleed has been known to occur regardless."

"But is that a problem?" The girl blinked. "I mean, if it's healing you, I don't see what the downside could be."

"Ah," her mentor grinned. "Remember what I told you a few months ago?" he asked. "Amadea, the problem is that the Navitas *does not regenerate.*"

Estelle opened her mouth to respond, but nothing came to her.

"Part of what makes soul bleed so dangerous is how quickly it happens," he went on. "Once it starts, you only have around fifteen minutes before it's too late. And even if you manage to get medical assistance in time, it almost *guarantees* you won't be able to fight anymore."

"Why not?"

"Well, I'm not an expert, but essentially, it's imperative that the soul's entire volume be filled with Navitas," he replied. "If it isn't, parts that are not in contact with it will dry out and become inflexible, which keeps energy from being able to move through properly.

"I can still use power, but it's nowhere near as strong. And I have to be extremely careful not to overdo it." He smiled. "For most Angels, overdoing it is not possible. But when parts of the lining dry out, they become brittle." He shrugged. "If I'm not careful, my soul could rupture, causing the whole thing to start up again—only this time, I'd have even less time to get help before it was too late."

Estelle frowned. "What do you mean by *'too late'*?" she asked. "What happens if it all drains out?" Her voice fell to a whisper. "Do you... die?"

"Oh, I wish," Antares chuckled.

Estelle's eyes went wide.

"Ah, sorry—" he rubbed his neck sheepishly, "—that was a bit morbid, wasn't it?"

"Antares."

"Let me start over," he said, waving his hands. "When the Navitas completely drains from an Angel's soul, they become what is known as a *husk*."

"A husk?"

"It technically refers to the fact that your soul is, quite literally, an empty shell. But the meaning runs deeper than that." He hesitated for a moment, then sighed. "You need to understand that your soul is... well, it's what makes you, *you*. Without it, you're..."

"An empty husk," Estelle whispered.

Antares looked up at her. "Yes," he said. "There's an entry in the journal that goes into this in more detail. The next one, I believe." He nodded slowly, and for nearly a full minute, neither spoke.

Estelle eventually broke the silence. "Antares, who is Lyra?"

"Oh! She was my mentor," he replied. "Your grand-mentor, if you will. Her Luminari was Vega."

A memory came back to Estelle at that moment. It was when she first told him what she had chosen as her Holy name, right before her first time on the surface. Familiarity flashed in his eyes as he smiled happily. It was only then that she realized his smile was also sad.

"She saved you."

Antares looked down, a sad smile on his face, the same as before, years ago. "Indeed, she did. At the cost of her soul."

The young Angel frowned. "You mean..."

"Yes," he sighed. After a moment, he began to speak again, his tone soft. "Amadea, I know how it feels to watch someone you care for Fall. It's a special kind of helplessness."

Estelle swallowed, her throat tight. "Did you ever see her again?"

He shook his head. "Even if I could, finding someone after they Fall can be challenging. Not *impossible*, but..." He shrugged.

"Right." Estelle paused. "Zye offered to help me with that."

"Oh, you told him?"

She nodded. "The night it happened. I would have gone to you, but— I don't know, he just came to mind first, so I went to him."

"In person?"

"Yes. He comforted me." Estelle winced. "Uh, kind of?" When the older Angel didn't immediately respond, she looked up and found him

377

grinning. The embarrassment hit her like a freight train. "I—I mean, it's not like—y'know, I just didn't—"

Antares waved his hands. "It's alright," he assured her. "Amadea, I'm happy you've found such a good friend in him. A bit surprised, yes, but happy nonetheless."

Estelle's face felt far too hot for her liking. She averted her eyes and muttered a squeaky "Thanks."

"So, he offered to bring Audelaire to the surface?"

"Oh, not quite." Estelle laughed nervously. "He offered to take *me* to Hell to see her."

The man froze and stared at her for a moment. Then he burst out laughing.

"Antares?" she squeaked, embarrassment returning full force. "What's so—"

"Sorry, sorry," he wheezed. "It's just... ahh. It's just funny."

"I gathered that, but what is it?"

"Nothing bad, I promise!"

"Then—!"

Antares raised a hand, stopping Estelle's upcoming anxiety attack. "Amadea, do you know how..." He gestured vaguely. "Protective, I should say, Demons are of Hell?"

The girl frowned. "What do you mean?"

"As someone who's been around a lot of high-ranking Angels, I can tell you, the few times when we tried negotiating with Demons, it's always been quite challenging." He shook his head. "Keep in mind, this was years before the Rapture. Everything needed to be on Earth, which is easy for them since they can pass as humans. Not so easy for us, however." He gestured pointedly back at his wings and halo, then sighed. "Anyway, the point I'm trying to make is that Demons have a surprisingly strong sense of collective responsibility. Consequently, they're usually reluctant to do anything that could cause others in their community to feel unsafe."

"Okay," she said, "I still don't—"

"Amadea, for Zylis to simply *offer* to bring you to Hell..." Antares chuckled and shook his head. "It almost sounds like a marriage proposal of some kind."

Estelle's blush flared up again. "It's—he's not—"

"I don't mean that literally, of course!" He put his hands up. "I'm quite certain Demons despise the very concept of marriage, anyway."

Somehow, that didn't make Estelle less embarrassed. She stuttered a moment longer before changing the subject. "What was Lyra like?"

Antares smiled. "Honestly, you're a lot like her," he said as he leaned forward against the chair. "Lyra Strix, like you, had black hair. She was strong, kind, and for some reason fascinated with dogs, specifically corgis."

Estelle giggled. "Zye likes cats. Black ones."

They talked for nearly two hours about nonsensical things, including the stories Estelle hadn't told him about, like Chandra. When Antares finally excused himself, it was with evident reluctance. Estelle was happy, though. Despite the ostensibly dark nature of certain parts of their conversation, the lighthearted portions left her feeling alright. It was nice to talk with Antares that way. At least for a little while, it was almost as though things were back to normal again.

It was enough to convince herself that things would be okay.

The following journal entry unlocked at midnight, and Estelle was on it almost as quickly.

Entry 7: 4700.1.29.500

I do not like the husks. They have a certain unsettling quality to them—somehow alive, yet simultaneously not. We've tried everything we can, but they don't respond. No talking, no movement, no response to stimuli whatsoever; they stare into space, breathing slowly, blinking occasionally. It's unclear whether their minds are still intact or whether they can hear what we say to them. We haven't been able to prove it wrong, either.

I try not to think about it too much, but it's been bothering me lately. There are times when I look into their eyes, and I *know* that these Angels are gone. That there's nothing left behind that hollow gaze—at least, nothing we can recognize.

But then I see that shine in their eyes during the tests, and I start to wonder. The pain sensitivity tests seem to be the only thing that promotes a response, albeit an involuntary one. Thankfully, due to their volatility, the pain inflicted during these tests is necessarily minor, which is a relief, I suppose. Even this much bothers me sometimes. I feel like I can feel their pain. Sometimes, I wonder if the Apostles forget that these are still Angels even if they no longer have a halo.

The hypothesis that the others seem to operate under is that the husks are not conscious.

I hope they're right about that.

For a few minutes, Estelle stared at the page in shock. Suddenly, her mind flooded with memories of the boy from level one—the one who had fallen ill, but by the time that was known, it was already too late—the flickering halo and vacant stare of his haunted her.

Is that what became of him? she wondered. *But I thought soul bleed only happened after sustaining severe damage. Maybe other conditions can cause it?* Estelle shook her head and sighed. *I'll have to wait until our next meeting to ask Antares about it.*

45

Scheduled

ANTARES WAS NOT IN CLASS.

At first, Estelle didn't think anything of it. Antares was absent more than most teachers. His status as a retired high-tier Angel meant he would occasionally be asked to travel to the innermost circles for special training events and teaching seminars. It wasn't unusual for him to disappear for a day or two every other month or so.

The fact that Estelle didn't know about it ahead of time made her a bit anxious, but it was easy enough to dismiss. Given the infrequency of their meetings, it would have been reasonable for Antares to have forgotten to mention it to her.

The second day made her a bit more nervous, but she remained calm enough to put her mind off it. When the third day rolled around, the sight of the substitute teacher strolling in made Estelle's heart lurch against her chest.

She barely focused for most of the day, which didn't bode well for her since it was test day, evaluating everything they had learned through the past year, especially what they had experienced while on the surface.

The only thing she was sure about was that because of the tests, Issac and Giovanna were too preoccupied to think about anything else, even Lilith's Fall. They buried themselves in the assignments and didn't allow anything else to occupy their mind. Estelle was not so fortunate.

She had been too afraid to ask where Antares was. Rationally, she knew that doing so wouldn't raise any suspicion and that it was normal for a student to wonder about something like that. But the paranoid thoughts in her mind all seemed to meld together in her state of panic.

Estelle cried out in pain as Issac popped her dislocated wing back into place. She was so out of it that she dislocated her wing against the edge of one of the rings on the flying field and wound up having to sit out for the rest of the day. Estelle wiped the tears from her eyes and did her best to regulate her breathing as her friend sat beside her with a sigh.

"How are you doing, Estelle?" Issac asked, after a moment. "I heard Antares was out sick."

Estelle tensed. "Oh, really?" she said. "Where'd you hear that?"

"I asked this morning. I guess it seemed strange for him to be gone more than two days in a row." He shrugged. "I don't want to jump to conclusions, but it seemed kind of…" He rubbed the back of his neck. "Well, serious."

Estelle felt a rush of cold through her veins. "I see…" she gulped. "Well, I hope that's not the case."

Issac hummed in agreement.

"Do you have any idea what he's sick with?"

He shook his head. "Sorry. I didn't think to ask." He nodded toward Mebsuta, their substitute, standing on the sidelines with a whistle in his mouth. "You could, though. He might know."

The raven-haired Angel hesitated. "I think I'll just go to his house to see for myself. When the break starts."

"Alright. Well, be careful. He might be contagious."

Estelle forced a returning smile.

After the tests were evaluated and announced, all Angels received a week off from schoolwork. It was intended for the teachers to focus on preparing for the next year of lessons and for the students to concentrate solely on the evacuation; however, if the Angels could, they tended to sleep in and relax.

After classes, despite seeming to fail nearly every test, Estelle walked from the school to her mentor's house. It was a short walk from campus, but it felt like it took an eternity. As she approached, she scanned over the windows, noting that one light was on out of all of them—the one in the study. Despite the circumstances, it made her smile.

Estelle ran up the steps to the porch and stopped at the door, taking a deep breath before ringing the doorbell and waiting.

And waiting.

Nothing. Estelle frowned as she felt a wave of nausea in her stomach. *Don't panic. If he's sick, it would make sense for him not to answer.*

After a few minutes, she tried again. She rang the doorbell, knocked, and even called out his name. But there was nothing.

Either he's not here, or too sick to get out of bed, the Angel thought, with a spike of panic. She managed to reel herself in a moment later. *Or he's just sleeping,* she reminded herself. *Stop jumping to conclusions.*

Estelle lingered on the doorstep for a while, but ultimately, she just had to head home.

Estelle stopped by his house again the following day, but nothing changed. Even the light in the study was still on.

She was trying her best not to panic as she sat on her bed. But the problem was that there were too many things that sent her into a spiral. If Antares was sick, how bad was it? Was there anything she could do to help him? Was he quarantining himself, or was someone making him?

Estelle groaned, falling back onto the mattress. She hated not knowing things. She hated not being able to find answers to her questions. But when she thought about it, since she was a low-level Angel and couldn't read over seventy percent of the books in the library, in retrospect, she should be used to not knowing things.

It was like that for nearly nineteen years, up until Estelle met Zylis. He made her question everything—challenged her to find answers to things that were far beyond her level.

Estelle sat up and reached over to grab the journal off the side table. She opened it to an entry she had yet to read.

Entry 8: 5900.17.4.1700

Things have been tense lately. It's been a while since any of us last spoke to God. The Apostles won't tell us anything, though; it would be a lie to say I didn't feel frustrated by it. It's just that I don't understand. It's such a departure from how things used to be. And I know that the Apostles likely feel paranoid. But frankly, if they fear that transparency could be a detriment if more third spheres Fell, then I'm afraid it might be a self-fulfilling prophecy. Already, I can sense my fellow level nines growing agitated and restless in the silence.

There's a rumor that the Apostles are looking into ways to modify Angels to prevent them from Falling. I choose not to believe them, mostly because I'm unsure how I'd feel if this were the case.

Estelle walked into the dorm building, her anxiety at an all-time high as another attempt to see Antares failed. He had mentioned before that someone was missing. Was he too preoccupied finding them that he went radio silent? But at the same time, Zylis mentioned Angels disappearing. Did Antares disappear, too?

"Estelle, what are you doing?" Issac called her from his spot on a chair in the common room. He was reading a book.

Estelle didn't bother reading the cover as she approached him. "I'm just…" she hesitated, realizing she was braiding her hair again.

She sectioned her hair into several chunks, braided them, and twisted each part around the other to make her hair look like a rose. She pulled at the strands hanging around her face. She wasn't sure if her hair even looked nice. She did it all on the way to and from Antares' house.

Her hands fell to the side. "It's nothing. I'm just stuck in my head."

He hummed as he took in her appearance. "Your hair, it's one of your more elaborate designs," Issac said, setting his book aside. "What's on your mind?"

"It's okay, I'm—"

"You're not fooling anyone, Estelle," he said, raising an eyebrow. "The more complicated your hairstyle is, and depending on how fast you change it for another, the more worried you are. And you were just about to change it, so," he patted the armrest, "tell me before you explode."

Was she really that obvious? Zylis had mentioned a couple of times that it was easy to read her when she played with her hair, but it couldn't have been that bad... *right?* Estelle sighed and took a seat on the armrest. She needed to quit the habit.

"I'm worried about Antares," she confessed. "He wasn't at school for the last days of studies." She sighed, but it morphed into a frustrated groan. "Ugh, I just want to know if he's okay!" The Angel covered her eyes and leaned back as far as she could without falling off.

"I'm sure he's just—"

"Issac, have you seen the repair kit?" Another Angel interjected, appearing seemingly out of nowhere and scaring Estelle.

She flailed a bit as she began to fall off the armrest. Issac reached over, grabbed her wrist, and pulled her back up.

"Sorry," Estelle breathed, sliding off her makeshift seat. "I used it last. I'll go get it for you," she said, already on her way.

"That would be great, thank you!" the girl chirped, smiling brightly. "I need to sew up a couple of holes in my cloak before I go to the surface tomorrow."

"I'm scheduled tomorrow, too," Issac commented. "First time since being back from the hospital."

Without meaning to, Estelle grimaced.

"I'm also supposed to go down the next two days..." Issac continued as Estelle ascended the stairs.

Until that point, her mind was filled with thoughts only of her mentor's health and the fact that they pulled back on every level two Angel visits to the surface because of the evaluation, which didn't make it a cause for concern. But as the thought grew, the more troubling it became.

Estelle had not been scheduled for an evacuation.

When was the last time I was sent on a mission? she thought, gripping the railing. To her horror, she couldn't pinpoint how long it had been since the last time she went to the surface.

Wait, that's not right, Estelle thought, reaching the top, her body going into autopilot, walking toward her room. *I was on the surface after Lilith's Fall.*

Her hand opened the door.

And I had a mission before then, a week ago.

Estelle blinked, the sewing kit already in her hand. She found herself staring down at the leather-bound journal. She took a deep breath, trying to gather her thoughts.

There must be a reasonable explanation why she hasn't been to the surface for a week. Was Regulus keeping her in Heaven? Did he see something that made Estelle seem likely to Fall?

She sat at her desk as the thought crossed her mind. *That's it, isn't it? They're erring on the side of caution because I witnessed Lilith Fall. They think I'm going to follow.*

Estelle set the repaired kit aside and opened the journal. *Might as well read this while I'm here.*

Entry 9: 5223.20.2.1023

It's hard for me to say whether it's better or worse than Hell at this point. Maybe it's the proximity of it, but I'm inclined to say it's worse. I know it's useless to dwell on it, but I wish the Demons could have at least tried to be more flexible. Operation Holy Devil might not have been necessary if they had been willing to negotiate on this.

I opened the hatch the other day. The fumes inside the place are truly something else—quite literally a misery agent. I'm still unsure if it's chemical, magical, or both, but it's potent. It's supposed to be alright, but I still hold my breath if I'm within fifteen feet of it. Last time I got a whiff of that stuff, I tried to go in. That's probably the worst part of it. When you're enveloped in it, you stop caring.

46

Food

It was Sunday, the fifth day since Estelle had first visited and the seventh since Antares' first sick day. Every other Angel in her class was down at the surface, fulfilling their duty of saving people and giving them safe passage to Heaven, whereas Estelle prepared a basket of food and a nice, soft blanket.

She was doing it as a gesture. Because Antares was in there, he just wasn't well enough for visitors.

That's what she told herself.

She wasn't much of a chef, as one would expect of an Angel, but she did her best. She got up early in the morning, dusted off the cookbook, and opened it up to a recipe for a simple soup. It took a while for her to get it right. Her first attempt, she had thrown out after accidentally pouring in an entire container of salt. The second, she had somehow burnt the seasonings.

It was a couple of hours before Estelle was satisfied that it was sufficiently edible. She put the soup into an airtight thermos, placed it in the basket, and buried it under the blanket. Though it was generally more socially acceptable for Angels to eat when ill, the fact that illness occurred so infrequently meant that most casual observers were not likely to assume sickness when an Angel was caught eating.

It was usually best to keep such things out of sight when in doubt.

Estelle wrote a simple, unsigned note that read, 'Get well soon,' tied a red ribbon around the basket handle, and was on her way.

It was still early when she arrived, so she didn't ring the bell. She set the basket on the doorstep and hoped Antares would find it. She crossed her arms and dug her fingernails into the flesh of her biceps as she strode away.

The light in the study was still on.

Entry 10: 5223.8.7.1023

I sat in to view the first test's results, and I decided to distance myself from this particular project. I know they're sinners, but that doesn't make it any less upsetting. I find it hard to watch people suffer, even when they deserve it.

The gas does more than I initially thought. Apparently, if you spend more than five minutes in there, your senses start to dull. By ten minutes, you can't sense anything at all. Not even orientation or where your limbs are located in space.

The subjects were fished out after about an hour. It was... disturbing. Neither of them reacted when they were dropped onto the floor. They were shaking and twitching a lot. One of them—the woman—had bitten off the tips of her fingers. The man was worse. When he came out, his chest and throat were spasming, and the lower half of his face was bloody. It took a moment for them to realize he was choking. When they managed to get him to cough the obstruction up, it turned out to be a large portion of his tongue. After washing his mouth out, it was discovered that most of his teeth were broken, supposedly as a result of him grinding them.

I guess this happens when someone loses the ability to sense their strength.

It took a few more minutes for them to start regaining their senses. I've never heard a person make a sound like that, and I hope I never will again.

I don't know. I know that punishing sinners is necessary. I'm just not used to having it at the forefront like this. I know that this is God's will. I don't need to understand it. But I can't help it. It keeps me up at night.

When I heard those two screaming, nothing about it felt holy.

The basket was still on the doorstep on Monday.

Tuesday as well. The porch roof kept it safe from the rain, but Estelle knew the soup would have spoiled. However, like a sacred item, she couldn't bring herself to move it.

She walked through the rain, hood up on the cloak, no longer pristine white. It was a warm summer rain. It was the kind of weather you would expect to see in the movies. Enticing small children to play in slow-growing puddles. Parents are watching under umbrellas, smiling with the sound of laughter. Or perhaps a scene where the love interests kiss under the downpour.

But for Estelle, it didn't feel like a magical moment in a movie. Despite having a cover to prevent herself from getting wet, droplets still ended up on her cheeks. They tasted salty.

She half wondered if Antares had taken the food but left the basket or put it all back once he was done. But logically, it didn't make sense. Everything from the blanket to the ribbon was untouched—left in the same position as if she had only just set it there.

Estelle walked into the dormitories and carefully hung up the cloak so as not to get anything else wet. She went up the stairs to her room and leaned against the door to close it. She didn't move for a while, taking deep, shaky breaths. When Estelle eventually walked further into the room, she noticed her sallvie breathed with life.

Wiping away tears, she settled down on her bed, book and pen in hand.

You better not be ghosting me again, Princess.

I'm not. I haven't gotten any assignments to the surface yet.

It's been more than a week. Are you still doing tests?

No. I finished those a couple of days ago.

Then what's the hold-up

I don't know. Everyone else has been getting evacuation orders every day.

She paused for a moment, then added:

I think it might be because I saw Lilith Fall. They're probably still worried about my state of mind.

That's incredibly stupid.

It might be for the best. I haven't been able to focus lately because Antares is sick, and I haven't seen him since last Sunday.

Are you sure he's not already dead?

Zye, I'm trying not to think about that! What if he is?! Should I

Before she could finish writing all her worries on the page, Zylis wrote over a couple of her words with his own.

Star, relax! I'm joking.

But consider this: he's a high-ranking Angel, right? He could be in some 'high and important' meeting or something. There's no need to go flying off the rails unless you're going to Earth, okay?

Okay. Yeah, you're probably right. Thanks.

I'm always right. Now, hurry up and get down here. It's getting boring without someone to tempt.

Despite herself, Estelle huffed out a laugh. She could practically see his smile and mischievous, glowing, red eyes.

Come Wednesday, Estelle was overwhelmed by all the uncertainty. Everything was the same. The light was on, and the basket was untouched.

"What if he's so sick he can't leave bed?" Estelle asked her friend as she paced the small room, thankful he had the day off. "What if he needs help but doesn't have the strength to move? What if he needs medical attention? What if—?"

"Estelle, calm down!" Issac interrupted. "You always assume the worst possible thing. It's most likely not even something to be worried about. He's probably just been busy helping the higher-tier Angels prepare for the next school year in the second sphere or something."

The Angel collapsed onto her bed and pulled at her roots. It was the same thing that Zylis had said. But something told her it was all wrong. More often than not, Antares told her where he was going and when he would be back, every time he was scheduled to be somewhere else. The likelihood that he was still sick was number one on her list of 'what ifs.'

"Like I'm one to talk," Issac started, "I'm no better than you when theorizing scenarios."

Estelle snorted, propping herself up on her elbows. "It's a miracle another Demon didn't show up," she giggled.

Issac rolled his eyes and pushed her over onto her back. "Antares was probably sick for a little while, but then needed to be someplace else immediately after he recovered."

Estelle nodded, forcing a smile. "Right."

"He's fine, Estelle," Issac assured her as he ran his hands through black hair, untangling any knots. "What's not fine was the woman who practically tackled me to the ground the other day."

As her friend recounted his latest mission to Earth, Estelle remained silent aside from the occasional hum, not concentrating on the story. It was hard when she didn't have any stories of her own to tell over the past few days.

The journal entries were not helping.

Entry II: 6102.18.6.1902

I can't do this anymore.

I've been afraid to even think about it until now, but things have gotten to the point where I can no longer stay silent. The Apostles are absolutely unconventionally out of line.

I could tolerate the idea when it was just the sinners being punished, but this expansion is grotesque. I know that preventing the leaking of intelligence is essential. Still, not every Angel who experiences high levels of corruption is a traitor, and to punish them as though they were is morally repugnant.

I've had enough. I need to find a way to speak with God directly. I need to hear Him condemn what they're doing here for the sake of my friends and my soul. Because honestly, I'm scared. These thoughts I've been having lately make me feel like a different person. I'm not sure how much the corruption has progressed. I'm too afraid to wash off the glue. Not even rosebay tea takes the edge off anymore.

I'll be on a mission tomorrow. We do not expect the fight to last long, but I must be careful. I need to hold on until I have a chance to speak with God. If things turn ugly, who knows what might happen.

On Friday, Estelle spent the entire day cleaning her room and the shared spaces in the dormitories, then braiding her hair in an intricate design that left half of her hair technically untouched while the braids wrapped around it—anything to keep her mind off her missing mentor. But there weren't enough things for her to do.

She glanced at the clock in her room. It read five o'clock. The other Angels would start returning within the next hour. With a heavy sigh, she decided to retrieve the basket that would surely still be sitting on Antares' doorstep.

It took her a while to get out the door and even longer to arrive at her destination as she deliberately meandered through the streets of Heaven, praying, by all odds, that it wouldn't be there anymore. That something would be different.

Unfortunately, something was different.

Estelle noticed as soon as the house was in sight, a few blocks away from the corner she always turned at. She was too far away to feel anything, but the fear that ramped up inside her was real.

The Vostarist stood still on the doorstep. He was facing away, but Estelle would know the look of the white cloak anywhere. Luckily, being so far away meant the Vostarist didn't notice her presence. But she wasn't about to push her luck. After a moment of shock, she turned on her heel and marched back the way she came.

Estelle couldn't walk more than five steps the entire way back without checking over her shoulder. The instant she got back, she made a cup of rosebay tea.

Her class began to file in afterward, and Issac talked about having the day off tomorrow before returning to the regular schedule of classes and missions. Estelle contributed to the conversation, but her mind was still back with the intimidating figure.

47

His True
Name

ESTELLE DIDN'T GET A CHANCE to open the journal until later that night.

She didn't even realize it was the last entry until she checked the back cover and found nothing written after it. It was odd, considering that the listed page number was only around halfway through the total thickness of the journal.

She was nervous as she turned to the listed page. The past few entries had shaken her enough to overtake her curiosity, and when she found it, a glance at the heading left her with an odd mixture of relief and fear. Because, unlike all the others, this one was addressed to her specifically.

Estelle,

Knowing where to start with this is difficult, but you've waited long enough.

First of all, I would like to apologize. I want you to know that I never meant for things to turn out this way. It wasn't part of any grandiose plan. Like you, I am fallible, but that does not excuse my getting you caught in the crosshairs. Six months ago, I did not have all the facts. I was unaware of the extent of the Apostles' actions, and my greatest regret is involving you before I had everything figured out.

I'm sure you're confused about some of the previous entries. The contents of this journal come from various sources. Some come from my mentor's notes, and others are from Vega's mentor. I transcribed them for you because I don't want the information I've gathered to go to waste if something happens, and because I think it's essential that you know what I know.

The short of it is that my mentor Fell to save me. I witnessed it myself. When an Angel Falls, unless a Demon specifically prevents it, they are automatically transported to Hell. However, a few months ago, I managed to confirm that there is no record of her soul ever having appeared in Hell. This suggests that the power was intercepted. The list of those capable of doing such a thing is very short.

At this point, I need to come clean about one thing in particular. When I initially suggested you work with Zylis, I told you it was because I thought demonstrating an ability to resist temptation would make your application for ascension stand out.

This is a lie.

The real reason was far more selfish. Back then, I was still searching for a way to confirm whether or not Lyra was in Hell. Due to the nature of my retirement, I cannot leave Heaven, and in the beginning, I had hoped that your connection to Zylis might allow me to circumvent those restrictions to achieve that goal. Of course, I wound up confirming it independently shortly after your partnership with him began. It was only then that I started to put the pieces together.

I know an apology for a mistake on this scale will probably fall flat, but I want you to know that I am deeply sorry. I am sorry for deceiving you, and I'm sorry for all the suffering that my choice has caused you. I could not have predicted how this would unfold, but that is no excuse. As your mentor, part of my job is to protect you. I have failed to do so, and that is something I will regret for the rest of my days.

As for this journal, please believe me when I tell you that I did not decide to tell you all of this out of a desire to cause distress. In fact, I think that you may be one of the only Angels capable of processing this information without succumbing to despair. Let me explain what I mean.

What you need to understand is that Falling is a physiological process: the dissolution of the soul's outer shell, which is held together by faith. It's an event triggered by either tactile corruption damage or specific emotional experiences, experiences that trigger the release of certain chemicals. For the vast majority of Angels, this can only occur under one specific circumstance: losing faith in God. When an Angel loses this, everything else comes crashing down. However, this does not seem to be the case for you.

Over the past six months, I've watched you grow to care deeply for Zylis. He has become your friend, someone you can trust, despite what he is rather than because of it. Your trust in him does not rely on faith in God. It is wholly independent of it. And though I obviously cannot know for certain, it is my belief that, as strange as it may sound, your relationship with him might be the reason you have managed to hold on for so long. Even if you lost every last shred of faith in God, you would still have something to believe in. Of course, this is all just a hypothesis, so I've done my best to remain cautious.

Now is the part where the "good news" ends. Because if you're reading this, I am already gone. I ask that you do not come looking for me. I ask that you do not attempt to rescue me. I'm painfully aware of the hypocrisy of this request. After all, I got myself into this mess in an attempt to save my own mentor, but I need to at least try to deter you from doing something courageous and stupid.

I know you well enough that you're probably already crafting a plan to save me, even as you read this. Fortunately, I've planned for this. As I'm sure you've noticed, this is not the last page of this book. There is quite a bit after this. I did not lock it, but I strongly suggest that you do not read any of it, as much of it is upsetting and not particularly useful for you to know.

However, it would be extremely useful to the Demons.

The most important thing I need to tell you is this: though I have done everything in my power to cleanse the situation of your involvement, it is still only a matter of time before they come for you, too. I've procured a serum that will wipe my memories to an extent, but no form of memory erasure, even that which God uses on his Angels, is entirely infallible. Persistent and sufficient probing will eventually lead to your being implicated.

If there's one thing I've learned from all of this, it is this: Falling is not the worst fate an Angel can meet. On the contrary, compared to the alternatives, it's quite merciful. I realize this is probably very shocking to read, but please try to understand that I would not be saying all of this if I thought there was a better way.

Estelle, for your safety, you need to Fall. Please. Before it is too late. Trust me when I say that it will be far worse if they get to you first.

Estelle, I love you as though you were my daughter. I'm so proud of everything you've achieved and want you to continue thriving. It is ultimately up to you, but I cannot stress enough the importance of this choice. I will buy you as much time as I possibly can, but there are many variables beyond my control.

I do not know how long it will have been by the time you read this. I tried to time it so this entry would unlock a few days after my disappearance, while still allowing you time to process each entry. If it's been under seven days, you have some time to think. I can probably hold out a bit longer than that, but there are no guarantees.

In the unlikely event that it has been more than twelve days, you need to operate under the assumption that you are in immediate danger.

At a minimum, you need to get out of Heaven. In the long run... It pains me to say this, but I cannot think of any other option. I know the idea is scary, but please think about it. Please make that choice before someone else makes it for you.

When the Apostles take you, they do not allow you to Fall.

Please take care of yourself.

Gabriel Leonhart

Estelle stared at the letter for a very long time. It didn't even register that she had turned the page four times to finish the message.

She froze. *The day Antares came over was a Sunday. He was gone the next day, making the last Monday in May the first day, so that's...* Estelle mouthed the days as she counted on her fingers. A chill ran through her like a block of ice had been dropped down her back underneath her clothes.

"Twelve days," she whispered. She glanced at the clock—*thirty minutes to midnight.*

Thirty minutes until the thirteenth day.

For a minute, she sat there, paralyzed. And then the hyperventilation began. Estelle gripped the edge of her desk as black spots appeared in her vision, her mind struggling to come to grips with it all.

They have Antares. They're going to do something to him. Some sort of interrogation. Is he okay? Are they hurting him? What if they've turned him into a husk? They wouldn't do that. They wouldn't. Not if they need information from him.

Her breath caught in her throat.

The place the journal described—with all the horrible gas—is he in there? They wouldn't—would they? Antares is susceptible to soul bleed. If they put him down there, he could hurt himself unless they restrain him. Unless something has changed.

Estelle's heart slammed against her chest. It felt as if all the blood had been drained from her body, and she could hear it rushing out through her ears. Estelle was shaking.

What do I do? What should I do? He told me to Fall, but I won't be able to return if I Fall. I won't be able to save him. I need to save him. Is it even safe to leave now? What if they catch me? Maybe I could—no, that won't work. Maybe—wait, no—What if they're already outside?

She felt her throat closing up, tears blurring her vision.

Think. Think, you idiot! You're running out of time! There has to be—

Knock, knock.

48

The Last Message

ESTELLE SCREAMED, FALLING OUT OF her chair as she frantically scrambled backward on the floor. *Void! This is it. It's over. I'm going to die. I'm going to die. I'm going—*

"Estelle?"

The Angel didn't process it at first.

"Estelle, are you okay?"

Issac.

Estelle struggled to stand up, nearly tripping over her feet as she went to open the door. Issac stood on the other side and looked at her with an almost fearful expression. Before he could even speak, Estelle yanked him inside.

"Woah, hey!"

Estelle shut the door, nearly catching Issac's ankle in the process.

"Estelle, what's going on?"

How do I answer that? Why did I let him in? Holy devil, this was a mistake. I made a mistake. This will just—

Issac grabbed her shoulders. "Estelle?" He studied her for a moment. "Crap," he muttered. "Estelle, I think you might be having a panic attack. You should probably sit—"

"No," Estelle reflexively shook him off. "Can't. I need to go."

"What?"

"I need to go," she repeated. "I need to get out of Heaven."

Issac's brow furrowed. "Why do you say that?"

"It's not safe."

"What isn't?"

"Staying here."

He faltered. "What makes you think that?"

Estelle's eyes flicked to the journal lying open on her desk.

Issac followed the path of her eyes and started moving toward it.

"No!" the girl shouted. Issac froze. "You can't; if you read it, you'll Fall!"

To say Issac seemed alarmed would have been an understatement. "I—okay." He nodded, putting his hands up. "It's okay. I won't read it."

Estelle relaxed slightly.

After a moment of uncertainty, Issac began speaking again. It was slow, careful, as though he were treading a verbal minefield. "Estelle," he started, "regardless of what that book says, you are safe right now in this room. You need to calm down. Take deep breaths. Can you do that?"

Estelle blinked and nodded after a moment of hesitation, but the tightness in her throat made it challenging.

"Don't force it," Issac told her. "Go slow." He demonstrated the action himself, breathing deeply through his nose and then out his mouth in a slow and steady rhythm.

Estelle nodded again and did her best to focus on that alone. After a couple of minutes, she gradually started feeling normal again, settling on the floor. Issac went into her bathroom, returned, and handed her a glass of water.

"Thank you," she mumbled, pressing the cool glass against her forehead.

Issac sat on the floor in front of her. "Are you able to talk about it?"

Estelle paused, the edge of the glass pressed against her lip. She wasn't sure how to explain it in a way that would have made sense while still being safe for Issac to hear. She didn't know what to tell him, and she expressed that to him.

Issac hummed, apparently thinking it over. "Well, if you don't think you can tell me everything, then tell me the version that doesn't make sense."

"You'll think I'm crazy."

"I've always thought you were a bit crazy," he deadpanned. "But I still trust your judgment. Mostly."

Estelle hesitated. "Uh, let me just—" She went to take a sip of water and then wound up downing the entire glass.

Issac stared at her, one eyebrow raised.

Estelle set the glass down gingerly, then took a deep breath. "The Apostles have Antares, and they're coming for me next, and if I don't leave soon, the Vostarists will take me, and I don't have a lot of time."

He looked at her for a long moment, expressionless. "Well, that's definitely crazy."

Estelle's shoulder slumped. "I knew you'd—"

"I didn't say I didn't believe you."

Estelle faltered. "So, you... do believe me?"

"I didn't say that either," he replied with a small smile. He dropped it a moment later. "That said, I can tell you believe what you're saying."

"So, you think I'm crazy."

"Maybe. That doesn't necessarily mean you're wrong, though." He shrugged. "What's the quote? I think I saw it in a book once." He used air quotes. "'*Just because you're paranoid doesn't mean they're not after you,*' or something like that."

That got Estelle to laugh.

"In all seriousness, I don't know if I believe you or not, but I guess it doesn't exactly matter," he said. "You're going to leave whether I help you or not, so I guess I will."

"Wait, what?"

"I said I'll help you," he said flatly.

"Issac," Estelle spoke slowly. "I'm pretty sure that's treason."

"It's only treason if I believe you."

She held eye contact with him for a while, analyzing Issac's oddly lighthearted expression. It wasn't that she didn't think she could count on Issac to help her if it came down to it. But it was unexpected for him to offer so readily without even bothering to try to talk Estelle out of it.

"Listen, Estelle," he sighed. "I had a lot of time to think while in the hospital. It's not like I've had some massive change of heart, but I'm trying to be less..." He trailed off, wincing. He paused, closed his eyes, and took a deep breath. "Anyway, all of that aside, if there's even the slightest chance you might get caught by the Vostarists, then yeah, I would rather do too much than too little."

"I... Thank you, Issac," Estelle said, smiling briefly.

"Do you have a plan for where to go once you leave?"

Estelle started to say 'no,' but then Zylis' words became known, echoing in her mind, and she bit her tongue.

A couple of seconds later, she cleared her throat. "Yes, actually. I do have a place in mind."

Issac looked at her expectantly.

She grimaced.

"Are you going to tell me?"

"I... I mean, do you want to know?"

He continued to stare at her for a while longer, blinking slowly. Pointedly. If Estelle hadn't known better, she would have thought the dark circles under his eyes had deepened.

"It's Hell, isn't it?"

Estelle made a face. "Uh, no comment?"

"Estelle—" Issac pinched the bridge of his nose, "—you know, I knew you were crazy, but... wow."

"It's not that crazy," she muttered. "Zye will protect me."

Issac scoffed. "*Uh-huh.*"

Estelle frowned. "I'm serious, Issac."

"Yeah, yeah, I know," he said with a bizarre, sarcastically sweet cadence.

Estelle watched as Issac began massaging his temples with his eyes closed and realized he was quietly counting to ten under his breath.

Afterward, he exhaled and looked up at Estelle. "I know," he repeated, that time sounding genuine. "I just don't like it, that's all, which is fine. I'm *allowed* not to like it. Anyway—" he suddenly stood up, "—do you own anything with a hood? Something dark, preferably."

Estelle noticed that Issac was already moving toward the door as though he already knew the answer. "I have a cloak, but it's white."

"Well, I have something you can wear."

Estelle stood. "Are you sure? It's possible you won't see it again."

"Oh, don't worry," Issac said. "From what I can tell about that guy's personality, I expect nothing less. Be right back."

Estelle opened her mouth to retort, but the door shut behind him before she got the chance. She sat there for a full minute watching the door, half expecting a Vostarist to march in and take her away before Issac's return.

Slowly, she stood up and grabbed her bag to start packing. A second later, the door opened again as Issac walked in with a dark blue cloak slung over his arm.

"How long are you going to be gone?" he asked, placing the garment on her bed.

"I-I don't know," Estelle said, shuffling over to her dresser. "But my bag will probably only hold a few days' worth."

She started grabbing at her clothes and shoved them in.

Issac quickly stopped her. "You can't just shove things inside," he said, taking over the packing. "We'll need to fold everything if you want things to fit."

"Right." She shook her head and moved to grab other things she'll need for the trip. It took an hour of searching, folding, organizing, and shoving things into her bag, but eventually Estelle was ready to leave.

"Wait, what are you doing with that?" Issac asked, stopping Estelle from putting a textbook in the bag. In truth, it was the sallbokvie.

She's told him before that Zylis and she have been communicating with each other apart from meeting up on the surface, but didn't go into specifics as to how that was done. But as Issac stared her down with a quizzical look, an idea popped into Estelle's head.

"I can't leave this behind," she said, "it's just as important as the journal."

"The one that you won't let me read?" Issac asked, more to himself, but Estelle nodded, nonetheless.

"Yes. And it's equally important that you find this on the surface." Estelle could see that Issac was even more confused than before. She continued, "Where are you scheduled to go on your next mission?"

He narrowed his eyes. "Estonia...?"

"Okay, I'll leave it there, near a church, for you to find later." Estelle watched has Issac opened his mouth to speak, but she beat him to it. "Please, Issac, trust me."

After a moment, he huffed a sigh and let Estelle store the book away in the bag. "What am I supposed to do with it once I find it?"

"Write in it."

Again, Issac looked at her as if she were insane. "Okay, I'll be sure to bring a pen with me, I guess," he said, sounding exhausted, grabbing onto the cloak's hood and flipping it up on Estelle's head. "Now, let's get you out of Heaven."

Issac led the way out of the dormitories.

There wasn't a curfew among Angels; they could stay awake for as long as they wanted or roam their respective spheres freely, just as long as they reported for missions or classes. And even though hardly anyone ever exercised that right, there was still a chance of being seen.

The Vostarists would be looking for Estelle, and possibly other higher-ranked Angels, like Regulus. So, Issac chose to lead her through less congested areas and was always first to check the streets before signaling for Estelle to follow. Thankfully, no one was awake.

It was around two in the morning by the time Estelle reached the surface. She ducked into the first intact building she saw, which turned out to be an old, abandoned house. She held the edges of the dark blue cloak Issac had lent her, trying to keep it from dragging through the piles of dust, broken glass, and who knows what else. She set down her bag, sat on a chair in the kitchen, and placed the sallvie on the dusty countertop.

Estelle found her pen and set it down beside the book. She didn't open it; instead, she took a deep breath, sighed, placed her elbows on the counter, and held her head in her hands.

Too many thoughts swirled around inside her head, too many things she had yet to process genuinely. Estelle's mind had been a mess even before the last journal entry. She had no reason to doubt the authenticity of the journal entries, but that didn't make it any easier to digest. It was like all those horrific things she had read about weren't quite real until she was hit with the possibility of Antares falling victim to them.

Antares's letter was a tangled ball of emotions and fears lodged in the back of her throat. Estelle hadn't even allowed herself to look at it again after the first time, as though she were afraid it would unravel and reveal something new. Something even more terrifying.

Everything. The lines, the stories, the implications of Lyra's Fall, the not-so-subtle endorsement of treason, the theories regarding Estelle's resistance to Falling, and the explicit push for her to Fall regardless. There was a part of her that couldn't wait to hand the journal over to the Demons, and yet another that wanted to clutch it tight to her chest and never let go.

Estelle was not going to Fall. Not tonight, not tomorrow. There was still too much she needed to think about. There was still so much she could do. But though she might make it through this stage with her wings and halo intact, she knew, on some deeper level, that it would change things. Estelle might still be an Angel when she emerged from the depths of Hell, but she wouldn't be the same person.

Estelle opened the sallvie and turned to a fresh page. She picked up her pen and pulled the cap off with her teeth. She clutched her wrist with her left hand to keep it steady.

Something ends tonight.

Estelle put pen to paper, knowing it could be the last thing she would ever write in the sallbokvie. And as she penned the message, she wondered, with the sort of humor one can only engage in under dire circumstances, what a passive observer might have thought if they were to read it. If someone—with no additional context—were to pick up the book and read through all of it up to the final point, she wondered what kind of story it would tell. Maybe they would read it as a tragedy.

Or perhaps, the start of something new.

I need you to take me to Hell

Estelle closed the sallvie and waited to see who she would become.

Acknowledgments

With the beginning of the Ethereal Intervention series, I find myself overwhelmed with gratitude for those who have supported me along the way.

First and foremost, I want to thank my biggest supporter, my husband. Your patients, humor, and unwavering love have carried me through countless late nights, unrelenting toddlers, and the unpredictable waves of pregnancy mood swings. You have been my rock, and I am endlessly grateful for your presence in my life.

Next, I extend my heartfelt thanks to my incredible Alpha and Beta Readers. Your insightful feedback, encouragement, and honest critiques have been invaluable in shaping this story. Without your dedication and support, Fall From Heaven would never have reached its full potential.

Finally, I am deeply grateful to my talented editor, K.F. Starfell. Your keen eye, creative suggestions, and meticulous work elevated my story beyond what I could have imagined. Thank you for bringing this vision to life with such grace and precision.

To everyone who believed in me, thank you from the bottom of my heart. This journey is just beginning, and I couldn't have done it without you.

E.L. Dawn is a passionate storyteller and avid adventurer at heart. Weaving enchanting tales of fantasy, adventure, and romance from the cozy corners of her home. As a devoted mother of lively kids, a loyal dog, and a loving husband, she draws inspiration from her vibrant family life to create worlds filled with magic, courage and heartfelt moments.

When she's not writing or chasing her kids around, she can be found exploring nature, brewing a cup of tea, or dreaming up her next epic tale. Self-published and proud of her independent spirit, E.L. Dawn loves connecting with readers who crave escapism and unforgettable journeys. She aims to transport readers to fantastical realms where bravery and love conquer all.

6e0eee33-ebdb-4f2a-a609-9e967c28e03cR01